A writer and book editor, Sandra Gulland was raised in the turmoil of the sixties in Berkeley, California, where she attended San Francisco State College and the University of California at Berkeley. After moving to Canada in 1970, she taught at a school in a remote Inuit village in Labrador before moving to Ontario to work in book publishing. She has been at work on the Joséphine novels for many years, travelling extensively to the places Joséphine lived, learning to read French and corresponding with period scholars. Sandra Gulland lives near Killaloe, Ontario, with her husband and two children.

The Many Lives & Secret Sorrows of Joséphine B.

Sandra Gulland

review

First published in hardback in 1995 by
HarperCollins Publishers Ltd, Canada

First published in paperback in 1999 by
HEADLINE BOOK PUBLISHING

10 9 8

THE MANY LIVES 7 SECRET SORROWS OF JOSEPHINE B.
is a work of fiction based on (and inspired by) the extraordinary
life of Joséphine Bonaparte.

ISBN 0 7472 6189 X

Printed and bound in Great Britain by
Clays Ltd, St Ives plc

HEADLINE BOOK PUBLISHING
A division of Hodder Headline PLC
338 Euston Road
London NW1 3BH

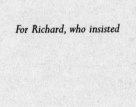

For Richard, who insisted

. . . the ghosts of our future
are unpredictable
and out of control
— *Wendy Rose*
from 'The Fifties'

I

Mademoiselle

In which I am told an extraordinary fortune

I am fourteen today and unmarried still. Without a dowry, what hope is there? Mother says the wind takes hope and dashes it into the sky, just as the big wind took our house, picked it up and dashed it, leaving nothing but debts in its place.

Oh, what a black mood has possessed me. Is not the celebration of one's birthday supposed to bring one joy? After dinner I took my leave and climbed up to my special place in the kapok tree. It was cool in the shade of the leaves. I could hear Grandmother Sannois and Mother arguing in the front parlour, the slaves chanting as they pushed the cane stalks through the rollers in the crushing hut, a chicken scratching in the honeysuckle bushes. I felt strange up there — peering out at my world, enveloped in gloom on my happy day.

It's the voodoo, surely, the bitter-tasting quimbois Mimi got me to drink this morning, a drink of secret spells. 'Something manbo Euphémie made for you,' she whispered. She'd knotted a red and yellow scarf tight round her head.

'Euphémie David — the teller of fortunes?' The obeah woman, the voodoo priestess who lived in the shack up the river.

Mimi pushed the coconut bowl into my hands. 'It will bring you a *man*.'

I regarded the liquid cautiously, for it smelled vile.

'Quick!' She glanced over her shoulder. For Mother doesn't hold with voodoo. Mother says the Devil speaks through the mouths of the voodoo spirits. Mother says the Devil is hungry for girls like me. Mother says the Devil sent her too many girls and is hungry to get one back.

So this is confession number one in this, my new diary, sent to me all the way from Paris by my beautiful Aunt Désirée: I drank a magic potion and I'll not tell Mother. I drank a magic potion and I'm filled with woe.

A note Aunt Désirée enclosed with her gift read: 'A little book in which to record your wishes and dreams, your secret confessions.' I shook the book over the table. Ten livres fell out.

'Confessions?' my sister Catherine asked. She is twelve now, almost thirteen, but even so, always into mischief. At convent school the nuns make a fuss over Catherine. They don't know it is Catherine who lets the chicken into the rectory, that it is Catherine who steals the sugar cakes before they are cooled. Catherine has the soul of a trickster, Mimi says.

'Tell us your wish,' my youngest sister, Manette, said, lisping through the gap in her teeth. I was saddened by the light in her eyes, for she is only ten, young enough to believe that wishes are granted.

I shrugged. 'My wish is the same every year.' I glanced at Father. He had spent the day with rum and absinthe and followed it with ti-punches all through the afternoon. 'To go to France.' Send Rose to France, my beautiful Aunt Désirée would write every year – send her to me, to *Paris*.

Father looked away. His skin was yellow; it is the malaria again, surely. So then I felt bad, for is it Father's fault he'd inherited only debts? Is it his fault he has been cursed with three daughters and no son, that Mother's dowry turned to dust in his hands, that his dream of sending me to France had never materialized for want of the price of passage?

'France!' Grandmother Sannois pushed her two pug dogs off her lap. 'I'd keep that girl well away from Madame Désirée.' Grandmother Sannois doesn't approve of Aunt Désirée, or any of the Taschers for that matter (*especially* Father). 'What's wrong with that boy over near Laniantin?' she said, downing her laudanum: seven drops in a jigger of brandy. 'What's wrong with that Beal boy?'

Algernon Beal! The fat boy we all call Algie.

'Monsieur Beal requires a dowry,' Mother said.

'Monsieur *de* Beal, I believe it is now,' Father said, 'the manu-facturer of shackles and branding irons, the owner of three gilded carriages, twenty-two fighting cocks, an English thoroughbred stal-lion and one dim-witted son.' Father coughed and emptied his glass.

'Monsieur *de* Beal and I had occasion to converse at the slave auction in Fort-Royal last month. He told me at *length* and in great *detail* how large a girl's dowry would have to be, how noble her bloodline, how abundant her bosom and intact her maidenhood even to dream of marrying his pimple-faced boy.'

Manette had her napkin stuffed in her mouth to keep from laughing.

'Well, there's always the convent,' Grandmother Sannois said.

The convent. Always the *convent*. Is this to be my future? I yearn for so much more! But it's too late now, I know, for on this, my fourteenth birthday, Aunt Désirée made no offer, and, for the first time since I can remember, Father made no promise . . . and I liked it better before, to tell the truth, with glittering false hopes to brighten my day.

24 JUNE

This morning I gave my ten livres to the slave-master to divide among the field hands. I am grown now and more aware of the sufferings of the world.

But Mother found out and got cross, accusing me of being like Father. 'Generous' Father who would let his family starve to feed a friend. 'Crazy' Father with his wild stories and dreams of glory. 'Dreams from the rum god,' she cursed. 'Promises like clouds on a summer day.'

Father who is never home. Already he's off to Fort-Royal – 'to play games with the Devil,' Grandmother Sannois said.

'To play games with the *she*-devils,' Mother said quietly under her breath.

SUNDAY, 29 JUNE

Dear Diary, I have been giving thought to my sins, making repentance.

I am guilty of wishful thinking, of extravagant imaginings.

I am guilty of gazing at myself in the pond.

I am guilty of sleeping with my hands under my bedsheets.

There, it is written. The ink is drying as I write. I must close this book now – I cannot bear to look at these words.

THE MANY LIVES & SECRET SORROWS OF JOSEPHINE B.

'Mademoiselle Tascher,' Father Droppet called to me after church this morning. 'Your grandmother asked me to talk to you.'

I fingered the pages of my missal. Outside I heard a horse whinny and a man shouting.

'You are coming to an age of decision,' he said. His big nose twitched.

'Yes, Father.' I could see the outline of his vest under his white frock.

He paused. 'I advise you to bend to God's will, to accept a life of service.'

I felt my cheeks becoming heated.

Father Droppet handed me a handkerchief. 'The life of a nun might satisfy that hungry heart of yours.'

Through the high open window I could see the head of the statue of Christ in the cemetery, His eyes looking up at the clouds. The hunger I felt was for fêtes and silk slippers, for the love of a comely beau.

He bent towards me. 'I was young once too,' he said. I could smell rum on his breath.

'I would die in a convent!'

Forgive me, Father. I backed away. At the door I turned and ran.

24 JULY

This afternoon Mimi and I were playing in the ruins* when Mimi saw a spot on my chemise.

I twisted and pulled my skirt round. Blood?

'It's the flowers,' Mimi said.

I didn't know what to do.

'Tell your mother,' she said.

'I can't do that!' Mother is proper.

So Mimi got me a rag and instructed me how to use it. She told me she washes hers out in the creek, early, when no one is around to see.

'Where we bathe?' How disgusting.

---

* The family home was destroyed by a hurricane in 1766. They moved into the *sucrerie*, the building used to boil down sugar syrup.

'Further down the river.'

I move around the house aware of this great cloth between my legs, thinking that surely everyone notices. This is supposed to be the big change in me, but all I feel is ill.

SATURDAY

Mimi is teaching me how to tell the future from cards, how to lay them out, how to know the meaning. Today we practised on my sister Catherine. The card in the ninth place was Death.

Catherine protested.

'It's not *really* death,' Mimi said, taking up the cards. She sniffed the air.

Later, I questioned her. 'Why did you stop?'

'Didn't you smell cigar smoke?' she whispered. 'The spirit of Death is a trickster. Never believe *him*.'

THURSDAY, 31 JULY

Dear Diary, something terrible has happened; it hangs over my heart like a curse.

It began with a lie. I told my little sister Manette that Mimi and I were going to the upper field to see if Father's ship was in the harbour yet. 'You stay here,' I told her.

Mimi and I headed up the track behind the manioc hut, but at the top of the hill we took the path that led back down to the river, towards Morne Croc-Souris. We hadn't gone far when Manette caught up with us.

'I told you to stay,' I told her.

'You lied. You said you were going up the hill.'

Mimi glared at her. 'Can you keep a secret?'

'I never tell!'

It was dark by the river; the moss hung thick from the trees. We heard a chicken squawking before we came upon the fortune-teller's shack.

'That's where the werewolf lives,' Manette said, taking my hand.

I looked at Mimi. 'Is this it?'

THE MANY LIVES & SECRET SORROWS OF JOSEPHINE B.

In front of the hut was a charcoal brazier. The air was thick with the smell of roasted goat. In the shadows of a veranda roofed over with banana-tree leaves, I saw an old Negro woman sitting cross-legged. Euphémie David — the voodoo priestess.

As we approached she stood up. She was wearing a red satin ball gown fringed with gold, much tattered and stained and too big for her. Her hair was white and woolly, standing out around her head like a halo. A rusty machete was propped up against the wall behind her.

Mimi called out something I couldn't understand. The old woman said something in the African tongue.

'What did she say?' I asked.

'Come,' the old woman said. A puppy came out of the shack and growled at us.

'I'll stay back here,' Manette said.

Mimi pushed me forward.

'Aren't you coming too?' I asked.

The two of us approached. What was there to be afraid of?

Entering the shade of the veranda, I was surprised how small the old woman was, not much bigger than Manette. Her loose black skin hung from her neck. She held a shell bowl in one hand — pigs' knuckles and coconut, it looked like — and was eating it with her fingers. She threw a bone to the puppy to finish. The old woman and Mimi began talking in the African tongue. I looked back over my shoulder. Manette was standing by a calabash tree, watching. A crow called out warning sounds.

Mimi touched my arm. 'She says your future is all around you.'

'What does that mean?'

The old woman went into the shack. She returned with a basket which she pushed into my hands. In the basket were a gourd rattle, a wooden doll, a stick, two candles, a bone, bits of frayed ribbon and a crucifix.

The old woman said something to Mimi.

'She wants you to pick out three things,' Mimi told me.

'Anything?' I took a candle, the doll and the crucifix out of the basket.

'She wants you to put them down,' Mimi said.

'On the ground?'

The old woman began chanting. I looked to see if Manette was still by the calabash tree. I shrugged at her. I remember thinking: see, there is nothing to fear.

The old woman began to moan, rolling her head from side to side, the whites of her eyes cloudy. Then she looked at me and screamed – a sound I will never forget, not unlike a pig being stuck.

'What is it?' I demanded. I was not without fear. 'Mimi! Why is she crying?'

The old woman was shaking her head and mumbling. Finally she spoke, slowly, but strangely. 'You will be unhappily married. You will be widowed.'

I put my hand to my throat.

The old woman began to shake. She shook her hands, crying out words I could not understand.

'Mimi, what is she saying!'

The old woman began to dance, singing with the voice of a man. I backed away, stumbling over a gnarled tree root. I fell to the ground and scrambled to my feet.

You will be Queen, she said.

In which I am punished

MONDAY, 4 AUGUST 1777

When I saw Father Droppet coming up the lane on his grey mare, fear came into my heart. I ran up the track to the manioc hut. Mimi was turning the big iron scraper.

'Father Droppet is here!' I said. 'Why? It's not a feast day.'

Mimi stopped turning the wheel.

'I made confession yesterday morning,' I told her.

'Did you tell?'

'About the voodoo witch?' I nodded.

'Did you tell I took you?' There was fear in her eyes.

'I *wouldn't*.' I turned, suddenly anxious. 'I wonder what's happening.'

I did not intend to eavesdrop. That was not my plan. But instead of going directly towards the *sucrerie*, I went down into the ravine. From my place in the kapok tree I could hear voices on the veranda – Mother, Grandmother Sannois. Then Father Droppet saying, 'You understand, this is a matter of . . . I don't have to . . .'

'Goodness!' Mother exclaimed.

Father Droppet said something I couldn't understand. I heard the front door open and close. Then I heard Manette's voice.

Manette! I strained to hear, but all I could make out was Grandmother Sannois saying, 'I told you. I told you this would happen.'

I heard the door open and close again and, before long, the sound of Manette weeping in an upstairs bedchamber. Then I heard Father Droppet say, 'If the Devil is permitted . . . You must . . .'

'But Father Droppet!' I heard Mother exclaim. I strained to hear more but a black finch landed on the branch above me and began to scold so vigorously I couldn't make out a word. I shook the branch to chase the bird away. Then, Father Droppet's voice: 'If you don't . . .'

It grew dark suddenly and began to rain, a light shower at first, followed by big, heavy drops.

'Yeyette!' I heard Mother calling.

I climbed down and approached the veranda.

'Why, it's Rose,' my mother said. 'You're soaking wet.'

Grandmother Sannois was slouched in a cane chair. Father Droppet was standing by the door with an empty glass in his hand. He nodded.

'What can you be thinking of, standing out in such a downpour. Go and put some dry clothes on and come back. There is something we must discuss,' Mother said.

Gladly I escaped. Catherine met me at the top of the stairs, an embroidery hoop in her hand. 'Manette says you will be Queen! She said the old witch told you. But she won't stop crying! What happened?'

I could hear Manette bawling even from the landing. I went down the dark corridor to the door to her room. I knocked. 'Manette? It's me.'

The weeping stopped but she did not answer.

'I won't hurt you, I promise.' I pushed the door open. She was huddled in the corner of the little four-poster bed. I stooped down under the canopy and sat down across from her. Her eyes were red and her nose was runny. I felt around in my bodice for a handkerchief and handed it to her. 'I know you told,' I said.

'You're not mad?' she asked, her breathing jagged. She glanced up at Catherine, who had come to the door.

I shook my head no. 'I should never have taken you there. Did you say anything about Mimi?'

'No!'

'Do you understand what might happen if you did, Manette? She'd be sold – or put on a field gang.' Or worse . . .

'I didn't say anything!' she sobbed, so hard my heart was full of fear.

The rain had stopped when I emerged on to the veranda. I could hear Mother and Grandmother Sannois bidding farewell to Father Droppet on the lane. I stood by the front door, my hands clasped

SANDRA GULLAND

12

in front of me, waiting. It sounded as if Father Droppet's grey was being fractious. I heard the stable boy cursing in the African tongue. The horse quietened. Then I heard the steady clip-clop of the horse's hooves on the stones.

Mother appeared on the path, Grandmother Sannois on her arm, the two pugs sniffing in the weeds behind them. They were wet and looked like big rats. Grandmother Sannois was saying something to Mother as they walked along. Then Mother looked up, saw me.

I held my breath.

'I'll tell her if you won't,' Grandmother Sannois said, lowering herself into the chair with the sisal seat. One of her pugs jumped up on to her lap and she pushed him off.

Mother turned to face me.

I bowed my head. I considered throwing myself at her feet. Was that not how it was done?

'And to think that you *made* little Manette go along with you!' she whispered, so low I almost couldn't hear her.

'Let me tell her,' Grandmother Sannois said.

Mother took a deep breath. 'Mimi, of course, will have to be—'

'No!' A violent emotion filled me. 'Mimi had nothing to do with it! I *begged* her to take me, but she refused. I was the one, it was only *me*!' My breath was coming in spurts; I could not still it.

Mother took the chain from round her neck, the chain with the big silver cross hanging from it. She took my two hands, put the cross between them. 'Look at me, Rose,' she said.

I looked into her eyes.

'Swear that you speak the truth.'

'Mimi is innocent. It is all my doing, all my fault,' I cried out, not untruly.

'She did not take you to see the unholy woman in the woods?'

I shook my head no, violently.

'Say it.'

'Mimi did not go,' I lied. The cross felt cold and heavy in my hands. I pushed it back into my mother's hands.

'Call the child down,' Grandmother Sannois said.

Mother sat down on a wooden stool. 'Come here, Rose,' she said. She pulled me down on the stones in front of her. She wiped several strands of damp hair from my forehead. Her touch was tender. 'Sometimes it's not easy to be a mother,' she said. Her voice was cold when she said, 'You will be put in the storm room, in the cellar. You will stay there for eight days.' She looked over at Grandmother Sannois and then back at me. She took a deep breath. 'You will be fed nothing but dry bread and water.'

I looked at her without comprehending. Eight days? Eight *nights*? In the cellar? 'Alone?' My voice trembled. In the *dark*?

Mother slipped the chain with the cross over my head. 'You will be needing this,' she said.

I've been sent to my room to await my fate. I am to eat supper with my family, and make my farewells. It will be my last meal.

Mimi and Manette are more upset than I am. Catherine, however, can only think of the fortune I was told. 'That *you* will be a queen, Rose. Imagine!'

My nanny Da Gertrude appeared, her face wet with tears. She crushed me to her bosom. Then she washed me with a fragrant liquid, beginning at my feet.

'Why?' I asked, for her method was curious. A floating feeling came over me, as if my body was not my own.

'This will protect you,' she said.

'I will be strong,' I said. The thought came to me: as befits one who will be Queen.

It was true, then, I knew, I *had* been cursed.

At supper I could hardly eat. After, everyone embraced me as if I was going on an ocean voyage. Grandmother Sannois presented me with her Bible. Da Gertrude grasped me so hard I feared my bones would crack.

Mother held the lamp high as we descended into the basement. It was cool, the air damp – old air. I watched where I stepped, fearing cockroaches. I followed Mother into the storm room – a large room with a narrow bed in it. There was a chair with a frayed wicker seat and a three-legged table propped up in one corner. On the table was a lantern, a candle, an earthenware jug and a cracked china cup. That was all but for one small opening high up on the wall, covered with a wooden shutter.

I set my basket down on the bed. I recognized the patchwork counterpane as one that Catherine and I had worked on together.

Mother put the lantern down on the table and felt with her finger to see if it had been dusted. She turned to me. 'Rose, I hope you understand why this is necessary.'

'I do,' I lied. I didn't know what to say.

She began to weep. It was more of a shuddering movement than a sound, for there were no tears. It seemed an unnatural thing. I put my arm round her shoulders. I was surprised how small she was. She wiped her face with the back of her hand. 'May God be with you,' she said.

And then she was gone and I was alone.

LATER

Dear Diary, it is night, my first. I pried open the shutters; the night sounds filled my room. Then I closed the shutters tight, for fear of the wandering night spirits, the hungry *mystères*.

I fear I am not alone. In the shadows I feel the presence of some spirit. I cannot sleep, will not sleep, for fear it will approach. My eyes open, ever alert, I watch the dark.

The oil in my lantern is low. I must blow it out, I know, forsake this island of light. Courage, I say.

Faith, I hear something whisper.

5 AUGUST

I woke at the sound of the slave-master blowing his conch shell up in the slave village. I lay there for a time, staring at the ceiling, looking for faces in the cracks. I thought I heard a voice and a giggle. I pushed the chair to the wall and opened the shutters. There, peering at me through the long grass, were Catherine's dark eyes.

'We have to be quick!' she whispered through the grate.

I heard Manette behind her. 'Let me see! Let me see!'

'Quiet!' Catherine hissed.

Manette's little face came into view. Her hand reached down. I took the handful of moist crumbs. 'A mango tart. I stole it!'

Then some more quarrelling and Catherine came back into view. 'How is it down there?'

'Boring.'

'Run!' I heard Manette cry out.

And then there was only grass.

6 AUGUST

Towards evening I heard a scratching at the window again. I stood on
the chair and looked out. It was Catherine again. She was crying.

'What's the matter!'

'You have to promise not to tell.'

'What *is* it?'

She started to speak but tears came. 'Just a minute,' she said,
taking out her handkerchief and blowing her nose. She pressed her
face closer to the grate. 'I went to the fortune-teller.'

'To Euphémie David?'

She nodded.

'But Catherine! How could you!'

'Just because she told *you* you would be Queen.'

'Did Mimi take you?' I was angry now.

'I went alone.'

'*Alone?*' I couldn't imagine anyone being *that* brave.

She was beginning to gasp now, sobs overcoming her. I stuck my
finger through the grate to try to touch her. 'What happened? Did
she say something?'

And then she told me. At first the voodoo priestess had told her
to go away, she would not say her future, she said she could not
see it. But then the old woman said an awful thing – that Catherine
would be in the ground before her next birthday.

'Mother's right, she is the Devil!' I hissed, but already Catherine
was gone, scrambling through the grass.

[UNDATED]

Is it the Devil or a kind spirit that takes the form of a bat? Last night
there were several. I have begun to feel dizzy and not at all hungry.
Why am I here? I can't recall.

[UNDATED]

I went for a walk. I remember an old woman's face. I remember
her eyes and dust on the back of her hand. I remember watching

as she picked through a basket of dried leaves and put them one by one on the earth in front of me. I remember her chant, her strange wail. I remember an earthenware bowl with two little hearts in it, swarming with flies. I remember seeing a maggot in the bowl.

Was this a dream?

I remember a crippled old woman standing, raising her arms. I remember her lifting a flask of devil-fire to her lips, drinking it like water. I remember her jumping up and down on the ground in front of me, swiping the air with her outstretched hands.

I remember the words: *You will be Queen*.

This must have been a dream.

TUESDAY, 12 AUGUST, LATE

It was Mother who came for me, at the last. I was lying on the bed. She stood at the door with a lantern in her hand. 'Rose?'

I did not answer. I tried, but could not — it seemed too hard a task.

She came to the bed. She was wearing a white gown and a white headscarf and by the light of the lantern she looked like an angel. 'You look like an angel,' I said, my voice strange, hoarse.

I felt her fingers fluttering over my face. I heard a snuffling sound. 'Oh, sweet Jesus!' she whispered.

I looked at her with confusion. Why was she weeping? I saw a brilliant light all around her. She was the Virgin Mary come to bless me. 'Maman!' I cried out, kissing her fingers, pressing her hand to my cheek, marvelling at her beauty.

In which the mystères *have their way*

I woke to the sound of a soft rap-rap-rap on my bedchamber door. 'Who is it?' I hissed, fearful.

The door creaked open.

'Father!' He was wearing a riding jacket, blue with gold buttons.

'I've ordered your pony saddled,' he whispered, so as not to waken Da Gertrude. Steam was rising from the earthenware mug in his hand. It smelled of coffee and rum. 'I want you to meet my new lady,' he said, tossing me a chocolate roll.

Father's new lady was a black mare with white socks – a bold well-built girl with big eyes, young still. 'Lady Luck, I've named her,' he said proudly. 'Won at the tables.'

I reached out to touch her muzzle. She jerked her head away. 'Sucre is small for me now,' I said. My little pony was standing by the wall with flies on her eyes.

'This one's a little hot for you,' Father said. I held the bridle as he mounted.

The horses snorted as we headed down the lane, shaking their heads against the flies. The sun had just come up; the shadows were long yet, the grass damp. A blue heron flew up as we approached the canefields, still in chaos from the harvest. On the far horizon, at the edge of the sea, the field slaves were working, preparing a field for burning.

'King Sugar,' Father said with an ironic smile, slapping at a mosquito. He pulled a leather flask from his coat pocket, tipped back his head.

Other planters lived like kings. Why did we have no fortune? But I knew the answer. Your father courts Lady Luck, Mother said. But the Lady mistreats him.

'Tell me a story about when you were at Court, Father.'

He groaned.

'The hunt story.'

'You know it by heart,' he said.

It was true. I knew the story of the hunt so well I could tell it myself. How the King set out each morning with his lieutenants and under-lieutenants, the gentlemen of the chase, his squires and under-squires and pages. How the dogs howled, how the King knew each by name. How the fine-blooded horses pranced in the morning mist – so many of them sixty men were needed just to give them water!

I leaned my head on Sucre's neck, inhaled her warm, clean scent. Imagine such a world. 'A story about the Queen, then,' I said. 'About the birth of the Dauphin.' About fire-rockets lighting up the night.

Father let loose his reins, allowed his mare to graze. 'Speaking of queens, I was told the most extraordinary thing.' He turned to look at me. 'I was told you went to see that old voodoo woman upriver.'

I sat up. 'Who told you that?' I tried not to sound alarmed.

'A woman in Fort-Royal.'

'Oh?' I didn't like my father talking about me with 'a woman'.

'It's said you will be Queen.'

I felt my cheeks burn. I looked away.

'So it's true,' he said. He held out the flask. I shook my head. 'You are looking a little pale, Rose, a little thin. Have you been ill?'

'No.' I'd been warned not to tell.

'You know, I wanted you to be a boy.' He took another swig from his flask. Then he laughed. 'But a queen might not be so bad,' he said, urging his mare into a walk. 'A queen might help pay off my gambling debts.'

'I was punished, Father!' The words leapt from me unbidden.

His saddle creaked as he turned to face me. 'Punished?'

Tears came to my eyes.

'For being told you will be Queen?'

I took a shaky breath. 'For talking to the Devil,' I whispered.

'The strap?' His voice cold.

I nodded. I wanted to tell him the truth, but I did not dare. I wanted to tell him about the room in the cellar, about the bats and the spirits and the faces in the night. I wanted to tell him about the voices. But it would only anger him, I knew, and there would be fights. There were fights enough.

'The Old Women did this?' That is what Father called Mother and Grandmother Sannois.

'Father Droppet made them!'

'The Devil be damned,' he cursed under his breath. His mare bucked as he spurred her, bucked again as she broke into a gallop.

I kicked my pony hard and held on, tears blinding me. Father cried out as I passed him at the hanging tree.

25 AUGUST
Catherine and I are getting ready to return to the convent school in Fort-Royal. Little Manette watches us enviously, offering to help, getting in the way.

We leave the day after tomorrow, in spite of the rains. The weather is hot and terribly humid. We have to push our embroidery needles through the heavy cotton cloth.

A WEEK LATER, 6.00 P.M. — FORT-ROYAL
Catherine and I are back at school again, back at dreary Dames de la Providence, back to Sister Gretch's scowls. Mass at seven, classes from eight until eleven, and again from one until five. Drawing and embroidery. Reading and penmanship. Lectures on virtue and modesty. My backside is sore from sitting all day on hard benches.

7 SEPTEMBER
This rainy season will never end. The streets are rivers of mud. Catherine and I are stuck here at the convent — we can't even go to Uncle Tascher's for Sunday supper. Instead we eat salt fish, the third evening in a row. A cockroach, the biggest I'd ever seen, was running under the tables. Catherine screamed, though I know for a fact she's braver than most boys. She stood up on the table and stepped into at least two dinner plates and sent her own crashing to the floor. If it weren't for Catherine, we'd die of boredom.

WEDNESDAY, 10 SEPTEMBER, 11.00 A.M.
This morning at bath Catherine lifted her chemise when the sisters weren't looking. I gestured to her to lower it, but she only giggled and did it again. Soon we were all being bad.

SUNDAY, 14 SEPTEMBER, 1.00 P.M.
After mass this morning we were led on a promenade across the Savane. The smell of the slave ships in the harbour was strong. And then, a disturbing thing. As we turned back, Catherine whispered, 'I don't want to die!'

'Your face is flushed,' I said, alarmed by her curious statement. 'Are you ill?' She looked inflamed.

Tonight Catherine was the first to fall asleep. This is the most worrisome sign. Usually she gets the paddle for staying up late.

TUESDAY, 16 SEPTEMBER
Catherine is so ill now, she has to return home. I have insisted I go with her. Sister Gretch told me I am using my sister's misfortune as an excuse not to go to school. It wouldn't be honest, dear Diary, not to say that there is some truth in what Sister Gretch said. I hate being at the convent school, but it is also true that I am worried about Catherine. I've been nursing her for two days. We leave in the morning.

22 SEPTEMBER – TROIS-ILETS
We've been home five days and Catherine's worse, always in a drowsy stupor. Da Gertrude has been making smelly salves to spread on her chest, but they haven't helped. All day Mother sits and watches her, fanning her with a big palm leaf. Every so often she sponges her all over with rum, her prayers filling the rooms with a monotonous drone.

23 SEPTEMBER
I found chicken feathers and bits of bone under Catherine's bed. Voodoo magic, I hope.

4.00 P.M.

Grandmother Sannois says Catherine has yellow fever.

Yellow fever! I try not to think of Madame Laveaux's little boy who died in the summer, try not to think what the slaves say, how Madame Laveaux pierced her dead boy's heart with a knife to keep the *bokor* from his grave.

FRIDAY AFTERNOON, 26 SEPTEMBER

The doctor finally came and looked at Catherine. He prescribed Hoffman's Drops with sugar. He said she's been seized by an ague that has been succeeded by a fever, but that it's not *yellow* fever, that there's nothing to worry about – but why is she getting worse?

I told Mother she should call the doctor back, but she said, 'What's the point? He'll just say the same thing and charge another livre.'

27 SEPTEMBER, 10.00 P.M.

Tonight Catherine was talking in a dream, crying out and screaming. Then she jumped out of bed and ran around the room. She thought little Manette was a giant crab trying to pinch her. Mother, Da Gertrude and I tried to hold on to her but she was strong. I couldn't believe it, she's so thin. Finally she weakened and Da Gertrude put some herbs in a pair of socks and tied the socks on to her feet. It helped, she went to sleep.

6 OCTOBER

Catherine gets worse. Manette and I are not allowed to go in her bedchamber. We stand at the door, but it's hard to see her through the nets.

THURSDAY, 8 OCTOBER

Tonight I sneaked into Catherine's room after Mother fell asleep. I sat on her bed under the nets and we talked, whispering in the dark. Before I left I took her hand.

'You mustn't touch me,' she said, pulling away.

'Imagine this. Imagine that I'm holding you,' I said.

She began to cry, so I put my arms round her and held her close. How could I not?

14 OCTOBER

Father came home late tonight. I heard him stumbling in and then I heard Mother: 'Catherine is dying and where are you? Getting drunk, you damn fool!'

Sheet lightning lit up my room and in the dark silence I heard the shrill whistle of the fruit bats. Catherine is *dying*?

15 OCTOBER

After morning chores I went down to the river, looking for Mimi. I needed her help. Mimi knew the ways of the spirits, the *mystères*.

She was up to her knees in the bathing pool washing linens, her flour-sack chemise soaked. Under a lilac bush the two pugs sat watching. A chicken was scratching in the mud nearby.

It began to rain. We took shelter under a tree laden with green oranges. The pugs scuffed around at Mimi's feet.

'Remember when we went to the obeah woman's hut?' I said.

'You think I'd forget?' She threw a pebble at the chicken, to shoo it away.

'I never told you something.' I paused. The rain was coming down heavily now, dripping through the leaves. I began to feel a little ill, the way I do when a wind starts up. 'The old woman told Catherine she'd be in the ground before her birthday this December. And now Mother says Catherine's—'

'*Catherine* went?'

'When I was in the cellar.'

'You never told me!'

'I *promised* not to tell.'

'That girl!'

'And now Mother says Catherine is . . .' I stopped, tears choking. 'What if what the obeah woman said comes true?' I blurted out. 'Can't you change it?'

'Undo it?'

'Yes!'

Mimi rested her chin on her knees, thinking. 'A paquets Congo,' she said finally.

'Yes,' I said, taking a breath. A paquets Congo, properly made . . .

I spent the afternoon helping Mimi gather the ingredients: a toad (which Mimi killed, not me), a tcha-tcha root, a bag of mombin leaves and some hairs I took from Catherine's comb.

'It must be buried under a mapou tree,' Mimi said, securing the bundle with a bit of red string, the type barren women wear at voodoo ceremonies. 'By moonlight.'

'I can't,' I said. 'Not at night.'

'It's safe if you keep your eyes down.'

'It's Mother.' Mother doesn't believe in voodoo, but she fears the mystères, the voodoo spirits.

'I'll do it then,' Mimi said.

'Alone?' I asked, in awe of her courage.

I don't know how late it was when Mimi climbed in my window. 'I did it,' she hissed, shaking me awake. I could hardly see her in the dark. 'I buried the paquets.' Faintly, through the steady drone of the rain, I heard drums.

'You're wet,' I said, touching her hand.

'I can't stay.' She tightened her kerchief round her head. 'There's a séance.'

I watched her climb down the mango tree, watched until I could see her no longer. I felt a chill pass through me, smelled the faint scent of a cigar. Trembling, I shut the window, pulled the curtains tight against the dark night.

15 OCTOBER

Father Droppet came today. I must have looked suddenly pale, for he guided me to the sofa in the parlour and suggested I rest for a moment. Mother came in then. She took his soaking wet cloak and hat. 'I was afraid you would not be able to make it,' she said. 'The roads are so bad.'

'The roads are bad,' he said.

He was in with Catherine for a very short time. When he came out, Mother offered him tea, but he said he must be on his way, because of the roads.

After he left I went to my bedchamber. I took the heavy wooden cross down from the wall and kissed it, pressed it to my heart. Don't take Catherine, I prayed. Don't. *Don't!*

16 OCTOBER

When I woke it was quiet in the house except for the sound of Mother crying and Father talking in a tired, sad voice.

I tiptoed into Catherine's room and I saw her lying there, still and all alone with no one fanning her, no one praying. I watched to see her chest rise and fall, her eyelids flicker, but there was no movement, only silence.

I willed myself to touch her, to wake her, but I could not. I stumbled back down the hall to my room. *Catherine is dead.* I began to shake.

I climbed out of my window and down the mango tree. I ran up the track to the slave shacks. Mimi was asleep on her straw pallet. She opened her eyes, seeing me slowly.

'You said it would work!' I cried. I hit her with my fist.

'Oh . . .' She grabbed my wrists, hard.

'Do something!' I was blubbering. 'Make her come back!'

Mimi began to cry then too. 'Oh, that little brat,' she moaned. She held me in her arms and rocked me, whispering, 'It's done, it's done. Rest now.'

7.00 P.M.

The rains stopped. 'We are blessed,' Mother said, her eyes shining. She washed Catherine all over with rum and laid her out in her festival gown on a patchwork counterpane. Father told me and Manette to go and gather flowers. We were bringing in baskets of roses, red jasmine, orchids and honeysuckle all morning. Mother laced the orchids through Catherine's hair and arranged the other blossoms nicely all around her.

'She looks beautiful,' Manette said, awed.

But so still.

Mother tried to get her best crucifix, the iron one with the tiny ruby in the centre, to stay in Catherine's hands, but it kept slipping to the floor.

'That will do,' Father said. I don't think he liked Mother fussing so.

Mother laid the cross on Catherine's chest and it stayed.

In the afternoon, neighbours began to arrive, gaping at our worn rugs. Later we began the journey to Trois-Ilets, two carriages and a wagon through the mud to the graveyard behind the church. The roads were perilous but it was so hot we dared not wait a day. One of the horses foundered in the deep footing and several times we had to stop to pull a carriage out of the ruts.

The sun was going down as the box was lowered into the tomb. My knees gave way as the top was fastened on. Da Gertrude helped me to my feet. All the way home, fireflies circled us. Circled us and circled us.

It is late now. The air is heavy with the threat of rain. I listen to the land breezes stirring the mango tree outside my window, the noisy *cabri-bois*. Father Droppet says Catherine's in Heaven, that she's with God. Yet I feel her in the wind, in the dark shadows. I feel her tears and I think, why *Catherine*? Why not *me*? The beating of my heart such a terrible sin.

SUNDAY, 19 OCTOBER

Mother and I took a potted ginger lily to town today to put on Catherine's tomb. Then Mother told me to go and sit in the wagon. When I looked back I saw her kneeling in the dirt. I ran to see if she was hurt. She had her fist in her mouth and her face was wet. It frightened me, seeing her thus. I didn't know what to say or do.

'Is there a God?' she cried out. I could see rage in her eyes.

I was afraid to answer, afraid that something I said might condemn Catherine to eternal Hell. 'We'd better go,' I said quickly, reaching out for her, fearful of what she might do in that holy place.

Once home I persuaded Mother to have a rum and syrup and got her to lie down. Her cry fills me still: *is there a God?*

My quill trembles and tiny blots of ink like a flurry of tears cover the page.

In which I suffer a bitter disappointment
& hope is offered anew

3 JANUARY 1778

Uncle Tascher came from Fort-Royal today with a buggy-load of
provisions: coarse cotton fabric for the slaves' clothing, black crêpe
for mourning clothes for us. Then he pulled a letter out of his vest
pocket – a letter from Paris! From Aunt Désirée.

Father read the letter. He looked up at his brother. 'It's about
Désirée's godson – the Marquis's boy.' He snorted. '*My*.'

'Are you not going to read it aloud, Father?' I sat down beside
Mother on the sofa. Outside a gentle breeze stirred the palms. Our
lovesick bull was bellowing in his pen.

Father began to read. In the letter Aunt Désirée informed Father
that the Marquis's son, Alexandre – 'handsome and well educated' –
was now seventeen. If he married, he would come into his mother's
inheritance, so Aunt Désirée has suggested he marry one of her nieces
– one of *us*.

At last! I thought. My prayers had been answered.

But then Father read out a part about Alexandre preferring
Catherine.

Catherine? 'But . . .' I stuttered. It was only two months ago we
buried Catherine.

Mother put down her mending. 'Let him have her then,' she said.
She is like that still – strange somehow.

Father paced the room. 'The young chevalier will command an
annual income of at least forty thousand livres.'

'Forty thousand?' Grandmother Sannois said, coming into the
room. 'Did he say forty thousand? Or four?'

Father stood by the window. 'Maybe they would take Manette
instead.'

'My thinking exactly, Joseph,' Uncle Tascher said, rubbing his chin.

I didn't understand. Why not *me*?

'Manette's too young,' Mother protested.

'Four thousand would be an acceptable income,' Grandmother Sannois remarked.

'Manette's *eleven*,' Father said. 'By the time—'

'Only just,' Mother interrupted.

'Eleven and a half. You're not being reasonable!' Father raised his voice.

Uncle Tascher coughed and poured himself a rum. 'Opportunities like this don't come along every day.'

'Why not *me*?' I said, standing.

Father looked uneasy. He sighed. 'Rose . . .' He glanced at the letter again. Then he cleared his throat. 'The chevalier has expressed a preference for a younger bride. You are too close to him in age – you wouldn't look up to him the way a wife should.'

Mother snorted.

'That's it exactly,' Father said. He stomped to the door. 'God help me!' He slammed the door behind him.

'I won't let you take my baby!' Mother cried.

I ran to my room. I started to throw things into an old haversack. I was going to run, I didn't care where. Anywhere. Even the empty slave shack down by the shore would be better than this. Even a cave in the mountains, with the runaways.

That's when I saw Manette, standing in the door sucking on a stick of sugarcane, her battered wooden doll under one arm.

'I thought you were playing outside,' I said. I didn't care about Manette, to tell the truth. I heard sniffles.

'I don't want to go!'

'Oh . . . You heard all that.' I took her in my arms. 'Poor little scarecrow,' calling her the name the slaves had given her.

SUNDAY NIGHT, 4 JANUARY

I woke to the sound of billiard balls knocking against each other, the sound of men laughing. Uncle Tascher and Father were in the games room. How late was it?

'Why one of *your* girls, Joseph?' I heard Uncle demand.

I went to the door, pressed my ear to the crack.

'Not that they aren't lovely,' he went on, 'and of baptismal innocence, both of them, but face it, a girl without a dowry? The lad must be desperate. And if he's such a fine specimen, why must he go halfway round the world for a girl he's never even seen? And a penniless one at that. If he's all our sister says he is, it seems to me he would have his pick of any of the pedigreed strumpets in France.'

'Désirée's no fool,' I heard my father answer. 'How old is the Marquis now anyway? Sixty? Seventy? When he hangs up his fiddle, Désirée will be—' Father made a rude noise.

Then Uncle Robert said something, but I couldn't make it out.

'If she can make this . . .' Father's words became unclear for a moment, 'she'll be legally related. And it wouldn't do, would it, for a *relative* to end her days in a charity hospital.'

I heard a chair scrape on the wood floor. 'I can see the advantage to Désirée, but why would the *son* go along with it?' Uncle Tascher asked.

'Does the boy have a choice? Until he's twenty-one, if his father tells him to jump in the Seine, he's got to jump in the Seine. And if our sister tells the Marquis to make his son go jump in the Seine, I believe the old bastard would do it. The Devil knows what she does for him in return.' He laughed.

'So you think young Alexandre is being forced into this arrangement?'

'Not so much forced as bribed. Happiness is an unlimited income, if you ask me. The only way the young chevalier can get his hands on his fortune is to marry. And my guess is that his piss-proud father told him (at our beloved sister's *suggestion*, God bless her), look, if you want my permission to marry, it must be a Tascher girl.'

There was another burst of laughter and the talk turned to slave prices. I climbed back into bed. I felt a strange tingling in my belly. What did Father mean, that Aunt Désirée had *done* something to the Marquis — something that made him do her bidding?

5 JANUARY

I told Mimi that Manette might be going to France to be married. 'She's scared,' I said.

'What's to be scared of?' Mimi asked, mashing the plaintain with violent strokes.

I wasn't really sure what it was Manette had to be afraid of, but I knew it was something – something to do with dogs climbing over each other, trembling in that pathetic way. 'You know, marriage duty.'

'Is she in flowers yet?'

I shook my head. 'What does that have to do with it?' All I know is that the cook isn't allowed to cure pork when she's in flowers.*

'Child, don't they tell you *anything*!' But Mimi didn't tell me anything either.

17 MARCH

Now Manette is ill – she has a fever, just as Catherine had. Mother says it's her fear of getting married that brought it on.

I crawl in under the covers beside her and try to cheer her. I tell her how grand it will be in France. I tell her about the wonderful dolls they have there, and how our beautiful Aunt Désirée will look after her. I tell her how handsome the chevalier is, how smart and how educated, how noble and how rich. I tell her how envious I am. (Oh, but I am!)

But in her fever she only cries. There are nights when I'm so afraid she will die, as Catherine did, in one big moment gone, just a limp body on a rumpled bed, no more or less than a rag doll.

23 JUNE, 9.00 P.M.

Father came back from Sainte-Lucie yesterday. Right away he and Mother got into a quarrel.

'But Manette never did want to go!' I heard Mother say. 'It was *you* put those words in her mouth.' She started crying that he *couldn't* take Manette from her, not so soon after losing Catherine.

---

* The belief that a menstruating woman could spoil a ham was maintained into the nineteenth century. Doctors published papers in medical journals theorizing that when a woman was menstruating her skin became moist, preventing the pork from taking in salt.

Father yelled, 'You crazy Creole women and your children!' I felt the walls shake as the door slammed shut.

24 JUNE

Father has relented. He wrote to Aunt Désirée, telling her he wouldn't be able to bring Manette, she was too ill to go, but how about me? He explained that I wasn't all *that* old, and already well developed.

'You know they may not like the idea, Rose,' he told me, sealing the letter with wax. 'After all, you're fifteen.'

'When will you find out?'

'It will take a few months for my letter to get there and what with the war on . . .' He stopped to calculate. 'Five months?'

I moaned. Five months! I want to know *now*!

In which I fall in love

SUNDAY, 19 JULY 1778
There is talk of a new family in town, a woman and her son. At church I saw them after Mass. The boy – about sixteen, I guessed, and comely – was watching three village boys chase a scorpion that had slipped under a pew. He fiddled with the handle of his cutlass, his long dark bangs hiding his eyes. His linen frock and leather breeches were patched.

'*Béké-goyave*,' Mother said under her breath, pushing me outside. 'Vagabonds!'

25 JULY
Mother allowed me to go with Mimi and Sylvester to market today. 'So long as your chores are done,' she said. We set off for town in the back of the ox cart.

It was busy in the village; I confess I was hoping to see the new boy, but there were only sailors who'd come over from Fort-Royal for the cockfights. I kept my eyes to the ground, the way the nuns had taught.

At the dock we bought a bonito and three coral fish from a fisherman with light frizzy hair. He stared at me while we went through his catch. Then he said something to Sylvester and laughed in a way that made me blush.

We walked back up to the village square to buy pawpaws, guavas, avocado pears and tapioca. At a table displaying pictures of the saints, little mirrors and beads, a woman told us about the runaway slave who had turned into a dog and eaten a baby on the Desfieux plantation. Just at the frightful part the new boy's mother arrived, followed at some distance by the boy, laden with parcels.

His mother nodded at me, her eyes deep set. 'I saw you at church,' she said. She talked like a nun, proper. Between sentences she pressed her lips together.

I nodded. She introduced herself as Madame Browder, a British name. The boy's name is William.

'We're at the foot of Morne Croc-Souris,' I told them.

Mimi spat on the ground.

'On the river?' Madame Browder asked, tucking a wisp of red hair under her plain white téte.

'Further on, La Pagerie.' From across the bay, I could see a gommier making its way slowly to the shore. A swarm of gulls hovered above it like mosquitoes in the rainy season.

'We're closer in towards town,' Madame Browder said.

'The old Laignelot homestead,' Mimi said. She was scratching the ears of a mangy dog. 'Neighbours, if you go by the river.'

I felt I should invite them for tea and cakes, but I dared not, remembering my mother's harsh words: *béké-goyave*. I was saved by Sylvester pulling up in the wagon. Hurriedly I took my leave.

'Sweet eyes,' Mimi teased on the way home, jabbing me with her elbow. 'I saw you making sweet eyes.'

SUNDAY, 9 AUGUST

William and his mother sat near the front in church this morning. Mother, Manette (who is better now) and I sat on a bench several rows behind. All through Mass I watched him, my heart fluttering like a trapped baby bird.

10 AUGUST

I sneaked down to the lower pond this afternoon for a swim. But when I got there I saw the new boy William Browder. He was fishing, his pantaloons rolled up to his knees. He started when he saw me, as if he shouldn't be there. He pulled his line out of the water, a long length of white horsehair attached to a bamboo pole.

'Caught anything?' It was hot and I longed to go in, but I didn't know if I should, now that he was there. Instead I sat down on the bank. I picked a long blade of razor grass and split it so I could whistle through it.

'How do you do that?' William Browder asked, rolling down his pantaloons.

I showed him and we sat whistling.

'Why did you move to Trois-Ilets?' I asked finally. *Cul-de-sac à vaches* — cow field — that's what we call it. 'Not that it's my business,' I added, in an attempt to show manners.

'It was hard for my mother in Saint-Pierre,' he said. He looked up at the sky. A hawk was circling. 'It's hard for her here, too.' He shrugged.

I'd heard that his mother used to be an actress, that she'd fallen in love with a sailor in the British navy during the Seven Years' War. Imagine having a mother like that, I thought. An actress! The shame and the glory of it. An actress couldn't be buried in a church graveyard, or even marry — the Church forbade it.

'You're English? But you don't have an accent.' I swatted at a red ant crawling up my arm.

'My father was from Scotland actually.'

I didn't know where Scotland was, but I was relieved he wasn't English. The English are not Christian — they eat children.

'I never knew him,' he went on. He stretched out on the grass, twirling a blade of grass between his fingers.

'Never?'

William looked at me. His eyes were the lightest blue I'd ever seen. 'I remember his face, remember him smiling. But that's all.'

'My father is rarely home, so I don't suppose it's that much different,' I told him.

'When I was young,' William said, 'I liked to think that my mother and father had loved each other very much, and had parted tragically. I thought that better than some long drawn-out marriage where the husband and wife only grow bitter and cold.'

A fish jumped from the water, making rings over the glassy surface of the pond. I thought of my own mother and father, of the bitterness between them. Had there ever been love?

William pushed his hair away from his eyes. 'I'm a romantic, I suppose.' He smiled. 'Like my hero, Jean-Jacques Rousseau.'

I got to my feet, uneasy. No one, most especially a boy, had ever talked to me about such things. I feared it was improper and didn't know how to respond. 'I must go,' I said.

'Yes,' William said, also rising. He stood before me, awkward and hesitant, no longer a mysterious young man, the son of an actress who had been tragically loved, but instead only William, a *béké-goyave* in patched clothes.

I hurried up the track. At the stone bridge I glanced back. William was watching me.

'Tomorrow?' he called out.

I ran up the hill, my face burning.

WEDNESDAY, 12 AUGUST

All morning I told myself: I'm not going to go, I'm not going to go. And then, after chores, there I was, heading for the swimming pond . . .

William grinned when he saw me coming down the track. I pretended to be surprised to see him there. I didn't know what to say so I sat on the bank and threw pebbles in the water. Then I ran home singing.

If anyone ever found out, I hate to think what might become of me.

I will never go again.

2 SEPTEMBER

Whenever I can I go to the fishing pond. William is often there. Mostly we sit and talk. I tell him how I long to go to France, to *Paris*, how I feel there is so much to experience and see, how exciting it is to be young and looking forward to it all, how hard to be told your dreams are impossible.

William is the same. He longs to see the world. He reads the journals that come over on the boats. He tells me all about the things that are going on in the American colonies. He talks of 'freedom' and 'equality'. He asks me what I think about it all, but I tell him I don't read, so how do I know?

'You don't have to read to know how you feel about something like freedom. It's in your heart,' he says, 'not in words on a page.'

This afternoon he read a passage from a book: 'Man is born free, but is everywhere in chains.'* '*Born* free,' he said. 'Imagine that.'

---

* From *The Social Contract* by Jean-Jacques Rousseau.

'Everyone?'

'Free *and* equal.'

'Slaves, too?'

'A master and his slaves.' He paused. 'A king and his subjects.'

'Is *that* what's written in that book?' I regarded it with apprehension, as if it might burst into flames before my eyes. 'But William,' I said, 'if that were true, the world would—' I stopped. I couldn't think of a word big enough.

'Yes!' he said.

FRIDAY, 18 SEPTEMBER

William and I have quarrelled. It started when I told him Mimi casts my cards, that she's teaching me how.

'How can your life be in those little pieces of paper?' he demanded.

'I just know the cards are right. I have seen that it is so.'

'You can't believe in freedom then,' he said.

'Show me freedom!' I cried, and he had no answer. For there is no such thing.

20 SEPTEMBER, 8.30 P.M.

William has apologized and I have accepted. He confessed that it distressed him to think that there might be no such thing as freedom, that everything was written. 'Then what would it matter what a person did?' he asked.

I told him about Catherine, that the old woman had told her fortune, and how it had so tragically come to pass. Then I told him about what the the old woman had said to me.

'Do you believe this is your destiny – to be *Queen* of France?' he asked.

'How frightful that would be,' I said. A flock of crows was making a racket in some bushes down in a ravine.

William picked a bough of scarlet bougainvillea and crowned my head. He stood back to look at me. 'You would make a lovely queen,' he said.

I turned away, for I felt so shamelessly beautiful in his eyes.

He made a mock bow. 'But who will be your king?'

The bougainvillea fell from my head. I stooped to pick it up. I stood and faced him, suddenly dizzy. 'You?'

Then he kissed me, and I allowed him to do so.

16 OCTOBER

This afternoon William and I hiked up the mountain in hopes of seeing the green flash.* We waited until just after dusk, but even so, we did not see it, for too much kissing.

SUNDAY, 1 NOVEMBER, ALL SAINTS' DAY

Oh . . . holidays, holidays, holidays, I'm so anxious for them to be over.

This morning, after lighting candles at Catherine's tomb, Mother, Manette and I returned to a holiday 'feast' at home: boiled green bananas and *féroce*. The *féroce* tasted terrible without salt, which we have had to do without ever since the British blockaded the port.† We said a prayer for Father, who is engaged in conflict in Sainte-Lucie.

I've not seen William for five days.

15 DECEMBER

The British have captured Sainte-Lucie. Father is safe – he's on his way home.

NEW YEAR'S DAY, 1779

Today I brought William a gift of ginger sweets. 'You have found the way to my heart,' he said. Sometimes he talks like that – like an old-fashioned knight.

It was hot so we stayed in the water a long time. When we got

---

* A narrow line of green that can occasionally be seen as the sun sets or rises. It is believed to bring luck to those who see it.
† France was unofficially supporting the American War of Independence against Britain by providing supplies to the American troops from Fort-Royal, so British ships had blockaded the port.

out we stretched out on the bank to dry. He untied my hair. Then he kissed me and held me close. There were no sounds, no birds singing, only the beating of my heart. I pulled away then, for it frightened me, this.

'Where have you been?' Mother said when I got home. The shadows had grown long.

'At the river with Mimi,' I lied.

'Your cheeks are pink,' she said. 'You're neglecting to wear your bonnet.'

It is night now, late. The hills are silent. I couldn't sleep so I got up and lit a candle and opened this dear little book, that I might write down the thoughts that burn in my heart.

I love William. I love William. I love William.

In which I am betrothed

FRIDAY, 29 JANUARY 1779

The letter from Paris came today. Aunt Désirée wrote to Father: whatever, just bring a girl, me or Manette, it didn't matter. 'We must have one of your daughters.' She urged Father to act with haste; the young chevalier might change his mind if forced to wait too long.

There was a note to Father from the Marquis as well: 'The one whom you judge most suitable for my son will be the one whom we desire.' He enclosed permission to have the banns read and left a space where a name should go.

Father looked at me. 'Well, Rose, your prayers have been answered,' he said, writing out my name on the form.

I looked away.

'What a funny girl you are. Always crying when you're happy.'

I wiped my cheeks with the back of my hand. 'Yes, Father,' I said.

31 JANUARY

At church this morning I saw William. I made our signal and he acknowledged it.

Back home, I hurried with my chores. I asked leave to go down to the river – with Mimi, I said, praying for forgiveness for lying, especially on a Sunday.

Mother consented and I was gone before she could think otherwise, down the track and into the forest. At the bridge I stopped, my breath coming in short jabs. Why was I running? I proceeded at a walk, my troubled thoughts catching up with me. What was I going to tell him?

William was fishing at the pond. He turned when he heard me on the path.

'I'm glad you could come,' I said, standing nervously beside him, like a stranger. 'I have something to tell you.' I heard the cry of a raven.

William pulled in his line. There was a live frog on the hook.

'Father received a letter from his sister in Paris,' I said. 'His offer has been accepted.'

'What offer?'

'I'm to be betrothed – to a man in France.'

William fiddled with the hook, trying to slide the frog off. He cursed under his breath and did not beg my forgiveness for doing so.

'I'm to go and live in Paris. I will be a vicomtesse.' In spite of myself, there was pride in my voice.

William looked at me. His eyes seemed unnaturally blue.

'Are you not going to say anything?' I felt uneasy.

William threw his fishing gear into his basket. 'Thank you for telling me? Is that what I'm supposed to say?' He untied his dusty donkey from a gumtree branch.

'William . . .' I put one hand on his shoulder.

He jerked away, pulling himself on to his donkey's back. Then he kicked her, taking off down the track at a trot.

I sat by the river, trying hard not to cry.

SUNDAY, 11 APRIL

This morning, after Mass, Father Droppet read the banns of marriage between Alexandre-François, Chevalier de Beauharnais, and Marie-Josèphe-Rose de Tascher de la Pagerie.

Manette made monkey eyes at me. Everyone turned to stare. I felt Father Droppet was speaking of someone else, not me.

Now this is the big news in the village: at last I will be married, and to a rich man in Paris, to a *Beauharnais*, the son of the former governor of all the Windward Islands. I will be Madame la vicomtesse. I am regarded as an adult now and I feel older, I admit.

8 MAY

Mother is having a dress made for me, in the Parisian style, an amaranthine brocade with gauze round the sleeves and neck. I'm not to wear it until I reach France. That way at least I'll have one thing decent to wear, she said. I go for my first fitting today.

MONDAY, 7 JUNE

Mother insists I learn a proper toilette. I'm to wear a *corps de baleine*, a whalebone corset with stays so stiff it pushes my bosom up and forces me to sit straight. It even hurts to breathe. 'When can I take it off?' I asked after one long hour sitting at my vanity, applying pommades.

'You must never take it off,' Mother said, showing Mimi how my hair is to be powdered. 'You are a woman now.'

23 JUNE

I'm sixteen today – how quickly youth passes. Mimi gave me tarot cards of my own as a gift. 'Blessed by holy water,' she whispered.

Carefully, I laid them out. In the tenth position was the hanged man, his hair hanging down.

'Life turned upside down,' she snorted.

SATURDAY, 10 JULY

Father is having difficulty getting enough money to pay for passage. I overheard him having an argument with Uncle Tascher. 'I've loaned you enough already, Joseph!' I heard Uncle say.

16 JULY, 3.00 P.M.

Father finally has enough money. Uncle Tascher gave in. Now Father has to find a ship that can take us. With the war on, it won't be easy, he says.

I worry, for his health is poor.

'You won't survive this voyage, Joseph,' I heard Mother tell him this morning. 'And then where will we be?'

'It's my only hope. Those doctors in Paris know things,' he said, coughing.

What if Mother is right? What if Father dies?

28 July

We leave in two weeks. Mother has had the two big sea chests hauled up to the parlour and there are stacks of clothing everywhere. There is so much to be done, deciding what to take, what to leave behind.

Mother is intent on sending Da Gertrude with me, but Da Gertrude begs to stay. The journey would kill her, she says.

'It's Lasyrenn that scares her,' Mimi whispered.

Lasyrenn, the voodoo spirit of the sea, the mermaid with the long black hair. Lasyrenn just below the surface of the water, calling.

29 July
Mimi's coming with me!

Sunday, 8 August
We leave for Fort-Royal the day after tomorrow, and the day after that we sail. At Saint-Domingue we will change over to the *Ile de France*, a naval store ship which Father warns might not be too comfortable. The frigate *La Pomone* will accompany us all the way to France, to defend us in case we're attacked by the British at sea.

'I don't like sailing when there's a war on,' Father told me, 'but if we wait for peace, we will never get there.'

It's scary, but thrilling – what if we were in a battle!

1.00 P.M.
A wind rises, bending the palms. The hot air rushes at my skirts, pulling my plaits loose, my dangling silver earrings. It is midday, but dark as midnight. Inside, in my room, I fasten the wooden shutters with some effort and light a wax taper on my toilette table. I scribble over the pages, seeking a path to my heart, one word, one name: *William*.

From somewhere a breeze catches the flame and snuffs it out, plunging me into dark.

9 August

Dawn was breaking when I got up. I slipped on my clothes and went out into the fields. Sucre was hard to catch. I had to use a custard apple to tempt her. Finally I got a bridle on her and headed off towards the river, my petticoats up around my thighs, my pony's warm body between my legs.

I waited by the stone bridge. Before long William came poking along the track on his donkey, reading a book. He was surprised when he saw me.

'Come up the mountain with me,' I said.

'You're betrothed.'

'I'm leaving tomorrow!'

That seemed to startle him.

I took the lead going up the slope. At the top of the path, where it opens into a clearing, I stopped. 'This is a good place.' I slid off Sucre.

'Good as any.' William tied his donkey to a coconut tree.

'You're not the only one who—'

'Who *what*? What is it that you feel, Rose?' He turned away. 'I'm sorry,' he said. 'I know it can't be helped.'

I pressed my forehead into his back. 'Do you think it possible we will always love one another?'

'Do not speak of love, I beg you,' he said, his voice full of tears.

We stayed on the hill until the mosquitoes began to swarm. He kissed me on my cheek. I longed for more, much more, but I no longer had the right.

We rode down the mountain, through the long shadows. At the bottom he turned to me. 'We never saw the green flash.'

I'd forgotten.

'Some other day,' he said, shading his eyes against the sun.

11 August – Fort-Royal

We were eight of us in the covered wagon – myself, Father and Mimi, plus Mother, Manette, Grandmother Sannois, even Da Gertrude. And Sylvester driving. Plus the two big sea trunks. So it was a wonder the horses could pull us at all. More than once we were up to the hub in mud and had to walk.

It was dangerously after dusk by the time we pulled into Uncle Tascher's courtyard. His wife came running down to greet us, her hair down and looking wild, Uncle Tascher behind her all red in the face.

We were all of us put in two rooms on the second floor. Uncle Tascher's waiting woman brought us cassava bread with sugar syrup and a saucepan of hot chocolate, to which Father added brandy from his hip flask. We ate and made ready for bed. As we said our evening prayers together, I could hear sniffling. Da Gertrude had her face in her hands.

I woke before dawn. I lay there for a time, dreaming. What will Monsieur de Beauharnais be like? I wondered. I imagined that he would be handsome and gallant, but perhaps a little shy, so that I would have to coquette a little to put him at his ease. I practised rolling my eyes, which I am told are my best feature, and kissing the back of my hand, but this only made my hand wet, and reminded me of William. I hoped that Monsieur de Beauharnais would be very much like William, only titled and rich, and that he would come to love me very much. As for myself, I know I will come to love him, for Da Gertrude says I could love a flea.

Grandmother stirred, poked Mother to help her up, and the day began. I went to the window and pulled back the heavy brocade. Our sailing ship was still there, beside the little fishing boats. One of the sails had been unfurled. I was anxious to be on deck, for what if a wind came and we were left behind?

For once Mother didn't have to tell me to get ready. Da Gertrude laced me into my best gown, the yellow one with the fichu I'd embroidered myself.

Mimi, still in her petticoats, joined us from the other room. 'I had a bad dream last night.' She wiped her sleepy eyes.

Da Gertrude threw her hands to her ears. 'Don't say that!'

'Hush!' Mother said, crossing herself.

Finally, we were ready, dressed in our church clothes. We'd eaten, had coffee and milk, said our morning prayers, which went on for so long my knees ached.

Uncle Tascher ordered two teams harnessed. His coachman (in new livery — very handsome) and Sylvester loaded the trunks on to an open wagon harnessed to two sleepy mules. Mimi, clutching her wicker basket, and a sniffling Da Gertrude climbed in behind. Sylvester swung himself up on to the driver's seat. Uncle's coachman – looking liquorish, in spite of the hour – helped us into Uncle's new carriage.

'My,' Mother said, touching the blue silk upholstery. 'Are you sure we are supposed to sit on it, Robert?'

Grandmother knocked on the glass to see if it was real and pulled down one of the shades to see if it worked. 'Pity it's that colour,' she said.

'Oh yes, oh yes, oh yes, do sit.' Uncle Tascher's wife arranged her pleated skirt of brown taffeta (from *Milan*). 'I never walk anywhere any more.' She looked in the glass to make sure her frightful red hair was well hidden under her lace cap.

'I feel like a queen in such a carriage,' I said. Then I slapped my hand over my mouth, for there was talk of my fortune still.

The coachman cracked his whip and the horses jumped forward, throwing us into a tumble.

As we approached the docks, Father took my hand. 'Nervous?'

'Mon Dieu,' Mother said. 'That ship's not so very big, Joseph.'

'We'll be changing to a bigger one at Saint-Domingue.' Father jumped down onto the dock as if he was a young man. He let down the metal step.

'A ship *and* an escort.' Uncle Tascher adjusted his hat, for he was Port Commander now. He took Mother's hand as she stepped down. 'They should be safe from attack.'

Sylvester pulled the wagon carrying Da Gertrude and Mimi up behind us. Our two sea trunks were loaded into a rowboat and suddenly we were all saying goodbye.

'Send me a doll!' Manette demanded, clasping me tightly round the waist.

I kissed her dear, tear-streaked face. 'You'll write?'

She nodded, but I knew she wouldn't.

Mother took my hands. 'You must remember to wash under your nails.'

'Maman!'

She put her hand on my shoulder. 'You'll be a good girl?'

I embraced her then. I feared she might cry.

Mimi and Father were already seated in the little passenger dinghy. Father was yelling for me to get in.

Da Gertrude took me in her arms. 'My baby!' I began to weep as well.

I kissed her wet cheeks and pulled away. A sailor with a beard helped me into the boat. Father handed me his kerchief. Mimi looked terrified. And then we were on the water, waving and throwing kisses.

I looked back. Da Gertrude had fallen to her knees and was praying. Mother stood silently beside Grandmother Sannois, her hands pressed to her chest. It was only Manette and Sylvester, at the last, who stood waving.

II

Vicomtesse

In which I come to the Old World

My knees trembled climbing on to the dock. I held on to Mimi to steady myself. I hadn't realized how frightened I'd been that we would never make it.

France! So many people, horses, carriages! A porter balancing a load on his head barked out to us to move. A newsmonger yelled from the edge of the crowd. It seemed strange, all these white faces rushing about, crying out words I couldn't understand.

Captain and the flag lieutenant helped with Father. He was so sick he could hardly walk. He has been taking a syrup of maidenhair and brandy concoction the ship's surgeon had made him, but it hadn't helped.

I asked a painted lady standing by some sea chests where we might hire a hackney coach but she only looked at me. 'She can't understand your dialect,' Captain explained, getting Father seated on a crate. He hailed a hackney cab and helped get us settled in a public house. He even sent word to Aunt Désirée that we have arrived. He said it would take about ten days for her to get here, maybe longer.

At first we tried to take a lodging in the Hôtel du Monarque, an airy and lightsome place with chandeliers, carpets and a buffet on which a few plates were set out. We were led into a parlour where a lady stood by the fire in a dress over a hoop so big I don't know how she got through the door.

We were all set to settle when Father, whom we had propped up in a chair, doubled over coughing and the innkeeper told us we couldn't stay. Captain, who doesn't hold his temper at the best of times, started to speak. I quickly assured him we would *prefer* to stay somewhere else. So here we are now, at the Hôtel Graves, which is at least clean, although not nearly so grand.

Father and I each have a room on the second floor, facing the street. Mimi was given a room by the stables and privies. I told the innkeeper, Madame Mignon Lodi-Clarion, a cross sort, and thin as a stick, that I wanted Mimi with me, that I needed her help during the night, with Father, but Madame insisted. 'We'll have the boy fetch her when you need her' is what she said, somewhat curtly.

The first thing I did after getting Father settled was ask to have a bath. Madame provided me with a hand-basin of hot water and some Joppa soap, immersion being unsafe, she said. I washed myself as best I could.

When poor Mimi came in she smelled like the barn. I let her use my water for a wash of her own, and then we put our small linens in. We draped them over chairs in front of the coal grate. It's so cold and damp I fear they will never dry.

THAT EVENING
All the people staying at this inn eat together. I went down without Father. We had cod's head with shrimps and oysters, and then mutton, eggs and a dish of broiled eels which I did not care for but forced myself to eat, to be polite. After the meal a man across the table rubbed his teeth with a sponge and scraper. I thought perhaps that was the custom here, but he was the only one who did it. Then he asked for the chamber-pot. Hastily, I took my leave.

THURSDAY, 14 OCTOBER
Father didn't sleep last night, suffering feverish dreams. He kept saying he *couldn't* die now.

I tried to get him to take some fish broth but he couldn't keep it down, coughing up blood. 'I'll get Madame.' I didn't want him to see me crying.

'No.' He fell back against his pillows.

I'm back in my room now, but I cannot sleep, listening for sounds on the other side of the wall. Listening for life — but fearing death.

THAT EVENING
At last, the doctor came, his tall assistant carrying his big bag. He

prescribed a tincture which Father's to take three times a day. That and his visit cost five livres! At least Father's not to be bled.

16 OCTOBER

Yesterday evening, after Father was asleep, I joined several of the guests in the front parlour. I taught them how to play piquet, which I learned on the boat. I was naughty and wagered a bit of money on it and won two sous from Monsieur d'Aelders, a dear old man from Dijon. I tried to give him the money back after, but he insisted I keep it, somewhat proudly. He's vowed revenge tonight!

Even Madame played. She was sipping wine and humming.

Everyone wanted to know what it was like to live on a sugar plantation: Madame said it was a well-known fact that an owner of a sugar plantation earned more money than a king. Monsieur d'Aelders wanted to know if it was true that the slaves went about naked.

'Not all the time,' I said, an answer that seemed to please him.

I told them that I've come to France to meet my fiancé. Madame told a story about how when she was introduced to her husband (who died six years ago), she was wearing false eyebrows, mouse skin ones. She didn't know it, but one eyebrow had fallen off! Her fiancé kept looking at her strangely.

I like Madame better now. She informed me that I may address her as Madame Mignonette. She told me how to get mildew out of linen: rub soap on it, scrape some chalk and rub that in and put it into the sun, wetting it a little. She says I might have to do it twice, but it should come out.

I told her I liked France, but that I had to confess that sometimes the smells quite overpowered me. She gave me a vial to hang round my neck. Inside there is flower water I can sniff. Also, I can dab little bits on my wrists and behind my ears and even on my bosom. She told me to dab it 'everywhere', wiggling her eyebrows. When she has time, she said, she'll show me how to dress like a *proper* French lady.

21 OCTOBER

Still no word from Aunt Désirée.

Shortly before noon Madame came to inform Father that there was a woman wishing to see him. 'Are you receiving, Monsieur?'

I glanced around his room, over his person. He had not been shaved yet and the room had not been freshened.

'Comtesse de la Touche de Longpré.' Madame stuck her nose in the air and wiggled her fingers, pretending to put on airs. 'The daughter of Madame de Girardin, she said to tell you.'

I looked at Father, confused. Wasn't Girardin the name of Mother's sister-in-law? I had only met her a few times. I remembered her as a haughty woman who treated Mother poorly.

Father groaned. 'Mon Dieu, Laure Longpré – Brigitte's daughter . . .'

My *cousin* Laure? I hadn't seen her since I was a child. She was much older than I was, almost fifteen years as I recalled, married and with children. I remembered that the boys used to ogle and follow her about, which she didn't discourage.

'Why in God's name would *she* be here?' Father snorted.

Shortly after, Madame Longpré was admitted, filling the room with a heavy iris fragrance that made Father cough. Quickly I opened the windows.

'Rose, how you've grown,' she said, accepting my offer of a chair. She was wearing a frothy pink dress looped in gauze with tassel decorations.

I curtsied, not knowing what to say. She was quite heavily made-up with jewels on every part of her, particularly over her bosom, which was displayed in such a way as to make one blush.

'How *charming* to have relatives in France,' she said. Her eyebrows had been plucked into a thin line and blackened with charcoal and the lids of her eyes were painted silver. 'I understand there may be a wedding soon.'

Father began to choke.

'Would you care for a dish of tea?' I said. 'Sweetmeats, perhaps?'

'No, thank you, child. I won't keep you. I can see that my uncle is not well, and as for myself, I must be returning home as I have only *recently* risen from childbed.'

Before Father and I could offer our blessings, Madame Longpré turned to me. 'In the last two years I have had the good fortune to make the acquaintance of your fiancé, Chevalier Alexandre de

Beauharnais, whom I assure you is the most *charming* young man one could ever hope to find.'

Father spat into his kerchief.

I searched my mind for something to say. 'A glass of wine perhaps?'

Madame Longpré smiled at me. She stood, taking up her pink parasol. 'When the chevalier does arrive, would you please be so kind as to convey to him my warmest congratulations. Inform him that it would be my *greatest* pleasure to tell him so *personally*.'

Immediately after Madame Longpré left, Father demanded a glass of brandy.

'Mother didn't mention that Laure Longpré lived here,' I said.

'I doubt that she even knows. Your mother and I are none too fond of the Girardins — and they, I must say, are none too fond of us.'

'Madame Longpré seemed *very* friendly.'

'Like a rabid fox,' Father cursed, downing the glass.

23 OCTOBER

Madame showed me fashion 'tricks' this afternoon. Mimi and I giggled, which Madame didn't appreciate, but we couldn't help it, especially when she showed us the false bottoms and bosoms. She showed me how to put a small cork ball in my cheek to fill it out where I'd had a tooth pulled. Madame does this herself, on the right side. (Now I understand why she's a little hard to understand sometimes.) She also showed me how I could glue little patches on my face to cover up my pockmarks. She gave me two small ones made of thick blue wool: one in the shape of a diamond, the other an oval. Then she showed Mimi how to tighten my corset for me by bracing her feet against the bedstead and pulling. We got me all done up with a bottom and a bosom and a tiny, tiny waist. I looked beautiful, but I couldn't breathe and I very nearly fainted!

26 OCTOBER

Aunt Désirée and Monsieur de Beauharnais will be arriving tomorrow! I fear I'm going to be sick.

In which I am introduced to my fiancé

Mimi and I spent the morning in my room fussing over my make-up, my clothes and hair. Every few minutes we would go to the window. At around eleven, I heard Madame's man-of-all-work talking loudly in the street. I looked out and saw a large woman being helped from a conveyance, but no sign of a young man – so I knew it wasn't them.

Then suddenly there was a woman at my door. It was my Aunt Désirée! I last saw her when I was only three or four, so I had no recollection of her, although I'd *imagined* her: my 'beautiful Aunt Désirée', the tall woman with golden hair who had bewitched a wealthy marquis. And now here she was – stout, cross and bossy.

'So.' She looked me up and down with a bit of a frown. 'You must be Rose.' She was wearing a red- and white-striped taffeta gown and a hat quivering with red feathers. She thrust me into a hug. I choked on the powder in her wig.

She wanted to know where Father was. 'That brother of mine – is he dead yet?' she barked.

I opened the sash doors to Father's room, hoping she wouldn't detect the scent of spirits.

'Joseph,' Aunt Désirée commanded, from the door, 'you're not to die!'

'I'm not *trying* to die, Désirée,' my father said, sitting up in bed with some evidence of discomfort, made the more so by his sister's vigorous greeting. I helped adjust the pillows behind his back. 'Where's the young chevalier?' he asked, a question that was foremost in my mind as well.

'I sent him on an errand.' Aunt Désirée helped herself to a cordial from the case near the bed. She looked me over. 'Are you going to hold your tongue, young lady? Your mother warned me you've got a bit of a tongue.'

I had to hold my tongue just then.

'Désirée, don't you be . . . Grand Dieu! I'd forgotten what a—'

'If I were you, I'd keep quiet, Joseph. I've already been attacked by Madame downstairs for the eighty-six livres you owe. And there will be other bills, no doubt.'

I sighed and went to the window. A barber covered in flour crossed the street, dodging a man on horseback. 'When will Monsieur de Beauharnais be returning?' I asked.

Aunt Désirée took me by the shoulders and turned me towards the light. 'None too soon, I hope. You're wearing far too much rouge. And what are these things you've got stuck to your face? Patches have been out of style since King Louis XV died!'

I glanced over at Mimi, who was standing by the door trying hard not to giggle. 'Madame has been helping me with my toilette,' I confessed.

'Madame downstairs? No wonder you look like a tart!'

I fought back tears. Aunt Désirée sighed and pursed her lips. I detected a flicker of affection beneath her crusty exterior. 'My dear child, you will find that your fiancé – should he approve of you, that is, and consent to this union – values *simplicity*, not artifice. He's a strong advocate, as the young man will *no* doubt inform you, of the "Cult of Sensibility", God help us all.'

She made this proclamation as if it was a badge of both honour and ridicule. I hadn't the faintest notion what she meant.

'What your Aunt Désirée is trying to suggest, Rose,' my father said, sinking back under the quilt, 'is that you change your toilette.'

And so it was that I received yet another lesson in how to dress like a proper French lady.

'There now, Joseph, what do you think?' Aunt Désirée pushed me to the foot of Father's bed. She had clothed me in a simple lawn dress and a straw hat covered with silk flowers.

'You've got her looking like a peasant, Désirée. Are you mad? She will catch her death in that get-up.'

The dress was not too different from the chemises we wore

back home, around the house doing our chores. I felt disappointed changing out of the amaranthine brocade gown Mother had had made for me, but Aunt Désirée insisted it was out of style and that Monsieur de Beauharnais would *never* consent to marry me if he saw me in a dress like *that*.

'You never did have taste, Joseph.' Aunt Désirée pulled at my side curls, trying to get them to fall in loose locks around my face – *à la négligence*, she called it. 'Although I must confess I rather agree with you in this instance. But whatever the Queen wears, all the young people follow, and God knows she's leading them on a merry chase.' She pulled a timepiece out of her bosom. 'Come now, child, we mustn't linger.'

I was more confused than nervous following Aunt Désirée down the stairs to the front parlour. The efforts of the last hours had bewildered me, and for some reason I wasn't expecting to meet Monsieur de Beauharnais at that moment – so when I saw a young man in uniform sitting on the sofa, absorbed in a book, I didn't think anything of it.

'Alexandre, if you please,' Aunt Désirée called out with a theatrical flourish, 'it is my pleasure to introduce you to my niece – and *your* fiancée.'

Monsieur de Beauharnais looked up, startled, as if he'd been waiting for a coach and suddenly it had arrived. 'Oh!' He put a bookmark in his little leather volume before carefully setting it down on the side table. He stood up.

'Mademoiselle Tascher de la Pagerie,' Aunt Désirée said grandly, 'Monsieur le chevalier de Beauharnais.'

I felt there had been a mistake. *This* young man was so *very* distinguished in his white uniform with silver facings. His hair (his own, not a wig – I like that) was brushed back from his forehead and nicely powdered. His nose was perhaps too long, but gracefully so. His arched eyebrows gave him an intelligent, questioning look. His eyes were dark, and quite deep set.

I dropped a curtsy all the way down to the ground (displaying my bosom to good effect, I confess) and on rising offered my hand as Father had taught me, delicately, with my little finger slightly raised. I smiled, remembering to keep my mouth closed,* which

---

* Like all the other members of her family, Rose had terrible teeth.

was not difficult, for I was terrified of speaking. Fortunately, Aunt Désirée was not. She stationed herself on the sofa and pulled me down beside her. Then she and Monsieur de Beauharnais talked about whether or not they should get accommodation elsewhere. Apparently Monsieur de Beauharnais was not content with the Hôtel Graves. Aunt Désirée observed that Father should not be moved; he needed to gather strength for the long journey back to Paris. Monsieur de Beauharnais said that in that case he would take a room at the Hôtel du Monarque. I turned my head from one to the other.

At that point Madame Mignonette stumbled in, carrying a basket of soiled laundry. She quickly perceived the situation and, stuttering, asked if we wished refreshment.

'What's wrong with that woman?' Monsieur de Beauharnais asked after she had left, backing out of the room in the most comical way. He pulled a cigar out of a silver case.

'She's no doubt a bit ruffled by the purpose of this meeting,' Aunt Désirée answered.

'She *knows*?'

'As far as I can ascertain, *everyone* knows.' Aunt Désirée rolled her eyes.

'Surely that wasn't necessary.'

Madame's maid came in with wine in a decanter, a little dish of marzipan and a plate of buttered burnt toast. I declined the wine and the sweetmeats, but accepted a piece of toast, eating it in little bites and trying to be ladylike, in spite of the crumbs falling on to my lap. Whenever Monsieur de Beauharnais happened to glance at me, I smiled and made sweet eyes.

I searched my mind for something to say. 'Madame Longpré came to call,' I announced finally. 'She said she would welcome the opportunity to see Monsieur de Beauharnais.'

There was a moment's commotion, for a bit of toast had caught dangerously in Aunt Désirée's throat. 'Madame *Laure* Longpré?' she asked, her eyes watering.

I nodded. 'Didn't Mother take care of her when she was a child?'

'Your mother and I together. Laure was a handful.'

'Still is,' Monsieur de Beauharnais said.

'What a pity that we won't be able to call on her,' Aunt Désirée said.

Then Madame Mignonette announced that supper was served. As I feared, the main course was eels. I noticed that Monsieur de Beauharnais was not fond of them either – so at least we have that in common.

Later we sat around the fire in the front parlour. Some of the others in the inn were playing whist. They were being so boisterous I sometimes had difficulty following what Monsieur de Beauharnais was saying – 'A groundswell of enlightened liberalism is sweeping the land,' or something like that. Then Aunt Désirée would nod and smile, and I would nod and smile, and Monsieur de Beauharnais would speak another sentence.

And so, in this way, my fiancé and I spent our first evening together.

28 OCTOBER

'Well?' Father demanded when I brought him his morning bowl of fish bouillon. (I've succeeded in persuading him to refrain from spirits – at least until noon.) 'The chevalier is to your liking?'

'He's a gentleman.' I pushed back the bedcurtains. 'And comely,' I added. My cheeks felt flushed.

'Indeed. I gather the ladies quite like him.'

'Philosophy is his passion,' I told him proudly.

'Mon Dieu – a *philosophe*?' Father sank back on to the pillows. 'Well,' he sighed, 'it could be worse, I suppose.'

LATER

This afternoon Aunt Désirée saw a notary. Now she has the authority to arrange the marriage herself, she said, 'should anything happen'.

Should Father die, she meant.

THAT EVENING

Monsieur de Beauharnais has gone to the country to call on friends from his regiment. Aunt Désirée has taken advantage of his absence to instruct me on how to be a good wife. This afternoon, after the midday meal (I'm not to eat with my fingers), she presented me with a book which I'm to study. In it are a number of essays on continence and obedience as well as one on how to prepare viands and address servants. She informed me that I treat Mimi too much as a familiar, that in order to command the respect due my station I must observe correct forms.

Also, as a grown woman now, I must take responsibility for the instruction of my servant: Mimi is not to spit and she is to refrain from using a word such as *pisspot* in polite company. She is to drop a curtsy when she sees me and address me as Mademoiselle de la Pagerie. After I am married she's to call me Madame la vicomtesse. Then Aunt Désirée demonstrated a curtsy and made Mimi practise until she had it right. Mimi has never been noted for grace and it was all I could do not to burst.

30 OCTOBER

Monsieur de Beauharnais returned from his visit to the country all good cheer, taking my hand and promising to be a faithful companion 'on the journey of life'. I said, 'Me, too,' and Aunt Désirée looked happy and clucked around us like a mother hen.

We played trictrac after supper. (I let Monsieur de Beauharnais win.) He is so educated and so talented, I am in awe of him. He draws portraits, he has a good singing voice, and he plays the harpsichord. He reads Latin, speaks German, and even a little English. He told me I have lovely eyes and called me 'mathia mou', Greek for 'light of his eyes', he said. I wish I knew something Greek I could call him.

31 OCTOBER, ALL SAINTS' DAY EVE

The doctor feels that Father has improved sufficiently to travel. We leave in the morning. Monsieur de Beauharnais has purchased a closed carriage for the journey. (For forty louis! So much!) It is dark green with black leather seats – *very* pretty. Aunt Désirée lectured him on the evils of going into debt but he said that the expenditure was necessary for Father's comfort. And, he added, 'If Mademoiselle Tascher and I marry, debt will not be an issue.'

If we marry?

In which I come to my city of dreams

Paris! As we crossed the Seine Father gave me a sou to throw in.
'Make a wish.'

'This *is* my wish.'

Paris is bigger and more beautiful than I had imagined, but
so muddy!

'Boue de Paris,' Monsieur de Beauharnais cursed, for a bit had
splashed on to the sleeve of his lavender grosgrain riding jacket.

'*Lutetia*, city of mud – that's what we call it,' Aunt Désirée
said.

I had to confess that there was a strange smell. Aunt Désirée said
one got used to it, but she cautioned me to be careful not to get any
mud on my skirts – it can burn a hole if left on too long.

We made our way at a footpace through crowded streets. I was
in a daze, taking it all in. It was cold; everyone in the market was
wearing shoes. A man in a beribboned wig was selling vinegar from a
wheelbarrow. A squat little soap dealer with a pockmarked face had
twisted pretty scarves together to hold up his buckskin breeches. I
saw a fish lady wearing a fluted cap.

And so many smells! So many sounds! Everywhere foot passengers
were talking, arguing, singing, but I couldn't understand a word
– it's French, but *poissard*, Aunt Désirée said, the language of
the market.

It was late by the time we got to the district of Monsieur de
Beauharnais's family home. The street lamps hanging on great
brackets were just being lit. The house is in a street so narrow
the carriage couldn't turn round. Aunt Désirée expressed warnings
regarding the neighbourhood. 'A short distance away thieves are

known to gather,' she said.*

The house is tall, with big shutters. There is a stone face of a woman above the front door. 'Vesta,' Monsieur de Beauharnais said, helping Father up the steps. 'A Roman goddess.'

'A *guiablesse!*' Mimi whispered, and refused to pass.

I grabbed her hand and pulled her in. 'There are no voodoo spirits in Paris,' I hissed.

Inside, it was very grand – more grand than Uncle Tascher's home in Fort-Royal even – with a big fireplace and many fine furnishings. In the front parlour white and gold brocade curtains hung from gold rods.

'Ohhhhh,' Mimi sighed. The slippery wood floors squeaked when she walked over them, reminding me of crick cracks.

Father took my arm. 'This will do?' he asked.

'It's like a palace,' I whispered. I had a sad thought of Mother and Manette, of our worn grey rugs.

'This way!' Aunt Désirée called out, following Monsieur de Beauharnais up a sweeping staircase.

Monsieur de Beauharnais's father, Marquis de Beauharnais, received us in his bedchamber. He was dressed in a flannel nightshirt and a quilted gold satin dressing gown. He was wearing an old-fashioned white powdered wig of thick curls which flowed over his shoulders and down his back. He was a lot older than I expected – in his sixties or seventies, I think – but he had an air of distinction, in spite of his state of undress.

I made a half-curtsy and accepted his offer of a chair by the fireside, where a tea board had been set.

'Content, Alexandre?' the Marquis asked, after we'd been introduced. I was relieved that Monsieur de Beauharnais answered in the affirmative.

'I believe you will find her pleasing,' Aunt Désirée said.

'I can see that for myself,' the Marquis said. He winked at me.

After a light supper and a family prayer we retired, weary travellers all. Aunt Désirée showed me to my room, which is large and filled with the most elegant furnishings. Father is in the room

---

* The once-prosperous neighbourhood was now quite poor, situated close to the entrance of the '*cour des miracles*' – a haven for beggars and thieves made famous in Victor Hugo's *Hunchback of Notre-Dame*, written in 1831.

next to mine so that I might easily tend him. Mimi is in a room on the third floor with the other household servants.

And so, dear Diary, I must blow out the candle. I hear church bells ringing. I am here, at last. *Paris!*

13 NOVEMBER

Father is more comfortable now that he's taken to bed and doesn't have to move, although he's none too happy about all the concoctions Aunt Désirée makes him take. In the morning he's to eat a paste of powdered rhubarb and currants. In the evening she brings him pennyroyal mixed with sugar. He doesn't mind that so much, but the poultice Mimi must smear on his chest is disgusting: bread mashed with milk, egg yolks and raisins.

14 NOVEMBER

The doctor spent only a moment examining Father. Nevertheless, he is confident of success. He prescribed half a grain of tartar emetic followed by a purgative when nausea commences. Father was pleased; he's to ingest claret as a remedy.

20 NOVEMBER

I've been ill, 'homesick', Aunt Désirée says. It was true. I'd been dreaming of home. 'Nothing an afternoon shopping won't cure,' she said.

So after our morning chocolate she ordered the carriage. Aubin, the footman, escorted us, running in front of our coach in his yellow petticoat with a fringe around the bottom and no breeches.* Mimi told me that there's wine in the silver ball on top of his staff and nothing at all on under his skirt! (Now every time I see him, that's all I can think of.)

Paris is a dirty, crowded city — but everywhere one goes there is gaiety. There are beggars *everywhere*. Some are quite aggressive.

* Breeches were difficult to run in so footmen wore skirts. They also wore bright colours so that they could be more easily seen in the dark.

THE MANY LIVES & SECRET SORROWS OF JOSEPHINE B.

Others play tricks to catch your attention. A gang of street urchins crowded us outside a billiard parlour until Aubin chased after them. One hit Aubin with his flute, on the leg, causing him to curse mightily.

I was overwhelmed by the beauty of all the things on display, all the trimmings and accessories, the laces, ribbons and silks. Everything I saw, I longed for – until I learned the price, that is. I did purchase a sketching pad and some charcoal at a stall in the market. The vendor reminded me of William, which brought on a mournful reverie in me. Secretly, I've started a portrait of him, but already I can't remember his face.

SATURDAY, 27 NOVEMBER
It is late. We've just returned from the home of the Marquis's brother, Comte Charles, who gave a reception on our behalf. I wore a new dress Aunt Désirée had had made for me: an ivory white silk, cut low – quite low! – with a tiny waist. (As tiny as I can get, anyway.) The sleeves have gold frogs on them, very pretty. The full skirt is tucked up by pretty little bunches of flowers, revealing a skirt of gauze and a quilted silk petticoat.

It took more than two hours for Aubin to get my hair piled up into what is called a hedgehog – in three waves over my forehead. First my hair was greased and combed over a wire mesh secured into place with pins. Then I went into the powder closet to be powdered (I almost choked). At the last he attached ribbons, feathers and silk flowers all over. In a wind, I fear I might topple! I'm to wear a cap over this heavy confection days and nights so that it will stay nice until after the wedding.

Before we left, I went to Father's room to show him my ensemble.

'It's too . . . !' He sighed, lay back on the pillows. 'You look *lovely*.' He smiled. 'Your mother would never approve.'

'This is Paris, Father,' I said, preparing his evening elixir. 'This isn't Trois-Ilets.'

'I should say,' he said, taking his glass. 'Remember to leave your gloves on.'

'And to sit up straight, and to keep my mouth closed when I chew, and to—'

'Have a wonderful time,' he said.

Everyone cheered when Monsieur de Beauharnais and I made our entrance. There were a number of guests: uncles, aunts, several cousins as well as friends of the family. I was introduced to Monsieur de Beauharnais's older brother, François. He's not nearly as good-looking as Monsieur de Beauharnais, nor as clever, but he seemed a gentle man, and very courteous. He looked distinguished in a black satin waistcoat with blue glass ornaments. He is married to Marie (his cousin), who is big with child. She looked ill and did not speak. Her hair, which was not dressed, was hidden under a cap ornamented with vulture feathers. They left soon after the meal, for Marie's time of confinement is approaching. Aunt Désirée told me that her first baby died not too long ago and that Marie has not taken it well.

There were a number of distinguished men and women there. A Monsieur de la Chevalerie* and his daughter were charming. Monsieur had spent his youth in the military on Saint-Domingue, so we talked of the Islands. Mademoiselle de la Chevalerie invited me to the next meeting of her Masonic lodge. 'We have feasts and perform good works.' Her hair was back-combed all around her face, giving her a woolly look.

Supper was elegant and abundant, served on a table laid with eighteen covers. We had sole fried, rump of beef boiled, boiled rabbit and onion sauce, jigget of mutton roasted with sweet sauce, batter pudding and drippings, macaroni and tarts all together with wine in abundance and brandy. By way of dessert we had filberts, apple pudding and some cheesecakes. So much! I was thankful for the severity of my stays, for surely I would have split a seam. As we dined, a violinist played.

After dessert, in the game room, Monsieur de Beauharnais and his brother played billiards while 'discussing' politics (it was more of an argument).

'Oh, politics, always politics,' Mademoiselle de la Chevalerie whispered to me. 'At the lodge we only talk of lofty things.'

I was tempted to advise Monsieur de Beauharnais on a more likely

---

* Jean-Jacques Bacon de la Chevalerie (1731–1821) was a celebrated Freemason. In 1773 he'd been Grand Orateur of the Grand Orient of France.

angle for a shot he was setting up, but held my tongue. He shot and missed, leaving the way clear for his brother to sink four running.

Someone began to play the harpsichord in the front parlour. 'Your fiancé may not be good at billiards,' Mademoiselle de la Chevalerie whispered as we left the game room, 'but he is so very charming. He is the favourite with all the ladies.'

In the parlour Aunt Désirée was playing the harpsichord as a woman sang. I was introduced to several people who had newly arrived. Soon Monsieur de Beauharnais and his brother joined us and the gathering became gay. At Monsieur de Beauharnais's insistence there was dancing, first a polonaise, which is a bit of a walk, and then contredanses, which are more involved.

'Alexandre is the best dancer in all of Paris,' one of the younger cousins said to me. A plain girl, she was strikingly attired in a lavender silk brocade dress with huge flounces and a bustle. Her braided shoes had little gold buckles on them that looked like flowers.

'Even the *Queen* has taken notice,' Mademoiselle de la Chevalerie whispered.

'The Queen?' I accepted another glass of champagne which a servant brought round. The three of us were sitting close to the musicians and it was a little difficult to hear.

Mademoiselle de la Chevalerie giggled behind her gold-painted fan. 'But then the Queen fancies any number of men.'

I was feeling a little light-headed and refrained from responding. I turned to watch Monsieur de Beauharnais move through the intricate forms. He *did* move elegantly. I could understand why everyone so admired him.

After the piece, which went on for over twenty minutes, Monsieur de Beauharnais invited me to be his partner for a polonaise. I declined. I love dancing, but these forms were entirely new to me. I feared I would embarrass him.

Nevertheless, it was an enjoyable evening. Even the Marquis seemed spry – I saw him dancing hatless.*

On the return, in the carriage (I had to sit on a low stool between

---

* Men who intended to dance wore a hat to a soirée. However, it was considered inappropriate for an elderly man to dance, much less to declare his intention to do so. It was acceptable, however, for an elderly man to be spontaneously recruited – to dance hatless.

the seats because my headdress was so high), Aunt Désirée informed Monsieur de Beauharnais that she had decided that the wedding would take place at her country home in Noisy-le-Grand and that she intended to arrange a special dispensation from the archbishop of Paris so that the banns wouldn't have to be read three times. 'This way, you and Rose will be able to get married before Christmas.'

'Excellent,' Monsieur de Beauharnais said. 'I shall talk to my accountant tomorrow.'

Before *Christmas*? So *soon* . . .

In which I am married & learn the facts of life

At nine the morning of my wedding I began my toilette. I allowed
four hours in order to indulge in a number of rituals: a wash with
water perfumed with jasmine (which made me homesick), a massage
(which made me ache) and a facial mask of cucumber and vinegar
(which made my skin blotchy). So right from the start my wedding
day was not as I had planned.

After being bled (not too much – just enough to give me a pale
complexion), my make-up applied (it took almost an *hour*), and my
headdress freshly powdered, Mimi and Aunt Désirée helped tie me
into a stiff, boned corset to which the paniers were fastened. I kept
bumping into the furniture. Over this came the dress: a white satin
gown with a train, embroidered and trimmed with lace. This was
fixed to the stomacher, an embroidered panel that goes down the
front. It wasn't easy, for the gown was tight. It was *torture* being
inside this construction.

Last, I slipped on my new shoes laced with silver and stood in
front of the looking-glass. I looked beautiful, but not radiant.

'You look like a bride!' Mimi said. She gave a squeal.

'You sounded like Da Gertrude just then,' I said, turning to see
my profile. Tears came to my eyes. How I longed for Mother and
Manette – and even Grandmother Sannois! If only they could see
me now.

'Don't cry! You'll spoil your rouge,' Aunt Désirée exclaimed.

Aunt Désirée and I went down to await the guests. I sat by
the window. My veil was secured to my towering headdress by a
pearl-studded cap which kept slipping.

First Abbé Tascher arrived, to stand in for Father, who was
too ill to come to Noisy-le-Grand with us. Then, shortly after,

Monsieur de Beauharnais's cousin Comte Claude, who brought word that François would not be able to attend as Marie was indisposed. Of course then we were all of us concerned that her time of confinement had begun, but we were assured that that was not the case. Three men in uniform arrived, colleagues from Monsieur de Beauharnais's regiment. They apologized that one of their number was unable to attend as he was suffering from an indisposition going around Versailles. Monsieur Patricol, who had been Monsieur de Beauharnais's tutor when he was a child, arrived a bit late and somewhat flustered, saying he'd had trouble with the wheel of his carriage. But he didn't put it that way. He said, 'There has been an apparent altercation with the drive mechanism.' I was struck by his eyes, which are protruding, and his ponderous forehead.

Finally Monsieur de Beauharnais came downstairs to join us. He looked elegant in a black silk coat, gold embroidered waistcoat and a lace cravat. I felt proud sitting beside him.

Aunt Désirée ordered refreshments. I sipped from a glass of champagne, now and again sighing from nerves, fearful that I might faint from the lack of air my corset was causing me.

We set out for the chapel. Some children cried out, 'Long live the bride and bridegroom!' The church was small and quite cold. We were received and Monsieur de Beauharnais and I said our vows. (It took longer to dress than to marry.) As we were leaving, the priest almost tripped on his robes thanking Aunt Désirée for the gift of two copper candelabras and six hundred livres, which he assured her would be used in its *entirety* to make up a dowry for some unfortunate girl of his parish.

Back at the cottage, the toasts began. Aunt Désirée touched her glass to mine. 'To the vicomtesse.'

I felt light-headed and had to lie down. I was still a little weak when I rejoined the guests. The men were teasing Monsieur de Beauharnais about the night that lay ahead.

It was almost midnight when the last guest departed. On Aunt Désirée's instruction Mimi accompanied me to Monsieur de Beauharnais's room. A fire had been laid, but even so it was chilly. In the dressing room, Mimi helped me out of my gown and into a new lace-trimmed chemise, which was lovely, although scratchy. 'You look like an angel,' she said. Mimi tucked my greased and powdered headdress under a boned calash. She began humming: *Calypso, you are a woman just like me . . .*

'How does that song go?' It was familiar.

Mimi sang, 'I caressed Sonson, fondled Sonson, I even went so far I nibbled Sonson!'

A dizzy feeling came over me. I grabbed hold of a wig stand.

'Are you all right?' Mimi asked.

'Yes.' Although I wasn't sure. I heard footsteps in the bedchamber, heard the door close, the bed boards creak. The light in the bedchamber suddenly went out.

'Ooooh!' Mimi hurriedly dabbed jasmine fragrance on my neck, bosom and behind my ears. Then she pushed me through the dressing-room curtains.

I was comforted by the darkness. 'I am here,' I heard Monsieur de Beauharnais say. I heard someone coughing downstairs.

I felt my way to the side of the bed. His hand reached out for me. 'You startled me!' I said.

'I'm sorry,' he said, pulling back the covers. 'I should have left a candle burning.'

I slipped under the covers, felt the warming pan at the foot of the bed. I was trying to think what to say. Was I supposed to say something? I was suddenly aware of the dull, constant ache of my bad tooth. Would I have to have it pulled? Did I have worms in my teeth, like Mimi said? Should I let Monsieur de Beauharnais kiss me if I did?

'What are you thinking?' Monsieur de Beauharnais asked. He turned on to his side, facing me. My eyes were growing accustomed to the dark. I could make out the outline of his head, his shoulder. He wasn't wearing a nightcap.

'Nothing.' I'd been thinking that in the morning I should rinse my mouth with urine to stop the ache. The thought made me ill, but if doing so would save the tooth— 'What are *you* thinking?' I asked.

'I'm thinking what a strange situation this is. We hardly know one another.' His words slurred a little.

I made a little laugh.

'Perhaps you would prefer to wait,' he said.

'Yes.' Was that what he wanted me to say? I wondered.

The room suddenly became brighter. The moon had come out

from behind a cloud. I could see his eyes. His lips were thin, a little disdaining, his nose prominent, giving him an aristocratic profile. My husband, the man for whom God intended me. I had only met him six weeks before, and now I was his wife.

'Perhaps if I just kissed you,' he said.

'Yes.' A pin had come loose in my headdress and was poking into my scalp uncomfortably.

He moved over to my side of the big bed. His head blocked the light from the window. I could no longer see his features. He put his hand on my shoulder. His breath smelled of brandy and cigars. His lips touched mine, and then he pulled away. Was that it? I wondered. Did I do something wrong?

'I forgot something,' he said.

He reached back and opened the cabinet beside the bed. 'Aunt Désirée doesn't want the sheets stained,' he said, handing me a cloth.

What was I supposed to do with it?

'Put it under your . . . you know.'

Under my bottom?

He lay down beside me. I felt him fumbling with my bed jacket. 'Do you mind?' he asked.

'Do you want me to take it off?' I didn't want to take it off.

He kissed my nose. I wondered, did he miss my mouth? His hand slipped into the bodice of my nightdress. His lips covered my mouth. Then he put his hand under my nightdress, found the place between my legs. I cried out, surprised. His fingers were cold. He kissed me hard. He pushed my nightdress up around my waist, got on top of me. His manhood felt warm against my skin. He poked it here and there. I lay still. I wasn't sure what I was supposed to do. Then I felt a sharp pain. I cried out and tried to pull away, but he held me. And then he was inside me.

He kissed my wet cheeks. He was moaning and moving around. I wondered how long it would go on. I tried not to cry, but it hurt! Then he clasped me to him hard, his feet kicking, and collapsed on top of me, groaning.

Had he had an attack? Was he dead? 'Are you all right?' I whispered. What had happened? He rolled over beside me, grunting.

Soon he was snoring. The image of William's face came to me, his smile. *You would make a lovely queen*, he had told me.

SANDRA GULLAND

Tears trickled down the side of my face on to the pillow. Was I a woman now?

1 JANUARY 1780, NEW YEAR'S DAY – PARIS
I have resolved to go to Mass every morning. I want to become a good wife. I have asked for divine help in this, for so often a pained expression covers Monsieur de Beauharnais's brow.

'What is it I do?' I asked Aunt Désirée. 'What is the reason?'

'*Reason*,' she said, correcting my pronunciation. 'You continue to drop your *r*s, Rose.'

Aunt Désirée wrote out a list of words. I am to practise them, recite them to her every evening. I try to accept her correction without temper, for I know that it is in *this* that I must strive – to obey without question, to become Madame la vicomtesse, a most excellent wife.

13 JANUARY
Monsieur de Beauharnais practises dance steps all the day long, watching himself in the big looking glass. He has been invited to the Queen's ball at Versailles . . . but I have not.

'Why?' I asked Father and Aunt Désirée. 'Why might *I* not go?'

'You haven't been presented at court, Rose,' Father said.

'Neither has Alexandre.'*

'But Alexandre is the best dancer in all of Paris,' Aunt Désirée said. 'This is quite an honour, Rose. You should rejoice on your husband's behalf.'

SUNDAY, 23 JANUARY
Monsieur de Beauharnais has returned from Versailles. He danced with the Queen!

* To be presented at court, one had to prove noble blood back to 1400. Alexandre's nobility was relatively new and made less impressive by the fact that the government was selling titles by the thousands in order to raise money.

THE MANY LIVES & SECRET SORROWS OF JOSEPHINE B.

Aunt Désirée looked as if she might faint. 'Alexandre, tell us the truth. You didn't dance with the *Queen*.'

It was true, he had, for one-quarter turn of a polonaise, he said.

'Did she touch your glove?' Aunt Désirée asked. 'This one?'

'Behold, Madame, I give you my blessing.' Monsieur de Beauharnais made an elegant sweep through the air and touched his hand to her shoulder.

We gathered in the front parlour to listen to his account. Even Father came downstairs to join us, interrupting Monsieur de Beauharnais to fill us in on details of proper royal deportment.

Monsieur de Beauharnais said the Queen is graceful – although she doesn't dance too much now that she is a mother, allowing herself only a few quadrilles or a colonne anglaise or two in an evening. When the King joins her he has to dance without turning his back to her, which gets him hopelessly mixed up and behind the music.

Monsieur de Beauharnais said the Queen is an accomplished hostess, keeping the young men from staying in the corners all night talking of horses and duelling.

Oh, there was so much that he told us, it is hard to remember it all: the Swiss Guards in starched ruffs, their spaniels on leashes; a door of glass so clear people almost walked through it; a room of maids to attend to dresses in need of repair; the firemen standing ready with buckets of water and large sponges . . .

All this evening I have been in a reverie. I imagine myself strolling, cooling myself with a fan of mother-of-pearl. Men in black velvet dance around me, their long plumes bobbing. I imagine the music, the women in court hoops twirling, the swish of silk on silk . . .

It is dawn. I have danced all night. Around the walls of the gilded room are the slumped bodies of the sleeping pages, the maids, the exhausted dancers. But still I dance . . .

TUESDAY, 29 FEBRUARY

Oh, sorrow beyond measure. One week ago Alexandre's sister-in-law, Marie, gave birth to a girl. Aunt Désirée and I have been going to Mass every morning, praying for the health of this infant, but in spite of our efforts, she died this morning, at seven days. This is the second infant Marie has lost.

Friday, 23 June, Saint John's Day

I am seventeen today. Monsieur de Beauharnais presented me with a ruby. Then he informed me that he must return to his regiment. 'How long will you be gone?' I asked.

'Six months.'

Six months!

18 July, 3.00 p.m.

Monsieur de Beauharnais is gone. He left a list of readings for me to complete: Agesilaus, Brutus, Aristides. I fall asleep reading.

25 July 1780 – Brest

Dear Rose,

I am glad you have been attending to your studies but disheartened that your efforts are not better reflected in your written expression. Are you sitting at the writing desk properly, as I showed you? Are you holding your quill correctly, bending your arm at the right angle?

As for content, I suggest you ask Aunt Désirée if she has a book of letters you might copy. In this way you might learn correct phrasing.

My heart is filled with longing for the one whom I hold most dear. In rapture, I fall asleep each night, pressing your image to my lips. Oh, that it were you! How cruel Time, who keeps us apart.

Write, Rose. Do not neglect your studies.

Your husband, Alexandre de Beauharnais, vicomte

2 August

I stood in front of the looking glass this morning, examining my belly, turning to the right and the left, trying to see if there has been any change. I should have started the flowers two weeks ago . . .

Thursday, 31 August

This morning when I woke, feeling sick in the way I do so often now, I decided it was time to talk to Aunt Désirée. After the midday meal

I asked her if we could talk. She invited me into her apartment. I sat down on the settee with some sense of formality. I told her I'd come to ask her advice.

She looked at me with a cautious but satisfied look. 'Yes?'

'How would I know if I were with child?'

I thought for a moment Aunt Désirée had stopped breathing, for the rise and fall of her chest is usually remarkable. She squared her shoulders and said, 'Very well,' and proceeded to ask me questions. When I told her I hadn't had flowers for over two months, she stood up and put me directly to bed, where she's been feeding me hot chicken broth and wine ever since.

The doctor comes every morning, to see Father. Hopefully he will release me from this prison.

1 September

The doctor prescribed ten drops of tincture of iron in the morning, meat two times a day, and a pint of beer or a glass of port with supper. I can get out of bed, but for two months I'm not to ride in a carriage.

I endure with joy. I am more than myself.

14 September, 7.00 p.m.

Monsieur de Beauharnais writes words of love now that he has received my news. But, oh, woe, I fear it is too late. A week ago I began to bleed – not much, but I was cautious and took to bed. The baby was held, Mimi said, kept from growing. She made a dragon's blood mixture that I dutifully ingested two times a day with powdered dried almonds mixed with the yolk of eggs. This went on for several days. Nevertheless yesterday I was seized with the most terrible pain. Mimi asked if she should fetch Aunt Désirée, but I insisted no.

So it was Mimi who was with me, for which I shall always be grateful. It was hard – it was *all* I could do not to scream – but Mimi knew how to help it pass. When it was over she prayed for me, not a Christian prayer, I confess, but a sweet crooning sort of chant about a woman's pain and the earth bringing life anew.

I wept the night through. I am no longer with child.

In which I am too much alone

1 NOVEMBER 1780, ALL SAINTS' DAY
At table the Marquis and Aunt Désirée talked of Marie's mother
'Aunt Fanny' who has recently returned from Rome. She's a writer
and keeps a *salon*. She has published a booklet, *Hail to All Thinkers!*
(which the Marquis *insists* 'one of' her lovers must have written) and
a romance called *Triumph of Love* (which Aunt Désirée forbids me
to read).

'Her salon stays open until five in the morning,' the Marquis
exclaimed. 'I'd like to know what people can be doing at that hour!'
It was a small entertainment to see him worked up so.

TUESDAY, 7 NOVEMBER
My room is full of the heavy scent of attar of roses, Aunt Fanny's
perfume. I confess to being captivated. Her face is tiny, giving the
impression of a fairy. She wears a frightful amount of make-up,
especially on her eyes, which are quite lively, never resting. She's
very *theatrical*. (It is hard to imagine that she is Marie's mother.
Marie is so timid.)

Her dress was simple, but she wore it without a corset — I
was shocked! There was a mannish quality to her hat, which was
mellowed charmingly by a wreath of flowers which she wore in
abundance in defiance of her age.

'So,' she said when we met, 'this is the beauty all of Paris will
be talking about.'

I blushed. Were that it were true! I don't believe I'll ever see
Paris, in spite of living in the heart of it.

She stayed for only one hour, drinking brandy in her tea. The

Marquis seemed only too willing to listen to her wild stories, in spite of his disapproval, which he made clear. She knows artists and politicians, philosophers and poets, all manner of people. She has just finished writing a romantic novel which will be published soon, and has already begun composing yet another. But mostly she was concerned about *me*.

'What events have you taken the girl to?' she demanded.

'Events?' Aunt Désirée asked.

'You know – *out*.' Fanny has a clipped and energetic way of talking. 'Lodge meetings, the fairs—'

'We're quite content to stay in,' the Marquis said.

'You didn't take her to the Saint-Germain Fair?' Fanny was clearly horrified.

'That's become so dirty,' Aunt Désirée protested. 'And the last time we went, we practically got run down by a carriage coming in through the gates at a gallop.' She turned to the Marquis to confirm this fact.

'Ermenonville is quiet – you could take her there.'

'I am perhaps the only person in France who is not enraptured with Rapture,' the Marquis said. 'Forgive me, but your hero Jean-Jacques Rousseau is not to my liking.'

'Young Alexandre and his dear tutor Patricol have not made a convert of you?'

'They have not.'

'They've not lured you to one of their Masonic meetings?'

The Marquis made a sputtering sound.

'He could never remember the password,' Aunt Désirée said, covering a disloyal smile with her fan.

'That wasn't the problem in the least,' the Marquis objected. 'It was all that nonsense about liberty and equality and brotherly love. And the red caps they wore were itchy as well as ugly.'

'Perhaps the theatre? You have taken her to some spectacles, surely.'

Aunt Désirée shook her head. 'Alexandre would not approve, I am afraid,' she said. 'Something to do with theatre fostering a sense of detachment in the modern age.'

Fanny hooted, a most unladylike snort. 'I suppose he would have us all out on the street, singing and dancing round Maypoles with ribbons! I'm weary of all this longing for the "Olden Days". One can take the precepts of Rousseau too far. The question, quite simply, is how can you bring this girl to Paris and *not* take her to the theatre?'

'Perhaps we could take her to the Théâtre Français,' Aunt Désirée suggested cautiously, glancing over at the Marquis.

'Mon Dieu!' Fanny said. 'The only show there worth watching is the King . . . and the Queen, sometimes, when he manages to drag her along to those tedious productions. "Ah, Virtue!" . . .' Fanny paraded across the room, demonstrating an actor reciting lines in the most superficial way. I turned to see Mimi giggling in the door.

'The Queen, on the other hand, who may not have sense but who at least has *taste*,' Fanny went on, 'is more likely to be seen taking in the entertainment on the Boulevard du Temple.'

'The Boulevard of *Crime* you mean?' the Marquis asked.

'Of course that's what we've come to expect of her,' Aunt Désirée said.

'Have you ever seen her?' I blurted out, revealing myself to be what I truly was: a star-struck girl from the Islands.

'What's to see?' the Marquis bristled.

'How can one *not* see her?' Fanny moaned. 'The woman is everywhere – at the theatre, the gaming tables, the concerts spirituels, the salons . . . not *mine*, of course, but I heard from Comte Clairon that she was at Comtesse d'Autricourt's, feigning disguise, which of course everyone sees right through. Poor woman. I feel sorry for her. Hope she's not allergic to cats.* Clearly she's not allergic to *men*. I understand she's moved into the little Trianon – for more *freedom* (Fanny indulged me with a wink) – where she can give full expression to her 'bucolic' affectations, playing shepherdess, tying pretty ribbons round the cows and sheep. It's all so fashionable, it makes me sick, frankly. Although I admit I couldn't stand being Queen for more than a minute. The palace is full of strangers watching the royal comings and goings as if they were on exhibit, relieving themselves in the corners. People even watch them eat –

* The Comtesse de Lingiville d'Autricourt ran what some considered the most brilliant salon in Paris, surrounding herself with Angora cats, each with a bright silk ribbon.

can you imagine?* Goodness knows *I'm* all in favour of giving up corsets – who can stand them? – but don't you think our Queen carries it a bit far?' Fanny did not wait for a response. 'But, of course, who wouldn't go wild with a man like King Louis for a husband? The only thing he's passionate about is food.'

'And carrying on like a child,' the Marquis muttered in turn, 'turning the fountains on strollers, for amusement. It's time His Majesty grew up, don't you think?'

'Did you know that in Strasbourg they've actually *minted* a coin showing our dear King with cuckold's horns?' Fanny said. 'It's true – a friend of a friend of mine has one.'

Fanny could have gone on and on, much to my delight, but Aunt Désirée changed the subject, informing Fanny that I was learning to play the harp, that I sang quite nicely and that I was interested in drawing as well. I was embarrassed to be paraded in this way, but eager, nevertheless, to be the object of Fanny's notice.

She insisted on seeing a drawing I've been working on, an island scene. Quite by accident she came upon one I'd done of the stone wall of the neighbour's house – the view from my window – and she laughed. She thought it showed originality and a sense of humour. 'Or a serious case of vapours.' She looked at me closely.

She noticed an open volume of Helvétius on a table. She asked if I was reading it. 'I'm trying to,' I confessed.

'Why?' she asked. 'Not that it isn't an admirable pursuit.'

'Monsieur de Beauharnais wishes me to,' I explained. 'He aims to educate me.'

'How good of him,' she said with a sarcastic tone.

'My spelling is terrible,' I said, defending my husband's intent.

'Voltaire's letters were *full* of spelling errors,' she said, noticing my guitar propped in a corner. 'Do you play?'

I somewhat reluctantly confessed that I did, for Monsieur de Beauharnais had given me to believe that only members of the lower social orders played such a primitive instrument.

'A guitar is lovely – so expressive. What pieces do you know?'

I told her I was trying to learn the cantatas of Clérambault but

* At Versailles, the public was allowed to watch members of the royal family eat. Crowds would race from one part of the palace to another in order to observe various courses being consumed by the different members of the royal family.

finding them challenging. 'I should think so,' she said, which was heartening.

She turned to me at the door. 'Tell me, my dear — what *do* you think of our fair city?'

I flushed.

'Don't be shy. Do you not think your misery is written on your face? As is every thought and emotion that comes to you? Really, you are the most transparent creature. But come now, admit it — one cannot be French and not love it.'

I felt she could see into my most private thoughts, penetrate my spirit, my very dreams. For all my life, had I not dreamed of France? Had not the word meant romance and all good things to me? 'I am, I confess, familiar only with these four walls,' I said.

'*That* we will have to remedy, my dear. You will begin by coming to my salon — tomorrow evening.' She raised a finger to still my objection. 'I *insist*. I will send my footman for you, at nine.'

And so, it is set. A *salon*? I don't even know what a salon is.

THURSDAY, 9 NOVEMBER
There were a number of men and women gathered in Fanny's parlour when I arrived — twelve, I counted. Fanny introduced me as a student of painting and music, which flattered my modest pursuits greatly. After supper, music was played and poetry read. There was lots of laughter and argument. All the while Fanny was stretched out on a silver and blue settee with a garland of flowers on her head, looking like a goddess. A poet named Michael de Cubières (short, with a booming voice and big lips) read some of Fanny's poems, which I didn't understand but everyone seemed to appreciate. I felt nervous, but of course quite proud once the reading was over and everyone praised her.

I can't begin to describe the interesting people I met and the vitality of the conversation. I felt tongue-tied, but nevertheless was kindly received. An older gentleman in a tight old-fashioned wig guessed immediately I was Creole.

'How did you know?' I asked.

'Your accent gives you away. And the intoxicating way you move.'

The intoxicating way I move, indeed!

THE MANY LIVES & SECRET SORROWS OF JOSEPHINE B.

MONDAY, 13 NOVEMBER

I have been to a meeting of a Masonic lodge — the lodge of the Triple Lumière. I went with Alexandre's brother François and Mademoiselle de la Chevalerie, whom I had met shortly before Alexandre and I were married. The banquet was elegant, the company delightful and but for the length of some of the speeches, it was a pleasant evening. A number of men and women from the Islands are members, so I felt very much at home. (There was even cassava bread served!) The songs were pretty, all about brotherhood and love.

Mademoiselle de la Chevalerie has promised to put my name forward. Already she showed me a secret hand signal. 'I tried this at the Saint-Germain Fair and *hundreds* signalled back,' she said.

'That many?' It was hard to imagine.

'If you are ever in distress, all you need to do is make a sign, and help will come,' she said with fervour.

SATURDAY, 18 NOVEMBER

Fanny took me to see a play tonight. She arrived early in order to help supervise my toilette. We were sipping brandy and being perhaps a bit silly, for Aunt Désirée stuck her head in and frowned at us. After the door closed Fanny made a funny face. Really, I've never met anyone quite like her.

Fanny gave her coachman orders to drive to the Boulevard du Temple. After what the Marquis had said — about it being called the Boulevard of Crime — I was looking out everywhere for ruffians, but it didn't take long for me to be overtaken by the gay spirit of the place. We were surrounded by tightrope acrobats, puppeteers, mime artists, performing animals — it was as if a circus had been let loose in the streets! Every balladeer and vendor had a song to sing — about liberty in America, about the Queen's naughtiness, and lots of songs about love, of course. There were even actors performing a sentimental sort of romance, a woman on one side of the street, a man on the other, yelling words to each other. It was impossible not to be swept up into the excitement of it all.

It was with some reluctance, therefore, that I entered the theatre, only to be drawn into still another world. After Fanny and I had seated ourselves in her loge – I was trying very hard not to look this way and that like a child at a fair – I noticed a commotion in the audience. Everyone was looking towards a loge at the front. It was the Queen!

I had a very clear view of her face. She is younger than I expected, not much older than myself, and pretty, with a kindly expression, almost shy. Of course I took in all the details of what she was wearing, especially her headdress, which was a most fanciful construction of mauve feathers that fluttered with every move she made. With her was a blonde woman and a tall, handsome man.

'That's Yolande de Polignac and the Comte de Vaudreuil,' Fanny whispered. 'She's the Comte's mistress. They have what is called "a secret marriage" – complicated, one would think, by *his* relationship with the Queen.' She looked at me over her fan.

'The *Queen?*' I whispered.

'And furthermore,' Fanny raised her eyebrows, 'it is my under-standing that the Queen and Yolande are . . .' Fanny held up two fingers entwined. 'If you believe what people say,' she went on. 'Which of course I don't.'

Just then the lights went out and the audience fell into a hush. I could hear a woman giggling in the loge next to ours.

'Is there someone in there?' I asked. For the curtains were drawn tight.

'In one's loge at the theatre, one may receive *anyone*.' Fanny rolled her eyes.

I heard another peal of laughter, followed by a man's low voice. 'You mean—'

'I can see I am going to have to give you one of my novels to read, darling,' Fanny whispered as the curtain went up. 'Disguised as a text on aesthetics, of course.'

The play we saw was *The Beaten* and I laughed so hard I feared my corset ties would break. In it, Janot, a servant, has a chamber pot emptied on his head. He tries to take legal action, but ends up in jail. It was terribly silly, but well done. Between acts there were speeches, singing and announcements.

Oh, I'm in love with the theatre! Fanny has promised to take me to another performance soon.

22 November

Monsieur de Beauharnais wrote to me: '*Labour omnia vincit improbus.*' I had to ask Father to translate it. 'Persistent effort overcomes all difficulties,' he told me. I should have known it would have to do with studies, and nothing whatsoever to do with *love*.

Saturday, 25 November

Fanny has had her newest novel published, titled *Abailard the Pretender*. We all went to a ballet tonight to celebrate — Fanny, my brother-in-law François (Marie is confined to bed), Aunt Désirée and even the Marquis. When the dancers leaped into the air one could see their garters. Fanny thought nothing of it, but I could see that the Marquis and Aunt Désirée were discomfited.

27 November

Aunt Désirée is reading Fanny's new novel to determine if I should be permitted to read it. I doubt that I shall — she makes the sign of the cross before picking it up.

7 December

Monsieur de Beauharnais sent word that he is coming home. I haven't seen him for five months.

Wednesday, 13 December, 11.30 a.m.

Today is our first anniversary. But already Monsieur de Beauharnais is gone again, on his way to join his regiment in Verdun. He was here for only four days.

In which I become a mother & discover a terrible truth

SUNDAY, 28 JANUARY 1781

Aunt Désirée and I were summoned in the night. Marie's labour had commenced. We hurried to her bedside, the horses slipping on the icy cobblestones. When we arrived, we were immediately taken to Marie's bedchamber where Fanny informed us that Marie had fallen into unconsciousness. Aunt Désirée was overcome with uneasiness and took leave of the room, Fanny following. Soon after, the child was born. The *accoucheuse* asked me to hold the infant while she tied the cord. The baby did not cry; her eyes opened, her blue skin slowly turning pink, the miracle of life in my hands. My tears fell on her cheeks.

The priest was delayed and Fanny was anxious that the infant quickly be baptized. I held the crying baby as Aunt Désirée poured water over her head, uttering the words, 'I baptize thee.' Her name is Émilie. We pray for her. I pray for her.

19 FEBRUARY

I'm with child again. I move with great caution.

28 February – Brest

Darling,

Joy filled my spirit on receipt of your wonderful news. Be sure to do all as the doctor instructs. I have asked Patricol to outline a programme of reading for you, for it is currently understood that a mother's thoughts will produce a result on the infant she carries, both for good and for ill. I do not need to remind you that any reading of novels is forbidden – especially romantic novels. Refrain from situations that occasion strong emotions, and above all, do not go to the theatre!

I have asked Aunt Désirée to obtain etchings of inspiring moments in Roman and Greek history to position beside your bed. In this way, by casting your eyes upon these heroic images, you will guarantee a good result. I forbid you to hire a wet nurse as the milk will influence the character of the baby. If mothers nursed their own babies, many of the ills of society would be eliminated.

I embrace you, *ma tendre amie*.

Your husband, Alexandre de Beauharnais, vicomte

Note – I suggest for this period of waiting you absent yourself from the company of Aunt Fanny.

7 MARCH

Fanny came by around eleven for tea. As she was going she put a small parcel in my hand. 'Don't tell Désirée,' she whispered. 'And certainly not your father.'

I've just now opened it. It's Rousseau's *Confessions*, which have been banned. I started reading it and was immediately shocked. I've hidden it under my mattress.

15 MARCH

Fanny came by before dinner. I didn't think I'd get a chance to ask her about something in *Confessions*, but finally Aunt Désirée went out to see how the cook was managing with the rabbits Fanny had brought and I got up the courage. 'You want me to explain?' she demanded.

I realized from the look on her face that I shouldn't have asked.

'You know how certain things can . . . *arouse* a man?' she asked.

Now it was my turn to blush.

'Well – for Rousseau, he fancied a bit of a spanking.'

I was shocked. 'You mean . . . ?'

'For a man like that, carry a birch rod and make him beg, I say.' She sat back on the sofa with a maternal air. 'Perhaps that's what your Alexandre needs,' she mused.

When Aunt Désirée returned I was in such a state of giddiness she grew alarmed on my behalf. After Fanny left and I was alone again I got out the book, searching for the passages that had previously eluded my understanding. In this naughty way I am pleasantly passing the Lord's day.

SUNDAY, 25 MARCH
Yesterday, the eve of Lady Day, I felt my child flutter in my belly like a butterfly. I grew still. It did it again, fluttering — oh, so faintly!

Mimi cast my cards. I will have a boy, she said.

A *boy*! I think of all the things a boy must do, all the things a mother must let him do, and I want to cry. Is this what being a mother means, this bewildering sentiment flooding one's heart?

SUNDAY, 15 APRIL
In church we learned that the Queen is expecting another child. There was much rejoicing. I felt the festivities as if they were for me, for I know what she feels, I know her joy.

18 APRIL
Monsieur de Beauharnais complains I haven't written, yet when I do my letters are corrected and returned. Now he suggests I send *all* my letters to him — even those I write to Mother and Manette — so that I might be instructed on correct spelling and construction. I cannot write at all, now, I am so distressed.

LATER
Father has suggested that Aunt Désirée help me with my letters to Monsieur de Beauharnais — she will write them out for me, to ensure that no errors are made.

30 APRIL
Monsieur de Beauharnais has accused Aunt Désirée of writing my letters for me. He is furious!

I received a letter from Monsieur de Beauharnais this afternoon, posted from La Roche-Guyon, the country estate of his patron, the Duc de la Rochefoucauld.

'But Monsieur de Beauharnais is in Verdun,' I told Aunt Désirée. Surely Monsieur de Beauharnais would not have travelled to La Roche-Guyon without coming to see us – to see *me*. It was but a short detour along the route.

'No doubt Alexandre was under orders,' Aunt Désirée said, but I saw doubt in her eyes.

'Under orders to live as he pleases without any regard for his pregnant wife,' I said angrily. Without any *love* for his wife.

'You must try harder, Rose,' Aunt Désirée said. 'It is a wife's duty to please.'

'Monsieur de Beauharnais is impossible to please!' I went to the window. Even the country vista did not soothe me. 'Laughing one minute, morose the next, serious and then frivolous, feverish and then cold – one never knows how it will be with him!'

Aunt Désirée sighed, putting down her lacework. 'We need help,' she said.

THURSDAY, 7 JUNE

Aunt Désirée sent Patricol, Alexandre's childhood tutor, to La Roche-Guyon to talk to him. Now Patricol has written to Aunt Désirée suggesting a solution to 'our' problem: that others get involved in my schooling. So now Aunt Désirée is hiring tutors for me. Everyone – even Father – is being recruited in this effort to educate me.

23 JUNE

I am eighteen today. It is terribly hot, and in my condition I suffer. Nevertheless, I've been trying to get through the first volume of Vertot's *Roman History* – but then the baby moves within me, inspiring a reverie.

My letters to Monsieur de Beauharnais report only my studies. I do not tell him of the changes in my heart.

My baby was born this morning – a boy, on the very day of my dear sister Manette's birth. A good omen.

It was a hard labour, more painful than I could have imagined, but the love I feel for this little creature, this little sucking thing, overwhelms me, puts all at peace. I clasp my squalling baby to me and sing sweet songs, baptizing him with tears of wonder. I curl under the covers with him, bringing him to my breast. He grabs at my nipple greedily, pulling the watery liquid out of me, and we are silent then together but for his chirps and sucking sounds. We fall into a sweet-smelling sleep, then, my baby and I, and I think, as we drift into dreams, this is Heaven, isn't it? Is this not what Heaven is?

LATER

'Rose, there is someone here to see you,' Aunt Désirée said. Something in her voice warned me.

Behind her I saw Monsieur de Beauharnais. I caught my breath. I hadn't seen him for – how many months? Eight? I'd lost count. He looked exceedingly well, dressed in an elegant black coat, a red-striped waistcoat and flesh-coloured breeches. The toes of his glistening black boots were pointed.

He smiled and tipped his top hat. 'My apologies. I intended to be here for the event, but—'

'No need to apologize, Alexandre. I wasn't expecting you,' I said.

'I recall that when you address me by my Christian name, it means that you are angry.'

'I am too tired to be angry.' I felt pressure in my breasts. Soon it would be time to nurse.

'I have a gift for you.' He pulled a jeweller's case out of his waistcoat pocket. Inside was a gold pin with a tiny image of himself painted on it.

Mimi came into the room, my baby bundled in her arms. She was startled when she saw Monsieur de Beauharnais.

'Alexandre, you remember—'

'Rose, of course I . . .' He faltered.

'Mimi,' I said, reminding him.

THE MANY LIVES & SECRET SORROWS OF JOSEPHINE B.

But his eyes were on the baby. 'And this is . . . ?'

Mimi gently put the baby into Monsieur de Beauharnais's out-stretched arms. He lifted the corner of the coverlet, looked upon the face of his son. Then he looked over at me, his eyes filled with tears. 'Have you named him?' he asked, his voice full of emotion.

'The honour is yours.'

'I would like him to be Eugène,' he said.

'I like that name,' I said. The baby began to fuss. 'He's hungry.'

Monsieur de Beauharnais put our son into my arms.

'Welcome home, Alexandre.' I touched his hand.

FRIDAY, 7 SEPTEMBER, 3.00 P.M.

Monsieur de Beauharnais is attentive. He goes on in a rapture about new life. He has studied the newest theories and is intent on doing everything properly. He talks of Rousseau, of nursing, of a child's 'development' – he talks of all the wrong a mother might do. He's in a fit of worry.

I want to take his head and place it on my heart. I want to say, do not be afraid. I want to stroke his fine, long hair and mother him – Monsieur de Beauharnais, my husband, the motherless one.

MONDAY, 22 OCTOBER

The tocsins are ringing, there is celebrating in the streets. The Queen has had her baby – a *boy*! One hundred and one guns were fired. Everywhere people call out, 'Long live the Dauphin!'

I clasp my baby to my heart and pray for the Queen. I do not envy her, for her baby is not her own. Her boy will be King. He belongs to God, to France – he belongs to us all.

23 OCTOBER

Last night I had a dream in which Monsieur de Beauharnais told me: 'You are not my only wife.'

I woke in a feverish sweat.

This morning I told Mimi about the dream. Her face is like water, it shows the slightest disturbance. So I watched her.

'What a crazy dream,' she said. But she had that look of caution.

'If there were some truth in it, would you tell me?'

'Ask Charlotte.' Charlotte is Aunt Désirée's cook. Charlotte is a gossip and wields considerable power, and not just with a knife.

'Mimi, don't make me suffer the humiliation of learning this from Charlotte.'

Mimi's dark eyes filled with doubt.

'Please!' For the truth was more and more evident.

Mimi collected herself before continuing, in that proud and silent way she has. 'Monsieur le vicomte keeps a mistress,' she said.

A *mistress*. It did not surprise me. Monsieur de Beauharnais was rarely home. 'Who?' I asked.

Mimi bowed her head. The light glittered off her black hair. 'Madame Longpré.'

'Madame Laure Longpré?' I stuttered. 'My *cousin* Laure Longpré?' I recalled the buxom woman who had called on Father and me when we had just arrived in France. I remembered her bosom adorned with gems, her frothy pink gown.

Mimi nodded.

'But she's so much older than Alexandre,' I objected. I was more confused than upset.

'There is more. There is a child, a boy.'

'Monsieur de Beauharnais is the father? How do you know this? Who told you?'

'Charlotte.'

'It's common knowledge? The Marquis? My father?'

'I don't know about your father.'

I sat down on the edge of my bed. I held my face in my hands. Then I stood up.

'Where are you going?'

I went downstairs. I found Aunt Désirée in the pantry, checking the supplies. 'May I talk to you?' I asked.

'Can it wait, Rose?'

I shook my head.

'Go to the front parlour. I will join you in a moment.'

I went into the parlour.

Aunt Désirée entered the room and sat down, her hands planted purposefully in her lap. 'Yes?' She had things to do.

'I just found out about Madame Longpré.' I was relieved that I was tearless and that my voice was steady. 'And about her child, Alexandre's son.'

'Oh,' Aunt Désirée said, with an appearance of calm.

'Does it not matter?' I asked, emotion breaking through.

'Laure poses no threat to you, Rose. Alexandre cares for you, if that's what concerns you.'

'How do *you* know?' A mean-spirited bitterness had come over me.

'Alexandre tells me everything.' Aunt Désirée sat back with a proprietorial air.

I stood. I felt light-headed and needed to lie down. Aunt Désirée reached for my hand. 'Rose, please – don't be so provincial.'

I headed for the stairs.

Shortly after, Father came into my room. I refused to look at him, attending to a drawing I was reworking. He sat down beside my writing table, toying with a split quill. 'Désirée suggested I talk to you,' he said.

I held the drawing out at arm's length. It was a portrait of Eugène. I was not content with the features.

Father coughed. 'I am told you are not happy.'

'I am perfectly happy,' I said. Nevertheless, I could not disguise the trembling of my lower lip.

'Rose, you were never one to be overly proud,' Father said, sighing. 'And more than once you were blessed with the strength of forgiveness. Look how many times you have forgiven *me*.' He smiled, stilled another cough.

'You are my father.'

'I am a man. You have to understand, it is not easy for the young chevalier—'

'Do not ask me to accept this, Father!' I stood up abruptly and went to the fire. I kneeled, picked up the bellows.

'It is natural for any man to have . . . interests,' my father went on, breaking the quill in his hands. 'But that doesn't mean Alexandre doesn't love you. A wife must learn to . . . to be accepting.'

The ashes blew back in my face. 'Do you think I do not notice when Alexandre puts his hand down the chambermaid's bodice? Do you think I do not know that he slips his hand under her skirts when she is doing his hair, that he visits her bedchamber? Do you think I do not know that he gave Vicomtesse de Rosin-Mallarmé his portrait? That he keeps a collection of silk stockings — victory trophies! — in his cupboard? Do you think I am blind? I see, I know — *and* I look the other way. But this, *this* is different. Laure Longpré is my *cousin*!'

I put the bellows to one side, stood up, brushing the ashes off my skirt. 'You said yourself that no good would come of Laure. Remember when she visited us when we first came to France? That child she had just given birth to was *Alexandre's*, Father. Remember how she asked *me* to invite Monsieur de Beauharnais to call on her? And I — so stupidly! so innocently! so *kindly*! — obliged her. Remember how he left the very next week? To visit friends from his regiment, he said!'

'If it makes you feel any better,' Father handed me a cap of whisky from the flask he carried, 'I believe I am to blame.'

I sat down on the footstool. The liquor burned going down. 'What do you mean?' I handed him back the cap.

'Laure's family, as you know, has long hated ours — resented the favours the Marquis bestowed on me, such as they were, all because I was Désirée's brother. I think it is no accident that Laure has meddled in your marriage. That family has spite in their blood. She is a cat, playing a mouse.'

'*Playing*, Father? This *game* will be the death of me!'

At five Monsieur de Beauharnais arrived home. I heard his voice in the entryway, heard Father's low warning tones, hushed whispers.

After a short time Monsieur de Beauharnais appeared at the door. 'Aren't you coming down for supper?'

I refused to answer.

'Désirée tells me you talked to her about Laure.' He came into the room.

Laure. Not Laure Longpré. Not Madame Longpré. But *Laure.* I pressed my hand to my lips to check the feelings that were rising in me.

'Oh, Rose, please!' Monsieur de Beauharnais had that same arrogance: *provincial*. It was *provincial* of me to be upset about such a thing.

'Don't take that tone with me, Alexandre.' There were wet spots on my dress, splotches from my tears.

Monsieur de Beauharnais walked to the window. 'It's stuffy in here.' He opened the window with some effort, for it tended to stick.

'How can you be so nonchalant!'

'You'll wake the baby,' he warned.

'*You*, who know so much about babies.' I turned away. 'When shall we tell Eugène that he is not your firstborn – on his fifth birthday? Or perhaps we should tell him sooner, on his third—'

'For God's sake, Eugène is my only legitimate son.'

'And Madame Longpré?' I could not stop myself. 'Who is *she*?'

'Do you want me to be honest?'

'I've had enough of deceit.'

'You are my wife.' He pulled aside a curtain and looked out on to the street.

'And . . . ?'

'And Laure is the woman I love.'

'Get out!'

'You wanted the truth!'

I flung a pillow, and another. I was trembling as I reached for a vase.

In which I come to the end of my endurance

13 DECEMBER 1781

'My daughter wears a long face,' Father said as I brought him his evening glass of claret. Ever since Monsieur de Beauharnais left for Italy six weeks ago, Father has been kindly.

'Do I?' I knew it to be true. It was the day of my marriage to Monsieur de Beauharnais, two years before. Our anniversary.

Father grabbed my hand. 'Come back with me, Rose.'

'To Martinico?' Father's health had improved and he'd succeeded in getting a small increase in his pension. Soon he would be returning home.

'Your husband does not honour you sufficiently.'

I was surprised by his words. Had he 'honoured' my mother sufficiently? 'I couldn't,' I said. Eugène was too young – the journey could kill him.

'Leave your baby with a wet nurse. You may send for him in time, when he is old enough to travel.'

Leave Eugène? It was the common practice, I knew. Yet I could not bear the thought. 'Forgive me, Father, but I could not.' My baby was my only joy.

Father looked at me for a long moment. 'You Creole mothers,' he sighed.

19 JANUARY 1782

Father left this morning. He didn't look back as the carriage pulled away.

I'm on my own now. I feel a lifetime older.

[UNDATED]

A feeling of loneliness continues to haunt me. This Easter week I have been examining my conscience. Monsieur de Beauharnais and I were united by God. Is it my right to question this union? I have vowed to the Virgin that I will write to my husband, and in my pitiful prose, which he so detests, I will offer him my heart.

25 JULY – NOISY-LE-GRAND

A courier came this morning with a message: Monsieur de Beauharnais was in Paris. Immediately I called for a carriage. I asked Mimi to prepare the baby. She dressed Eugène in his sailor suit – an ensemble intended for a child one year older. I kissed his fat little nose. He rewarded me with a smile, his feet kicking. I tried to nurse before I dressed, but I was too anxious. Eugène fretted and began to cry. 'I will try again on the way,' I told Mimi, handing Eugène back to her. Nervously I prepared my own toilette, choosing a cream silk visiting suit and a big straw hat with wide cream ribbons that tied under my chin. The jacket was a little tight for me.

All the way I thought of what I was going to say. At the edge of a wood I instructed the driver to pull into a shady glen. This time Eugène was hungry enough to nurse no matter my emotional state. I held a handkerchief to my other nipple to keep from staining my jacket. 'I'm nervous,' I told Mimi.

At the Hôtel de la Rochefoucauld I presented my card. Mimi stood behind me with Eugène, humming to him. I adjusted his funny little sailor hat, which had fallen down over his eyes.

'Rose.'

I turned. It was Monsieur de Beauharnais, standing in the open doorway. He looked stylish in a double-breasted waistcoat embroidered in gold. I offered my hand. 'It's good to see you, Alexandre.' The baby let out a squeal. Mimi lifted him into his father's arms. For a moment I feared Eugène might take fright in the arms of this stranger, but he didn't. He stared at the gold buttons on his father's waistcoat, reached out to touch one.

'Is it all right to hold him this way?' Monsieur de Beauharnais asked nervously.

'He's a strong, healthy boy, you will not hurt him,' I said, following him into the parlour.

Monsieur de Beauharnais touched the baby's chin with his finger. Eugène rewarded him with a grin. 'He smiled at me! Do you think he knows who I am?' Eugène began to fuss. 'I must have done something wrong.' Monsieur de Beauharnais handed his son to Mimi. Eugène began to howl.

'Is there somewhere I could walk with him?' Mimi asked.

'The garden is through those doors,' he said.

I removed my hat, touched my hair. Monsieur de Beauharnais filled a pipe with tobacco. I sat down, for my knees felt insecure. 'How was Italy?' I asked.

'Rainy.' He paused. 'Lonely.'

In spite of my prayers, I could feel anger rising within me. I willed such feelings away. They were the work of the Devil, not of God. For within me, too, was the longing that had become so much a part of me. For the sake of my son, for my own sake, I wanted my husband with me. For this, I was willing to forget, to give my heart anew.

Monsieur de Beauharnais lit his pipe, sucking in air through the stem. 'I received your letter,' he said, exhaling smoke.

There was a moment of silence. I heard my baby shriek from outside. Eugène, happy again.

'It was the reason for my return.'

I stood, went to the window, looked out. I feared I might say the wrong thing.

Monsieur de Beauharnais put his pipe down on the fireplace mantel. 'I . . . I know it has not been easy for you, Rose, but on my travels I've had time to reflect, to examine the past . . . and to consider the future.' He cleared his throat. 'I have decided . . . that is, I have made the decision, to forsake a certain woman.'

A certain woman. I turned to him. 'Will that be difficult, Alexandre?'

He came to me and kissed me, lightly at first. 'No,' he said. I put my hand on the back of his neck. He embraced me with feeling. My heart weakened.

I heard my baby crying. I pulled away. Mimi was at the door, holding a crying Eugène in her arms. 'I could come back later,' she said, grinning.

Monsieur de Beauharnais ran his fingers over his hair. 'No, come in . . .' He kissed my hand.

We have returned to the country, Monsieur de Beauharnais and

I, Mimi and our son. Now and again a voice of warning sounds in me; I do not pay it heed. I am intent on putting loneliness behind me.

1 SEPTEMBER
I woke with the most delicious feeling of warmth, curled next to my husband, a sense of peace filling me. I am with child again . . .

3 SEPTEMBER, EVENING
Eugène's first birthday. I've had the most shattering news. Monsieur de Beauharnais has applied for the position of aide-de-camp to the governor of Martinico.

'But Alexandre, our son is too young. I couldn't leave him behind. And if I'm—'

'I don't think it would be safe for either of you.'

'You would leave us?'

'I have much to gain in taking this opportunity—'

'And *everything* to lose,' I cried, which set the baby howling.

7 SEPTEMBER
This morning I woke and Monsieur de Beauharnais was gone. He had left in the night.

10 DECEMBER
I've learned that Laure Longpré, now a widow, is on the same boat as Monsieur de Beauharnais, also headed for Martinico.

A feeling of bitterness overwhelms me. I have been betrayed.

I pray for strength. I must endure – for my boy's sake, for the sake of the child within me.

10 APRIL 1783
In the morning I gave birth, earlier than expected. She is red, frail – she sleeps the sleep of the dead.

After the cord was cut, after the *accoucheuse* had washed her with red wine and wrapped her in cotton wool, Mimi bathed me with a fragrant tea. I began to say something but she silenced me. A woman who has just given birth should never speak. 'Else a wind come inside you,' she said.

I closed my eyes, my lips. I closed my heart. A wind has already come inside me, a storm carrying tears.

11 APRIL

My baby was baptized this afternoon. Fanny, as godmother, has suggested the name Hortense. It is not a name I care for. I am too weary to object. I had to sell a medallion in order to pay the priest.

I don't remember feeling this way after Eugène was born . . . so sad, so sad.

22 APRIL — NOISY-LE-GRAND

Hortense is not growing. The doctor insists I put her in the care of a wet nurse. He has recommended Madame Rousseau in the village here.

'A wet nurse in Noisy-le-Grand would be better than one in Paris,' Aunt Désirée said, in answer to my concerns. 'In Paris the wet nurses starve their charges. They take in laundry and overexert themselves, which spoils their milk.'

I regarded the screaming baby in my arms. She'd sucked for hours and, even so, writhed with discontent. Was my own milk spoiled? Could grief spoil a mother's milk?

So today Aunt Désirée and I went to interview Madame Rousseau. Her abode is humble but clean. No animals are kept inside. She has a one-year-old boy (healthy, I noted), still nursing but ready to wean, she assured us. Her bosom seemed ample — she displayed it for inspection.

'I can come for your baby this evening,' she said.

So soon? 'I was thinking tomorrow,' I said.

'This evening would be better,' Aunt Désirée said. My baby's crying distressed the Marquis, I knew.

Hortense was wailing when we returned. Mimi was pacing the floor with her. I took my miserable baby from her, put her to suck, but in a short time she was screaming once again. I walked her in the garden for over an hour, until mercifully she fell into an exhausted sleep. If Madame Rousseau's milk will ease my baby's cries, I will rest content.

24 APRIL

I am ill, in terrible pain still, I have not slept. After my baby was taken from me, Mimi bound my breasts, but even so, one became inflamed, my milk blocked. The doctor has been coming each morning to bleed me. After, I am able to sleep, but wake weeping.

Eugène brings me leaves torn from the lilac bush in the garden. His sweet kisses are my only consolation. That and the news that my baby has stopped crying. I have been advised not to visit her until my milk dries.

Who would have thought this would be such a heart-wrenching process? I keep one of my baby's nightshirts under my pillow at night, press it to my lips as I sleep, inhale her sweet scent. My longing to hold her is so strong it makes me ill. I mourn for mothers everywhere.

30 JUNE

The Marquis has received several letters regarding Alexandre's dissolute behaviour in Martinico, where, he has learned, his son drinks, gambles and consorts publicly with a number of women (not only Laure), oblivious of the disgrace to his family name. Dangerously enraged, the Marquis composed a letter to the King demanding that his son be arrested under a *lettre de cachet*. With some effort Aunt Désirée apprehended it before it was sent.

2 SEPTEMBER

I was finishing the embroidery on a vest for Eugène when Mimi brought me an envelope. 'It's from your husband,' she said.

'A courier brought it?' It was unusual for a courier to come so early.

'A woman.' Mimi stared at the floor. 'Madame Longpré.'

'Madame Laure Longpré?' Was she not in Martinico? 'She came

here?' I regarded the envelope in my hand. It smelled of iris powder. I broke the seal and slipped out the paper.

It was a letter — a letter from Monsieur de Beauharnais.

'What is it?' Mimi asked, perceiving my distress.

'Monsieur de Beauharnais has ordered me out of the house . . . into a convent. He claims—' I stopped. I could not say it. Alexandre claimed that Hortense was not his child.

'Allow me to fetch Madame!'

I did not protest. I felt myself weakening. Aunt Désirée came rushing into the room. She took the letter from me.

In it Monsieur de Beauharnais called me a vile creature. He accused me of having had numerous affairs as a girl. He claimed I'd lain with a man the night before I left to be betrothed to him, and with another in Saint-Pierre on the voyage to France. He claimed to have proof.

Aunt Désirée sank into the chair beside me. 'Mon Dieu,' I heard her whisper.

I felt the world become heavy around me.

III

Madame

In which I am banished to a convent

29 OCTOBER 1783

'The fee is six hundred livres a year for a room, eight hundred livres for board,' the Abbesse of the abbey de Penthémont informed us. She is a small woman of middle age, pretty in spite of a pocked face. She speaks with that particular cadence that identifies a member of the highest level of the noble class.

I nodded. I had expected it to be more. The convent of Penthémont was an elegant establishment for aristocratic ladies in distress. The Princess of Condé had been a boarder there.

The apartment that is available is parlour number three, on the second floor, overlooking a stone courtyard. The rooms, four in number, are not large, but sunny and simply furnished. Through two huge oak trees I could see the glittering dome of the Invalides.

Aunt Renaudin felt along the windowsill for dust.

'Satisfied, Madame?' the Abbesse inquired with a forgiving smile.

I move in at the end of November.

1 NOVEMBER

'Why should *you* move out!' the Marquis stormed. He can't even look at me without sputtering. His son has disappointed him in the most grievous way. Since returning to Paris, Alexandre has refused even to speak to his family. As a result, the Marquis's gout has flared.

I am touched by his loyalty, yet what can I do? By law I must do as Alexandre commands, in spite of the fact that he hasn't contributed an écu towards my support since he abandoned me over a year ago, in spite of his dissolute behaviour, his attack on my honour.

Eugène burst into tears when I told him. He wants to stay with 'Papa', he wept, his beloved Marquis. How can I explain?

27 NOVEMBER
We've moved, Mimi, Eugène and I. 'I want to go home!' Eugène cried when I showed him his new bed.

1 DECEMBER
Yesterday morning I received an elegantly scribed invitation to dine with the Abbesse.

Her rooms are on the ground floor, directly below my own. We were joined by three other boarders – Vicomtesse de Douai (tall, elegant), Duchesse de Monge (witty, plump) and Madame de Crény (tiny, sweet). We enjoyed an elegant meal of fresh oysters, brochette de rognons, foie gras aux truffles and, last, a fondue, which was put on the table in a casserole with a chafing dish and a spirit lamp. Afterwards we sat by the fire drinking *les régals à gloire* – a hot coffee and cognac drink that is popular now.

That evening there was a gathering in the apartment of Vicomtesse de Sotin. Monsieur Beaumarchais, the playwright, attended. After readings and song there were the usual discussions concerning the weather, theatre and politics. Then we got on to the more relaxing pursuits – gossip and games. (The Abbesse is unbeatable at trictrac, I discovered.) I feared the sound of our laughter would disturb our neighbours, but the Abbesse said I need not be concerned – that over the years they have had to become accustomed to it.

Life here is not at all what I expected.

TUESDAY, 2 DECEMBER, 11.00 P.M.
This afternoon, taking in yet another one of my dresses (I've become thin), I informed Aunt Désirée that I intended to seek a legal separation.

Aunt Désirée looked concerned. 'A separation, Rose? Have you any idea what that would entail – the social stigma that would attach to you and your children?'

'Yet you obtained a legal separation from your husband.' In the first year of her marriage, Aunt Désirée's husband had tried to poison her.

'And I have paid the price. Many a time I have been excluded from gatherings. It matters not at all if a woman is innocent. She has been tarnished and is not considered fit for *proper* society.' Aunt Désirée put down her needlework. 'And what if Alexandre proved contentious, Rose? Are you willing to expose the details of your private life for all of Paris to see? A woman is rarely the victor in such a battle. Even if you were beaten black and blue, it would be viewed as your husband's right – and your *duty* to be submissive to his wish, *whatever* his wish might be.'

'Am I to do nothing?' I demanded, jabbing the needle into my thumb by mistake. With some effort, I refrained from cursing. 'Alexandre has attacked my honour in an entirely public way.'

'But what of your son? Think how it will affect him. Eugène is old enough to understand the taunts of his playmates.'

'Think how a stain on my honour will affect him. Imagine what it will be like for him, having a mother who is forced to live in a convent until the end of her days. And what of Hortense? Her prospects for a good marriage will be seriously diminished. A legal separation is my only alternative – both for my sake *and* for the sake of my children.'

Aunt Désirée sighed. 'I will pray for you, Rose.'

8 DECEMBER, LATE AFTERNOON

This afternoon I met Monsieur Joron, King's Counsel and commissioner at Chastelet, to make official my record of complaint. He came with his father* and his secretary. It was trying, laying bare the failure of my marriage, but they were tactful and put me at my ease.

Monsieur Joron told me that it will take a few months for an order for a separation of person and dwelling to be issued, and that I shouldn't expect settlement for more than a year after that. Until then, I must live according to my husband's wishes.

* Monsieur Joron's father described Rose in the following way to his wife: 'a fascinating young person, a lady of distinction and elegance, with perfect style, a multitude of graces and the most beautiful of speaking voices.'

'One full year?'

The secretary transcribed my testimony in his careful hand. I was asked to read it over and sign each page. 'How shall I sign?' I asked. 'As Beauharnais, or Tascher de la Pagerie?'

'However you prefer.'

I wrote: Tascher de la Pagerie.

And so it is – my marriage undone.

13 DECEMBER – NOISY-LE-GRAND

We are at Noisy-le-Grand for a few days. Four years ago Alexandre and I were married here, shared the bed I sleep in now. I remember so clearly the first time I saw him, a handsome young man reading Cicero's *Treatise on Laws* in the salon of the Hôtel Graves in Brest. It seems another world, another time – another Rose.

After Eugène woke from his nap we walked to Madame Rousseau's to see Hortense. She giggled in her brother's clumsy embrace. I held them both in my arms. How can I regret a union that has given me two such beautiful children?

MONDAY, 22 DECEMBER – BACK IN PARIS

The women at the convent make a fuss over me. Their warmth puzzles me. Well-bred, wealthy and titled, they are much above my station.

'They perceive a natural elegance in your demeanour,' the Abbesse told me this morning. (I read to her; in return she helps me with my enunciation.) 'And, too, there is nothing so rewarding as an avid student.'

An avid student I confess I have become. I long to feel at ease in this world, among these women – but there is so much to learn: how to bow, how to enter a room, how to take a seat, how to speak. Quietly I observe the way Vicomtesse de Douai orders her coach, how Duchesse de Monge bows (and for whom, and how low, depending), watch for whom her footman opens both double doors and for whom only one is opened, listen to the way the Abbesse speaks, her aristocratic inflection.

In the privacy of my room, I practise before the long looking glass, bow deeply to my image in the glass. 'Don't laugh!' I tell Mimi, who watches me with a mocking smile.

4 FEBRUARY 1784

Alexandre is suing for the return of my jewellery, including the medallion I had to sell in order to pay for Hortense's baptism. He claims that it was part of his inheritance, that I had no right to sell it.

I am so distressed I cannot sleep. Alexandre provides nothing for my support. I am increasingly desperate for funds. Every day, it seems, there is a creditor at my door. Yesterday I was presented with a bill for jewels I had never even seen. I gave the man Alexandre's address and directed him there, trying not to reveal my rage.

23 FEBRUARY

Fanny called early this morning, her heavily powdered face streaked with tears. Her daughter Marie has suffered yet another infant death. The youngest, Amédée, died in the night, succumbing to a fever. She was not even two. It was three-year-old Émilie who'd discovered her 'sleeping' sister.

'Can you come with me?' Fanny asked. 'I can't face her alone. Not again.' This is the third child Marie has lost.

It was Alexandre's brother François who came to the door to meet us, wearing a nightcap and a blue waistcoat over a bedgown. He looked distressed. I don't know why this surprised me, for he is a man of feeling, with a tender regard for children. He led us into Marie's bedchamber, where she was resting on a chaise longue, a dish of tea on the side table. She was pale, without expression, like a dead person herself. Little Émilie was sitting quietly beside her mother, looking confused.

We were told that the child was in her bed in the next room. I stayed with Marie while Fanny went to help prepare the body, the sobbing nanny assisting.

After the priest came, and then the doctor (who prescribed laudanum drops for Fanny as well as for Marie and François), I left, taking little Émilie back with me to Penthémont. Mimi, Eugène and I fuss over her gently. Even so, she refuses to speak.

2 MARCH

Eugène has worked his magic on Émilie. She follows him every-where. She is a bright little thing, a little pixie with fair pink cheeks and coal-black hair and eyes – but oh, so serious! Only Eugène can coax a smile from her.

'I'm afraid we will have to take Émilie back home soon.' I broke the news to him gently. 'To her own mother.' Marie was in need of her now, in need of her one surviving child.

10 APRIL – NOISY-LE-GRAND

Hortense is one today. She's walking!

27 April 1784 – Noisy-le-Grand
Dear Madame Beauharnais,

  I am returning the money you sent me. Your husband came for a visit last week and paid for two months. He brought some pretty baubles from the funfair for the baby. She didn't make strange at all. He sang her a ballad and danced about with her, which made her spit up but he didn't mind too much. You never mentioned your husband. I hope I did the right thing.
                                  Respectfully, Madame Rousseau

TUESDAY, 11 JANUARY 1785 – NOISY-LE-GRAND

Aunt Désirée has received word that Alexandre would like to see Eugène. 'And he would consent to see me as well,' she said, examining the letter.

The Marquis snorted. 'How good of him.'

'I think you should go,' I told her.

Aunt Désirée spent the morning getting ready. She settled on her blue silk robe with a black velvet cape. I lent her my hat with the blue ribbons, which complemented the dress nicely. She was flustered, which brought some colour to her cheeks.

I dressed Eugène in his best clothes. 'Am I going to church?' he asked. He is too young to grasp the situation. To him, 'father' is the Marquis – why should it be otherwise?

Aunt Désirée returned at nightfall looking relieved. Eugène was quite excited about the bounty of presents this 'stranger' had heaped upon him.

'Alexandre asked if I could bring Eugène once a week.' Aunt Désirée took off her hat and tidied her hair.

'What do you think?' I asked.

'It might help.' She paused. 'Although there will be no changing his mind.'

I stiffened. Even if Alexandre were to relent, could my heart open? 'And you? How did you find him?'

'Oh, he was full of pretty words.'

I knew Alexandre's pretty words. 'But his heart was not there?'

Aunt Désirée looked at me, her eyes filling with tears. 'How can that be?'

FRIDAY, 4 FEBRUARY

Today, as I returned from my clothier, Mimi rushed to me in the most terrible state, crying out in the African tongue.

'Speak!' I demanded. She had fallen to her knees. 'Mimi, *mon Dieu*!'

'The boy! He's gone!'

I could not comprehend. Eugène? *Gone?* What did that mean?

In a rush her story came out. She'd allowed Eugène to play in the courtyard, as was our custom. Every few minutes she looked out. Eugène had been beating on a drum and the din served as a means of keeping track of him. She'd gone into her room to search for a particular colour thread. When she came back out she noticed that the courtyard had become silent. She looked out of the window. The courtyard was empty.

She ran down to the courtyard and out through the iron gates – which were closed, she assured me – and on to the street. Eugène was nowhere to be seen. She questioned the tenants, but could get no answers. She ran for the Abbesse, but she was out.

I went to the open window, looked out at the empty courtyard. 'Eugène!' I called out. I hurried through our rooms, looking into every closet, under the beds. I could not believe that Eugène was not there. It was then that I noticed a piece of paper sticking out from under the carpet. Apparently it had been pushed under the door. I picked it up, knowing even before I read it what it would reveal.

THE MANY LIVES & SECRET SORROWS OF JOSEPHINE B.

It was from Alexandre. He had taken Eugène.

It did not take long to send for a fiacre and find our way to the
Rochefoucauld town house on Rue de Seine. The big doors to the
courtyard were still open, the horses had not yet been unhitched.
A footman in livery opened the door.

Alexandre came to the foyer with a cautious look. We hadn't seen
each other since he'd left my bed in the night, two years before.
He looked the same, if pale and thin, no doubt from the lingering
effects of the malignant fever he had contracted in Martinico. He
was without a wig, his hair long, hanging about his shoulders.

'I've come for Eugène.' I tried to calm myself.

'I won't have my son growing up in a house of women!' he
said.

'Then permit me to live elsewhere with him!' I cried.

He turned his back, commanding the footman to shut the heavy
door. Mimi pulled me away.

5 FEBRUARY

I've notified the authorities. A hearing has been set one month from
today, but until then I am powerless. Alexandre, as the father, may
do as he pleases with Eugène.

Mimi has gone to stay at Alexandre's in order to look after Eugène.
I am unbearably alone here.

SATURDAY, 7 FEBRUARY

As I was packing to go to Noisy-le-Grand, tiny Madame de Crény
called. She was in need of diversion, she said. Her coach had been
tied up in traffic at Saint-Sulpice for over an hour. 'An enormous
wedding.' She removed her hat. She was wearing a travelling suit
of grey silk with abundant lace trimming that overwhelmed her tiny
figure. At her neck and elbows were huge pink-and-white-striped
bows. 'General Arthur Dillon and that woman with the bosom.
Creole, I am told. Perhaps you know her. Apparently she met Dillon
in Martinico. Her name is Longbeau, Longpried . . . something like
that. She chews candles, I've heard.'

Laure Longpré.

'You should have seen the equipages. The Queen and King signed the wedding contract.' Madame de Crény rolled her eyes. 'Even Duchesse de Monge's sister couldn't get *that* honour, and she practically lives with the Queen.'

I sat down, stunned. The Queen and King? Signed their wedding contract? Alexandre's bloodline wasn't even noble enough to permit him to sit in a royal equipage. 'Madame Longpré is a cousin of mine.' I paused. 'My husband fancied her,' I said.

'Oh . . . ! Was *she* the one?' Madame de Crény said sweetly. She took my hand. 'And now she has married General Dillon?'

I recalled the deranged expression in Alexandre's eyes. 'Curious,' I said, 'is it not?' Curious and cruel.

3 MARCH

After Mass this morning the Abbesse came to my door. 'Your husband wishes to speak with you.'

'Alexandre?' Tomorrow both Alexandre and I are to appear in court. Why would he come at this time? 'Is Eugène with him?'

The Abbesse shook her head. 'You must consider whether or not *you* wish to speak to him.'

'What harm might there be?'

'If you do consent to receive him, Rose, I recommend that you do so in the presence of your lawyer.'

'I'll agree to nothing, I promise you.'

'You'll receive him?'

'If you will stay with me.'

'That is wise.'

She was gone for what seemed a long time. When Alexandre entered, I was puzzled by the look in his eyes. It has always been difficult to interpret Alexandre's emotions, and this time was no different.

The Abbesse settled herself into a chair by the door. Alexandre seemed uncomfortable about her presence, and for a moment I thought he was going to protest. Then he spoke. 'Rose, after a period of deliberation I have come to the conclusion—' He stopped to clear his throat. 'I have come to the conclusion that I have been in error.'

I was shocked by his confession, but remained, nevertheless, cautious. How many times has Alexandre fooled me with his golden words, jewels given but not paid for?

Alexandre turned to the Abbesse. 'I have come to comprehend the . . . grievousness of my actions – while I was in Martinico, and again, most recently, in taking Eugène. I have no defence,' he went on, addressing me now, 'but that I was possessed by emotions I could not control. I have vowed to make amends. Eugène will be returned to you shortly. At the hearing tomorrow I will plead guilty, for it is guilty I stand before you.'

There was silence but for the steady ticking of the clock. 'Madame de Beauharnais – if I may address your husband,' the Abbesse said.

I nodded.

'Vicomte de Beauharnais, I urge you to continue in this line of thinking. It can only bear fruit. The appearance of a *fiat lux** in one's life helps not only oneself, but all those around one, and puts in motion any number of blessed events. But it is not to this purpose I wish to speak. I would advise your wife to accept your apology – but only were it to be expressed in a more tangible form, such as an equitable and prompt settling of accounts overdue. But at the same time I would caution her to be aware of the benefits that might accrue to *you* in light of your confession of guilt, for your sins might perhaps be judged less severely, and you might stand to gain in this way. Is this not so? Tell me truthfully,' she went on, 'how does your lawyer feel about this . . . this "confession" of yours?'

'Abbesse, respectfully,' I interrupted. 'I thank you for your counsel. I will hold your words close to my heart. But at this moment I would like to have a word with my husband in private.'

The Abbesse looked at me with concern.

'I promise I will not do anything foolish,' I whispered, accompanying her to the door.

She touched my shoulder as she departed.

I closed the door behind me and turned to Alexandre, pulling my shawl round my shoulders. 'Alexandre, tell me what this means – I have lived with uncertainty too long.'

'I am prepared to give you whatever you ask, Rose. I look back with regret on the things I did, the things I said. I can only conclude

---

* She is referring to Genesis, 'Let there be light.'

that I was not myself. Perhaps it was the delirium I suffered in Martinico, occasioned by the fever.'

Relief filled my soul, followed by caution. I recalled the Abbesse's words. 'What will you be demanding at the court hearing, in the way of a settlement?'

Alexandre turned his face to the embers in the fireplace. 'I will agree to anything. A public apology, an admission of error, a monthly allowance, your freedom to live where you please . . . whatever you require.'

I went to the window. A bricklayer was working on the courtyard wall. 'And in exchange?'

'I only ask for custody of my son, when he turns five.'

Eugène!

'You will have Hortense,' he pleaded. 'Can't you grant me Eugène? A boy needs his father. He will need what I can teach him. You know that, Rose. For the boy's sake.'

For the boy's sake . . .

In which ill fortune plagues us

12 March 1785 — Fontainebleau
Darling!

Congratulations! Who would have imagined that a woman could take her husband to court and win!* How unthinkable! All the ladies are in a fever of excitement over your victory. I've been told that even the Queen talks of it. You are a heroine now!

I've finally persuaded your aunt and the Marquis to join me here in Fontainebleau. The estate Désirée has leased on Rue de Montmorin is well located, and big — stables for twelve horses! And all for the price of some Paris hovel, no doubt.

Is it true that you intend to join us soon? I pray that it is so. My salon here in Fontainebleau could use your lively heart.

Your loving Aunt Fanny

24 March 1785 — Fontainebleau
Dear Rose,

With the proceeds from the sale of Noisy-le-Grand, I've been able to secure a long-term lease on an estate here in Fontainebleau. You will love it. There is a lovely suite of rooms for you and the children overlooking the garden.

You will be pleased to know that Alexandre paid us a call to inform us personally of the results of the settlement. He and

* The separation agreement stipulated that Alexandre would pay Rose an annual allowance of five thousand livres plus an additional one thousand livres for Hortense's expenses up to the age of seven, fifteen hundred livres thereafter. (Unfortunately, this was rarely paid.) As for Eugène, the agreement stipulated that Alexandre would take custody when the boy turned five.

his father have come to terms. What a great joy this is to me. Already I can see an improvement in the Marquis's health.

Do join us soon. The garden, quite large, is much in need of your special attention. The prices are reasonable and there isn't all that disagreeable mob one encounters in Paris now.

We miss Eugène. Alexandre told us a number of charming stories — it is clear that he is quite fond of the boy. As for Hortense, he made a point of mentioning that he would like 'his daughter' (his exact words) weaned from her wet nurse. I told him it would be best for her to be weaned after you move. I know it is hard to wait, but it is not an easy process. Best to be settled first.

Your loving Aunt Désirée

22 JULY, SAINT MARY MAGDALEN'S DAY — FONTAINEBLEAU

How quiet Fontainebleau is — so unlike Paris, which never rests. This morning I took my morning cup of chocolate into the garden, breathing in the cleansing air. I could hear the soothing clip-clop of the chimney sweep's horse, the creaking of the rag collector's wagon. From somewhere close a cock crowed. We will be happy here.

24 JULY, EVENING

This afternoon Madame Rousseau, the wet nurse, brought Hortense. The good woman bawled leaving 'her' girl behind, she has formed such a strong attachment. When Hortense saw the carriage pull away she began screaming as if she was being tortured. This horrible state lasted for over two hours.

Now, at last, she has fallen into an exhausted sleep. I look upon the face of my daughter with apprehension. Will she ever love me?

FRIDAY, 23 SEPTEMBER

Father writes that there has been no income earned on La Pagerie, or even on the Marquis's properties in Saint-Domingue.*

* Joseph acted as manager of all the Beauharnais properties in the Caribbean. Unfortunately, he was not a good one.

'No income at *all*? But how is that possible?' Aunt Désirée exclaimed when I read out the letter. 'How are we to manage?'

Indeed. Already my debts are mounting. Alexandre hasn't paid support for four months. He recently bought a country property in the Loire from his brother and claims to have no cash. And now, without income from the Islands . . .

4 MAY 1786

A Madame Croÿ came to call this afternoon. She'd sent a letter from Paris a week ago requesting an audience on a matter she said concerned us.

She is a humble woman of quiet composure. Although her clothes were tattered, she wore them with grace. She was nervous in our company, but when she perceived that we were kindly, she was able to speak her mind.

Her daughter, a married woman with three children, is about to have another. She explained that her daughter intended to put this baby into the charities, for she could not afford to provide for it. Madame Croÿ was concerned about this possibility, for she knew what the fate of that child would be. Indeed, more than half the babies given over each year die.*

'Why have you come to us?' I asked.

'Because the Vicomte de Beauharnais is the father—'

'Alexandre?' Aunt Désirée interrupted.

'I do not believe he would deny it.' The spots of rouge on Madame Croÿ's cheeks were garishly bright in the afternoon sun.

I sat back. I had falsely assumed I would no longer be affected by Alexandre's reprehensible behaviour. I was mistaken.

'You're not going to suggest that *we* take the child,' Aunt Désirée said.

'No – I thought perhaps you . . . I thought if you could help—'

'Financially, you mean.' Aunt Désirée sighed.

'It wouldn't take much, but it is more than I can offer. I had to sell my winter cloak to purchase a coach ticket to come see you today.'

* Approximately forty thousand babies were abandoned a year.

'How much would your daughter require in order to keep the child?' I asked.

'I do not believe she has the heart for it,' Madame Croÿ said. 'I am ashamed to say so, but the baby would be better in the care of a foster parent. I do laundry for a woman, a Madame d'Antigny, the wife of a goldsmith, but a *paresseuse* – she has no children of her own. She might be willing, were the financial needs looked after.'

'You have discussed this with her?' Aunt Désirée asked.

'Aunt Désirée, I think we should talk to Alexandre,' I said.

6 MAY

Alexandre arrived in the rain. He'd set out from Paris the day before, but the roads were so muddy a linchpin had been lost from one of the fore wheels and they had had to stop at an inn along the way.

He'd been alarmed by my use of a mounted courier. 'Bad news always comes fast. Is it Father? Do not keep me in suspense, I beg you.' His yellow velvet frock coat was splattered with mud.

'A Madame Croÿ came to see us,' I said.

Alexandre leaned his sword against the wall. 'Do I know this Madame Croÿ?' Aubin cleaned the mud off his boots.

'She claims you enjoyed an amourette with her daughter.' Aunt Désirée appeared in the doorway behind us, wearing a brocade dressing gown over her corset and petticoat. She'd interrupted her toilette to come to the door, her hair greased but unpowdered.

Alexandre groaned.

'You recall?' Aunt Désirée asked.

He sighed with exasperation and entered the parlour. 'I believe you mean Darigrand – a certain Geneva-Louise.' He sat down by the fire, blowing into his hands and rubbing them together. 'It's so cold out there! Who would believe it's May? What's come over this country? The weather has become so unpredictable!'

The parlourmaid came to the door. 'Would Vicomte de Beauharnais wish for something?'

'I'll have a pint of claret – warm.'

'Alexandre!' Aunt Désirée said. 'It's not yet eleven.'

'And *you* haven't been travelling for days in this miserable weather. When you think of the nonsense they concern themselves with, you'd think they'd work out a way to heat a diligence.'

I sat opposite him, ready to speak of the subject at hand, when Mimi came to the door holding Hortense's hand, Eugène following behind, carrying a toy crossbow he'd made the day before from sticks and bits of string.

'Take the children away,' Aunt Désirée told Mimi.

'Please allow a moment.' I knew how much his father's visits meant to Eugène. Hortense squirmed to escape Mimi's grasp.

Alexandre examined Eugène's crossbow.

'Do you want to try it?' Eugène asked.

'I must talk with your mother and Aunt Désirée first.'

Mimi picked Hortense up, setting off a howl. 'You will see your father soon,' I assured her.

After the children had gone, the three of us sat for a moment in uncomfortable silence. Aunt Désirée cleared her throat. 'Madame Croÿ is concerned about the welfare of the child,' she said finally.

'The child?' Alexandre stood in front of the fire. There were only a few small sticks on a deep bed of ash – they gave off little heat. 'What child?'

'You don't know?' I asked. Aunt Désirée and I exchanged a confused look.

Aunt Désirée explained: 'Madame Croÿ claims that her daughter – Madame Darigrand – is soon to have your child.'

Alexandre sat down in a chair, crossing and uncrossing his legs in an agitated manner.

'Alexandre,' I said, 'you look upset. Please explain.'

'I . . . knew Geneva-Louise – or Madame Darigrand, as you so honour her – for a period of six months. I wasn't the first and I won't be the last. We broke off, and a month later she came to me, claiming to be with child.'

'Why does this news surprise you?' I asked.

'Because I gave Madame Darigrand a considerable sum of money to . . . to *resolve* her condition.'

'I see.' Aunt Désirée crossed herself. 'And what do you propose to do now, Alexandre?'

'I told Madame Darigrand I wanted nothing more to do with her,' Alexandre said, 'and certainly nothing to do with a child.'

'But, Alexandre,' I said, 'you are the father of that—'

'I did not journey all the way from Paris to be lectured,' Alexandre said. He strode back into the hall.

'Hortense and Eugène will be heartbroken if you leave!' I cried out, running after him.

He stayed. I promised not to mention Madame Darigrand again.*

10 AUGUST
We are besieged by financial troubles, which I greatly resent for I consider money one of the least important things in life. Yet the want of it can certainly be distracting.

The Marquis's Saint-Domingue plantation is not earning, nor La Pagerie in Martinico. Aunt Désirée and I have written letter after letter to Father, but without solution. He claims it's the British, the weather, inflation . . . all adding up to the same result: no income. I've had to depend on Alexandre's contribution, which is rarely forthcoming. There are times when I am entirely without . . .

3 SEPTEMBER, 1.15 P.M.
It is said that autumn is beautiful in Fontainebleau, but the charm is dulled for me in this season. In three hours Alexandre will arrive and we will partake of the refreshments the cook has made in honour of Eugène's fifth birthday. I've just finished decorating the cake, fulfilling his request for liquorice comfits all around on top. Oh, how my heart went out with each comfit I placed, how the tears started as I positioned each candle.

4 SEPTEMBER
Eugène and Alexandre left this morning, Eugène holding on to his new book bag, looking very grown-up but for the baby blanket he clasped in his other hand. I tried hard not to cry, for he might cry in turn, and that would have distressed him, I knew, trying so hard to be big. We are all of us trying.

---

* In June, Marie-Adélaïde (Adèle) was born. Monsieur and Madame d'Antigny became her foster parents. Rose contributed to the child's upkeep. In 1804, Rose – as Empress – arranged Adèle's marriage to a Captain Lecomte, and provided her with a farm as a dowry and a trousseau.

WEDNESDAY, 3 JANUARY 1787

Creditors pester our door like flies in autumn. Years ago, the Marquis's annual pension was set at one hundred and fifty thousand livres. In the last decade, it was reduced to twelve thousand. And now, because of the impoverishment of the government treasury,* it has been further reduced to under three thousand livres a year.

Three thousand! How can the Marquis and my aunt be expected to live on such a sum? After all his years of distinguished service, is this his reward? I have written to the Minister of War to try to persuade him to have the pension increased. We are renting a house that can stable twelve horses, but can't afford to keep a pair.

The Marquis maintains his humour: 'I used to think someone impoverished if he couldn't enjoy the privilege of raising three armed men. I'll soon be so poor I'll have to stay in bed while my breeches are mended.' He's in bed all the time anyway; it's unlikely he'll ever wear out a pair of breeches again.

1 MAY 1788

The letters from home are distressing. Father is not well and now Manette is seriously ill. Mother begs me to come home – her words have an ominous tone. I must go, surely . . . but how can I leave Eugène?

TUESDAY, 27 MAY

We've received the most bewildering news: the Island properties have been earning a profit. According to information Uncle Tascher provided, last year La Pagerie earned seventy thousand livres.

'Seventy thousand! Why hasn't Joseph sent you your share?' Aunt Désirée demanded. 'Has he sent you anything?'

'He's been ill. No doubt—'

'I wonder if the Marquis's properties earned a profit as well.' She began pacing in an agitated state. I no longer feared that she might faint.

'If only I could talk to him,' I said.

Aunt Désirée stopped. 'You must go, Rose.'

* France was bankrupt in part because of its support of the American Revolution.

'To Martinico?' I stuttered.

'I would gladly go myself were it not for the Marquis's health.'

'But—' What about Eugène? Alexandre would never permit me to take him. 'But Eugène is coming in a few weeks to spend his summer holiday with me.' I'd been looking forward to it, making plans.

'Yet it is precisely for his sake that you must go, Rose. It is his inheritance, his future, after all.'

I was at a loss. I longed to see my family, my ailing father and sister, but the very thought of an ocean voyage made me ill. 'It would cost a small fortune to go,' I said. Last week Alexandre had informed me that he didn't have the two thousand livres required to pay for Eugène's schooling. As well, my own debts had mounted.

'It will cost you *not* to go.'

'But it's almost June. I would have to leave immediately.' It would be dangerous to be at sea in August, the month of hurricanes.

'Exactly.' Aunt Désirée dipped a quill in the inkwell. 'The Marquis may be feeble but as a former commander in the navy there are a few things he can arrange – I should think passage on the next ship to Fort-Royal would be one of them,' she said, writing out a note. 'There.' She sprinkled the letter with sand and shook it clean. 'Take this up for his signature and I'll send it out on the next post.'

2 JUNE

It has happened very quickly. Passage has been found. I've borrowed six thousand livres for the journey. In addition, Aunt Désirée will loan me one thousand livres. Already she's found a buyer for my harp – that should help pay for Eugène's tuition.

And so it is set – Mimi, Hortense and I will be leaving in a few weeks for Paris. From there it will be a three-day journey by coach to Rouen, where we'll take a river barge to Le Havre to wait ship.

There is so much to do, so many things to remember to do, so many things to worry about.

I told Hortense last night, at bedtime. She likes the idea of a boat. She is five now, and a strong girl.

Mimi is ecstatic, of course.

I can't believe we are doing this.

Hortense and I are in Paris, saying our farewells to Eugène and Alexandre. We leave for Le Havre in the morning.

It was difficult explaining to Eugène that we are going to be away for a very long time. 'I must see my father and my sister,' I explained. 'They are ill.' He is only six; it was the explanation he could most easily understand.

He said he would come and visit us, and I had to explain that he couldn't. 'Your sister and I will be on the boat for a very long time, just to get there.'

I gave him a music box with a toy soldier that popped up. I turned the box over. I'd had an inscription engraved on the bottom.

'I can't read it,' he confessed.

I pointed to each word as I pronounced it: 'For Eugène, whom I will always love, Maman.'

He turned the box over in his hands. 'Is that all?' he asked.

'That's all,' I said, too close to tears to say more.

In which I return home

THURSDAY, 3 JULY 1788

As we approached the open sea it grew dark. Soon there was a great wind and one of the sails began flapping, making a cracking sound. Quickly the men began taking down the sails.

'Get below,' a flagman yelled. 'Take the child!'

I grabbed Hortense for fear the wind might snatch her away.

The swells were growing. The rain began hitting us violently. Just before I climbed down into the passage, I looked out to sea. In the dark I could see a darker dark, a thickening of wind and rain. Then, a deafening roar; the rain had turned to stone. Mimi appeared, falling down the ladder behind us.

We stumbled into our cabin as best we could, for we were thrown from one side of the narrow passage to the other. Hortense cried out; I held her too tightly. I braced myself against the bunk. I could feel the sickness rising within me. We'd sunk into the pit of Hell, into an elemental fury. 'Mimi!' I called out.

'I am here.' A voice in the dark, barely discernible over the frightful howling. I felt her curled at the foot of the bunk.

The sickness filled me again. I fought it, weakly. Oh, please, God, I prayed, shameful for having neglected Him.

We emerged into the light, giddy with the memory of terror. The deck was covered with stones of ice, glittering like a wealth of diamonds. And, as far as I could see, the undulating surface of the sea, smooth and untroubled.

[UNDATED]

We've hit a calm, and are helpless, unmoving. For two days we've not moved, merely drifted. I never thought I'd pray for wind.

I feel cut loose from the world, detached. The most horrifying thing might happen and I would never know.

When I think about this, looking out on the vast watery surface, standing on the deck under the bright and crowded stars, when I think of the enormity of it all and the meaninglessness of my own small life, I am both sickened and comforted.

'Time is longer than rope,' Mimi says, a Carib proverb. And now I understand.

7 AUGUST
At last, we've caught a wind. It pulls us forward. With the rising and the falling of the waves, the sickness fills me again. I tolerate it gladly. I'm anxious to be done with this voyage.

[UNDATED]
We're approaching Martinico. I can smell it. I stand on the deck and pretend it is the wind that brings tears to my eyes.

10 AUGUST
Sighting the mountains, I held Hortense in my arms and wept. 'Is that 'Tinico?' she asked, perhaps four times before I gave up answering.

Mimi leans on the railing and stares, as if turning away would cause this vision to disappear.

Oh, my beautiful island – in the midst of such a great water.

11 AUGUST – FORT-ROYAL
We pulled into port in a torrent of rain. Uncle Tascher braved the weather to meet us, drenched.

The roads were rivers of mud. We made it with difficulty to his new estate in the hills, where the house slaves relieved us of our mud-splattered clothes. Hortense escaped and went running through the rooms in her petticoat (Mimi chasing after), much to the delight of her cousins.

I was astonished by the luxury of Uncle's home. He is Mayor

now, as well as Port Commander. 'And all he has to do is keep the young men from killing themselves off in duels,' his wife said, giggling. Her time of confinement is approaching, it is clear.

Uncle seemed cheerful in spite of his gout, inflamed due to the rain.

12 AUGUST
The bay was too rough to cross by gommier so we made the trip to Trois-Ilets overland in a carriage.

A 'carriage' I say – it was more of a partially covered wagon, crudely fashioned from canvas, and leaking terribly whenever we were overcome by a squall. Hortense, bounding with eagerness, flung herself from one side to the other in spite of my efforts to still her. At last she fell into an exhausted sleep, her sweat-damp head on my lap, and I was left with my thoughts.

Now and again the sky cleared and the sun came out, illuminating the thick foliage with an intensity I'd forgotten. The smell was dank, fertile, salted by the sea. I was in a reverie of emotion for all I had missed and was missing still. The incessant noise of the cicadas, the bullfrogs croaking, even the buzzing of the mosquitoes was like a song I'd been longing to hear. I felt I'd been a lifetime away, and was assaulted by memories both of pleasure and pain.

Coming into Trois-Ilets, I asked Morin, the driver, to stop in the square in front of the church. The market women were there, as before, selling fruit. The fishing boats were moored down the hill at the pier. Behind the church, the bright white of the tombs, littered with flowers and trinkets. Nothing had changed. Only I had changed – thinner, dressed in elegant silk and lace, wearing a bonnet that hid the sadness in my eyes.

Mimi cried out – she recognized one of the women in the market. She climbed down out of the wagon and sprinted across the square, her skirts pulled up to her knees, in one instant forgetting the ladylike saunter she'd acquired in Paris.

Hortense sat up, wiped her eyes. 'I'm thirsty,' she said.

'Maybe one of the market women would sell us juice.' I climbed down from the wagon, took Hortense in my arms. Her clothes were damp from the heat. 'This is the church I was baptized in.'

'It's little.'

'Yes.' It looked small to me, too. I pressed her to my heart, inhaling the sweet scent of her damp hair, kissed her nose before lowering her to the ground. 'Do you want to come inside with me?' I took her hand, dirty now.

'And then juice?'

I nodded. I had forgotten her thirst.

We climbed the three steps to the door. It creaked as I pulled it open. The dark interior was cool – and empty, for which I was grateful. We stood together, made the sign of the cross (Hortense so sweetly), walked down the aisle, the sound of our footsteps echoing on the black-and-white tiles. 'I'm just going to say a prayer and we'll go,' I whispered to her, edging into the second row of pews.

'A prayer for what?'

'For juice, for you,' I teased.

'Mother!' She frowned, alarmed, for she perceived my jest, and no doubt believed jesting in church a sin.

'For thanks, for our safe journey,' I whispered, adjusting my skirts and kneeling. And for the soul of my dead sister Catherine. And for my ailing sister Manette and my ever-ailing beloved father. And for my mother, who held them all in her arms, both the dead and the dying. And for my own small soul.

After a moment I rose. Hortense was sitting on the bench beside me, her eyes pinched shut, her brow furrowed, her hands clenched in a fist under her chin. I touched her shoulder. Her eyes flew open. 'One moment.' Her eyes shut tight again.

'And what was it *you* were praying for?' I asked as we emerged into the light. Mimi was already in the wagon, sharing a mango with Morin. Flirting, I thought, by the way she moved.

'For Father.' Hortense jumped three steps in one leap.

'Alexandre?' I was taken aback. I took her hand and we headed over to the market.

'For his blessing.' Hortense looked around the market. Trunks of felled banana trees, thick with green fruit, were stacked next to a basket of overly ripe mangoes, buzzing with flies.

I asked the eldest of the women if she had juice. She smiled a toothless grin and pointed to the pile of ripe oranges stacked before her. She hadn't understood and my memory of the African tongue had abandoned me. I took three oranges, gave the woman a coin.

SANDRA GULLAND

'An orange will be wonderfully juicy,' I told Hortense, who was about to object. 'For his love, you mean?' I stripped an orange of peel and gave her a segment, popping one in my mouth as well. The sweetness of the fruit brought on a distant recollection of standing in this very market, sucking on an orange after Mass on a Sunday morning. A girl with an aching heart, sucking orange segments and watching the door of the church, searching the crowd for a boy named William. I took Hortense's hand and headed back to the wagon.

'Yes – for you.' The juice from the orange dribbled down her chin.

I stopped under the shade of a manchineel tree.

'For him to love you,' she said.

I heard Mimi laugh. I looked towards the wagon. The two horses were asleep on their feet. 'You prayed for your father to love *me*?'

Hortense looked confused. 'Was that bad?'

'Stay,' I told Mimi, hoisting Hortense up on to the wagon seat, taking care (without success) not to soil my skirts on the muddy wagon wheels. 'We're fine back here,' I added, handing two oranges forward, one for Mimi and one for Morin.

The road leading out of Trois-Ilets was as rough as I remembered it, the wagon almost overturning. Before long, we came to my family's canefields, black with ash. In the distance, a field yet to be burned, and, beyond that, newly planted coffee trees.

'All of this belongs to my family,' I told Hortense.

'It's burned.' She stood on my lap to look.

'They do that to scare away bugs and snakes.'

'Snakes!'

At the river we had to get down. The horses refused to put hoof to the old wooden bridge. They had to be coaxed and in the end whipped, but finally they made a bolt for it, cantering across in a lather of fear, the wagon clattering behind them.

We climbed back in. I noticed a gang of field slaves in big straw hats labouring in a field – replanting likely. 'Do you recognize anyone?' I asked Mimi.

'I can't see that far.' Mimi threw an orange peel into the canefield.

THE MANY LIVES & SECRET SORROWS OF JOSEPHINE B.

'Turn left up ahead,' she told Morin, adjusting her skirt. 'By the cabbage palms.' She turned to me and grinned.

The horses slowed, beginning their ascent up the gentle slope. The road was more overgrown than I remembered it, the moss hanging heavy from the trees, reminding me of dreams. As we passed the kitchen gardens, several of the Negro women waved.

'They aren't wearing tops.' Hortense pressed her hands over her eyes.

'It's hot working in the sun.' My own clothes were already damp, the heat was so intense. As we neared the homestead it began to rain, a soft, cooling shower more like a mist. I fussed over Hortense, cleaning her face, attempting to push her unruly hair under her new hat.

'It that it?' she asked, pushing her hat back off her head. I turned as we pulled up in front of the old stone building – the *sucrerie* my family called home. I nodded wordlessly, climbing down, looking upon the graceless structure with a stranger's critical eyes. The massive stone chimney seemed to tower above us, ominous and dark from the rain. One corner of the veranda roof had given slightly.

Where were Mother and Father? I searched for some sign in the windows, but they had all been shuttered against the midday sun.

It was Da Gertrude who came first to greet us, running down the path from the crushing hut screaming, 'They're here! They're here!' Her big arms circling like a windmill, her big lower lip quivering, catching first Mimi and then me in a hug so hard it forced the air right out of me. She twirled me round, admiring my Parisian finery. 'Lord, girl, look at you now, a *lady*! But you're too thin!' She was weeping now, uttering cries in the African tongue, a musical clicking sound. She had aged in the nine years I had been away, her face etched with lines like crevasses in an ancient hillside. But her eyes were bright, her spirit as clear as my heart remembered. In her arms I felt myself a girl again.

And then, magically it seemed, we were surrounded by all the household slaves, by the familiar faces of my youth, crying out in the cooling mist. One after another they took us in their arms, did joyful little dances all about us. 'Oh, look at you both, so elegant! Look! Even the little girl is in ribbons! So precious in her little hat!' Sylvester was there, elderly now, but as comical as ever, his pipe extinguished by the rain. My heart was full to bursting with the love I felt around me. I had been starving for them all and hadn't known it.

Embarrassed by the choking emotion that had welled up in me, I searched in my velvet bag for a handkerchief. 'And this is Hortense,' I said, wiping my eyes.

'Oh, and when she smiles!' Da Gertrude pulled a section of cane stalk out of her pocket. 'Have you ever sucked on a sugarcane?'

Hortense regarded the stalk suspiciously, looked at me for approval.

I kissed her dirty cheek. 'Chew it. It's like a comfit.'

With a rush of wind, the gentle mist turned to pelting drops of rain. I ran with Hortense for the shelter of the veranda, Da Gertrude chasing after.

'Mother? Father?' I lowered Hortense to the ground. I was puzzled by their absence.

'Your father's not well.' Da Gertrude pushed open the heavy door to the refinery. She'd taken Hortense's hand, wooed my girl with her big-hearted magic. I followed, stepped inside.

The floor of the boiling room was littered with cane stalks. I was struck by the familiar scent of sugar syrup, the sound of buzzing flies. I saw the stairs that descended into the cellar – to the room where I had been punished. Had that really happened?

I heard voices up above. I headed up the rickety wooden stairs. It was dark on the landing. 'Mother?'

She appeared before me, as stern as I remembered her, but for her eyes, which were etched with something different, I knew not what. She was wearing a brown muslin gown of a simple design and a white fluted cap.

'Look at you.' She took my hands in hers. She stood back and appraised me. 'You're thin, Rose.'

'And you.' She was so much older than I remembered her, older than I'd ever imagined her being.

'Only *you* look like a lady of fashion.'

Her hands felt rough, dry. 'Have you seen Hortense?' I asked. 'The child?'

We both turned at the sound of Hortense's giggle. Da Gertrude came striding up, my girl on her shoulders. Hortense was grinning, one hand covering Da Gertrude's left eye, the other still clutching the sugarcane stalk. 'I used to carry you this way, Rose,' Da Gertrude said. 'Remember?'

I smiled, reaching up to take Hortense. I cradled her in my arms, turned to Mother. 'My girl,' I said.

Mother reached out a finger, stroked the smooth skin on Hortense's arm. Hortense was suddenly still, sucking on the cane stalk. 'She's lovely.' Mother's eyes were glistening. 'She takes after her father, doesn't she?'

'Yes.'

'I'm not a man!' Hortense said.

I let her down. 'She's big for her age,' I said, 'healthy — quite bright. And *active*,' I sighed, watching Hortense spinning circles on the slippery wooden floor.

'Having a child in the house will be good for us,' Mother said. 'We are all of us too old here.'

I heard a voice boom from the parlour: 'This must be Yeyette's girl!' It was Father, addressing Hortense no doubt, who had spun into the other room.

'No,' I heard Hortense answer. 'Who is Yeyette?'

'You don't know!'

I followed Mother into the parlour. There was Father, leaning on a tasselled cane, addressing Hortense. He was wearing a patched hunting jacket over a nightdress. At his feet snuffled one of the pugs, now white around the muzzle and quite thin. Grandmother Sannois had died almost three years ago, the other pug the year after.

'She's not Yeyette any more,' Mother said. 'She's a woman now.'

'Father!' I kissed him on both cheeks, taking care not to bump his cane. He looked so weak — so fragile. 'You look wonderful,' I said.

Father looked down at Hortense. 'Now you would never do such a thing, would you? Tell an ugly old man that he looked wonderful. The *wonder* is I'm still alive.' He paused for a moment, studied my face. 'My, but you have become so very, very lovely.' He turned to my mother. 'Claire, who would have thought that that scrappy, plump, dirty-faced little thing would ever have turned into this!' He swung one hand wide, too wide, for he began to lose his balance.

Quickly Mother was at his side, one arm round his back, her

shoulder braced under his arm. Father started to cough. 'You're too flamboyant, Joseph,' she said, pounding his back with her fist.

Da Gertrude appeared with a tray. 'Some juice – and sugar cakes,' she announced. 'But I bet you don't like sugar cakes,' she said to Hortense.

'Yessss.' Hortense swung her skirts. 'Yes I do!'

Mother nodded towards the landing. 'Manette's in her room, Rose.'

'Go,' Father said, waving me away. 'She's been waiting.'

'Rose, she is—' Mother didn't finish her sentence.

I traced my way through the dark rooms, thick with the scent of sugar syrup, the musky faint scent of mould, the sound of flies buzzing at every window. At the end of the narrow passage was the door to Manette's room. I stood for a moment before opening it. I remembered standing before this same door, listening to the sound of Manette weeping. Now, there was only silence.

It was dark in the room. One shutter had been closed. Manette was lying on top of the bedclothes in a stained white muslin shift, her long dark hair dishevelled, wet tendrils curling around her neck. A plump Negro girl I didn't recognize was sitting at the foot of her bed, fanning her lazily with a palm-tree leaf.

I approached the bed slowly. I tried to put on a brave face, but tears broke free as soon as I caught my sister's eyes. I pretended my tears were tears of joy – but they were not. Oh, my little Manette, how she has wizened and aged, an old crone in a young woman's body.

Manette spoke slowly, pushing the words from her with some effort. 'Rose . . .' She stopped. She took my hand. 'I'm sorry,' she whispered.

I laid my head on her hollow belly. Already I knew there was no hope.

In which storms rage

17 AUGUST 1788

As the Carib chief approached, the slaves went running. He stood in the lane in his loose shirt made of old flour sacks, his long hair blowing in the wind. Mother stood to greet him.

It was a windy morning, without mosquitoes. The leaves of the gumtree fluttered to the ground.

I could overhear little, understand nothing. He spoke to Mother in his language, an ancient tongue beyond my understanding, and my mother answered him in kind, slowly and with some effort. He turned and left, the back of his shirt stained with sweat.

I went down to the veranda.

'There's a storm coming.' Mother stood looking out towards Morne Croc-Souris.

'Does he always come?'

'Once before he came.' She turned towards the *sucrerie*. 'Before the big storm.'

The big storm. Seventeen sixty-six. I was only three at the time, yet even now, when a wind rises, a sick feeling comes over me. All through my childhood, I'd heard stories of the wind that had blown our house away, the rain that drowned an entire town, the wave that swallowed a hundred ships whole, not even a shoe washed up on the shore.

'We must see to the shutters,' Mother said.

The morning hours turned frantic. The field gang was called in, the house slaves alerted, the children in the garden crew located, the animals put back in their stalls.

After the midday meal, the air thickened. The wind howled. A wooden bucket on the veranda clattered across the stones. Drops of rain splashed hard against the shutters. A chicken screeched, caught in the rising gale.

We descended into the stone cellar, the air heavy with the odour of rotting potatoes. I was sickened for a moment entering that dark room – the room in which I had been kept as a girl, the room of my imprisonment. The bed was still there. The three-legged table was gone. I reached up to make sure the shutters were tightly fastened.

Sylvester carried Manette down the narrow steps, put her down gently on the bed. She looked around dreamily. Mother put the pug dog down and arranged the bedclothes over her. Mimi and I sat on a straw mat, our backs against the rough stone wall. Da Gertrude squeezed in beside me, trying to hold on to Hortense, who nevertheless wiggled free to chase a lizard. Father squatted by the door drinking pétépié from a bottle, his cane by his side.

Everyone was crowding in, the house slaves and their children in with us, the slave master and the field slaves in the other basement room.

A blast of wind rattled the window. The slaves in the other room began to chant.

'I want to go in there,' Hortense said.

'What happened to the lizard?'

'He lost his tail and ran away. I want to find Max.'

'See if Max can come in here.' I wanted Hortense near me.

'You're letting Hortense go in there?' Mother had her Bible open on her lap. The chanting in the other room had grown louder. Someone had started beating on a drum. 'I wish they'd stop,' she sighed, closing her eyes.

'She's gone to find a friend. She'll be back.'

Mother started to say something but then there was a terrible roaring sound. The beam above us cracked. Mother clutched her cross.

I looked over at Da Gertrude. Her upper lip was beaded with sweat. I thought of the dark nights I had trembled in her arms, suckled her milk, slept in her bed. When I was an infant she'd protected me from the ants that had infested our island, swarming the hills and valleys, consuming everything in their path. She'd held me during every storm, singing prayers to the howling winds. I took her hand.

'So now it is *you* who comforts me,' she said.

We emerged at dawn, squinting against the sun, faint from terror and constant prayer. Four chickens were perched in an uprooted orange tree. Deep cracks had been etched in the earth, like a network of snakes. Everywhere a thick carpet of torn trees and bushes – even the giant kapok tree had fallen, crashing across a river now raging with debris. The devastation was everywhere, frightening in the early morning light.

Hortense began to cry. 'My cricket cage!'

'Hush,' I said. We had survived.

LATER

We spent all this day picking through splinters. The slave huts have been destroyed. There has been considerable damage to the stables and the crushing hut as well. The stone kitchen shack only suffered two broken windows and a deluge of water. Two horses, nine cows and a goat are missing. The sow was badly injured and had to be slaughtered, so weak she did not even squeal.

19 AUGUST

We've received word from Fort-Royal. The roof of Uncle Tascher's house was blown off and the furniture ruined. But no one hurt, thank God.

14 SEPTEMBER

Mail – *at last*.

> 16 July 1788 – Fontainebleau
> Darling!
>
> Two weeks after you set sail we had a dreadful hailstorm – in July, the hottest month of the year! Imagine. Really, we begin to think France is being visited by a destroying angel.* The ice stones were so big they killed birds and ripped the branches off the oak trees in the Luxembourg gardens. My servants are blaming the priests, for ineffective influence.

* Fanny is plagiarizing, something she was known to do with regularity. The statement about the destroying angel was in fact made by the great economist Mirabeau.

THE MANY LIVES & SECRET SORROWS OF JOSEPHINE B.

My darling pixie of a granddaughter Émilie, quite tall for seven, continues to thrive. I had Eugène over the other day as well – the two are a charm for the vapours.

A million kisses, your loving Aunt Fanny

18 July 1788 – Fontainebleau
Dear Rose,

We've been busy attending to finance and health. It is maddening how much time these two matters consume. Fortunately, with respect to health at least, I am beginning to make progress. A doctor suggested I take purgatives and clysters, followed by Peruvian bark. I am following his programme with excellent results. I am enclosing three ounces of this bark at a cost of ten livres, which I will add to your father's account. I urge you to get Joseph (and your sister?) to take it. As well, restrain him from consuming milk foods and salt meat – not to mention spirits.

The situation here worsens . . . there was a dreadful ice storm which destroyed the crops, just when everyone had been praying for grain. No doubt this is God's punishment for the riots in Paris. My chambermaid's brother vows he saw Henry IV's statue bleeding.

Do not neglect to say your prayers – morning and night – as well as your hours. Have you talked to your father regarding the accounts? We anxiously await news.

Your loving Aunt Désirée

5 July 1788 – Paris
Dear Rose,

A quick note (I have a meeting to attend) – I have decided to enter the realm of politics. It is a labour I do willingly; my country needs me.

Your husband, Alexandre Beauharnais

Note – Eugène is well.

Sunday
Chère Maman,

Ice came out of the sky. Are you coming home yet?

A thousand kisses, Eugène

29 JANUARY 1789

A talk with Mother, regarding the accounts. She is reluctant to bring in anyone from outside.

'What can be the harm?' I insisted. Father wasn't able, Mother was unwilling and I had no experience, much less knowledge.

'Our only problem is your father's debts,' she said. 'His *vice*.'

But at last she relented. She has agreed to allow me to consult Monsieur de Couvray, an accountant of merit in Fort-Royal.

MONDAY, 16 FEBRUARY

I have been reviewing the accounts in preparation for my trip to Fort-Royal. There are a number of mysteries. Father was blustery at first, refusing to respond to my questions, accusing me of ignorance. Gently, I persisted, pointing out discrepancies. At last he broke down. Much of the money had gone to cover gambling debts — but not all. Some covered mistakes he had made managing the plantation. It was the blunders he was ashamed to admit, not the gambling losses — the 'debts of honour' he insists are a result of courage, not weakness. 'It takes strength to play deep,' he said, 'to risk one's fortune on the turn of a card.' (I refrained from pointing out that it had not been *his* fortune he'd put at risk.)

In spite of his disclosures, there was a sizeable portion left unexplained. 'There must be more, Father.'

He confessed: four years ago he'd had an amourette with a sewing woman in Rivière Salée. The woman had given birth. He was beholden to look after her.

I didn't know what to say. 'Did she give you a son?' I asked finally. He'd always wanted a son.

'*Another* daughter.'

I had a half-sister.*

'She's almost three, pretty.'

---

* Marie-Joséphine Benaguette, 'Fifine', born 17 March 1786, to Marie-Louise Benaguette. Eventually Rose's mother took the girl into her own home and in 1806 Rose, as Empress, provided her with a dowry of sixty thousand livres.

THE MANY LIVES & SECRET SORROWS OF JOSEPHINE B.

'Does Mother know?'

Father nodded. 'Your mother is a saint,' he said.

TUESDAY, 17 MARCH – FORT-ROYAL

Hortense, Mimi and I arrived in Fort-Royal shortly before noon, splattered with mud. Hortense and I changed before joining my aunt and uncle for the midday meal. After, my aunt excused herself, 'for my beauty nap,' she said. Then Hortense and her cousins were dispatched with their nannies on an outing to the shore, giving me an opportunity to talk privately to my uncle.

I took a sheet of paper from my basket. 'There are two individuals I would like to consult while I am here. Perhaps you could tell me how they might be reached.'

Uncle Tascher studied the names, twisting one point of his enormous moustache. 'Monsieur de Couvray? It is likely that I will see him this very evening, at the Masonic meeting. If you like, I could set up a meeting.'

'Excellent.' The palms of my hands were damp. 'And the other . . . ?' I asked.

'Monsieur William Browder?' Uncle Tascher looked up. 'An English name – I recall seeing it somewhere. Oh, yes – *Captain* Browder. He's enlisted in the navy, I believe, as a translator, if I'm not mistaken. I can't imagine what benefit consulting him would be.'

'His family used to be our neighbours,' I said, my voice tight. 'There's a field that has always been shared for grazing, a common – until now, that is. The current tenants have claimed it entirely for their own use.'

'But surely this is a matter for the courts.'

'A costly procedure, although perhaps a necessary one. In any case, I will require documents, information—'

A butler with silver hoops in his ears came to the door, nodded to Uncle Tascher, and disappeared.

'If you'll excuse me,' Uncle Tascher said, rising. 'My presence is required at Government House.' He handed the paper back to me. 'My secretary, Monsieur Dufriche, will be able to tell you how Captain Browder may be reached.'

I retired to my room. The chambermaid, a girl with dirty hands and an unpleasant odour, helped me take off my dress. My petticoats were damp from the heat. I asked the girl to return in an hour and stretched out under the canopy of gauze netting. A gold cross hung from the bedcurtains.

Forgive me, I prayed.

In which I confront the past

I was seated at the writing desk in Uncle's study when Captain Browder was announced, earlier than expected. 'Tell him to come in.' I smoothed the lace ruffles over the bodice of my silk chemise. Suddenly it seemed too formal.

I opened a book, a volume of Greek history, in order to give the appearance of industry. I cannot begin to transcribe the tumult of my thoughts. I feared I would love him; feared he would disappoint me. Neither thought gave my heart ease.

The leather of my chair creaked as I turned. William stood in the doorway, a shabby black-plumed hat in his hand. His unpowdered black hair was secured at the back with a ribbon. His frock coat, ill-fitting, was patched at one elbow. I remembered my mother's words: *béké-goyave*.

'Captain Browder,' I said. I extended my hand.

William crossed the room, bowed. 'Madame la vicomtesse.' He smelled of horses.

I withdrew my hand, more for fear he would notice the dampness of my palm than from any sense of propriety. 'How good to see you. Please, sit down,' I began, the worn phrases affording comfort. 'Would you care for a brandy?' I asked.

'No, thank you.' He sat down on the stool by the door to the garden. The stool was too short for him. He turned his hat in his hands, studying me.

I looked away. I had forgotten how unnaturally blue his eyes were. 'I was grieved to learn of your mother's death,' I said. Hanged, it was rumoured, by her own—

'She got what she wanted,' he said.

I was disconcerted by the bitterness in his voice.

'To be free of it all.' He flung his hat on to a low table next to him.

Freedom. William's God. His was a life of the sea, a life of freedom, no doubt. Freedom from comfort, freedom from love?

'Did you find happiness, Rose?' he demanded.

'Yes . . .' I paused, shrugged. 'No. My husband and I have separated,' I said.

'I'm not surprised.'

My cheeks burned. It seemed the entire island was aware of Alexandre's misconduct, Alexandre's accusations.

'Did you love him?' he asked boldly. Too boldly, I thought.

'I was willing to love him,' I answered finally.

'That's not the same, is it?'

'Your dimples are still there, I see,' I said, changing the subject. I felt I had made a mistake.

'So my daughters tease me.'

'And your wife?'

He smiled. For a moment I saw the William I knew. 'She puts up with me,' he said.

'Is that so very difficult?'

'I have yearnings, she says.'

'Yes.' I studied his face. He still had that boyish look.

'Do you ever think of that fortune you were told?' he asked.

'It comes to me in dreams sometimes.' *You will be unhappily married.*

'Good dreams?'

'Bad dreams.' Terrible dreams.

'I have a confession to make,' he said, after a moment of hesitation. 'I wasn't going to come today. But then I changed my mind. I decided I wanted to prove something.'

He was interrupted by the sound of a child's voice, footsteps approaching. Mimi and Hortense appeared at the door. William stood.

'Hortense would like . . . to go down to the pier, to watch the boats,' Mimi stuttered, her face revealing her surprise.

'That would be fine. Captain Browder, this is my daughter, Hortense. And you remember Mimi? Madame Mimi we call her now.' For Mimi was clearly in a family way.

'Of course I remember.' He bowed.

'Grand-maman says that it is not proper to bow to slaves.' Hortense pushed her straw hat back off her forehead.

'Hortense! It's not proper for a child to lecture an adult.' At six, Hortense had an overly rigid sense of right and wrong and seemed intent on informing everyone how they should behave.

'Perhaps Captain Browder is what we call "A New Thinker",' Mimi explained to my daughter. 'Men like that do things differently.'

'Oooooh.' Hortense regarded William with apprehension.

William nodded. 'I might even stand on my head.'

Hortense studied him for a long moment and then let out a little laugh.

'Forgive us for interrupting – I can see you are busy.' Mimi backed towards the door, pulling Hortense along with her.

'Busy doing *what*?' I heard Hortense demand in the other room.

'I must apologize.' I tidied the papers on the desk. 'My daughter was rude.' I had seen a quill earlier, but now I could not find it – it was not in its holder. I was surprised to note that my hands were trembling slightly.

'I should be going. I shouldn't be here.' William was standing by the window, looking out at the garden.

'I did want to talk to you about that field.'

William withdrew a document from the pocket of his waistcoat. 'This will give you what you need to know.' It was a letter of agreement regarding use of the common.

'Do you wish me to return it?' I stood.

'I have no need for it.'

'You were saying something, before we were interrupted.'

'I don't recall.'

I paused. 'That you came here today to prove something.'

'It wasn't important.'

'That wasn't my impression.'

He cleared his throat, looked at me. 'I came here today with the intention of proving that I no longer loved you.'

In the silence, I heard a crow call out four times. I thought of all the nights I'd dreamt of him, the conversations I'd had with him in my mind. The questions I'd wanted to ask, the stories I'd wanted to tell. But the man who stood before me was not William. 'I think you should go, Captain Browder,' I said.

Captain Browder took his hat. 'I was mistaken,' he said, turning at the door. 'I still love you. Good day, Madame.'

LATER

Monsieur de Couvray was shown into Uncle's study shortly after four. When he recovered from the discomfort of having to discuss matters of business with a woman, we set to work going over the La Pagerie accounts, reviewing the assets, the land. The low sugar yield indicates exhaustion of the soil, as I suspected; certain fields must be allowed to go to flower and to be replanted from seed.

His other suggestions were less palatable, and I suspect will be so to Mother and Father as well. He observed that there were a number of children in our slave population, our 'thinking property' was the term he used. 'It is more economical to buy slaves than to breed them,' he said.

'It is not intentionally done.'

'Perhaps measures should be taken to . . . to inhibit production.' He wiped his palms on his buckskin breeches. 'Overall, looking at these figures, it is clear that the cost of keep is high in proportion to the work accomplished.'

I knew this to be true. Several of the slaves were now either infirm or elderly, I explained.

'If a slave has ceased to be productive,' he said, 'it is wise to encourage him . . . to *go* on.' He puffed on his pipe; the fire had gone out.

'Go?' I was confused. 'Go *where?*'

He circled his fingers impatiently. 'You know . . .'

'You don't mean . . . killed?' Surely I'd misunderstood.

'No! Goodness. I wouldn't use *that* word. After all, the methods are humane, and if they are suffering—'

'Monsieur, I do believe my mother and father would be loath to employ such a practice, and I, for one, loath to suggest it.' We talked a short time longer, for the sake of form. I showed him to the door.

SATURDAY, 21 MARCH

I was packing to return to Trois-Islets when Mimi brought me a letter. 'Did this come to the house?' I asked, alarmed. I took a seat by the window.

Mimi shook her head, her dangling earrings making a tinkling sound. 'In the market. He asked me to give it to you.'

I broke the wax seal.

Madame Beauharnais:
   I have discovered information regarding your family's use of the common. It is urgent that you be apprised of it.
   At your convenience.

Your servant, Captain Browder

I put the letter on the side table.

'He asked if it would be possible to arrange a meeting,' Mimi whispered.

I looked down at my lap. My hands looked like the hands of an old woman.

'Something about a green flash.' She looked at me with a puzzled expression.

I held my breath. 'Tell him no,' I said.

2 APRIL – TROIS-ILETS

We've been back in Trois-Ilets for over a week. A feeling of disquiet continues to haunt me. As a youth one dreams of love; by the time one wakes, it is too late.

I've been going for walks in the morning, after chores, in search of solace. In the cool of the forest, my spirit is soothed but not healed. Often I head down the river, towards the sea, but this morning I followed the track towards Morne Croc-Souris. Before long I had come upon it – the clearing by the side of the river, the wattle-and-daub shack collapsed, a frangipani bush flowering where the door had been.

You will be unhappily married.

Not far from the rubble I saw a crude wooden cross stuck in a mound of earth covered over with stones. A grave.

You will be widowed.

A wind through the forest shook the leaves, a bird called out

THE MANY LIVES & SECRET SORROWS OF JOSEPHINE B.

warning. I approached the pile of stones. The ground was littered with crumpled pieces of paper, feathers, a chunk of bone.

You will be Queen.

I felt a cool wind come through me. I was possessed by a light sensation, a feeling of floating on water.

You will make a beautiful queen, a boy had once told me.

In which two worlds claim my heart

4 January 1789 – Paris
Chère Maman,

It has been cold for three weeks. I saw a dead man, frozen.
We go walking on the river. When are you coming home?

A thousand kisses, your son Eugène

3 April 1789 – Paris
Dear Rose,

A quick note – I have been elected to the Estates General,
a representative for the Blois nobility. A spirit of optimism has
permeated our land. It's electrifying!

Your husband, Deputy Alexandre Beauharnais

Note – The drawing of Hortense was well executed. Your
technique is improving, although the shading would have been
more effective in a charcoal, I thought.

And another – I enclose a pamphlet by Sieyès, *What Is the
Third Estate?* I recommend you study it.

15 April 1789 – Paris
Darling!

I've moved back to Paris – it's so thrilling here now! It's the
'Roman Republic' all over again – the Goddess of Love rules.
Everywhere one goes there is great celebrating, dancing around
bonfires. To walk down the street is to become intoxicated by
profound sentiment, embraced by everyone one meets, rich
and poor, young and old alike.

My salon will never be the same. Where before we talked
of Beauty, we now talk of Equal Representation.

Your loving Aunt Fanny

Note – How can you stand being away from the opera for so long?

11 AUGUST

I've been reading the journals that came over on the last boat. I was saddened to learn that the Dauphin died – yet no one seemed even to notice, much less care. I grieve for the Queen. A boy so like Eugène.

Eugène. I grow ill with a longing to hold him again . . . I have been in Martinico for one year.

20 July 1789 – Fontainebleau
Dear Rose,

Both Alexandre and François have been elected to the Estates General. Now whenever the two brother deputies visit on feast days, they have a frightful row. The Marquis refuses to even discuss political concerns any more, claiming to find 'all that' distasteful. 'All that' will go away soon, he says, and everything will be back the way it should be. He burned all the books by Rousseau in the house, even the signed copy of *Discourse on Inequality*. I hate to think what is going to happen when Alexandre discovers it missing.

At least we aren't in Paris – there are twenty thousand troops there now. The strumpets are getting rich, no doubt. As well, every beggar and thief in France has come to the city, swarming at the slightest opportunity. Each district – all sixty of them – has drawn up its own army to keep order. I've taken to carrying a pistol in my bag, even here in Fontainebleau.

Don't forget your prayers.

Your loving Aunt Désirée

Note – You've heard about the riot at the Bastille? Fanny promised she would retrieve some of the stones for me. I'll save one for you, if you like.

10 August 1789 – Versailles
Dear Rose,

What were before disconnected jottings have now become a fluid system of philosophy, an ether that connects the present to the past. I have long understood how the Roman Empire gave way to the feudal system, which in turn gave way to the modern monarchies. Such a study reveals the oppressive nature of our laws. But it is only now that I begin to understand that it is the Roman Republic in all its glory that we seek to rebuild.

Would that my family could understand the profound nature of the task before us. Unfortunately, they are blinded by history and by the traditional greed of our class. In joining with other enlightened nobles (La Rochefoucauld! Lafayette! The Duc d'Orléans!) to renounce our feudal privileges, I was forced to choose between my family, on the one hand, and my country, on the other. Oh, what a night of profound heroism! What sublime sacrifice! May the night of 4 August burn in my heart for ever.

The sacrifice of my father's regard, of my brother's fraternal embrace is a loss I must bear. The Revolution demands that each citizen make a personal offering for the good of the Nation. I submit with tears of virtue in my eyes, knowing that my pain will be rewarded.

> With a noble heart, your husband, Deputy Alexandre
> Beauharnais 'an honourable and virtuous Republican'

Note — I urge you to study the pamphlets I have forwarded, open your heart to the truths you will find therein. One — *A Few Thoughts on the Nature of Reason & Revolution* — I wrote myself. I have worded it simply so that a woman might understand, for I am not of that group that believes women incapable of abstract reasoning.

Sunday
Chère Maman,

I have my own sword now. My tutor says I might need it. When are you coming home?

> A thousand kisses, Eugène

9 DECEMBER

A Creole man was found dead in a clearing in the woods near Fort-Royal, together with the head of a butchered pig. Blood had been spilled over his hands. Three days before a slave had died on his plantation, imprisoned in a sweltering hut in the sun without food and water.

I hear drumming in the slave village. The moon casts a ghostly light. I see a fire up on the hill, hear shouting and singing. I know the song:

> Never, never, I'll not forget the ranks of Africa.
> Never, never, I'll not forget their children.

I despair.

10 October, 1789 – Fontainebleau
Dear Rose,

The Marquis and I have not been well. Our nerves suffer from the distressing reports in the journals.

I am ashamed of my sex. Women – thousands of them, it has been reported – forced our King and Queen to move into that horrid palace in Paris, and now everyone of quality is talking of leaving France. Even the King's brothers have fled, even Madame de Polignac, the royal governess, abandoning her charges. (How could she do that?)

But that isn't all of it. Monsieur Ogé, that mulatto from Saint-Domingue, went before the Assembly to demand equal rights for mulattoes – and *succeeded*! One delegate even suggested that the slaves be freed!* Everyone, it seems, has lost their reason. If the slaves were allowed to go free, we'd be penniless!

Pray for us . . .

Your loving Aunt Désirée

Note – Fanny's son Claude and his wife have had a baby girl.†
Send your condolences.

23 JANUARY 1790
Morin, Mimi's lover and the father of the child she is carrying, was

---

* This delegate was hanged when he returned to Saint-Domingue.
† Stephanie Beauharnais was later to be adopted by Napoleon and wed to the Grand Duke of Baden, which made her a Grand Duchess of the Court of Würtemberg.

killed in a riot in Fort-Royal. There is nothing I can say to comfort her, for it was men of my race who murdered him.

I stood at the door to her whitewashed hut watching her crumple into the arms of the slave women, listened to their collective moans – and I, who am like a sister to her, was forced to turn away, tears running down my cheeks.

Drums in the mountains. As a child, the steady beat lulled me into sleep. But tonight I do not feel comfort in such sounds. Tonight I hear anger, and a terrible, terrible grief.

5 November 1789 – Lake Maggiore
Darling!

Michel de Cubières and I are in a delightful Alpine spa. (Remember Michel? The poet with the big lips?) Every evening we play faro in a casino in the village, where a shocking amount of money changes hands. But what is life if one is not prepared to cast all to the winds? One must be brave to be so foolish.

The Austrians have been threatening to set up a 'cordon sanitaire' across the mountains to keep 'dangerous ideas' from coming over from France. Were it not for my mindless chatter and Michel staying quiet – for once! – I doubt very much that they would have let us into their backward little paradise. Fortunately, they neglected to look in the basket that contained the political pamphlets Michel intends to distribute on the streets of Rome.

Take care of yourself, darling. I hear your husband has become a Hero of the Revolution. How dashing!

Your devoted Aunt Fanny

Note – Claude's wife had a girl. He's not taking it well, which disappoints me. I thought we were beyond all that.

1 FEBRUARY

Mimi lost her child. I went to see her in the infirmary, but she was in a fever and did not comprehend that it was me. I sat beside her for a time, cooling her with strips of linen soaked in rum. She was talking in a dream: *Never, never, I'll not forget* . . . *Never, never* . . .

THE MANY LIVES & SECRET SORROWS OF JOSEPHINE B.

Oh, my dear Mimi, how my heart goes out to her. I pray, I pray.

11 November 1789 – Paris
Dear Rose,

I have been elected one of three secretaries to the Assembly. I am both honoured and challenged. Fate, surely, is the author of a scheme of such heroic dimensions.

I am enclosing a copy of the *Declaration of the Rights of Man*, suitable for framing. I consider involvement in its creation one of the achievements of my life.*

     Your husband, Deputy Alexandre Beauharnais

Sunday – Fontainebleau
Chère Maman,

Papa's name is in the news-sheets. I've not seen him for two weeks. Are you ever coming back?

     A thousand kisses, your son Eugène

3 FEBRUARY

Mimi has emerged from her fever, wrapped in sorrow like a ghost. The slave women hover around her protectively whenever I approach. 'Go away! You curse her!' I do not persist.

7 December 1790 – Chambéry
Darling,

The Italians were positively *wild* about my poem 'To Frederick the Great on the Death of Voltaire'. That and one of my novels (*Abailard the Pretender*, wouldn't you know – the most naughty of all my works) is being translated into Italian and will be published there soon. I'm a writer of the world now!

---

* France took the American Bill of Rights one step further. Where Americans proclaimed men free and equal in *their* country, the French proclaimed men free and equal *everywhere*.

How is my goddaughter Hortense? I am enclosing a leatherbound copy of Erasmus's *Manners for Children* for her. It is, at the least, egalitarian. Encourage her to copy the lovely script – the first step towards becoming a writer.

As you perhaps already know, Marie and François have separated, for reasons of *philosophy*. Philosophy! At least when my husband (God rest his soul*) and I parted, we did so for reasons of sentiment.

Your loving Aunt Fanny

23 FEBRUARY

Mimi has been put on the field gang, Mother informed me this afternoon.

'How could you do that! Mimi belongs with *me*, with Hortense!'

Mother put down her needlework. 'Apologize for your temper. Mimi asked to be put in the fields.'

'But *why*?' I could not comprehend. Field work was a killing labour.

'I can only presume it is because she has turned against us, because of our race. Were it not for your sensibilities, Rose, I would have sold her, or at least had her whipped. Hate is a dangerous thing in a slave.'

I left the room in tears.

17 December 1790 – Fontainebleau

Dear Rose,

The Marquis and I have suffered a collapse of nerves due to the distressing news about François and Marie. The Marquis is terribly upset, going on about the morals of the young, the stain upon the family name, the lack of commitment to values. I hold my tongue, but in my heart I grieve: for is this not the fruit of our own sins? I have been going to Mass twice daily and to my confessor weekly. I urge you to do the same.

Your loving Aunt Désirée

Note – I am enclosing a bill for one livre, the new paper money

---

* Claude de Beauharnais, the Marquis's brother and Fanny's ex-husband, died on 25 December 1784.

we are required to use now, but it's not worth one sou – hold on to your gold.

WEDNESDAY, 3 MARCH

The island press has been restricted for fear that any further mention of 'liberty' would be dangerous. Even the journals we receive from Paris must be hidden away.

'Your husband's letters should be burned,' Mother said. She does not approve of Alexandre's views. 'As well as Madame Fanny's.'

'Along with her novel, perhaps?'

'Indeed,' Mother sputtered, crossing herself.

I smiled, for I have seen her glancing into it when she thought no one was looking.

30 December 1789 – Fontainebleau

Dear Rose,

Thank you for the lovely Christmas gifts – the Marquis loved his bamboo cane and already the bottle of La Pagerie rum has been consumed. I adore the silver bangles, but especially the set of enamel buttons painted with island scenes – they brought on a feeling of reverie in me. And a *crate* of coffee beans! What indulgence!

Eugène loved all the presents you sent (really, Rose, you must try to refrain from such excess), but the item that pleased him the most – to our own discomfort, I confess – was the foghorn made of shell.

Your uncle reports that you have been diligent in your efforts to organize the finances and the management of the properties. You must be having some success, for already we have received a banknote. This money is very badly needed. You can't imagine how expensive everything has become. It is *impossible* to live on even twelve thousand livres a year now. *Nom de Dieu!*

How is my brother's health? How is your sister Manette? I have sent my gardener on a pilgrimage to Chartres to seek cures. He is devout; I have hope of some success.

It has been a gloomy holiday season. No one entertains any more – everyone stays home.

Remember – don't neglect your prayers . . .

Your loving Aunt Désirée

Christmas Day
Chère Maman,
  Thank you for the foghorn. I have decided to become a sailor. That way I can come and see you and my sister Hortense.

Eugène

21 MAY

As I write at this little table in my room, listening to the heavy dripping of the rain, I wonder if it's possible I ever left this island. France seems like a dream to me, more distant than my childhood.

I sleep with Eugène's miniature under my pillow. Tonight I could not find it. Fear takes my heart – will I *ever* see him again?

In which we flee under cannon fire

3 June 1790

A mulatto uprising in Saint-Pierre. In his sermon this morning, Father Droppet questioned the existence of a soul in the Negro. After church, talk of weapons. I sleep with a pistol on my side table.

30 July

Today Mother said, 'You must go, Rose – take your daughter, return to France.' Her eyes were dark, I could not see her thoughts. 'This is no place to raise a child.' She pushed a cloth bag across the table at me.

It was a bag of coins – the coins she counted so religiously every day. 'I cannot.' I pushed the bag away. How could I abandon her with violence threatening, with Father and Manette so ill?

'The British are going to attack. If you don't go now, you will never see your son again . . .'

Tears came to my eyes. 'But—'

'I will not mourn *you*!' And then, her voice low, almost a whisper, 'I will not bury *all* my daughters!'

Later

With a heavy heart I have written to Uncle Tascher, asking if it is possible to obtain passage to France . . .

That evening

Uncle Tascher sent back a prompt reply. It is difficult to get passage to France at this time, he said, but not impossible. The openings come quickly, without notice. I must be in Fort-Royal with my movables packed if I am serious about leaving. He advises me to come immediately, for there are rumours of a blockade. 'In these turbulent times,' he wrote philosophically, sadly I thought, 'nothing is as it seems, nothing is as it should be.'

1 AUGUST, NOON

Mother was on the veranda when I went to her this morning, darning socks that had been darned many times before. 'You are leaving,' she said. She looked out over the garden of flowers I'd tended, the blooms drenched by the rain.

I nodded, turned away. I have become weary of tears.

6 AUGUST

We've been packing. All day Hortense has been fighting with Da Gertrude over a rag doll she wants to take with her, but Da Gertrude insists it will bring bad luck. 'It was out all night in the light of the moon!' she said with great fear.

7 AUGUST

This evening, after dinner, I brushed and braided Manette's hair, the dark plaits falling over her shoulders. I read to her from *Paul et Virginie* until she fell asleep. I sat for a time with the book in my lap, the flame from the candle flickering from the breeze from the open window, looking out at the moon rising behind the tangled branches of the mango tree. Manette and I climbed that same tree when we were children. How does one say goodbye?

TUESDAY, 10 AUGUST

I awoke shortly before dawn. As if by some miracle, it had stopped raining. Quietly I slipped down the stairs and out of the *sucrerie*, down to the bathing pond. I put my chemise and my kerchief on the wet rocks and slipped into the clear water, gasping until I became accustomed to the cold. A frog scuttled into the grass, but other than that there was not a sound but for the tree ferns rustling in the breeze. The scent of the orange tree filled the air.

When the turtledoves began to coo, I emerged, heart heavy. It was time. I dressed and made my final rounds, stopping to talk to the house slaves. To each I gave a livre. I left three louis with the slave master to divide among the field hands. I knew Mother would not approve so I asked him not to tell.

I told Da Gertrude to give Mimi my emerald. 'Heal her,' I said. Open her heart. Da Gertrude began to cry. I wrapped my arms round her.

'Go!' she said, pushing me away.

I went to Father's room.

'So,' he said.

I sat down on the straight-backed chair next to the bed. It was wobbly, for one of its legs kept coming loose and had been secured, not too successfully, with hemp. A foul odour filled the room, a smell I had become accustomed to, 'the smell of death', Mother called it. But I had become too immersed in the mechanical routine of Father's care to think of such things.

I took his hand, for I felt comfortless entertaining such thoughts. His skin felt dry, thin – like the delicate texture of a snake's discarded skin. 'Is there anything I can get you?' I asked, for my devotion had taken this form: service.

'You've done enough.' His eyes were grey. 'Enough for a dying man.'

I began to protest, uphold some vain lie – but I knew it would be disrespectful to deny him this, the reality of his passing. I nodded. 'I will miss you, Father.'

'Princess.' He squeezed my hand.

The memory of my childhood fantasies came back to me then, the enchantment of my father's stories, told to a dream-struck girl in a hammock under a mango tree, fanning herself lazily with a palm-tree leaf. I kissed his cheek. 'My King.' I swooped into the courtly curtsy he'd taught me as a girl, regally kicking an imaginary train aside as I turned to go.

He was laughing silently as I left. For a moment I saw that spark again. I did not say goodbye.

At the very last I went to Manette, who was asleep. She looked graven, old, her bedclothes tangled. I did not have the courage to waken her. I kissed her forehead and left. I will never see her again.

It was still very early, only eight in the morning, when Sylvester drove the cart round to the front of the *sucrerie*. I helped Hortense scramble on to the seat. I turned to Mother. 'You will come, to France . . . ?' I could not say 'after' . . . after Father dies, after Manette.

She clasped my hands, hard. I climbed into the wagon. Sylvester cracked his whip, the horses pulled forward. As we neared the stone wall, I looked back. Mother was no longer there. I watched the house recede, searching for her face in the windows.

13 AUGUST – FORT-ROYAL
Aunt Tascher is frantic, the house in chaos – there are open packing cases in every room. She and the children are moving to the country, she explained. 'It's not safe here!' We left our sea trunk in the carriage house – we will be leaving soon too, I hope.

Hortense and I are sharing a room on the third floor. It is hot – but private. I am sitting at a desk in an alcove overlooking the harbour. Through the rain I can dimly make out where the four warships and several merchant ships are moored. Uncle will be home late. He has much trouble now with government matters and the general restiveness in the population. Tonight he will be able to tell us the situation with respect to our departure for France.

3 SEPTEMBER – GOVERNMENT HOUSE
There have been riots in town. At a fête yesterday, Governor de Vioménil refused to put on a tricolour cockade, claiming that he would prefer to die a thousand deaths – which resulted in such violence that he was forced to retract his statement and put on the ribbon, 'this pledge of peace, union and concord!' he proclaimed. All this to the sound of musket fire over his head.

A Te Deum was sung and all appeared to be at peace again, but even so, Uncle Tascher has insisted that Hortense and I move into Government House. It is safer for us here, he said. We do not go out any more.

MONDAY, 6 SEPTEMBER

There has been an uprising. Uncle Tascher imprisoned the revolutionaries, but then the guards released them and opened fire on
the town.

I was at Government House when it happened. Governor de
Vioménil ran from room to room, yelling at everyone. Madame
de Vioménil fell to her knees, praying loudly. I took Hortense up
to our room and read to her from *Fables of La Fontaine*, trying to
ignore the sounds of musket fire. All the while I was trembling.
Then the parlourmaid came running up the stairs with the news
that Uncle Tascher had gone to talk to the rebels in the Fort.

Hortense and I ventured back downstairs to the front parlour
where everyone had gathered. The messenger who finally arrived
from the Fort was a thin man wearing a dirty wig. 'Baron Tascher
has been taken hostage,' he announced theatrically. The rebels had
imprisoned my uncle and were threatening to kill him and every
person in the town.

I was helped to a chair. 'What did he say about Uncle?' Hortense
demanded tearfully. 'What does "hostage" mean?'

The governor was frantic. Aides on all sides were trying to offer
him advice. His wife ran after him, yelling, 'You can't go!'

He stomped into his study and slammed the door. 'He is intent
on killing himself!' his wife wept. The musket fire began again,
shattering what little confidence we had managed.

Soon after the governor left. His plan was to take refuge at Gros
Morne, a village on the way to Trinité, and from there gather support
to attack. His wife locked herself in her bedchamber and refused to
come out.

I lay in my bed in our little room with Hortense in my arms,
trying to calm her, listening to the sound of musket and cannon
fire, praying for Uncle Tascher. Long after Hortense had finally
fallen asleep, I was startled by a knocking on the door. 'Who is
it?' The night candle threw ghostly shadows.

The door opened – it was the chambermaid.

'Is there news?' I whispered, fearing for Uncle Tascher's life.

'A letter from Commander du Braye.' She handed me a sealed
folded paper. 'I was told it was urgent.' There was a sudden retort
from a cannon, followed by grapeshot.

'Commander du Braye?' A friend of my uncle, Durand du Braye

was the commander of the *Sensible*, one of the warships in the harbour. 'What time is it?' I asked.

'Five?' she answered sleepily. She set her lantern on the side table.

Anxiously, I broke the seal. I had difficulty reading the handwriting for there were big blotches of ink on the page. They were going to set to sea, I finally made out. I must join the ship at once. Commander du Braye cautioned me not to tell anyone, *especially* not the servants. One of his crew would be sent to meet me at Shell Point, south of the village.

I looked up at the chambermaid. She had such a sweet expression – how was it possible that she could be my enemy? 'That's strange. He regrets to inform me he must stay in the harbour until given permission to leave. Why would he wake me for this?' I asked, colouring.

The girl shrugged, successfully puzzled.

When she closed the door behind her I got out of bed. How was I to get a child to the shore without being noticed? I put on a petticoat and two dresses, one over the other, as best I could. I had some gold coins in a little cloth bag. I tucked this into my bodice. I would not be able to take much. I wrapped my rosary and a nightdress in a kerchief along with some of Hortense's clothes and the doll she is so attached to.

It was time to wake Hortense. I almost had her dressed before she began to stir, slumping over on to the bed with every move. 'We're going on a boat,' I whispered to her. 'We must be quick.' I pulled her to her feet. 'Can you walk?' She was too heavy to carry far.

A loud crack from a musket startled her awake. She nodded. I took her hand and opened the door. We slipped down the stairs. In the hall a footman was snoring into his chest. I put my finger to my lips, indicating to Hortense that she must be very quiet. I heard a shout out on the street.

I stooped down and kissed her, stroking wisps of curls away from her eyes. 'We must be brave,' I told her, pulling her hood over her head.

She trusted me completely; it broke my heart, her faith. I led her across the room and slowly opened the big oak door. I was relieved that the footman continued to slumber, our footsteps nothing compared to the turmoil outside.

SANDRA GULLAND

It was as I closed the door behind us that the reality of battle struck me. A smell of sulphur filled the air. Cracks of grapeshot broke the morning silence. I pulled Hortense forward. There was no time for hesitation. We had only to cross the Savane to get to the shore. It had stopped raining. The ground was soggy under our feet. I skirted the mud puddles. I was beginning to think we might make it safely when cannon fire broke out, followed by a shower of mud at our feet.

Death, so very close.

It is said that at such moments, time stops. I think I will never forget looking at Hortense then. I saw her as a baby, and as an old woman too. Then the spell broke and I moved, slowly, as if coming out of a dream, the dawn beautiful and clear before us. Suddenly I saw a bright green ribbon of light across the horizon. 'Look!' But as quickly as that it was gone.

At Shell Point there was a man waiting in a rowboat. I lowered Hortense into his big hands. There were shots all around as we made our way over the dark water. When we reached the ship, the man climbed the rope ladder up to the deck, Hortense under one arm.

Cannons fired as the sails were unfurled, but by then we were out of reach and I was below deck, Hortense pressed to my fluttering heart.

I felt the sails catch wind, the ship surge forward. The sound of cannon grew faint. From somewhere up above I could hear a man singing, drunken and off key: *Ah, ça ira, ça ira, ça ira . . .*

IV

Citoyenne

In which I am reunited with my son

FRIDAY, 29 OCTOBER 1790 – TOULON
We've arrived. We're on land again. I am writing this at a table
by a crackling fire. The table does not tip, the ink does not spill
. . . for that matter, my hand does not tremble, my stomach does
not turn.

Mal de mer for seven weeks! Even now, if I close my eyes, I see
a mountain of water towering darkly over me. Whosoever is an
atheist has never been to sea.

Our trials are far from over, however. Our meagre clothing
– suitable for hot summer days in Martinico, not chilly autumn
evenings in France – is stained and torn. Nor have we a sou
for bread or bed. Fortunately I was able to borrow a sum from
Commander du Braye and that together with some money kindly
loaned to us by Captain du Roure-Brison* will enable us to make
the long journey to Paris.

At least we're alive, I remind myself. Two times the ship took fire
– two times good luck they say, luck we were in need of, for it was a
stormy crossing. In the Strait of Gibraltar we ran aground. Had not
everyone on board – including Hortense, who insisted on 'helping'
– pulled *mightily* on a rope to pry us loose, we would surely have
perished. I have rope burns still.

I will never set foot on a sailing ship again.

30 OCTOBER
'Voilà, Madame,' the clerk at the post station said with a rough

* Captain Scipion du Roure-Brison was on the crew of the *Sensible*, the ship that
returned Rose and Hortense to France. He is thought by some historians (lack of
evidence notwithstanding) to have been Rose's lover.

southern accent, handing me the tickets for two places on the mail coach to Beaucaire. He was wearing leather over his lace cuffs, to protect them.

'Beaucaire? But we wish to go to Paris—'

'That's as far as I can get you.' He threw up his hands. 'From there . . . who knows! Everything has changed! Everything is being "improved" – the measures, routes, the *procedures*. I don't even know what district I'm in! But the road is good,' he added, perceiving my confusion, 'if the bandits don't get you, that is.'

'Bandits!' Hortense gasped, grasping my hand.

After purchasing the coach tickets I was able to locate a seamstress who would make capes for us quickly (and reasonably). Aboard ship Commander du Braye had been kind enough to lend us some woollens. I can't say that I was unhappy to return them – they were itchy and smelled of fish. He urged me to accept the loan of a pistol, however – 'You travel without the protection of a man, Madame.'

I declined, at first. Then he told me a story I wish I had not heard and I accepted his offer.

'Make one deep inside pocket,' I instructed the seamstress. For the pistol.

SUNDAY, 31 OCTOBER, ALL SAINTS' DAY EVE – AIX

After early-morning Mass – prayers for surviving the voyage by sea, prayers that we will survive the long land voyage that lies ahead – Commander du Braye escorted us to the post station. I was thankful for our newly made capes, for they disguised our stained and tattered robes.

I very nearly wept saying farewell. Commander du Braye pushed a basket into my hands: a bottle of wine, a roast chicken, some pickled plums, six hard eggs and a two-pound loaf of bread. 'Baked here in Toulon,' he assured me, for the ship's flour had long become rancid. I accepted his offer reluctantly – we owe him enough as it is.

We were fortunate to get a seat with our backs to the horses. Even so, there were jolts. Shortly before the second post station the route became quite rough, with postillions at the foot of many a hill to help us over. Several times I feared we would tip. At one pass through the mountains, after the second station, we were asked to walk. One of the passengers – a young man who had been partaking of a flask – refused, letting off his pistol for sport, which caused the horses to bolt and almost overturned the coach with the young man still in it. Once the horses had been recovered, the young man and the driver got into a fearful row – the driver threatening the soldier with his whip. Suddenly the soldier burst into tears and threw his arms round the driver's neck, apologized profusely for abusing a fellow citizen and offered him his flask.

'Why are they hugging now?' Hortense whispered as we, the shaken passengers, climbed back into the coach.

It was late afternoon when we were finally let down at the post station in Aix. We will resume our voyage at dawn. This inn is dirty, and the meal of half-raw little thrushes was not to our liking. Hortense carefully inspected the buns for insects, as has become her custom.

MONDAY, 1 NOVEMBER, ALL SAINTS' DAY – BEAUCAIRE

Between Aix and Beaucaire we overturned. Only small injuries, but I'm exhausted. Fortunately, our bedsheets here are clean and there appear to be no fleas. We share a room with a clock mender and his wife. I fear there might be improprieties.

FRIDAY, 5 NOVEMBER – MONTÉLIMAR

We have been on a river barge for three days. It is pulled by a team of placid oxen – Joseph, Jos and Jean, Hortense has named them. It is a common flat boat, a large raft-like vessel. In the centre is a shelter under which all the luggage, cargo and passengers are sheltered. Below deck is a stable of sorts for the oxen (we smell it).

It seemed an entirely tranquil, if slow, method of travel and I was congratulating myself on my wisdom when we came to Pont-Saint-Esprit, where the river runs under the arches of a bridge with great force. We accepted the driver's invitation to disembark and walk along the banks with the hoggee – a peasant boy of twelve – until the bridge had been safely navigated. I was apprehensive for the sake of the animals as well as our driver, but the beasts swam calmly under the arches, the driver sitting between the horns of the lead ox.

But that, I am content to say, has been our only excitement. Hortense is in good spirits – a better traveller than her mother, I confess, who is overcome by *mal de mer* at the slightest movement. She loves the barge, for she may run about and yell to the ox-boy, who endures her attentions with patience. Now and again I try to induce her to sit, for the sake of my fellow passengers, holding her on my lap and entertaining her with stories of her big brother Eugène, whom we both grow increasingly anxious to see.

'And Father,' Hortense demands, wriggling impatiently again. 'Tell me stories of my *father!*'

Alexandre . . . I sigh. Where do I begin?

THURSDAY, 11 NOVEMBER – LYONS

We've been able to secure a seat (only one – Hortense will have to sit on my lap) on a mail coach headed towards Paris – a fairly smooth road, I am told. We should be in Fontainebleau in five days, weather permitting. And then Paris! And then *Eugène*.

FRIDAY, 12 NOVEMBER – MÂCON

I'm writing this in bed, by the light of a dirty tallow candle. Hortense is limp at my side, wheezing sweetly. The floor of this inn is covered with fleas, the bedlinen dank with the sweat of others. Lice keep me awake, scratching like a monkey. Endure, endure, I tell myself, shivering with the cold, reluctant to part with five sous for coal.

15 NOVEMBER – PONT-SUR-YONNE

At supper tonight there was talk of highwaymen just south of Fontainebleau. In the woods there, four coaches have been taken. A few of us have decided to take another route, through Provins. From there, we are told, we can take a coach to Paris. I have posted a letter to Aunt Désirée informing her of the change in our plans.

ONE STATION PAST PROVINS

Two men on our coach, one a farmer, the other a surgeon, talk between them of politics. They pass a news-sheet back and forth.

Now and then a woman, a dealer in candles and cotton bonnets, joins in their conversation and an animated discussion ensues. They talk of the National Assembly.

I listen and remain silent, but I cannot control Hortense. She blurted out that her father was a delegate, a representative of the nobles.

'Does the child speak truly?' the woman asked. For we do not look the part.

I nodded in Hortense's defence.

'There are no more nobles,' the surgeon said. He is a young man with no teeth and a hairy wart on his chin. Later, as we passed what appeared to be the burnt-out ruins of a fine old estate, he pointed to it. 'The home of a noble. Perhaps it was your home?' He laughed nastily.

At the pewter basin in the post station, I whispered to Hortense that she was not to speak to that man, when his companion, the farmer, came up to us. '*Tu t'appelles Madame Beauharnais, n'est-ce pas?*' He asked if my husband's name was François.

I was reluctant to answer.

'Alexandre then?' he persisted.

I must have revealed the answer in my eyes, for the burly man threw himself upon me. He turned to the others, crying out: '*Madame Beauharnais! La femme de député Alexandre Beauharnais!*'

His friends the surgeon and the dealer in bonnets came over and the three of them displayed considerable pleasure at this news. The surgeon apologized for his rude conduct and offered me his cider. I accepted, but with confusion. It is apparently a good thing to be the wife of Deputy Alexandre Beauharnais, but I am too embarrassed to ask why.

17 NOVEMBER – MORMANT
Tomorrow – Paris! I can't sleep.

THURSDAY, 18 NOVEMBER – PARIS
Fanny's hôtel on Rue de Tournon was badly in need of repair. A window on the second floor had been boarded over. I looked for some sign of life. The once-elegant neighbourhood was deathly

quiet. A dilapidated carriage passed pulled by a mismatched pair of nags. The carriage emblems had been painted over. Tattered ribbons hung from the leather traces.

Hortense tugged on my hand, pulled me to the big wooden doors, yanked on the bell rope. Soon we heard someone fumbling with the latch and one of the big doors swung open. Before us was a woman, dressed exquisitely in a green silk ball gown festooned with mauve and blue ribbons. Even her hair was done up in the old style, elaborately piled and powdered, decorated with flowers. But the set of her coiffure was slightly off: a wig out of kilter, I thought. Behind her, in the courtyard, was a broken-down carriage with one wheel off.

'May I help you?' she asked. She spoke with an accent – a German accent, I thought.

'Is Comtesse Fanny de Beauharnais in?' I asked, embarrassed by our clothing, fallen to rags.

'Whom may I tell her is calling?' She had a musical voice.

'Her niece, Madame Rose de Beauharnais.'

'And Hortense!' my girl said boldly.

Suddenly, from across the courtyard, there appeared a plump woman with wild white hair, her face covered over with rouge. Fanny!

'*Ortensia!* My baby!' Fanny stooped down to look into Hortense's face. Hortense offered her godmother her hand. Fanny gave it a loud kiss, leaving a bright smear of rouge on Hortense's skin.

Fanny embraced me in the Italian manner, with great vigour. She smelled strongly of attar of roses. 'It *can't* be you,' she said, leading the way into the house. I detected a hint of wine on her breath. 'Forgive me, darling, but I've just returned from my Italian tour with Michel.' Her voice reverberated through the half-empty rooms.

From the stairway I heard a hiss. I looked up. A girl of about eight or nine stood on the landing, dressed in a white cotton gown. 'Émilie?' I recognized the pixie face, the big black eyes: Fanny's granddaughter, Marie's only surviving child. She'd grown tall in the two and a half years since I'd seen her, her limbs long. She gestured to Hortense.

'Remember your cousin Émilie?' I said. Hortense hesitated only a moment and then ran up the stairs.

I followed Fanny through a swinging door into the kitchen. There, seated at a painted table, were a man and a woman. The man's hair was short and unpowdered and he was wearing a peasant's smock.

'Rose!' A woman in man's clothing stood to greet me, her loose curls caught back informally in a linen bonnet. I was astonished to see that it was Marie, Émilie's mother – timid, proper, shy Marie. But something had changed, for the woman I saw before me was quite bold, and certainly not *proper*.

'Why, it's Alexandre's wife!' the man exclaimed. He had big lips and his voice was booming – surprising in a man of his short height. Michel de Cubières, the poet. I had met him at one of Fanny's receptions years ago. He poured a glass of red wine from the bottle in the middle of the table. There were three empty wine bottles lined up on the counter.

Fanny handed me the glass. 'Oh, Rose, you have missed the most glorious fêtes.'

'The most glorious *Revolution*!' Michel exclaimed, hitting the bare tabletop with his fist.

'Am I not going to be introduced?' the aristocratic woman asked from the door.

'Princess Amalia, Madame Beauharnais; Rose, Princess Amalia.' Marie broke off a piece of bread on a platter. 'Come, Rose, eat. We're enjoying the servants' day off.'

They all laughed, as if this was a joke.

'But Princess Amalia is my servant now,' Fanny protested.

Princess Amalia? The woman in the wig made a full court bow. I felt I had walked on to a stage in the middle of a comedy and did not know the lines.

'I've come *up* in the world,' Fanny said in a stage whisper. 'Princess Amalia de Hohenzollern-Sigmaringen is now my kitchen help.'

'And *we're* helping clean out the wine cellar,' Marie said, her eyes shining.

Michel de Cubières raised his glass. 'To house-cleaning!'

Fanny pulled out a chair for me to sit on. I backed away. 'I must go,' I said, stuttering, 'to the Collège d'Harcourt. I am anxious to see Eugène.'

'Collège d'Harcourt?' Princess Amalia asked.

'But Rose, darling,' Fanny stuttered, 'you . . .'

'Is . . . is there a problem?' Suddenly I was fearful.

Michel burst into laughter. 'I suggest one of you ladies give Madame Beauharnais a looking glass.'

How delirious to be clean. How shocking to be full. I've become too accustomed to hunger. After a meal of slipcoat cheese and skerret, and a change into clean linen (provided by Marie) and a walking dress (provided by Fanny), I felt renewed.

Renewed, but far from rested, I might add, for every move I made (even into the water closet) I was followed by Marie, who felt called upon to provide a minute-by-minute account of every political event of the last six hundred days, as well as Fanny, who kept interrupting her daughter to give me a minute-by-minute account of her recent Italian tour. Finally, I was forced to interrupt. 'I must go,' I said.

It was not yet three in the afternoon. There was time.

The Collège d'Harcourt is a large institution. Aristocratic, militaristic: there was a sentry at the gate. Everyone was in uniform.

I wandered into the centre court, looking into each boy's face. I feared I would not recognize Eugène, feared he would not know me. He was nine now. He'd been only six when I last saw him.

I knocked on the door to the office. I was introduced to the headmaster, Monsieur de Saint-Hilaire, a portly man in a vivid red frock suit. I explained who I was and my business there. Monsieur de Saint-Hilaire bowed and offered a chair, but I refused. 'I haven't seen my son for two and a half years, Monsieur.'

After mentioning the tuition, long overdue apparently, Monsieur de Saint-Hilaire ordered a thin boy with boils on his face to escort me to the study hall. I followed the boy through several corridors to a room occupied by only three students. In the far corner was Eugène, glumly hunched over a chalkboard. He seemed older than I had pictured him.

I gave my guide a sou and he ran off. It was then that Eugène looked up, his curly hair falling on to his forehead. He glanced at me and went back to his work with a resigned expression. I was filled with confusion, for no maternal feeling came to aid me.

I stepped back out into the corridor, out of view, and leaned against the wall. I felt short of breath and suddenly unsure. Nothing had prepared me for this – this indifference on my part, this lack of love. I felt tears again, but this time they were tears of dismay.

I resolved to trust whatever Providence offered. I went to the door again. I called out to Eugène this time, softly. He looked up, stood and came to the door with a questioning look. I detected a moment of recognition in his face – but he was insecure, unsure of his young memories. I extended my hand to him. 'It *is* me,' I whispered, leading him into the hall, out of view of the other students who were watching us. 'Maman.'

He did not know what to say. I stooped so that I could better see his face. 'Did you get the cricket cage I sent you – for your birthday?'

Eugène looked down at the stone floor and pushed the toe of his boot into a crack. I put one hand on his shoulder. The memory of him came to me forcefully then, through the fragile feel of one bony shoulder. 'Oh, my boy,' I whispered. I took him in my arms and he clung to me, as if he would never let me go.

Little by little the pieces fall into place, the parts make up the whole. Myself, my boy, my girl.

Arriving back at Fanny's, we three sat in the big empty salon on the big empty sofa, a tiny touching cluster down at one end, telling little stories. Shyly. Getting to know one another again.

At nightfall I shook the big feather quilt out over them and sang to them, one childhood song after another. I kissed them once and then again – and then again and again. How can there ever be enough?

It is late now as I write. The night is clear; the street lanterns sparkle like diamonds in the dark. From somewhere I hear the sweet sound of a Provençal flute mingled with a violin and a cello. The light from the fire touches the faces of my sleeping children.

A church bell rings, Paris sleeps. But before I blow out the candle, I vow to remember this, this night, to remember that whatever life holds, it is really only this that matters, this fullness of heart.

In which I discover my husband a changed man

MONDAY, 22 NOVEMBER 1790

Fanny had tickets to the National Assembly and insisted that I go. 'Watching the Assembly has replaced theatre,' she said. She was wearing a bold ensemble entirely of red, white and blue. 'My revolutionary toilette.' Apparently the Revolution is the style now in fashionable circles. 'Charming, is it not?' She made a clumsy pirouette. Even her gloves matched. 'And besides, my dear Rose, it is time you saw your husband.'

It was a beautiful morning, cold but bright. We hired a fiacre to take us to the river and across to the Tuileries. The Assembly meets in the former Palace riding school next to the terrace of the Feuillants's. convent. Everywhere there were deputies in black. The gardens were crowded with vendors selling pamphlets and news-sheets, lemonade sellers shouting, 'Freshly made!' People of all classes pressed to gain entrance.

Inside there were public galleries above the Assembly chamber. Fanny chose a bench that was cleaner than others and spread out a cloth for us to sit on. I noticed a number of elegant women dressed as for an afternoon stroll in the Bois de Boulogne. Intermixed were men and women – mostly women – of the serving class, even market women in one section.

I scanned the faces of the deputies below.

'He isn't here yet,' Fanny said, in answer to my thoughts.

A deputy stood and with an air of authority went to the front of the chamber. A woman behind us cursed. I must have flinched, for Fanny leaned over and whispered, 'You should have been here *last* year – she'd have been armed with a pike.' She pointed to a man on the far side of the hall. 'See Robespierre? He's the one in the powdered wig.'

'The tiny aristocrat?' The man I saw was wearing a pale green frock coat and a white lace cravat. He was sitting very quietly with his hands folded in his lap, watching everyone.

Fanny scoffed, snapping her fan shut. 'He should have been a priest.'

Suddenly there was a tumultuous cheer. I leaned forward to discern what had occasioned the commotion. Fanny pointed to a man who had just entered.

'The peasant?' I asked. He was a thin man dressed in a coarse linen tunic and wearing wooden clogs.

'That's Deputy Luzerne. They're cheering because he came *dressed* as a peasant. There's François! In the fourth row. He's wearing one of those dreadful pigtail wigs and a king's hat. Can you see him?'

I placed François by the white plume of his round beaver hat.

But where was Alexandre?

Fanny nudged me in the ribs, nodded towards the far entrance. A man was standing in one of the doors, his long hair curled about his shoulders. He was dressed in a black coat and nankeen pantaloons. It was Alexandre.

'Stop watching me,' I protested.

'You still fancy him. Confess.'

'You're making up romances.' If Fanny wanted to see love in my expression, nothing would prevent her from doing so.

Fortunately, Fanny's attention was distracted by a flurry of shouting from the floor. Two men had stood and were yelling with considerable vigour at another deputy. Finally, order was restored – but with difficulty.

Fanny explained: 'Some deputies, your husband among them, are proposing that the clergy be elected officials, government employees. The subject gets them wonderfully heated, don't you think?'

'The clergy – *elected*? But the Pope would never consent to such a proposal,' I said, shocked at the notion.

'Who's asking the Pope?' Fanny hissed.

Speakers for and against alternated. Alexandre was the sixth to go to the podium. He expressed himself most persuasively. France was facing financial ruin, he began. The poor were starving, yet the clergy continued to enjoy an exorbitant lifestyle at the people's expense, free from taxation, free from any allegiance to the state. The nobles had given up their special privileges. So in turn must the clergy . . .

Then Alexandre's brother François spoke, in opposition. He was not as eloquent as Alexandre; his voice did not carry and he was hard to understand. Nevertheless, I found, to my confusion, that I could see his point as well. He argued that in principle such concepts made sense, but in practice the solution proposed was unthinkable. One could not expect men of God to forsake allegiance to the Church.

From there the discussion became extreme, with both sides becoming vociferous. The woman sitting behind us began cursing again. At last the debate was brought to a close, but without resolution.

'It's that tithe system that gets the Church into so much trouble,' Fanny ranted as we were exiting. 'If the clergy would only exert a little self-control – but no, they have to live like kings. And at whose expense, I ask you? And all those gloomy parades! Why do they have to clog up the streets *every* Sunday? Aren't feast days enough?'

'I'd hate to be at a family gathering when this comes up,' I said, thinking of Aunt Désirée, who was so devout, and the Marquis, who demanded loyalty, whatever the cause.

We followed the crowd into a large central hall. Alexandre was standing with a group of deputies. He looked up and returned to his discussion.

'He doesn't recognize you.' Before I could stop her, Fanny was pushing her way into his group.

Alexandre turned to me with a quizzical look. He broke away and in two steps was in front of me. 'Madame Beauharnais,' he said, 'what a surprise. I learned just this morning you were back.' He pushed his fair hair out of his eyes. 'I was beginning to fear you would never return. Hortense is with you?'

'She is anxious to see you,' I said. I adjusted my gauze fichu; Marie's dress was too small for me. 'I thought you gave an excellent speech.'

Alexandre glanced towards the hallway where two men, deputies, were trying to get his attention. He looked at me with an apologetic shrug. 'I'm sorry, but I must go. You're at Fanny's?'

'For one more week. I've had difficulty obtaining seats on the post coach to Fontainebleau. I'd like to take Eugène with me, for the holidays, if, that is—'

We were interrupted by a plump little man in a white dimity waistcoat.

'Deputy Dunnkirk, you're *just* the man I need to see,' Alexandre said. 'I'd like you to meet my wife, Madame Beauharnais.'

'Your *wife!*' The man gripped me in the comradely embrace that seemed to have become customary in France.

'Deputy Dunnkirk is a *banker* — be kind to him,' Alexandre winked.

'The ladies are all *so* kind to me,' the little man said sadly.

Alexandre took my hand. 'Tonight? You'll be in?' He disappeared into the crowd.

'I didn't know Deputy Beauharnais was married.' Deputy Dunnkirk sneezed into an enormous linen handkerchief.

'There you are, darling!' Fanny pressed her thickly painted face between us. 'I didn't know you knew Emmery.'

'Deputy Dunnkirk, forgive me if I appear abstracted,' I said. 'I have only been in Paris for a few days, and it is really all so . . .'

'Indeed. We are all of us in a state of confusion. I very much doubt that we will ever recover.'

Fanny laughed too loudly. 'Dear, dear Emmery. Why do I never see you?'

'You were in Rome, with that wild man. On a tour of propaganda, I am told, preaching to the unenlightened masses . . .'

'I'm beginning my evenings again, this coming Monday,' Fanny said. 'I will simply *die* of grief if I don't see you there.'

I looked at her. 'Monday!' That was only in four days.

'But you don't even have a cook,' I exclaimed, as we waited outside for our fiacre.

'*Mon Dieu!* I'd forgotten!' Fanny said, fanning herself furiously in spite of the cold.

THAT EVENING

I spent most of the afternoon preparing for Alexandre's visit. I bathed, found a suitable dress, this one a loan from Princess Amalia, one of her *less* formal creations — a teal silk with ivory ribbons and lace, quite the confection. Hortense tried on all of Émilie's big-girl dresses and finally settled on a horrid pink one. It is far too big for her but she will not be persuaded otherwise, especially after Eugène told her she looked 'lovely' in it.

Alexandre arrived after supper. Proudly, Eugéne performed

civilités – showing his father to a seat in the front parlour, ordering refreshments. Hortense refused to leave my side, clinging to me, her eyes never leaving the face of this stranger, her father. She would not allow him near her.

'She will get over it,' I assured him, after the children had been taken to bed. I sounded more confident than I felt, for in truth I find Hortense difficult to predict. 'You will be pleased to discover that she is quite bright,' I told him, 'and possesses a number of remarkable abilities.'

'I wish I could say the same for our son.' Alexandre stood in front of the fire, warming his hands.

'Perhaps Eugène takes after me in the matter of school.' I stared into the flames, the heat warming my face.

'He certainly has your nature.' He cleared his throat. 'Kind, generous . . .' He studied me for a moment. 'Charming. That colour quite suits you, Rose.'

I flushed.

'Do you ever think of me?' he asked.

'I often think of you.'

'Do you think of me *kindly*?'

How honest was I willing to be? 'You are an easy man to care for, Alexandre.'

'You make it sound facile.'

'Is that a fault?'

'I wish you to know that I am a changed man; I feel I have risen from some magnetic slumber. I am intent on putting the foolishness of youth behind me.'

We talked for some time of the changes in his life – of his health, the lingering effects of the fever he had suffered in Martinico, which had made a military life untenable. A political career was his only alternative. 'Fortuitously,' he said, for politics had become his passion. 'I should like to tell you more,' he said, pulling out a timepiece, 'but I promised the Duc d'Orléans I would help prepare a petition. Oh – I almost forgot. I have something for you.' He reached into his waistcoat pocket, pulling out an envelope.

'It's from *Mother*?' I recognized the writing.

'Apparently it was delivered to our old hôtel on Rue Neuve-Saint-Charles.'

I broke the seal, scanned the contents. Uncle Tascher was safe. Father, Manette, were alive.

'It is bad news?' Alexandre asked, alarmed by my tears.

'No, yes.'

'Good news?'

I laughed, handing him the letter to read. 'I'm to protect myself against you,' I explained.

'Me?'

'Unless, of course, I succeed in reforming you.'

23 September, this year of our Lord, 1790 – Trois-Ilets
Dear Rose,

I trust that my prayers have been answered and that you and Hortense have completed your journey safely. Your father and sister continue to weaken, in spite of my prayers.

Your uncle Tascher was released shortly after your depart-ure and in time the rebels were subdued. The disturbance, however, continues. I have had to take measures to ensure discipline with the slaves.

The government in France is godless. I have reason to believe that your children's father may be of their party. It is the duty of a mother to help that which is of God overcome that which can only be the work of the Devil. For the sake of your children, Rose, pray for Alexandre's salvation.

There is increased talk of war. It may be some time before I am able to write to you again. The British continue to blockade the port. It was only through smugglers and the will of God that I have been able to get this letter to you, should you receive it.

Your mother, Madame Claire de Tascher de la Pagerie

WEDNESDAY, 24 NOVEMBER

Everyone has been recruited to help Fanny prepare for her reception. Princess Amalia's brother Frédéric – *Prince* de Salm-Kyrburg – and I were asked to write out the 'at home' cards. He's a charming man, quite short, with no chin at all. He was happy to do it, he confided. He and his sister have just built a mansion on Rue de Lille – Hôtel de Salm it is called.* In his *drôle* German accent he complained that it smelled of plaster, that his sister was for ever engaging him in discussions about wall-covering, and that he welcomed any excuse to get out. 'Who wants to stay at home all day with servants who snicker at you behind your back?' he said.

'At least you *have* servants,' Fanny interrupted. She was covered with flour and seemed a little jolly. She'd been in the kitchen all morning with Jacques, her man-of-all-work, training him to cook, a vocation for which he showed enthusiasm if not promise. I suspected she'd been sipping the cooking wine.

'You mean *masters*,' Frédéric said, indulging his passion for paradox.

27 NOVEMBER

Fanny's evening started out well, in spite of many disasters: the goose overcooked, the cake fell in upon itself and a curtain in the front parlour caught fire.

Quite a few people came, and the mix was invigorating. Royalists socialized with radicals, artists with bankers. A number of the guests were deputies from the National Assembly. As Alexandre's wife, I am held in high esteem. One deputy even assumed I would be in a position of influence and asked if I would speak to Alexandre on a certain matter.

I was struck with how things have changed. Where before people paraded finery, now they boast of economy. Where before our distractions were *bouts-rimés* and charades, now people amuse themselves with talk of politics . . . and, of course, what is now called 'economics': national product, inflation, public debt. (It seems that everyone is writing a plan of finance to save France.)

There were a few poets present, fortunately, several of whom were persuaded to recite from their latest creation – which of course they just happened to have with them. Fanny even got me to play her harp, which I did quite badly, I confess – I haven't practised for some time.

Even so, Deputy Emmery Dunnkirk, the banker Alexandre introduced me to at the Assembly, was effusive in his praise (between explosive sneezes). We talked for some time. He believes he might be able to make contact with Mother, in spite of the British

* Now the Palace of the Legion of Honour.

blockade – in any case, he will try. He has clients who have dealings with the Islands, so he is not unfamiliar with the difficulties.

It wasn't until after supper that Alexandre arrived. He joined me in the front parlour. 'I was impressed by your article in the *Moniteur* today,' I told him. It was a long dissertation on the need for better hospitals.

Alexandre was about to say something when we were joined by a man with an enormous moustache, a deputy from Poitou. 'Deputy Beauharnais, you devil, you never told me you had such a lovely wife!'

'Rose, I must say, you've made quite an impression on all my comrades,' Alexandre said. 'Everywhere I go—'

'Alexandre, I didn't know you had arrived!' Alexandre's cousin Marie interrupted. She was wearing red and blue cockades all over her bodice, the badges of a revolutionary.

'Deputy Beauharnais, how charming to see you!' Princess Amalia joined in. Her hair had been arranged in the old style, stacked high and heavily powdered. Silk ribbons and feathers were stuck into it everywhere.

'Are there hairdressers who still know how to dress hair like that?' the deputy from Poitou asked.

'*Hélas!* There's a flour shortage and *she's* pouring the stuff on to her hair,' Marie said.

Prince Frédéric, who overheard, was about to say something in his sister's defence when we were joined by Deputy Dunnkirk and another deputy, a Monsieur Lyautey, and the discussion turned to the new land tax.

Alexandre and Frédéric excused themselves – they were late for a meeting of a debating society,* 'formed under the auspices of the virtues,' Alexandre said, putting on his hat. 'I will see you and the children in Fontainebleau? Over the holidays?'

'My pleasure.'

He took my hand and kissed it with a tender show of feeling. 'The *pleasure* will be mine.'

---

* 'The Friends of the Constitution' – formerly the Breton Club, and soon to become known as the radical and powerful Jacobin Club. In the interests of clarity, all references have been changed to the 'Jacobin Club'.

In which I suffer a great loss

WEDNESDAY, 1 DECEMBER 1790
Fontainebleau is a ghost town. The palace gardens have grown wild, the long grass rampant. Gypsies are camped there.

Nevertheless, it was a joyful reunion; the Marquis stuttered, Aunt Désirée wept. They exclaimed how Hortense had grown, pampering her with a multitude of kisses.

The Marquis is frail, as one expects of a man of seventy-six. Indeed, it is a blessing he is with us still. I was relieved to find Aunt Désirée strong in both body and spirit. Their house showed signs of neglect — it is clear that they are getting by on very little.

It did not take Aunt Désirée long to bring up the subject of Alexandre. She has cut out all the articles about him in the news-sheets and pasted them into a big book which she proudly displayed, turning the pages reverently.

She did not say how she felt about his views. I wonder if she thinks of such things. Yet how can she not? Alexandre supported forsaking feudal rights — this alone has cost the Marquis a great deal. And now Alexandre supports the Church being made a government institution. Does Aunt Désirée not understand what this could mean?

'Look at this one,' she said. 'His name is mentioned five times.'

'It's wonderful,' I said, turning the pages.

THE NEXT DAY
Aunt Désirée and I had a talk this morning — about finances. It was impossible to put off. We had to decide what to do about Adélaïde d'Antigny, Alexandre's six-year-old illegitimate daughter we are both of us supporting. It is hard enough to support ourselves. Nevertheless, I could not accept cutting off the girl's care entirely. Aunt Désirée urged me to be firmer with Alexandre. I was making

it too easy for him, she said. 'If you were to demand more, perhaps he would see the benefit of a reconciliation.'

'Perhaps I do not wish a reconciliation.' I turned my attention to my needlework.

'Yet you care for him.'

'As do any number of women.' Alexandre's 'successes' were legendary.

Aunt Désirée cleared her throat. There was a moment of silence. 'Surely you do not prefer to remain single.'

'I believe I have no other option.'

Aunt Désirée put down her lacework. 'Rose, there is something you should know,' she began, as if she was about to reveal a confidence. 'A wise woman does not allow her husband's "amusements" to disturb her, a wise woman closes her eyes. In allowing her husband his freedom, she dominates him!'

I confess I did not know how to respond. I knew my Aunt Désirée to be a woman well versed in the art of getting her way, but I had never suspected that she supported her actions with *philosophy*.

Aunt Désirée, sensing that she had captured my attention, went on. 'Alexandre has a taste for tumultuous sensations, he is easily carried away – but surely such excessive sensibility is only proof of a good heart. A family that has suffered the stain of separation can never be repaired. The dishonour will endure for generations to come. I tell you this most painful fact out of the wisdom of my own experience. Rose, you owe it to your children to do everything in your power to bring about a reconciliation between yourself and your husband – the man to whom you were united by *God*.'

Now, past dark, I sit in the quiet of my room. The memory of Aunt Désirée's lecture brings a smile to my heart, but the intent of her words brings dismay. I would give my life for my children – I would not hesitate to die for them – but would I live with Alexandre for them?

The lantern throws a flickering light on the walls.

In the light I see security, but in the shadows I see grief . . . in the shadows I see defeat.

13 December 1790 – Paris

Dear Rose,

I note that today is the eleventh anniversary of the day

on which we were wed. I am writing to commemorate that union, which has brought forth two beautiful children into the world.

I intend to come to Fontainebleau for the holidays. No doubt my Royalist brother plans to come as well. It is almost impossible for us to communicate now without becoming heated, but for the sake of family harmony I will attempt to put thoughts of Truth aside.

Your husband, Alexandre Beauharnais

Note – Make sure Eugène perseveres daily in his studies. Do not allow any exceptions, for in this way his natural inclination towards laziness takes root.

CHRISTMAS DAY

Alexandre arrived laden with gifts, including a jewellery case for Hortense and enamelled boot buckles for me. Hortense ended in a frenzy of emotion, weeping her heart out in her room. It was just too much, this sudden regard from this stranger, her father.

I understand her confusion.

SUNDAY, 26 DECEMBER

What a terrible evening. Aunt Désirée is in the parlour with the Marquis, giving him ether, trying to calm him.

It began after supper, over coffee. The Marquis asked François how things were going in the Assembly. I believe it affronted Alexandre that his father had not asked *him*. In any case, Alexandre interrupted to point out the causes *he* has furthered. It was at this point that François suggested that Alexandre inform their father of his views on the clergy.

'Well, Alexandre,' the Marquis asked, '*do* you believe priests should forsake the Church?'

'It is possible to read on his countenance all his projects, Father,' François said. 'Alexandre not only supported that motion, he was one of the deputies who advocated it.'

'Why *should* the clergy be exempt?' Alexandre countered. 'It is equality we believe in, yet it is inequality we further—'

'Pretty words,' François interrupted, 'but they dangerously evade the issue. Honour is not unknown to men of religion. What will you do when the priests refuse? Put them to the lantern?'

Aunt Désirée excused herself from the table. I found her in the parlour, arranging and rearranging the religious relics on the mantelpiece. From the dining parlour I heard Alexandre exclaim, 'And that reality is starvation!'

'Is it true?' Aunt Désirée looked paler than I had ever seen her. 'Does Alexandre believe that the priests should *renounce* the Pope?' She sank into the chair by the grate. She shivered; the embers did not heat the room. I heard voices from the dining parlour again: François and Alexandre. And then, the Marquis: 'I will not have it, Alexandre *de* Beauharnais!' pronouncing the 'de' with great spite.*

There was the sound of china breaking. Alexandre strode forcefully down the hall. He banged the front door shut behind him, shaking the walls. As the sound of his horse's hooves grew faint, Aunt Désirée gave way to tears.

FRIDAY, 31 DECEMBER

Alexandre returned on the last day of the year. He'd ridden a bay gelding all the way from Paris.

'I didn't want to start the New Year unluckily,' he told me, taking first Hortense and then Eugène into his arms.

'Did you bring me something?' Hortense asked.

'Of course,' Alexandre said.

Eagerly the children tore open their gifts: a riding whip for Eugène and a blue velvet bag for Hortense.

'And for your mother.' He handed me a parcel. Inside was an embroidered muff.

'It's lovely.' I kissed his cheek. Eugène and Hortense ran out of the room, giggling.

Alexandre poured himself a brandy. 'Has my father forgiven me yet?'

---

* After the nobility lost their feudal rights (a decree Alexandre supported), it was no longer appropriate to indicate heritage in a name: hence Alexandre *de* (of) Beauharnais became, simply, Alexandre Beauharnais, a man without lineage. Some individuals got round this by incorporating the 'de' into their last name — 'de Moulins' becoming 'Demoulins', for example.

'He's so forgetful now. He probably can't remember what happened.'

'I brought him a copy of Hume's *History of England*.'

'You're giving him a book written by a *Protestant*?'

Alexandre slapped his forehead. 'I didn't think.'

'How long can you stay?'

He made a face. 'I've a meeting in the morning, in Paris.'

'On a Sunday? On New Year's Day?'

He sighed. 'Making history is so time-consuming.' He confessed he was uneasy about a speech he planned to give at the Jacobin Club the following week, on the subject of public education. He feared no one would attend. When Robespierre spoke, tickets had to be purchased in advance, but for an unknown such as himself—

There was a commotion in the hall. Suddenly Aunt Désirée rushed into the room, her hat still on. 'Alexandre!' She looked pale. 'Have you heard?'

'Heard what?'

'You don't know?' She rummaged around in her basket, her hand pressed to her chest.

'Aunt Désirée?' Was she all right?

She pulled a news-sheet out of her basket. 'Two thousand Creoles have been *murdered* in Saint-Domingue! By slaves!'

'Murdered?' *Two thousand?* I put my hand to my mouth. Mon Dieu.

Alexandre took the journal from her. Cap-François had been destroyed, the road to the city lined with the bodies of slaves – ten thousand killed, he read.

Ten thousand? Had I heard correctly?

'We're ruined!' Aunt Désirée rummaged through the writing desk. 'I thought there were some salts in here.'

'Behind the quills,' I said.

'Our properties are at some distance from Cap-François,' Alexandre called out as she headed up the stairs to the Marquis's rooms.

I stood by the fireplace, staring into the flames.

'This is unfortunate,' Alexandre said. He was standing at the window, clasping and unclasping the pommel of his sword.

'Yes.'

'Perhaps you should be sitting down,' he said.

'I will be all right.'

THE MANY LIVES & SECRET SORROWS OF JOSEPHINE B.

'I insist.' He cleared his throat. 'I bring . . . other news.'

I felt apprehensive. I sat down.

'You understand that it is difficult to get mail in or out of Martinico. The British have set up a blockade.'

Martinico? I nodded. 'Deputy Dunnkirk has been trying to contact my family.'

'That's why I came.' Alexandre took the chair beside mine. 'Emmery asked me to tell you that in spite of the civil war there, he has been able to get through.'

'There's a *war* in Martinico?'

'You didn't know?'

My heart began to flutter. 'You've had news, Alexandre?'

'Yes.'

I felt a tingling sensation in my fingers. 'Is it my sister?'

'No.'

'Tell me!'

'Your father . . . He—'

I pressed my hands together.

'I'm sorry, Rose. Your father exchanged worlds last November.' He put his hand on my shoulder.

I could not catch my breath. *Father.* Tears came to my eyes.

Alexandre took a handkerchief out of his waistcoat pocket and handed it to me. 'No doubt you were expecting this. Your father has been ill for a very long time.'

'No!'

1 JANUARY 1791

The New Year. It is quiet. No fêtes, no grand balls, no receptions. Instead of perfumed water, stagnant pools fill the fountains.

I wake with a sense of loss. I think of Father, a man so given to dreams.

What did his life mean, in the end?

My mother hated him.

Harsh words, but reality must be respected. And the reality of my father's life was: he suffered, he achieved nothing.

In which Alexandre is a hero

21 JUNE 1791 – FONTAINEBLEAU

On my way to the perfumer this morning a placard on a tavern wall caught my attention. In bold letters was the name Beauharnais. Alexandre has been elected President of the National Assembly.*

Immediately I returned to the house. Coming in the door I called out to Aunt Désirée. I summoned the children, who were in the garden. 'I have news of your father!'

Aunt Désirée came to the landing.

'Is the Marquis in his room?' I asked.

'It's about Father!' Eugène called out. He had tracked mud on to the carpet.

'Is Alexandre all right?' Aunt Désirée asked.

'It's good news.'

Aunt Désirée ushered us all into the Marquis's apartment. There, I told them the news. I had to repeat it three times.

'My son? Alexandre? *President* of the National Assembly?' the Marquis exclaimed in disbelief. 'But that's not possible!'

I assured him it was so. Other than the King, there was no one more powerful, more important in all the land.

WEDNESDAY, 22 JUNE

I've been anxious, sleepless without news. *Something* has happened, for the gates to Paris have been closed; no mail, no journals, no couriers have been allowed in or out. It was whispered the King and Queen had fled the country – an unthinkable thought.

* Although Alexandre's term of office would be for only two weeks – the position of president rotated – this was a prestigious honour.

It was only this morning, at the procession in town for the feast of the Holy Sacrament, that Aunt Désirée and I were able to obtain a copy of the *Moniteur*. There our fears were confirmed: on the night of the twentieth, in disguise, the King and Queen and their two children escaped by means of the subterranean passages of the palace kitchens. It is thought that the royal berline headed for Varennes.

Quickly we returned to the house, for there was danger of the mob becoming heated. In the Marquis's bedchamber, Aunt Désirée read the journal reports out loud. It was with considerable pride that we learned that Alexandre was being credited with holding the country together — 'with a firm and steady hand'.

Aunt Désirée read, 'President Deputy Alexandre Beauharnais has organized the effort to capture the King—'

'*Capture* the King!' The Marquis was taken with a nervous seizure.

'Not to capture, but to *free* him!' Aunt Désirée rushed for the ether.

The King has not *fled*, he's been 'abducted'; he's not to be *captured*, he's to be 'freed'. If only reality could be changed so easily.

23 JUNE

This afternoon after supper — a lovely repast in honour of my twenty-eighth birthday — we were alarmed by sounds outside on the street. Aunt Désirée's chambermaid went to the window. 'There's a crowd in front of the house.'

'In front of *this* house?' the Marquis asked.

The children ran to the window. I jumped to my feet, nearly knocking a vase on to the floor. 'Get back!' I commanded.

'They're crying out "Dauphin"!' Eugène said, confused.

'*Mon Dieu*,' Aunt Désirée whispered. 'They mean Eugène.'

'Because of Alexandre?'

'But the Dauphin is not *here*,' Hortense protested. 'Is he not in Paris?'

I could not answer, my terror was so acute. The mob was calling my son Dauphin — the future *King*.

27 June 1791 — Paris
Dear Rose,

    Thank you for writing such a very kind congratulation.

And please, forgive me for neglecting your birthday. I am in a delirium. I've not had any sleep for four days. The events of this last week have been overwhelming, for myself as well as for the Nation.

In moments of despair I recall Rousseau's words – that the best part of Virtue is to accept the yoke of necessity. And so it is with those of us who were born to the nobility, born to bear arms. How enlivening to be relieved of this slavery, to choose, instead, to risk life in honour of that which is True and Just. The sacrifices that we make for the Revolution will be a great benefit to mankind. With the love of Virtue spurring us on, how can we be defeated?

Your husband, Alexandre Beauharnais

30 JUNE

François has taken on the role of the King's defender in the Assembly. 'He's going to get us all hanged!' the Marquis sputtered.

Yesterday it was Alexandre's *condemnation* of the King that enraged him.

The brothers fight it out over the King's head on a national stage. Beauharnais *for*, Beauharnais *against* . . . If it isn't one son, it's the other.

6 July 1791 – Paris
Dear Rose,

I have been ill, having exhausted my system during the crisis. Thank you for enrolling Eugène in the Collège d'Harcourt for the autumn. I had entirely forgotten. I agree that Hortense would benefit from more formal instruction at this time as well. You will see to this? Not too costly, however.

Your husband, Alexandre Beauharnais

18 July 1791 – Rue de Tournon, Paris
Darling!

It's late, almost midnight, but I feel compelled to write. Alexandre gave a wonderful speech at the Jacobin Club tonight – so uplifting! We were all of us there to applaud him: Marie,

Michel de Cubières, Frédéric. Even Princess Amalia came to hear him, in spite of her Royalist leanings. Afterwards we all went to the Café Covazza in the Palais-Royal. There Alexandre informed me that you intend to move to Paris, in order that your children might be educated.

Although transported with joy at the thought of seeing you and your wee darlings more often, I thought it would only be fair to warn you what Paris is like right now. It seems we are for ever swinging from one extreme to the other, beginning with the sublime and ending in the tragic. Observe:

The week began with the grand fête and procession moving Voltaire's remains to the Pantheon – another of the brilliantly theatrical events orchestrated by the painter David. (Have you met him? He came to my salon once.) Of course I had to go – you know how I feel about our Apostle of Tolerance. The service began in the Masonic Lodge of the Nine Sisters, then wended its way through a number of triumphal arches to the site of the old Bastille. There the coffin rested overnight.

By the time Michel Cubières and I got back on Monday morning, the roses, myrtles and laurels had been stripped. Representatives of the sections and clubs had turned out in togas and red wool caps (like those awful itchy ones we have to wear at Masonic meetings). The coffin was loaded on to a chariot and pulled to the Pantheon by a team of white horses. I melted with tears.

Thursday, another fête at the Bastille, this time for the Fête de la Fédération. We didn't go (how unpatriotic) but that night the sky was fairly blooming with fire-rockets.

And yesterday, as if we must be punished for enjoying ourselves excessively, there was the tragic riot on the Champ-de-Mars. It began as a peaceful assembly – Marie was there with one of her women's groups to sign a petition in favour of a Republic. It got out of hand when two men, spies (or so it is thought), were discovered hiding under the central platform, and were promptly lynched. So Lafayette called out the National Guard, someone in the crowd yelled 'Fire!' and now more than fifty are dead.

Thank God Marie was not harmed! Over the course of the day I virtually emptied my bottle of laudanum. It did not help in the least that it was washing week here and the two women I'd hired to help kept disappearing to go off to some fête or demonstration or riot. And now, all these dreary funerals.

If, despite my warnings, you persevere in this matter of your children's education and move to our entertaining city, I recommend you contact Madame Hosten, a Creole widow with three children (only one home still, I believe). I've been told that she has just purchased a hôtel on Rue Saint-Dominique (not too far from Hôtel de Salm), and is looking for someone to help share the expenses. It's in a good district – there, at least, the neighbourhood ruffians aren't out cutting off cats' ears. You will find her a genial woman and will most assuredly not regret my sending you to her.

Your loving Aunt Fanny

26 July 1791 – Rue Saint-Dominique, Paris
Dear Madame Beauharnais,

Your welcome letter was received yesterday. I take the liberty, through your aunt Madame Fanny Beauharnais, of addressing a few lines to you relative to the inducements of my new abode.

The house is large, divided into two apartments, with rooms for domestics on the third floor. My daughter (age twelve) and I occupy the ground floor. The upstairs suite is small but sunny. There is a walled-in garden. The Church of Saint Thomas Aquinas is immediately behind us.

It will give me much pleasure to see you at our residence next Monday evening in order that you might view the accommodation. Hoping to have the pleasure of welcoming yourself and your family as neighbours, I am,

Yours, very truly, Madame Hosten

TUESDAY, 2 AUGUST – FONTAINEBLEAU
As arranged, I called on Madame Hosten on Rue Saint-Dominique, in order to view the apartment. A maid in a day gown of worked muslin answered the door and was about to speak when a huge and somewhat imposing woman appeared behind her. She was wearing

THE MANY LIVES & SECRET SORROWS OF JOSEPHINE B.

a fencing mask and carrying a sabre in her hand. 'Who is it?' she asked, removing the mask. Her voice was gentle, in contrast to her stance.

'Madame Beauharnais.' I put forward my card, somewhat nervously, I confess. 'I believe I am expected.'

'What island are *you* from?' the woman exclaimed, recognizing my accent. She put down her sabre. 'No, let me guess. Martinico?'

She was Madame Hosten – and she's from Sainte-Lucie. Her family even knows Father! After showing me the rooms – they are perfect, quite sunny – she invited me into her downstairs parlour for ginger sweets and a glass (or two) of pétépié. We talked for hours.

Her name is Aimée. Although big (huge!), she is graceful in manner, dainty even. She has an acid wit, quite droll. She is thirty – only two years older than I am – widowed, yet managing quite well on her own with three children, two boys aged fifteen and sixteen (serving an apprenticeship in the military), and a girl of twelve, Lucie, still at home. I feel I've found a friend.

1 SEPTEMBER – PARIS

I'm exhausted, we've moved. I've hired a scullery maid, Agathe Rible, a meek creature who stutters. I assure her she has nothing to fear, but she only quakes all the more. Already her trembling has resulted in three glasses shattered.

14 SEPTEMBER

In the Assembly today the King pledged an oath of allegiance to the constitution. Firecrackers have been exploding all afternoon. The Revolution is over!

Alexandre joined us on Rue Saint-Dominique to celebrate. I took his cloak and hat at the door. 'Congratulations,' I said, embracing him. He looked flushed and his breath smelled of brandy. No doubt there had been many toasts proposed at the Jacobin Club.

Eugène came sliding down the banister and jumped into his father's arms. 'You won!'

Alexandre laughed. 'We all won.'

Hortense came leaping down the stairs after her brother, three steps at a time. 'Won what?'

'A constitution,' Eugène told her officiously.

'You must feel proud of what you've accomplished,' I said, upstairs in our new parlour. It had been an exhausting effort, I knew, to craft a constitution – one that gave France the best of two worlds, a Republic with a monarch. 'And relieved.'

'It remains to be seen if the King can actually work with it.' Alexandre tapped tobacco into his pipe, lit it. 'Sharing power will be trying to him, I expect. He was raised to rule his subjects, not to be beholden to them.'

'If he is wise, he will use this opportunity to unite France,' I said.

'Wisdom is not inherent in kingship, regrettably. And now, no doubt, all the Royalist countries will be sending in their troops to save him from this horrifying development . . .'

'You believe there will be war?'

'Undoubtedly.'

'Austria?'

He nodded. '*And* Prussia, *and*—'

There was a sudden clattering on the stairs. Hortense and Eugène burst into the room. They'd caught a frog in the garden. Alexandre and I helped to make a 'home' for the little thing out of a travelling basket. Then, after a meal of mutton, we took the children to the show of paintings at the annual Salon. As we entered the second gallery, there it was: Alexandre's portrait, paired with that of Deputy Robespierre. Eugène and Hortense were of course most pleased, although they fail to comprehend the prestige that attends such an honour. We admired the likeness, which is excellent.

On the way home, we walked along the river, exclaiming as each fire-rocket exploded. Lovers strolled languidly by. The memory of being introduced to Alexandre came back to me then – Alexandre so young, so worldly, so dashing in his white uniform, myself a nervous girl from the Islands, so anxious to please, so willing to offer my heart.

A fire-rocket burst directly overhead. I started, clutched Alexandre's arm. We laughed. The children, their cheeks pink, went running on ahead. A pleasing portrait, I thought: a man, his wife, two children, out for an evening stroll.

FEBRUARY 1792

It's as Alexandre predicted: we've become a country under siege. Austrian and Prussian troops assemble at our borders, preparing to march on Paris, preparing to rescue us from democracy. Preparing to rescue our King.

15 MARCH

I've been overcome with the vapours. Daily I am bled. Hortense and Eugène hover, bringing me drinks of barley-water. Night falls. Alone, I pull myself to my feet, fall to my knees in front of the holy-water stoup. I have not had news from home for over a year. In the silence, fears grow, bloom, take shape.

I resist the cards, resist the temptation to look. But control was never my friend. I dig for them in the writing desk, in the upper corner of the top drawer, next to the bottle of ink. Pretending calm, I lay out the first card.

The Falling Tower: the stones falling, the men tossed and turned as if by some force beyond their control.

I did not need to see the rest: the Wheel of Fortune, Death, the Star turned upside down.

Manette is dead.

I put the cards away.

Manette — dear little one — I see you in the stars, I see you skipping over the boulders in the river. *Wait for me!* you cry out — to me, your big sister. *Wait for me!*

20 APRIL

Paris has become an armed camp. The Church of Saint Thomas Aquinas is being used to assemble munitions: on the pews, guns, muskets, swords, bayonets, even cannon balls are stacked. One sees men with pikes everywhere. Boys too young to fight stand in lines to sign up. Eugène watches them with envy. I pull him away.

21 APRIL

I woke with a feeling of foreboding, so when Alexandre arrived unexpectedly this morning, I felt threatened by vapours. 'You're in uniform.' I heard footsteps in the street, a woman calling out, distant drumbeats. The fear I'd felt on waking was with me still. 'Married men do not have to serve, Alexandre. I don't understand.'

'The Republic is in need of officers.'* Alexandre put his hands on my shoulders. 'Rose, please, don't ask me to go into battle without your blessing.'

It was a solemn moment, broken by the discovery of something wriggling inside Alexandre's greatcoat. I cried out. Alexandre drew an animal out of his pocket – a horrid-looking pug, no bigger than a rodent. It had a fawn-coloured body and a black head. 'It's a King Charles,' he said. It squirmed out of his hands on to the rug. It was sniffing at my feet, making snorting noises, as if it couldn't breathe. 'A dog like this is worth ten louis,' Alexandre said proudly.

I called for Agathe, my timid chambermaid, but she wouldn't go near it – it looked too much like a rat. 'It's only a puppy,' I chided her, picking the little thing up and heading for the children's room, motioning for Alexandre to follow.

'Is it a dog?' Eugène asked, examining its corkscrew tail.

'Does it bite?' Hortense this time, holding out her hand to it. She squealed when it licked her. It growled. 'Is it hungry?'

'Can we keep it?' Eugène asked.

Alexandre looked at me: would I?

I held out my hand to the little thing. It licked and nipped me, its teeth harmless but sharp. Its nose was flat, pushed into its face. It was a repulsive creature – yet it charmed me. 'Fortuné. That's what we will call him.'

I do not need to say more. We – Alexandre, the children and I – passed the morning together most enjoyably. When we bid him farewell, it was with regret. I gave him a stone I'd had since childhood, a talisman.

'I will keep it with me always.' He hesitated at the door as we were parting. 'May I kiss you, Rose?'

'Say yes, Maman!' Eugène exclaimed.

I embraced my husband.

* Before the Revolution, all officers had been aristocrats. When the Revolution came, most fled. There were few men left in France who had been trained to lead an army, fewer still with any experience.

'May God be with you!' Hortense cried out as Alexandre passed through the gate. She burst into tears.

'Come now,' I chided, drying her cheeks, 'a soldier's daughter must not weep.' Nor a soldier's wife.

In which we are at war

23 APRIL 1792
There is a curfew in Paris now. By ten the city is dark, silent but for
the sound of the guards' boots on the cobblestones and cats fighting
in the alleyways. From somewhere I hear a church bell ring out one
note, a lovely, melancholy sound – and so rare now. Most church
bells have been melted down for munitions.

25 April 1792 – Valenciennes
Dear Rose,

I have been assigned to General Biron's staff. Only a fraction
of the available troops have been assembled here for fear of
risking the safety of the fortified towns. The result is that
the war plans are to be executed with very small numbers.
On learning this, I had a will made up. I am forwarding
it on to you, sealed. It is not to be opened until such
time as . . .

Your husband, Alexandre Beauharnais

2 May 1792 – Valenciennes
Dear Rose,

Forgive me for alarming you. And thank you for your
prayers. If I'm to die of anything, it will most likely be
frustration. How am I to make soldiers of these farm boys?
When they get hungry, bored or have a little fright they take
up their muskets and head home.

Give the children my love. I keep your talisman with
me always.

Your husband, Alexandre Beauharnais

4 May

Alexandre has been in battle against the Austrians. His conduct was praised in the *Moniteur*. Proudly, I showed the article to the children. We have attached a large map to the wall of the dining area where we trace his progress. We are also making a book of clippings from the journals, which is already thick, for the *Moniteur* publishes articles about Alexandre's patriotism daily.

17 May

Alexandre sends letters which he instructs me to burn. The revolutionary armies are small, he confides, ill-equipped and untrained. Suspicion rules. The troops do not trust their officers, the officers do not trust their troops. One general was forced to call off a bayonet charge because his troops voted against it, another was murdered by his own men. *By his own men.* Grand Dieu.

Tuesday, 19 June

This evening I heard a commotion. I looked out: the streets were jammed with horses, carts filled with possessions. What had happened? I ran downstairs to Aimée's suite.

'Oh, the King has everyone upset,' she sighed, stretching out on the chaise with remarkable calm. She was in her white fencing clothes, her sabre on the floor.

Her chambermaid appeared at the door, carrying a portmanteau. 'I'll be needing my pay.'

Aimée gave me a disgusted look. 'They're all in a panic, every last one of them.' Reluctantly she went to her writing desk.

'Others have left?' I asked.

The chambermaid cursed. 'The Austrians march towards Paris and our own King is going to open the gates wide to let the butchers in! Well, I won't be here!'

Aimée offered the woman paper money but she insisted on coin.

'There goes another one,' Aimée sighed when the door slammed shut. 'Let's get out the brandy.'

21 June

My chambermaid woke me this morning with excitement in her

voice. 'There was trouble last night.' Agathe handed me a bowl of hot chocolate. 'The palace was invaded!'

'Invaded?'

'The people ran in, took over.' She wasn't stuttering.

'Agathe, explain, please.'

Slowly I got the story. Yesterday's feast-day festivities had turned to violence in the night. A mob of men and women had invaded the palace, demanding that the King bring in troops to protect Paris from the Austrians.

'Is the Queen safe?' I asked. 'The children?'

Agathe looked at me suspiciously. I realized my mistake. One should never show sympathy for the royal family, especially not for the Queen.

28 JUNE

Agathe insists that the Queen is plotting to burn down the Assembly while all the deputies are in it, that muskets and gunpowder are stored in the basements of all the nunneries. And now Hortense will no longer eat bread. 'I might die,' she said, for Agathe told her the priests plan to murder everyone by poisoning the holy bread.

'Mademoiselle Agathe told you that?'

Hortense looked at me with a horrified expression. 'Maman, it is *Citoyenne* Agathe now, not Mademoiselle.'

My daughter, the revolutionary. Now she refuses to speak during meals. It's the patriotic way.

MONDAY, 2 JULY

Aimée and I went to the Comédie-Italienne to see *Unforeseen Events* with Madame Dugazon playing the soubrette. Princess Amalia had offered us the use of her loge.

'The Queen is expected to be there,' Aimée said.

'I didn't think the Queen went out to the theatre any more,' I said. She'd let all her loges go months ago, something people held against her.

'There's been pressure on her to make an appearance.'

Our loge was directly across from the one the royal family was to use. There was applause when Her Majesty entered, accompanied by her children – the Dauphin, a sweet-faced boy of about seven, and Madame Royale, almost a young woman now. The King's sister Madame Elizabeth and another woman, the children's governess, I guessed, were also with her.

Throughout the performance I watched the Queen's face. It was hard to believe she was only in her thirties, she looked so very aged. The Dauphin, a charming child dressed in the regimentals of the nation, sat on her lap. Now and again the Queen kissed the top of his head. He kept gazing up at her face – he seemed perplexed by her tears.

In the third act, the soubrette and the valet sang a duet. In it Madame Dugazon exclaimed: '*Ah! Comme j'aime ma maîtresse!*' looking directly at the Queen. Three men in pantaloons jumped up on the stage and threatened the singer.

The Queen's guard hurried the Queen and her entourage out of the theatre. It was, of course, impossible to continue the performance after that.

THURSDAY, 19 JULY
The Austrians have cut off supplies to Paris – we are entirely without. We whisper – not of gossip, but of grain: where it might be found. (Those who know stay silent.) Every day there are riots for food.

Santerre, Commander of the National Guards, has proposed that all dogs and cats be disposed of, arguing that the food they eat would be better directed towards people.

'What about *pain bénit*?' Agathe argued. Every Sunday, thousands of loaves of bread are blessed by the priests and left uneaten. 'And what about hair loaded with flour powder? What about that!'

My timid maid is timid no longer.

SUNDAY, 22 JULY
The warning cannon on the Pont-Neuf has been firing every hour. An hour ago a man on horseback, an official caller, yelled out in the street, '*La patrie en danger! La patrie en danger!*'

The Austrians are coming . . .

The streets are clogged with carriages. Everyone is trying to get

out of Paris, but it is impossible – the gates have been closed!
Nobody is allowed in; no one allowed out. We are trapped.

8 AUGUST

I have not slept for a week. It's so hot Agathe claims she saw the
river boiling. Each day I try to get passes to get out of Paris, but
have been unable. The gates are *still* closed!

10 AUGUST

Last night masses of people were in the streets. The children were
sent home from school this morning. Then, at around nine this
evening, just as Frédéric, the Princess, Aimée and I prepared to
sit down to supper together, the tocsins began to ring.

Frédéric was intent on going to see what was happening. Aimée,
Princess Amalia and I tried to dissuade him, but he insisted. Aimée
offered him her sabre.

'No, it would look too aristocratic,' Frédéric said, taking a meat
cleaver instead.

It was almost two in the morning when he returned. The tocsins
were still ringing. There was talk of a demonstration at the Palace
at daybreak.

'*Another* demonstration?' I asked.

'Who is calling it?' the princess asked.

'The Commune.' Frédéric's cheeks were pink. Vats of wine had
been set in the street in front of the section house.

'For what purpose?' I feared the Commune.*

'To arrest the King.'

Arrest the King?

I took a seat. I could not comprehend. Arrest the King? But the
King *was* the law.

The tocsins began ringing again at dawn. I went to the window,

---

* The Commune was the municipal government of the city of Paris. Conflicts
arose because the city government, which tended to be radical (urban-based), felt
that the conservative (rural-based) national government was not doing enough to
protect Paris. The Commune, therefore, felt justified in taking control.

pulled back the curtains. A group of men, ruffians, were in the street, two carrying pikes. One was wearing the blue tunic of a dockman of Marseille. He saw me at the window and screamed, 'Death to the aristocrats!'

I backed away from view. From far away I could hear the faint sound of a musket being fired, followed by grapeshot.

Somewhere, a battle had begun.

LATER THAT EVENING
The Commune has taken over. Hundreds have been killed, hundreds more arrested.

'We've *got* to get out,' I whispered to Aimée. 'Get the children out.' But how? Who could we trust?

'I've heard that there's a place by the Allée des Invalides, near the Boulevard, where the wall is low. Maybe we could get over there.'

'Climb over?' We would have to run through fields in the dark. Eugène and Lucie might be able to, but Hortense . . . ?

No matter how we think it through, it's too dangerous. So we're staying, preparing for the worst.

In which I take desperate measures

MONDAY, 13 AUGUST 1792

I was on the balcony when a coach and four pulled into the courtyard. A footman helped lift an elderly woman down. I could not make out her face under the hood of her cape.

A short time later, Agathe brought me a calling card scented with lavender. It was the Comtesse de Montmorin, whose elegant fêtes at the castle in Fontainebleau had so charmed me, whose dear clumsy husband, Comte Luce de Montmorin, the governor of the castle, I'd found so endearing. Why would she be calling on *me*? I wondered, untying my morning cap and reaching for a wig.

The Comtesse's trembling hand clasped mine. 'Comte de Montmorin has been arrested — by the Commune!'

'Your husband?'

'They've confused him with Monsieur Armand de Montmorin, the Minister of Foreign Affairs!'

Bungling, forgetful, sweet old Comte Luce de Montmorin — how could anyone have mistaken him for a diplomat? 'Which prison?' I asked, shaken.

'The Abbaye.'

The *Abbaye* — it was but a short distance from our home; Eugène, Hortense and I had walked by it the day before. All the windows had been boarded over.

'Nobody knows anything! I am desperate. To whom can I turn?'

FRIDAY, 17 AUGUST

Finally, a response from the Tribunal Jury that has been set up to review the arrests of 10 August. I've been granted an audience this coming Monday with Citoyen Botot, one of the seven directors. I have notes scattered all over the dining-room table, formulating arguments, pleas. My bed is covered with gowns pulled from the cupboard in an effort to select a suitable ensemble. What does one wear when begging a life?

18 AUGUST
This morning, as I entered the kitchen, I thought I saw Agathe hastily shove something under the counter. Later, I went to look. It was a pamphlet, official in its presentation, written by an unwhiskered patriot. It claimed that a plot had been uncovered to assassinate the good citizens of Paris during the night of 2 September to come. According to the pamphlet, this treacherous scheme is to be carried out by aristocrats and priests with the help of those in the prisons, whom the aristocrats and priests intend to set free.

A fabrication, surely. Yet who would promote such a lie? Who would promote such *fear*?

MONDAY, 20 AUGUST, LATE AFTERNOON, 3.30 P.M.
Citoyen Botot is a tall, baby-faced older gentleman with a smug, well-fed look. I felt I had met him before.

'I used to sell dental water on Rue des Noyers,' he said. He spoke with a hint of a lisp.

L'eau de Botot – of course. 'I consulted you years ago,' I said.

'Did my remedy help?'

'Yes,' I lied.

'My uncle invented it,' he said proudly.

He was sympathetic about Comte Luce de Montmorin's mistaken identity but informed me there was little he could accomplish alone. He suggested I attend a reception being held at the home of Deputy Paul Barras in four days. Several members of the Tribunal Jury would be there, he said.

'But I have not even been introduced to Deputy Barras,' I said.

'It will be my honour to do so,' Citoyen Botot assured me.

TUESDAY, 21 AUGUST
Agathe came back from market today flushed with excitement. She'd

seen a man's head cut off – by guillotine.* 'The crowd booed!' she said, her pallid complexion pink. 'It was over too quickly.'

23 AUGUST
The children came running into the parlour this afternoon much in a fright. They had heard that our troops to the east had fallen to the Austrians.

'Is it Father?' Eugène asked.

I assured him no, his father was safe.

'But what about us!' Hortense cried.

'It's not the *Austrians* you should fear,' Agathe hissed. 'It's the priests and aristocrats in the prisons who will hold the knife to your heart as you sleep.'

Hortense began to wail. It took some effort to calm her.

'Dismiss Agathe,' Aimée insisted later that night. We were sitting in our little garden sipping claret, watching the moon and the stars come out.

'It's too dangerous. I dare not.' Many, now, are betrayed to the authorities by their domestics.

FRIDAY, 24 AUGUST
Tonight, the reception at Deputy Barras's. Princess Amalia has offered to lend me one of her beautiful gowns. I have taken a herbal remedy in an attempt to calm the fluxations of my stomach. I must go, whatever my condition.

EVENING
Citoyen Botot and I were shown into an elegantly furnished entryway hung with Gobelin tapestries. An older man of about forty approached us, trailing a sword. He walked with the studied

* Beheading, formerly the privilege of the aristocratic class, was made available to all social classes by means of the guillotine. It was created by Dr Guillotin, who died of grief over the abuse to which his humanitarian invention had been put.

grace of a ballet instructor. He embraced Citoyen Botot, caressed his cheek. 'And who is this lovely lady you've brought for me, François?' With a theatrical flourish, Deputy Barras kissed my hand.

'Ah – the famous Deputy Barras.' I dropped a deep curtsy.

'I hate to think what I might be famous *for*.' He smiled, removing his gold-rimmed lorgnon from his right eye. A diamond on his middle finger caught the light. He was wearing skin-tight yellow silk breeches, high black riding boots and lace everywhere – *very* Ancien Régime. Hardly the revolutionary I had expected, from all I had heard.

'Are there so very many possibilities?' I asked. He smelled strongly of spirit of ambergris.

'Innumerable.' By the light of the torches his face was angular, sculpted, with high cheekbones. A sensitive-looking man with sorrowful, puppy-dog eyes. 'My dear Botot,' he said, taking my arm, 'would you be offended if perhaps *I* introduced this lady to my guests?'

As we entered the parlour, I paused to admire a painting by Greuze.

'Later I will show you my collection,' Deputy Barras said. 'I have an eye for beauty—'

'A weakness, some call it,' Botot whispered.

Deputy Barras smiled, a boyish lopsided grin that was rather endearing. 'Speaking of beauty, I see you are wearing one of Citoyenne Deperret's creations,' he said, noting the intricate lace-and-ribbon design on the shoulder of my gown. 'A brilliant designer, but temperamental, I've been told.'

'She *is* brilliant,' I said. I dared not reveal I had borrowed the ensemble.

Throughout the evening Deputy Barras was quite attentive. (I suspect him of being more interested in the show of seduction than seduction itself.) After the third toast to the Republic I was sufficiently emboldened to express my concerns regarding Comte de Montmorin's arrest. I was encouraged by Deputy Barras's response – more than the dismissive 'We'll see', in any case. He made a point of introducing me to four members of the Tribunal Jury who were present. By the deference they paid Deputy Barras, I could see that it would be wise to cultivate his friendship . . . and no hardship, certainly. He amuses me.

TUESDAY, 28 AUGUST

Tonight it begins. No carriages, no horses on the streets after nine. A crier on horseback proclaimed that the searches would begin at midnight.

What do we have to hide? Aimée burned a quantity of love letters. She read the more private passages out loud before throwing them into the fire. 'I wish I had love letters to burn,' I said. Alexandre's letters are more like sermons, extolling the virtues of the Republic.

'Leave his out where the authorities can see them,' Aimée said.

Agathe watched us furtively and suddenly I wondered: is my chambermaid a spy?

29 AUGUST

It was after one in the morning when the search party came, a group of twelve men pounding on the door. The leader was a Citoyen Wimpfen, a vendor of skins I remembered seeing at our section office. They went through our rooms, insisting that we wake the children so that they could search their beds, stabbing the fur coverlets with their daggers.

Aimée offered them old wine in a decanter and cold river pike. 'You'll need this for the hard night's work ahead, citoyens,' she told them, pouring out generous glasses which flushed them finely. She is good at this. As for myself, I was afraid they would perceive my trembling.

29 August 1792
Citoyenne Beauharnais:
    Regarding the arrest and imprisonment of Citoyen Montmorin, you have been granted a hearing before the jury in one week, on the fourth day of September, at three in the afternoon.

Citoyen Botot
Director, Tribunal Jury

THURSDAY, 30 AUGUST

Thousands more have been arrested – clerics, priests, aristocrats. 'We're next,' Aimée said, strapping on her fencing mask.

28 August 1792 – Valenciennes

Dear Rose,

I have been promoted to maréchal de camp at Strasbourg. I depart tomorrow. I do not know how long it will take to get there as I will be inspecting the garrison towns en route. Do not worry, I have an excellent horse.

Give my love to the children.

Your husband, Alexandre Beauharnais

2 SEPTEMBER

Austrian troops are a two-day march from Paris. Panic has taken the city. In a back room, on a small oak table, Aimée and I assemble weapons: a meat cleaver, Aimée's fencing sabre, Commander du Braye's pistol. I touch the cold metal, imagine the worst. Could I? Would I?

MONDAY, 3 SEPTEMBER, EVENING

Eugène's birthday, his eleventh. The sound of the tocsins filled the air, the slow passing of the hours marked by cannon.

I pulled the curtains and forbade the children to look out. Calmly I proceeded, pinning up ribbons in celebration of birth, reciting prayers to ward off death. Daggers ever at the ready, I went about the day: children fed, linen mended, bedclothes aired. In little ways one conquers fear.

But now, the children asleep, I wait by the window and watch, listen and wait, the pistol on the table before me. In the dark, fear rules. What would I do if attacked? Would I have the courage to take a life? How are such things done?

4 SEPTEMBER

It was two, perhaps three in the morning, when I heard faint laughter and went to the window. The stars and the moon hovered over the city. Tranquillity, I thought, but then, in the dark I saw flickers of light moving. The city was vibrant with flambeaux.

Two boys appeared in the street below, laughing with drunken pleasure.

I looked closer.

They pulled, they pulled, they staggered and fell, they laughed and pulled again.

What was it they pulled?

It was then that I saw. It was the body of a man they were dragging, his long legs white, naked under a black habit – a priest.

I retched and turned, I gasped for air.

As soon as the sky lightened, I changed into my street clothes, pinned on my cockade. I set out for the Rue de Lille. Frédéric was a member of the National Guard. He would know.

It was Princess Amalia who received me, in spite of the early hour. She, too, had not slept. She led me into the garden where she invited me to sit under a blooming acacia. There, in a setting of peace and beauty, she told me what had transpired in the night. The men and women in the prisons had been slaughtered.

I felt faint. 'The Comte de Montmorin? He is in the Abbaye—'

Princess Amalia took my hand.

Mon Dieu. I had had an appointment to go before the jury that very afternoon. And now it was too late.

It was then that the princess told me that she and Frédéric were planning to escape France.

'But how? The gates, the guards . . .'

'Frédéric has been able, at great cost, to get passes to Saint-Martin. From there we believe we can get to England.'

England. The enemy. But who was the enemy now? The enemy was everywhere.

'You'll . . . you'll lose everything.' Their estate, the Hôtel de Salm, everything they owned would be taken by the state, everything but the clothes on their backs.

'Everything but our lives.'

'Take us with you.' The words leapt from me without thinking. 'Me and the children.' It was a terrible and fearful thing to do, a terrible and fearful thing to ask someone to do, but I was obsessed with one thought only: to get Hortense and Eugène out of France, to safety.

'Oh, Rose, we couldn't. It's impossible. You would need a passport.'

'The children, then.' Tears came to my eyes. 'You could pretend they were your own.'

She reached for me, alarmed. 'Rose?'

I began to tremble.

Princess Amalia looked up at the sky. She took a breath. 'Yes.'

Aimée and Lucie were in the hall when I entered. I looked away.

'Is something amiss?' Aimée put down her market basket.

'I'm not feeling well,' I said. Princess Amalia and Frédéric were leaving at dawn. I'd promised not to tell. In any case, I did not want to. I feared complications, logic – truth. I feared guilt, for thinking only of my own. I hurried up the stairs.

Eugène greeted me with a hug. Hortense ran in with a drawing she had just made. They seemed so very young. A terrible feeling began to rise up in me.

'Maman?' Eugène asked.

I gathered strength. 'I have news. I've arranged for a holiday for you both, with Frédéric and Princess Amalia.' I had to see this through, and calmly, I knew. Otherwise I would alarm them.

Eugène appeared pleased. I was relieved.

'But I want to go to school,' Hortense said.

'There are no more schools. Remember? The schools have all been closed.'*

'You're not coming?' Hortense's voice had that high quavering pitch.

I took her in my arms. 'I will join you soon,' I lied. I kissed the top of her head. Don't cry, I told myself. Don't cry!

It is midnight now. The light from the lamp burns low. I curl strands of the children's hair round my fingers, press them into a locket. Eugène's curls round my finger easily; Hortense's is fine and straight, it defies confinement.

They are sleeping. Eugène is sprawled across his bed, all long

* Two weeks earlier (18 August 1792), all religious institutions had been closed by the state. This included most of the schools, which had been run by the Church.

SANDRA GULLAND

legs and arms. He sleeps soundly, without movement. I do not fear for him.

It is Hortense who still needs me, Hortense who will suffer. She is curled in a tense ball, her face frozen into a frown even in sleep. I thank God that Eugène will be with her. He has heart enough for us all.

5 SEPTEMBER

It was dawn when we set out, Eugène and I taking turns carrying the canvas haversack. I tried to maintain a festive attitude. The coach and four were in the prince and princess's courtyard, waiting. The driver was not in livery and the family crests had been painted over for fear of drawing attention.

Poor Frédéric was flustered. He couldn't get his sword to tie properly. Eugène helped him. Then the children and I sat down, out of the way, while the princess supervised the packing. So much had been stuffed into a trunk that the valet was unable to close the lid. Princess Amalia was obliged to take a number of robes out.

At last they were ready. I helped the children into the coach. I kissed them and closed the door. The driver cracked his whip, the horses pulled forward. Hortense waved. Eugène pressed his lips to the glass, to make a funny face.

That was the last.

Quickly I headed home. Nearing the Church of Saint Thomas Aquinas, I heard a child singing, a melancholy soprano much like Hortense's sweet voice. I stopped.

I would light a candle, I thought, say a prayer . . . a prayer for safe journey, for my children, but within the dark chapel my intention was thwarted. Labourers were dismantling church ornaments. In a corner a table had been set up and a line of young men had formed: army recruits. At the pews at the front a cleric and several old women were sorting army uniforms.

I stood in the archway, confused.

Two of the labourers moved by me, carrying a heavy statue of the Madonna between them. 'Pardon,' one said. They loaded the statue on to a handcart and began to pull it away. The labourer in the blue tunic waved to me, as if in a procession.

I recalled Hortense waving. *Goodbye. Goodbye, Maman.*

For how long?

For ever?

A feeling of panic came over me. I fell to my knees. The cleric and one of the old women came to my aid. The cleric supported me as best he could to a pew, urging me to rest. 'I must go.' I pulled away.

I do not remember making my way to Rue Saint-Dominique. I do not remember climbing the stairs. All I remember is standing at the door to the children's room. Scattered all over the floor were Eugène's toy soldiers. One of Hortense's dolls was slumped in a corner.

'Oui?' Agathe was bent over Eugène's bed, as if to straighten it. There was a hollow in the pillow, where Eugène's head had been.

'No!'

Agathe looked at me in confusion.

'Please.' Softly this time; I had alarmed her. 'Don't.' I reached for the door handle to steady myself.

'I'm not to make up the bed?'

'Not just now.' My voice was quavering.

Agathe regarded me with suspicion. 'I see.' She backed away.

I closed the door behind us, turned the key, took a breath. I would have them with me still, their familiar disorder, their rumpled bedclothes – their scent, the imprint of their bodies on the pillows . . . evidence, of their existence.

In which I become a good Republican

8 September 1792
Aimée is horrified by what I've done.

'I *had* to!'

'You could have at least talked it over with me.'

The truth was, I had been afraid to tell her, afraid she'd try to talk me out of it. Afraid she'd say: what about Lucie? What about *my* daughter?

'I promised not to tell.'

'Rose, don't you see? This puts you in such peril!' she ranted, close to tears. 'And what about Alexandre? I hate to think what's going to happen to *him* when the authorities find out.'

Alexandre – *mon Dieu*.

Sunday, 16 September
Rain, and more rain. I spent the morning in bed, listening to the crackling of the fire, the steady dripping of the rain on the roof, alone with my sad thoughts, a devouring ennui.

At around eleven I must have fallen asleep, for I was dreaming of home, of the salty water of the bay, the tangle of the mangroves . . . I awoke with a start. Outside, on the street, I heard a child's voice, a girl's bubbling giggle. How cruel, I thought, for a child so like Hortense to call at my window.

I heard the impatient prance of a horse's hooves on the cobblestones, the front door open, a boy's voice. Was it possible? I went to the landing, clinging to the railing for support. There, in the entryway looking up at me, were Hortense and Eugène.

'Maman!' They clattered up the stairs and into my arms. I clasped them hard, disbelieving. They were confused – and perhaps a little uneasy – by the intensity of my welcome, my tears.

'Father wrote a letter for us to come back,' Hortense explained. She seemed pleased by this.

'Alexandre?'

Princess Amalia came in the front hallway. Frédéric was behind her, looking harassed. He was wearing his National Guard uniform, now tight on him. I motioned to them to be cautious, for Agathe had come to the landing with a basket of linen.

'Would you like Agathe to make you a hot chocolate?' I asked the children. They followed her happily down into the kitchen. I opened the double sash doors to the parlour. Princess Amalia and Frédéric followed me in, Frédéric checking to make sure there was no one behind the curtains. I closed the doors behind me. 'What *happened*?' I whispered.

'We received a letter by courier close to Saint-Paul,' Princess Amalia said in a hushed voice, taking off her feathered hat. Her heavily powdered hair was dressed in an elaborate pouf. 'From Alexandre. He demanded that the children be returned to Paris at once.' She took a document out of her basket and handed it to me. 'It arrived two days before we were to depart for England.'

'Alexandre sent you this?' I sank on to the sofa. 'How did he find out?'

'*You* didn't inform him?' Princess Amalia glanced at her brother. 'We thought . . .'

'Is it possible the government knows?' I asked.

'They have spies everywhere,' Frédéric said bitterly.

I didn't know what to think. I was overwhelmed with joy to see Hortense and Eugène again, yet alarmed by the perilous situation into which they had been returned. 'But *you* could have gone on to England,' I told them.

'Someone had to accompany the children,' Princess Amalia explained.

'There was no one we could trust,' Frédéric said.

It wasn't until they had left that the enormity of Alexandre's action struck me. The lives of our children, of dear Frédéric and Princess Amalia, have been put at risk. I penned Alexandre a letter of rage and regret. I watch as it burns in the fire.

SANDRA GULLAND

21 September 1792 – Strasbourg

Rose,

How can you say that I do not understand the situation in Paris! I understand it clearly: the Parisians were overcome with an irrational panic. The Austrians would never have attacked! But even so, to send the children to England? Can you imagine what that would have meant to my career? As a former aristocrat, daily I am required to submit proof of my loyalty.

Your much enraged and offended husband, Alexandre

FRIDAY, 21 SEPTEMBER

Aimée is intent on my safety. 'You're to become a good citoyenne, a model Republican.' She's put a red cap and a worsted linen cockade by the door – not even a silk cockade will do – 'for *whenever* you go out'.

I groaned.

She took the liberty of suggesting that I find a less attractive cape to wear in the streets. 'Any show of wealth is dangerous,' she said. 'Even clean *linen*.' She gave me a cape she'd found in a used clothing shop. It is worn and patched, an unbecoming dirty yellow. 'Perfect. You look horrible.'

SATURDAY, 22 SEPTEMBER

The new Republic dawned wet and dreary. The streets are crowded with people milling about in the rain, sharing wine, singing, celebrating the new Era of Liberty. Dressed in Roman tunics, ragged old army uniforms, mouldy court gowns, they link arms and roam from one neighbourhood to the next.

Aimée has cluttered the front parlour with revolutionary newspapers and magazines. 'For our salon,' she explained.

'*Our* salon?'

'Every Tuesday evening, revolutionaries welcome,' she said, scratching out a guest list. 'They're a rowdy bunch – it might even be amusing.'

26 SEPTEMBER

Our 'salon' was a success. There were seventeen guests. Fanny arrived first (looking fashionably rustic). She came with Michel de Cubières (looking fat), her daughter Marie (looking thin) and a Citoyen Lestaing (looking wealthy), a mulatto widower from Saint-Domingue who appeared to be on more than friendly terms with Marie. (Everyone pretended not to be shocked.)

Marie informed me that she has filed for a divorce from François under the new law. 'It's easy!' She was wearing a working woman's cap with an enormous tricolour cockade stuck to the front. 'When are you going to divorce Alexandre?'

'I hadn't thought of it,' I said. In spite of everything, I still felt Alexandre *was* my husband – the father of my children.

A number of deputies had been invited, including Deputy Barras, who arrived in the company of Citoyen Botot and Deputy Tallien, all of them in spirits.

Deputy Barras kissed my hand. 'Citoyenne Beauharnais,' he said, his big eyes mournful. 'I regretted learning of your friend's . . .'

Citoyen Botot looked equally stricken. 'The timing . . .' he lisped. He shrugged.

'I have been meaning to write to you both,' I said, 'to thank you for your help.'

'Should aging libertines be trusted in the company of a lady?' a young man in a red frock coat interrupted. Inordinately tall with a bristly head, he moved like a cat.

'Did your mother give you permission to go out tonight, Tallien?' Deputy Barras asked, setting up a table for cards. Citoyen Botot laughed.

'Deputy Tallien is *Secretary* of the Commune?' I asked Aimée later, when I had a chance. 'But he's so young.' Although gentle in appearance, his manner is one of a gay blade: sarcastic, irreverent, a bit of a wit.

'Hardly five and twenty, the son of a valet. But comely, is he not? And educated, apparently. His father's master made the mistake of educating him. I'm told he quotes Plutarch as well as any noble. In fact, it's said the master *is* his father. Do you not see something aristocratic in his profile? In his nose? A gentle, good-hearted man, by the *looks* of him, but ruthless, they say – one of the Commissaires. Did you hear about that nineteen-year-old woman from Saint-Denis? Disguised as a delegate, she was apprehended in the Assembly carrying sulphuric acid – intended for his face.'

'He's a Septembrist?' I thought of Luce de Montmorin, his violent death. How could we have invited a *Septembrist* to our home?

'But influential — he'd be the one to ask about passes out of the city for Princess Amalia and Frédéric.' Aimée squeezed my arm. 'It's said he fancies aristocratic women.'

After innumerable toasts to the Republic, I invited Citoyen Tallien to join me in a game of écarté. He has a weakness for gambling, I perceived. I pleased him greatly by losing. After two games (at a cost of seventeen livres) I summoned the courage to put forward my request on behalf of my friends.

'And allow your friend Frédéric to join the army of the enemy?' Tallien responded.

I had to smile.

'Forgive me if I fail to see the humour,' Tallien said.

I explained: 'This is perhaps the first time my friend has been regarded as an asset on the battlefield.' Dear Frédéric had a reputation for being a coward. He had even had the dishonour to be dismissed from the volunteer National Guard.

Levity or no, Tallien said he doubted that passports could be obtained.

'But there *must* be a way.' Were it not for me, Frédéric and Princess Amalia would be in England now, they would be safe.

30 September 1792 — Strasbourg
Rose,
    How can you accuse me of valuing my own safety over that of my children! I would die for them! And as for Amalia and Frédéric, they are better off in Paris.

                                                            Alexandre

2 OCTOBER
This afternoon I went to Deputy Tallien's office, to ask him once again about passports for Frédéric and Princess Amalia. I was kept waiting for some time. He was working on the layout of *L'Ami des citoyens*, the revolutionary news-sheet he publishes, he explained when finally he consented to speak to me. He had a deadline to meet, he said.

'Some other time?' I inquired, making the bold step of inviting him to supper.

'Perfect,' Aimée said when I told her, offering to keep Eugène and Hortense in her apartment for the night.

THAT EVENING

Deputy Tallien is gone; my virtue intact. Tarnished, perhaps, but unbreached.

We spent the evening together, sharing two bottles of wine, which Deputy Tallien clearly enjoys. We played piquet and talked – of the Republic, the constitution, the future. Under a gentle demeanour is a young man who longs to make a difference. He is fervent in his belief in the Revolution, dedicated to a vision of a better world.

'The moderate deputies maintain that the radicals aren't heeding the past,' he said, 'yet the moderates ignore the present. They refuse to see the poverty that surrounds us.'

'It is difficult to understand how one could *not* see it.'

We talked of our families, our hopes and aspirations. 'You are – twenty-four? Twenty-five?' I asked. 'Do you not seek a wife?'

'I seek the wife of a brigadier-general,' he said sweetly.

'You know what I mean.' I smiled.

'I believe I am incapable of the emotion they call love.'

I looked at him, surprised. 'That must be a sad feeling.'

'It is a secure feeling.' He stood to go. 'You've not asked about the passes for your friends.' He pulled a paper out of his waistcoat pocket. 'I've arranged for two to be issued.'

The light from a candle reflected in his eyes. 'You are kind to have done this,' I said.

'Not many call me *kind*.'

'I have another request to make,' I said, made bold by wine. 'Regarding a girl named Anne-Julie de Béthisy, in the Port-Libre prison. She's only nineteen.'* A weeping Marquise de Moulins had contacted me three days earlier about her niece, imprisoned when the girl's family returned from Germany.

---

* Anne-Julie de Béthisy was the cousin of the Abbesse de Penthémont. Rose had been introduced to the girl's aunt, Marquise de Moulins (or Demoulins), in Fontainebleau.

Tallien smiled. 'One gets the impression your list may be long . . .' He leaned towards me.

I stooped suddenly to take up his sword, handed it to him. 'I believe it is time you fell in love,' I said.

He sighed, put a hand to his heart. 'Everyone seeks my downfall.'

I laughed. He left content; I am relieved.

THURSDAY, 4 OCTOBER
Frédéric and Princess Amalia departed this morning, quietly, before I could bid them farewell.

9 OCTOBER
This evening I received a note from Frédéric: *Alas, we're back.*

I hurried to the Hôtel de Salm. Frédéric came to the door. He'd been weeping. 'It's hopeless. We'll perish!'

Princess Amalia entered. She told me what had happened. They'd set out for Amiens, but at a post station near Clermont their papers had been questioned. No amount of persuasion – 'Or gold,' Frédéric interjected – could persuade the station master not to turn them over to the authorities. Fortunately, the precinct commander was more lenient and let them go, provided they returned immediately to Paris.

'And so here we are, in the gayest prison in all of Europe,' Frédéric concluded, waving an embroidered handkerchief through the air. 'At least *here* we may go to the opera.'

FRIDAY, 12 OCTOBER
A military coach pulled into our courtyard this morning.

'Lieutenant Soufflet,' Agathe informed me. 'He has a message from your husband.'

'From Alexandre?'

'*Oui, oui.*' Lieutenant Soufflet remembered to remove his hat. He seemed a boy – no more than fourteen or fifteen. '*Oui,*' yet again. He felt around in his pockets and handed me a letter.

I recognized Alexandre's hand. 'I can no longer trust you. I do not have to remind you of the law.'

'I am to take General Beauharnais's son back to Strasbourg with me.' Lieutenant Soufflet spoke these words resolutely, as if he had been practising.

'Eugène is to go to Strasbourg? With you?'

'*Oui*.'

'Now?'

'*Oui, oui*.'

'Surely there has been a mistake!'

I read the note again. *The law*. As the father, Alexandre could command his children back to the dangers of Paris, entrust his son on a long and perilous journey in the care of a boy, expose him to the dangers of a garrison town. I put the note in my pocket. I understood: I had no choice.

Lieutenant Soufflet and I left to fetch Eugène at the joiner's workshop in the Faubourg Saint-Antoine, where he has been serving as an apprentice, as required by the Commune. The fragrant smell of wood filled the room. Eugène, busy at a table at the back, did not look up.

I explained to Citoyen Quinette the purpose of my call. He called Eugène over and told him he was dismissed. Eugène looked alarmed. He enjoyed his apprenticeship more than he had ever enjoyed school.

'I will explain,' I said.

The large, official coach and the handsome team of horses impressed Eugène, as did the uniform Citoyen Soufflet was wearing, his jaunty hat and long, shiny sword. Eugène brushed the sawdust off his clothes and climbed on to the leather seat.

We returned to Rue Saint-Dominique. It took less than half an hour to prepare. Proudly, Eugène strapped on his sword. Hortense pushed a drawing into his haversack. I checked over the basket of food. 'No eggs?' Agathe went to see if there were any hard-boiled.

Lieutenant Soufflet was growing uneasy. It was time. It was raining so we said our farewells at the door. I feared tears, but was instead startled — and, I admit, saddened — by Eugène's enthusiasm. He was going to join his father at the front. What could be closer to a boy's heart?

In which we grieve for our King

Eugène sends brief, mournful letters. Life in Strasbourg is not as he imagined. Instead of being 'on the front' — in tents and around campfires, which is how he imagined it — he is enrolled in Collège National, a revolutionary boarding school which he loathes even more than the aristocratic ones.

Hortense struggles over a sash she is making for him. She misses him greatly. We all do.

16 NOVEMBER
I have spent most of this week interviewing applicants for the post of governess for Hortense. This afternoon I asked my mantua-maker if she might be interested. Her name is Marie de Lannoy, of the ancient Lannoy family of Flanders (she insists), a homely, vain woman with claims to being an aristocrat. She chatters incessantly, but she can read and I'm desperate. As a former seamstress for the Queen, she will also be able to teach Hortense a trade, fulfilling the legal requirement. She starts next week.

MONDAY, 19 NOVEMBER
'*Mademoiselle* Lannoy, *s'il vous plaît.*' She is stout, with a pockmarked face, buck teeth and bad breath. She has insisted on a bedchamber on the second floor, objecting to the one on the third. Already the cook is cursing, for she sent her mutton chops back three times. No '*tu*' or '*toi*' for this lady, not even to the children, much less to Fortuné, who tried to bite her.

Agathe, our stuttering revolutionary, is the only brave soul among us. She alone refuses to be cowed, boldly addressing her as '*Citoyenne* Lannoy' and taking the liberty of bestowing upon her a vigorous fraternal embrace — much to Mademoiselle Lannoy's obvious discomfort. I confess I was amused.

22 NOVEMBER

Mademoiselle Lannoy will not speak to Agathe. 'I will have nothing to do with a Jacobin,' she told me firmly.

'Must I remind you,' I told her, 'my husband is a Jacobin as well as a brigadier-general in the revolutionary army. We are a *Republican* family.'

I have insisted that she take Hortense to all the revolutionary festivals and allow her to play with the bookseller's children. I sound more patriotic than I am, I confess, but Lannoy's arrogance brings out the revolutionary spirit even in me.

18 November 1792 — Strasbourg

Dear Rose,

Thank you for your 'olive branch' — nor do I want to quarrel. It is important in a time such as ours that all factions be eliminated. We must stand united against the Enemy, against the oppressors of Freedom.

Eugène seems to have adjusted and is showing more of a Republican spirit.

Your husband, Alexandre Beauharnais

MONDAY, 26 NOVEMBER

We've become a house of spies. Agathe spies on Lannoy, Lannoy on Agathe. Hortense spies on them both.

Last week Hortense informed me that Agathe sneaks out after *petit déjeuner* each day — and I've discovered that it is so. Agathe does go out, and furtively so, around ten in the morning. An hour later she is back, her cheeks flushed, her chores undone.

Now I have discovered where it is that she goes. It's the guillotine that draws her, across the river in the Place Louis Quinze – Place de la Révolution now – where daily crowds gather, the vendors selling lemonade, the children playing prisoner's base, the old ladies gossiping as the heads fall.

29 NOVEMBER

This morning I went to my dressmaker on Rue Saint-Honoré. It was with a sinking heart that I saw a cart approaching, three men and a woman on their way to the guillotine, one of the men a youth, really, quite young and weeping, another man doing his best to console him. Five boys were following behind the cart, dancing the farandole.

Shaken, I crossed the street and traced my way back to the palace gardens. There I sought an empty bench under a chestnut tree and sat for a moment, my heart gripped by sorrow. Not far from me, under another chestnut tree, a toy-seller was setting out a tray of tiny guillotines, the kind Hortense and Eugène had often pressed me to buy and I had unpatriotically refused.

I could hear the sounds of the crowd gathering in the Place de la Révolution. Now and then a group would break into song and others would join in and the song would grow in strength and joy. It was a bright and shining morning, and if one could erase the image of the knife, one could not imagine a more innocent festivity.

A cheer sounded and then the cry, 'Long live the Republic!'

A head fallen.

What have we become?

22 November 1792 – Strasbourg

Dear Rose,

Victory has crowned our arms! I was confident my commanding general, the great Custine, would conquer Mainz – but Frankfurt as well! This victory proves the virtue of our cause. Our Republic will carry the banner of Freedom to all the nations of the world, throw off the oppressive yoke of tyranny! This news has made my job of training the new recruits easier. With glory in their hearts they tackle their work with enthusiasm.

Eugène has been ill with a fever, but is now recovering.

Your husband, Alexandre Beauharnais

THE MANY LIVES & SECRET SORROWS OF JOSEPHINE B.

8 December 1792 – Strasbourg

Dear Rose,

Celebration has turned to shame. General Custine's troops were forced to fall back on Mainz, where they are trapped for the winter. Many of my men have deserted. There are rumours that Custine will be arrested as a result. Don't believe what you read in the journals.

Your husband, Alexandre Beauharnais

23 DECEMBER

It was with some difficulty that Hortense and I made our way to Fontainebleau for 'Christmas'. (We dare not call it that now – it is not Christmas we are celebrating, but *Unity*, the official designation.) Most of the horses have been requisitioned for the armies, so the wait for a seat on the post coach was considerable. I thought to hire a hackney but the drivers were charging four times the normal rate, well beyond our means. So when Frédéric and Princess Amalia offered us the use of their coach and four, I accepted.

And so it was that Hortense (with Fortuné), Lannoy and I set off in such fine style. Although Frédéric and Princess Amalia had long ago taken the precaution of painting over the aristocratic emblems, there was no disguising the fine wood inlay around the windows. Was this the reason the officials at Porte-Saint-Martin would not allow us to pass through? Or was it Lannoy's haughty demeanour? Or Fortuné's incessant growling? Whatever the cause, the guard was reluctant to believe that our papers were authentic. We had to turn back and try another gate. The detour added two hours to our journey. By the time we arrived in Fontainebleau we were dangerously chilled.

Aunt Désirée burst into tears upon greeting us – it has been many months since we last saw her and the time has been fraught with worry. The Marquis's beard, which used to be grey, has turned a shocking white.

'Don't call him Marquis,' Aunt Désirée cautioned fretfully. 'It's *citoyen* now.'

I suppressed a smile.

WEDNESDAY, 26 DECEMBER

The King's trial has begun. 'It's an insult!' Lannoy exclaimed. 'The

King can do no wrong!' She is convinced that the compromising papers found in the iron chest were put there intentionally by Jacobins.*

'Pray hold your tongue, Lannoy!' I whispered, urging her to use caution in her expression. It has been made a crime punishable by death to show support for royalty. 'A governess needs her head.'

'Fig,' she exclaimed. 'Fig, I say.'

She has certain endearing ways, but one has to look for them.

LATER

This evening I was visited by a market woman, a *poissarde*. The scent of attar of roses gave me pause. In the parlour, she let down her hood. It was Fanny. 'Why are you in disguise?' I asked, alarmed.

'I've come to warn you,' she hissed, motioning me to be silent. 'François has fled. He tried to free the King.'

'Mon Dieu.' I lowered myself on to a chair. '*Free* the King? From the Temple?' I mouthed these words.

Fanny nodded, taking a pencil and paper out of her basket. *He was part of a group*, she wrote. *A conspiracy*.

I was so stunned by this news I could hardly comprehend. Alexandre's elder brother, cautious, quiet, honourable François, had taken the ultimate gamble, the one flamboyant, desperate act of a hero. He had risked his life to free the King.

Fanny pushed another scrap of paper into my hand. *He's gone over to Germany – to join the émigré army at Koblenz!*

I threw the notes into the fire. Would François and Alexandre bear arms against one another then? Would they carry their quarrel unto death?

I heard a door close in the hall. Agathe. I motioned to Fanny to be cautious.

Fanny held out her hand. In it was a gem, a diamond. The lights danced against her skin. 'I will take only metal coin, citoyenne,' she said loudly, showing a command of a market accent I did not know

* On 2 November, secret correspondence between the King and the Austrians was discovered in a locked iron chest hidden behind a wooden wall panel in the Tuileries Palace.

she possessed. (Had I not been in such a state of alarm, I might have found it amusing.)

'Is it genuine?' I asked, loud enough to be heard. 'What are you asking for it?'

'Not half its value.'

'You talked to François?' I whispered when I could be sure that we were alone again.

Fanny nodded. 'He came to say goodbye to Émilie. He gave me a letter to give to his father. I am going to try to get out to Fontainebleau tonight. The Marquis must be warned.'

Of course. We would all be under suspicion now. 'But *how*?' The barriers had been closed all week.

Fanny glanced towards the hall. 'I know a sewing woman who lives by a break in the wall,' she whispered, 'once used by smugglers.'

I heard soft footsteps in the hall again. 'And so, my good woman, how much *do* you want for this?'

Fanny scribbled something on a piece of paper: *I'm going into hiding.*

The harsh reality of our lives came home to me then. It was possible — I could not admit to the fact that it was even *likely* — that I might never see Fanny again. The tears I'd been fighting overwhelmed me.

Fanny put the diamond in my hand, pinched my cheek and was gone.

15 January 1793 — Strasbourg
Dear Rose,

I am shocked and appalled to learn of my brother's defection. The enemies of the Revolution are too cowardly to face the problems of our day; they look, instead, to the past, to the Age of Chivalry, the Crusades, fancying emigration a modern Crusade. They claim the King is in danger of being guillotined. Absurd! The rage of Europe would be heaped upon us! How foolish do they imagine us to be? They insist that in taking up arms against their own countrymen, they act honourably. They delude themselves!

François has put the entire family in danger, cast the stain of the traitor over us all. I fear he might try to contact my father. If a letter is received, it *must* be turned over unopened to the officials at the section office. Make sure he and Désirée understand the importance of this.

My brother's inheritance, all his property and possessions, will be confiscated now, of course, leaving Marie and their daughter Émilie penniless. It goes without saying that Émilie's prospects for a good marriage have been for ever dashed.

I can't believe it has come to this . . . I close in despair,

Your husband, Alexandre Beauharnais

TUESDAY, 15 JANUARY 1793
The King has been found guilty – of *treason*. Lannoy is profoundly indisposed. We've been giving her hysteric water to revive her.

'Will they kill him?' Hortense asks. 'Will they take his head?'

I assure her no. However much the French love liberty, we hold our good King Louis dear.

17 JANUARY
I was at my perfumer's shop on the Rue Neuve des Petits Champs when I heard some commotion on the street. A caller on horseback cried out: 'The King must die! The King must die!'

I turned to the shopkeeper. She burst into tears and ran from the shop. I walked out of the door into the brilliant winter sun. Others, too, lined the street. We looked at one another in shocked silence. Our *King* must die?

21 JANUARY
The drums began at dawn. I closed the curtains, but I could not keep out the sound.

Lannoy stayed in her room, praying. Agathe took her a dish of tea.

We heard the drums roll three times. Even Hortense grew silent. I held her in my arms.

The King is dead. We have killed our King.

In which my husband's star rises and falls

28 MAY 1793
Deputy Tallien called this evening, his bristly hair uncovered in spite of a gentle spring rain.

'What is it?' The wife of a soldier always fears news.

'Your husband is going to be promoted,' he said.

'Promoted?' It was only two months ago Alexandre had been made General.

'Commander-in-Chief of the Army of the Rhine.'

'*Commander*-in-Chief?'

'It's to be announced in the Assembly tomorrow.'* Tallien leaned his sword against the wall.

'Can nothing be done to stop it?'

'This is quite an honour, citoyenne.'

I held my tongue. Now, almost three in the morning, I cannot sleep. Alexandre — Commander-in-Chief? I should rejoice, yet fear is the emotion that fills me. A quill is Alexandre's weapon — not a sword. I see myself in a widow's habit, I see my children in black.

29 MAY
I saw Tallien in an archway, his bright tricolour plume setting him

---

* In fact, Tallien uses the term 'Convention'. During the Revolution, the name of the elected body was changed several times: on 17 June 1789, the Estates General became the National Assembly, which in turn became the Constituent Assembly in the autumn of that same year. With the adoption of the new constitution, on 1 October 1791, the elected body became the National Legislative Assembly, which on 22 September 1792 became the National Convention. In the interests of making the text less confusing for the reader, the word 'Assembly' has been used throughout.

off from all the deputies in tall black hats. He told a clerk to show me to a private loge, which, to judge by the luxury of its fittings, must have once belonged to the royal family. It was more like an apartment, with a water closet and even a fireplace. There were three women there, one in scarlet satin with a daring décolletage. They introduced themselves as guests of Deputy Barras, '*en mission* to the south, alas,' the woman in scarlet said.

We fell to watching the proceedings. When Alexandre was proclaimed Commander, Tallien jumped to his feet and applauded. The approval was far from unanimous, however. 'Let us be perfectly clear, citoyens,' yelled a deputy from the back of the hall. 'It is the *Vicomte* Alexandre *de* Beauharnais who has been proclaimed . . . an *aristocrat.*' Menacing hisses followed this declaration.

'Congratulations, *Vicomtesse*,' the woman with silver paint on her eyelids said.

'Citoyenne, *s'il te plaît*,' I said, and quickly rose to go.

3 June 1793 – Strasbourg
Dear Rose,

I have been acclaimed, but feel far from secure. The war waged on the battlefield is simple in comparison to that waged in the Assembly. It would be helpful if you made contact with the members of the Committee of Public Safety – Deputy Barère I know is one. We were colleagues together in the Estates General. He could prove useful, but be cautious: in the early years, he had suggested a throne of diamonds for the King, yet at the King's trial he insisted the Tree of Liberty be refreshed by royal blood. No one can be trusted.

Your husband, Alexandre Beauharnais

TUESDAY, 11 JUNE
I'm exhausted. Every morning I write letters – letters of appeal, letters of guarantee. Every afternoon I sit in on the Assembly sessions, meet members of the various committees. In the evening I go to the salons the men of influence frequent. I smile, I nod, I inquire.

In this way the wife of Commander-in-Chief Beauharnais has

succeeded in getting the sequester lifted on the home of Citoyenne Montlosier and her three children, a stay of execution for Citoyen Dolivier, the release of Deputy Hervilly and the award of a position in the postal service to Citoyen Basire, whose daughter begs coins on the Pont-Neuf. In this way the wife of Commander-in-Chief Beauharnais fights a war of her own.

13 JUNE
The Austrians are gathering strength. Alexandre's letters are disturbing. He is concerned about what might happen if he must lead his men into battle. 'My troops are ill-equipped, ill-clothed and ill-fed. I am doing everything I can to train them, increase their morale, but I fear for them. We stand thirty thousand against three hundred thousand, and prayer is no longer the fashion.'

SUNDAY, 16 JUNE, 3.15 P.M.
Aimée is jubilant. She has succeeded in negotiating a marriage contract for Lucie, now fourteen, to Jean-Henri de Croisoeuil, thirty-four.

'Monsieur de Croisoeuil? Isn't he a Royalist, a counter-revolutionary?'
'But disgustingly *wealthy*.'

15 June 1793 – Fontainebleau
Dear Rose,

As you insisted, I have hung a copy of the Declaration of the Rights of Man in a prominent place in our parlour – fortunately, the Marquis cannot see well enough to notice – and just this morning I made a donation to the municipality in exchange for an affidavit declaring my patriotism. But I draw the line at attending the Temple of Reason!

I have been trying to persuade the Marquis to send a donation to the Jacobin Club here, along with the patriotic speech which you so thoughtfully provided, but he refuses. On this matter you will have to speak to him yourself.

I am having great difficulty getting our certificates and papers in order. (Perhaps you have my baptismal records? They would be in the bottom drawer of your escritoire.) Already I have suffered some harassment on this account. At every turn one is required to present papers and passes and if there is the slightest inconsistency . . . !

When are you coming to see us here in Fontainebleau? We miss Hortense. I know how busy you are with all your good works, but do try. We are frantic . . .

Your godmother, Aunt Désirée

21 June — Fontainebleau.

Aunt Désirée is uncharacteristically undone. She has been walling up valuables in a corner of the cellar, late at night when the servants are asleep. Both she and the Marquis showed visible relief to see me, and great joy to see Hortense again.

My pass permitted me to stay for one week. This gave me time to talk to Aunt Désirée, determine what should be done. She fears they are under surveillance due to François becoming a major-general in the army of the émigrés. Were it not for the fragile condition of the Marquis's health, they would go into hiding.

'What are we to do?' Aunt Désirée demanded, showing me the extreme unction kit she kept hidden in a crockery pot in the scullery: a hollowed crucifix which held two candles, a few cotton swabs and a vial of blessed oil — in case the Marquis died. 'Camp in some third-storey garret?' She carefully put the crucifix back. 'It would kill him!'

So they keep quiet, pay their help well (better than they can afford), and do nothing to draw attention to themselves.

I was anxious to get them to register loyalty to the Republic, as a protection against arrest. If they didn't, it would certainly not count in their favour. At first the Marquis refused. He could *never* vow allegiance to a government he could not support. 'A noble stands by his words.' It took considerable persuasion to get him to relent.

The journey to the section house was perilous. Aunt Désirée and I had dressed the Marquis as best we could, taking care that he did not look too dignified. With some effort I got him to sport a *bonnet rouge*. I rehearsed them both on what they were to say and reminded them to use the familiar form. ('To someone I don't even know?' the Marquis demanded. 'How rude.') When the clerk at the section office addressed him in the familiar and refused to take off his cap in respect, I trembled. Fortunately the Marquis was too confused to quarrel and Aunt Désirée too nervous. They made their oaths with the appearance of sincerity, and as we came back out into the hot summer sun I congratulated them both.

'For what?' the Marquis scowled, pulling the *bonnet rouge* from his head.

Quickly, I took the hat from him; I feared he might throw it to the ground. I hung it on a branch of the liberty tree outside the section house – a common act of patriotism. 'How generous of you to give up your hat for the Tree of Liberty, citoyen,' I said loudly, for the benefit of some young men passing by.

Slowly we made our way home; as for myself, I am giddy with relief.

25 June – Paris

Deputy Tallien came to our salon tonight. It was in the early hours, after a shocking amount of money had been exchanged at faro, that he told me, in confidence: 'Your husband's star continues to rise. He is now being considered for the position of Minister of War.'

'For *all* of France?'

'You are not pleased?'

'They will murder him. *That* should please me?'

Deputy Tallien gave a careless grin. 'They will murder us all,' he shrugged, playing his last card.

Thursday, 27 June

In the Assembly today Alexandre was nominated for Minister of War. A number of deputies jumped to their feet in protest, including Robespierre. Deputy Barère went to the tribune in front of the President's box. He read out several of Alexandre's patriotic statements to the papers, accounts of his zeal. Then another deputy came forward. He argued that Commander-in-Chief Alexandre Beauharnais was too valuable to be made Minister of War. He should stay with the Army of the Rhine and continue on to glorious victories. Another deputy countered that if Commander-in-Chief Alexandre Beauharnais could achieve so much at the head of one army, think of what glory would be France's were he placed at the head of *eleven*, as Minister of War.

Eleven . . . *mon Dieu.*

When several deputies protested, yelling that it was an *aristocrat* who was being considered for one of the most powerful positions in the Republic, Deputy Barère jumped up, cried out, 'He is my friend! He is my friend!'

The nomination was accepted.

I am ill; I have taken to bed. All our armies were losing. To be Minister of War at this time means certain death. I have sent a message by courier to Alexandre, begging him to decline.

TUESDAY, 30 JULY
Our Tuesday night salon was somewhat strained. The sudden surrender of our men at Mainz to the Germans, the failure of Alexandre's troops to rescue them, the dishonour to the Republic threw a feeling of gravity over the evening.

'I have something to show you,' Deputy Tallien whispered to me, guiding me into the music room. 'A billet your husband sent the Committee. I think you should see it.'

He handed me the note – one page, only half of it filled. In brief, blunt words Alexandre expressed rage at the surrender of our troops at Mainz, blaming the commanders there, calling for their execution, demanding that their heads be sent to the enemy. Indignantly, he insisted that the government accept his resignation, his offer to break his sword.

I handed the letter back. I felt uneasy with Alexandre's blame of the disaster on others, his call for vengeance. 'Apparently he is ill,' I said.

'How convenient.' Deputy Tallien folded the note, slipped it into his waistcoat pocket. 'The enemy attacks, one million Frenchmen prepare for battle and your husband wishes to resign his command.' His tone was sarcastic. 'This does not reflect well on him, citoyenne. Indeed, you should be aware that the word "traitor" has been spoken.'

'Commander-in-Chief Beauharnais should rather have led untrained troops against a professional army ten times their size? He should have led his men to *slaughter*?'

'One leads, willing or not,' Deputy Tallien answered. 'It takes courage to face one's own death, but even more so the death of others. We are learning this lesson well.'

Our conversation was interrupted by a woman and two men, one of whom was in uniform. 'Why should dancing no longer be permitted on the streets?' the woman complained, running her fingers lightly across the harp strings.

'It's the other outlawed pleasures* that concern me,' the man in uniform said. His companion laughed.

'Deputy Tallien, darling.' The woman took his hand, began a little dance around him. 'Why no dancing, pray?'

'Robespierre doesn't care for pleasure, I've heard,' the man in uniform said.

'Robespierre doesn't care for women,' the other man said.

'Shall I tell Deputy Robespierre you said that?' Tallien's eyes were on the woman, her revealing décolletage.

I stared into the empty fireplace, oblivious of their gaiety. What would become of Alexandre now?

SATURDAY, 10 AUGUST

We were awoken at dawn by artillery fire announcing the Festival of Unity.

One must attend these events lest one's patriotism be questioned, so late in the afternoon Aimée, the children and I set out, dressed in Republican garb. We hired a fiacre to take us to the site of the Bastille. At Port-Saint-Paul we were slowed by a procession of men, women and children trudging along in the heat carrying posies of wheat. We decided to get out and follow behind. At the intersection of Rue Saint-Antoine and Rue des Tournelles there was a giant level (signifying equality?), under which everyone was expected to walk. It reminded me of the type of thing one sees at Freemason meetings, and equally mysterious.

On the rubble of the former prison a giant statue of a woman had been erected – Mother Nature. She had a curiously mocking expression, squeezing her bosom with her hands, water gushing out. It was all Aimée and I could do to maintain a suitably reverent

---

* The revolutionary government frowned on prostitution as a remnant of the corrupt Ancien Régime.

attitude. The children, of course, began giggling. I wasn't entirely unhappy when Aimée's daughter Lucie became ill and we had to return home. Later Aimée confessed the reason for her daughter's malady: the girl is with child, and not by Jean-Henri, her fiancé, but by the stationer's son.

'What will you do if the engagement is called off?' I asked.

'Kill her,' Aimée said, lunging, her sword arm extended.

13 August

Jean-Henri has at last consented to marry Lucie, despite his young bride's dishonour. 'No doubt the fear of proscription was the motivating factor,' Aimée observed wryly. 'Vive la Révolution!'

18 August

Lucie is married, at last. The union was blessed to the sound of the crowd in the Place de la Révolution – the mob cheering the execution of General Custine, Alexandre's former commanding officer. He had lost a battle, so off with his head. In spite of the heat, I closed all the windows.

Daily Alexandre sends letters to the Assembly demanding that they accept his resignation. Daily they refuse.

21 August

The Assembly has *finally* accepted Alexandre's resignation – but he is to stay at a distance of thirty leagues from the frontiers, twenty leagues from Paris, a criminal.

I was in the public galleries when the announcement was made. Immediately Deputy Tallien got up and left. I caught up with him in the gardens – with some effort, for his legs are long and he walks with impatience.

'There are other concerns!' he said. He stopped, mercifully. I caught my breath. 'Your husband's resignation, the restrictions on his movements are no longer the issue,' he said. 'What *is* a concern is his *head*.'

'You are cruel!' I was angry at his flippancy.

'Far from it, citoyenne,' he said. 'Have I not kept from you the accusations that have been brought against your husband? Have I not held my tongue?'

'Do you think I do not know!' The Army Commissars of Strasbourg had accused Alexandre of spending his time with whores when he should have been preparing for battle. I knew that. I knew more. I knew he'd played court to the daughter of an Army Commissar, Citoyen Rivage – Rivage the Rich, he was commonly called. Rivage the Revenger, I would call him now.

'There are more serious charges,' Deputy Tallien said. 'Some are saying that your husband, an aristocrat in collusion with his brother François, *intentionally* let Mainz fall, *intentionally* betrayed the Republic.'

'Who would speak such slander?'

'Deputy Robespierre, for one.' Deputy Tallien looked behind him. I followed his gaze. Two men, deputies, stood at the fountain, watching us.

Deputy Tallien spoke in a hushed tone. 'Citoyenne Beauharnais, if I may, as a friend – it would behove you to become invisible. The radicals are going to succeed in pushing through their Law of Suspects, giving the Committee of General Security the power to imprison without *trial*, without *reason* even!'

'Are you not on this committee?'

'No longer – the more radical members have taken control. I caution you not to draw attention to yourself. If you were wise, you would retire from your charitable activities, from your efforts to save all the good people of Paris. *Leave* this city.'

I believe I turned pale, for he clasped my arm. 'You *must* listen to me! I won't be here to help you. I'm leaving in the morning.'

'Leaving?' I confess I was dismayed. I'd become dependent on his help, his protection.

'For Bordeaux. *En mission.*'

'Congratulations.' I didn't know how to respond. 'Bordeaux is lovely.'

'Any place other than Paris is uncivilized, in my opinion.'

'Will you be gone long?'

'Long enough to tame the population, convert the provincials, bring them to heel.' He made a comical gesture.

I smiled. He was a boy in so many ways.

He pulled out his timepiece. 'I'm expected at a meeting in Rue

Saint-Honoré. We're having a guillotine made. The contractor, a German, assured us that it would be ready, but now, of course, he is full of excuses.'

A *guillotine*. I reached for my friend's hand. I knew him to be well-meaning, a patriot, yet he was so very young, too young for the power he wielded, the intoxicating power over life and death. 'Beware, my friend. Don't—'

He stooped to whisper in my ear: 'It is *you* who should beware.'

1 September 1793 – Hôtel Croisoeuil, Croissy
Dearest Rose,

Lucie's pregnancy is not going well. She has been confined to bed. I have moved to Hôtel Croisoeuil in order to care for her and manage the household. I thought this would be a temporary measure, but now I begin to see that it could go on for some time. As a result, I have been forced to consider what should be done with my château here, and it occurred to me: why don't you move into it? Croissy is safe . . . and I miss you!

Love and a thousand kisses, your dearest friend, Aimée
Note – My fencing instructor has finally 'cut me' (as we say in the Islands). I feinted but did not parry. *Touché!*

24 SEPTEMBER
Agathe woke me in the night. She'd heard knocking.

'Is it a search party?' I asked, frightened.

'It's at the back door.'

I drew the dagger from under my mattress. I put on my dressing gown. Agathe had disappeared. I lit a candle and went to the door. 'Who goes there!'

There was no answer. I heard a noise. 'Speak, I pray you!'

'Rose?'

I held my breath.

'Rose – is that you? *Please*, open the door!'

The voice was familiar. I opened the door a crack, the knife at my side. There, by the light of the moon, was my husband.

'Alexandre!' I opened the door. He was drenched from the rain. 'It is forbidden for you to be in Paris! Why are you here? You are in danger of arrest. Is Eugène with you?'

Alexandre paced. 'I had no idea it was like this in Paris now! There are guards everywhere! How am I going to get out?' He'd lost weight. His face looked gaunt and there was a feverish look in his eyes.

'Alexandre, where is Eugène?' I grabbed his arm.

He looked at me. 'Eugène?'

Had he been drinking? I could not smell alcohol.

'At school,' he said. He strode into the drawing room. He pulled the curtains to one side, peered out.

'You . . . you *left* him, in *Strasbourg*?' I demanded, following him. 'But Alexandre, he's only twelve! He can't—'

There were shouts outside on the street. Then a knocking at the front door. 'I must get out of here!' Alexandre exclaimed. He leapt towards the kitchen.

'Alexandre . . . !' But before I could stop him, he was gone. 'Take care!' I cried as the kitchen door slammed shut.

In which I try to escape Paris

26 SEPTEMBER 1793
We are in Croissy, at last, in this lovely château on the banks of the Seine. The sky is streaked the most amazing shade of pink. We will be safe here.

4 OCTOBER – CROISSY
He is here, at last. We sit together, Hortense and I, and look upon him in amazement. He is taller than I remember, all legs – and so beautiful to look at, this boy of mine, my son.

He made his way from Strasbourg, in the company of an aide. He carries a sword and knows how to use it. He sits a horse boldly and knows how to tame it.

He regards me shyly – his mother, a *woman*. He becomes fretful when I weep.

10 OCTOBER
Every morning at eleven Aimée comes for a bowl of tea. Often, Abbé Maynaud de Pancemont from the 'church' across the road joins us. He is a tall man, lanky, his thin ankles sticking out from under a patched white cape draped in the Roman style.

'It's an Italian *riding* habit,' he assured me. For priests are not permitted to wear robes. He enjoys a bit of rum and is fond of romantic poetry. He has an engaging smile, a big toothy grin. This morning the three of us played whist and made chit-chat on a matter of great importance in our village: my gardener's courtship of my neighbour's valet's daughter.

There is an air of unrestrained joy about Abbé Maynaud de Pancemont, so it was with disbelief that I learned he'd been in Carmes prison during the September massacres. He was one of the few to survive, his long legs enabling him to leap the wall to safety, to escape the carnage, the murdered bodies of his colleagues stacked ten deep.

We are all of us in hiding here.

17 OCTOBER

The Queen has been guillotined, accused of crimes beyond imagining.* Last night she appeared to me in a dream, handing me her head.

'No!' I screamed.

I sat up in the dark, my heart pounding. The night candle had burned down and the moon threw ghostly shapes against the walls. I thought I was in Martinico. I thought I could hear drums, chanting.

I heard a noise outside my door, saw a light moving. I began to tremble.

'Madame?' It was Lannoy, a candle in her hand, her white face framed by her ruffled nightcap. 'I heard a scream.' She set the pewter candle-holder down.

'Oh, Lannoy,' I wept. 'Our Queen!'

25 OCTOBER, 2.00 P.M.

Yet another new dictate from the 'Nouveau Régime' – we do not have weeks any more, but *décades* of ten days.† What day is it? What

---

* The Queen was publicly accused, among other things, of taking her eight-year-old son into bed with her and teaching him how to masturbate, to which she responded, with tearful dignity, 'I appeal to all mothers here – is such a crime possible?' She was convicted of aiding and abetting foreign powers and conspiring to provoke civil war within France.

† To further separate France from the Church, the Gregorian calendar was replaced by a 'Republican' calendar, dating from 22 September of the previous year (1792), the date the Republic was proclaimed.

month? I do not know. Is it *vendémiaire*, the month of vintage? Or *brumaire*, the month of fog?

This change has made everyone cross. This new, more 'natural' order, this romantic calendar of fog, frost, wind and snow, of meadows, flowers, heat and fruit, is nothing but more work. Where have our feast-day Sundays gone? Where our days of rest?*

'It's a plot to befuddle us,' Abbé Maynaud said, and perhaps he is right, for befuddled we certainly are. The measures have been changed, the names of our coins, our streets, our deities and now our days. 'They're even revising the next life,' he complained, for he has been required to put a sign on the graveyard that reads: Death is eternal sleep.

26 OCTOBER

A great sadness has fallen over the village. Two weeks ago a flower vendor here went to Paris to testify on behalf of her brother and has not been seen since. Rumours were she'd been arrested for coming to his aid and now it is said that she was guillotined. There is a black mourning wreath on several doors in the town, this in spite of the law threatening death to any who grieve a victim of the guillotine.

One hears stories of this sort often now. In most instances I feel it wise to question the veracity of the account, but sometimes, one wonders . . . what if they are *true*?

FRIDAY, 1 NOVEMBER, ALL SAINTS' DAY

As I made my way past the church this morning – on my way to Hôtel Croisoeuil to call on Aimée – Abbé Maynaud beckoned for me to enter. Inside, candles were lit. Although the hour was early, five women were on their knees. 'In honour of "Reason",' he whispered, winking. It is All Saints' Day, but we dare not say so.

I lit candles for Catherine, Manette and Father – and another for the soul of our Queen. I tremble writing these words.

---

* Before the Revolution the French had over thirty feast days a year in *addition* to Sundays and Mondays. Under the new revolutionary calendar, there was one day off every ten days plus five or six '*jours complémentaires*' tacked on at the end of the year – a considerably heavier workload.

Eugène brought me a note today, passed on to him by the postmaster. The wax seal was clumsily made, but it had not been broken. The script was studied, careful, composed – a child's hand. It was from young Émilie, in Paris, informing me that her mother had been taken to prison.

'What is it?' Eugène asked.

I was hesitant to tell him.

'Your Aunt Marie has been arrested. She's in Sainte-Pélagie . . .'

'In *prison*?' He was horrified.

'She is innocent,' I quickly assured him. 'She has done nothing wrong.' How was I to explain? Marie's crime: to have been married to an émigré. That, apparently, was enough to condemn her. Her divorce, her revolutionary activities, her work in support of the Republic were of no importance, apparently. 'I must go to her.'

'To *Paris*?' Eugène asked. I could see fear in his eyes.

This evening I showed the note to Aimée. 'Your son is right,' she said. 'It's too dangerous in Paris now. You must not draw attention to yourself.'

'But how can I *not* go?'

My valise is packed. I leave in the morning. Quietly.

SUNDAY, 3 NOVEMBER – PARIS

It rained the entire way to Paris. At one point, where the road was badly rutted, I feared the post coach might go into the ditch. We passed a convoy of grain, escorted by the National Guard. Peasants followed it, on foot, wolves circling prey.

At Fanny's hôtel on Rue de Tournon, I was received by Citoyen Lestaing. Marie's 'friend' had apparently moved in.

'And to what do I owe the pleasure of this call?' he asked. He is a slight man, with haunted eyes. He was wearing a white satin dressing gown embroidered with a Roman motif.

'Émilie sent me a note – about her mother.' I accepted the offer of a bowl of veal broth. 'How is Marie?'

'I send the chambermaid to the prison each day with clean linen. She reports Marie is well.'

'You've not seen her?'

I heard footsteps behind me. I turned. There, in the hallway, with one hand on the banister, was twelve-year-old Émilie.

'I got your note, Émilie,' I said.

'You should not have bothered your aunt,' Citoyen Lestaing said.

I went to Émilie, took her hand in mine. It was cold. 'Have you seen your mother?'

'Émilie!' I looked up into the face of a Negro woman of enormous proportions standing on the landing. The nanny. Émilie ran quickly up the stairs.

'The child is excitable,' Citoyen Lestaing said. 'It would disturb her to visit a prison.'

I turned to him, my heart jumping in my chest. 'I appreciate your concern, Citoyen, but I am going to see Marie,' I told him, 'and I will be taking Émilie with me.'

It was shortly after two when Émilie and I set out. When we reached the iron gates to Sainte-Pélagie prison, I took her hand. 'You don't have to come in with me.'

Émilie clasped the parcel she'd brought to her chest. She had that same pixie look I remembered from when she was a baby. 'I want to,' she said.

'You are a brave girl.'

The gaoler was a big man with a red face. He directed us to the guardhouse where we waited in the company of two men. They were kindly and smoked outside, on the steps. Émilie and I sat side by side on a truckle bed with a rough woollen blanket pulled over it. Soon the gaoler returned, out of breath from climbing the steps. Marie was behind him.

She looked dishevelled, her dress soiled, the tricolour cockade on her bodice frayed. She attempted to tidy her hair.

'I am here to help,' I said, sensing her shame.

'Citoyen Lestaing did not come?'

'He was concerned it would distress you,' I lied.

Émilie pressed her parcel into her mother's hands. It contained clean linen and a silver fork, knife and spoon. There was also a porcelain cup, a small box of sewing implements, a novel by Richardson.

The gaoler examined the contents. He saw the knife and took it from her. He opened the small box and removed the scissors. 'It is time,' he said.

Émilie embraced her mother.

'You must not be a burden!' Marie said.

'We're working to get you out,' I told her. I kissed her dirty cheeks. She took off her cockade, shoved it angrily into my hand.

Now, it is late. I am filled with concern. Deputy Tallien is in Bordeaux. Deputy Barras is in the south, I am told, Citoyen Botot with him. To whom can I turn?

5 NOVEMBER

'You are suggesting that *I* make an appeal to the Committee?' Émilie flushed. I doubted momentarily the wisdom of my proposal.

'It is more likely that the Committee will be persuaded by a petition delivered by the prisoner's daughter,' I said.

Émilie and I spent the morning preparing. We wrote out the petition, rehearsed. 'Imagine that you are in a play,' I coached her, for as shy as Émilie is, she blossoms on stage. 'Imagine that the members of the Committee are in the audience.'

She made a dramatic, pleading gesture.

'That's it!'

Shortly before three I accompanied Émilie to the Tuileries. We were told that the office of the Committee was in the southern section. My heart was pounding as we walked down the wide marble corridors. I thought of the Queen, of her footsteps on the very stones I touched. I thought of her children, orphans now, growing up in a dank prison, alone.

We sat in the anteroom with all the other petitioners, Émilie folding and unfolding her notes. At last her name was called. I gave her a little push. She went through the double doors.

When the doors opened a short time later, it was a sad, diminished Émilie I saw. 'I've failed!' she wept. 'What if I've failed!'

10 NOVEMBER

Executed this week: Olympe de Gouges, Duc d'Orléans, Citoyenne Roland. Tomorrow, Citoyen Bailly, the astronomer.

SANDRA GULLAND

How can this go on? Even cows cannot be induced into Paris, the smell of blood is so strong.

LATER
I leave for Croissy in the morning – without Émilie. I could not persuade her to leave Paris, the city of her mother's imprisonment.

MONDAY, 13 JANUARY 1794 – CROISSY
Abbé Maynaud looked solemn this morning.
   'Is something wrong?'
   He handed me a letter. The seal was broken.
   'It was broken when I received it,' he said.
   It was from the Committee. 'You read it?' I asked.
   'It's not good news.'
   I scanned the letter. Émilie's appeal had been turned down. No reason was given. I turned the paper over in my hand. So few words, but they meant so much – that a woman, a mother, would stay imprisoned, endanger her health, her heart, perhaps go to the guillotine, lose her head as a drunken mob cheered.
   Abbé Maynaud guided me towards a chair. 'A glass of brandy?'
   'No!' I pulled away. 'I must pack my valise,' I said.

14 JANUARY
I applied this morning for a pass. 'So you want to go to Paris again.' The postmaster used a tiny model of a guillotine to cut a length of string. He laughed.
   I glanced uneasily towards the door. Two men stood watching me.

FRIDAY, 17 JANUARY – PARIS
I am exhausted. It is early evening, a cock is crowing. I've taken claret to calm my nerves. I will write in the morning. For now, I can't . . .

What happened:

As I entered the grand hall, I encountered a most disturbing sight – a long line of men, women, children even. From the bedding and baskets of food, I gathered that some had been there for a long time. I went to the head of the line. 'I wish to speak to Deputy Vadier,' I told the guard. Vadier's signature had been on Marie's arrest warrant. He and Alexandre had worked together in the Assembly, I recalled.

'So do all these others,' the guard smirked.

I handed him a letter I had written. 'Would it be possible to have this delivered to Deputy Vadier then?'

The guard opened the big double doors. He gave my envelope to a man in blue velvet sitting at a desk. The man looked up at me briefly.

I smiled: *please?*

He looked away. No doubt he received such looks all day.

There was nothing to do but wait. Now and then the big oak doors would open and the man in blue velvet would call out a name and one of our number would enter. This kept up our hopes that we would be summoned ourselves.

A few members of the Committee would come and go. Robespierre was one of these. He was wearing a striped satin waistcoat. A woman threw herself to her knees in front of him. She was pulled away by the guards.

Towards noon I began to despair. I saw a man approach – a man I recognized. Deputy Barère! I ran after him, called out his name. He turned.

'Citoyenne Beauharnais.' There was something in his face that warned me.

'I've been here all morning, hoping to speak to Deputy Vadier.'

'We are exceedingly busy.' He ran his hand through his thinning hair, which he had combed to disguise a bald spot.

'If I could just talk to him . . .'

He shook his head, gave me a look of alarm: *don't insist.* 'I'm afraid that's not possible.' The big oak doors closed behind him.

It was nearing five in the afternoon when my name was called. I went to the head of the line. The guard handed me an envelope. I broke open the seal. Inside was a note: 'Green salon, north side.' Signed 'B'.

It took some time to locate the green salon. When I gave the guard my name he opened the door: I was expected.

Deputy Barère was seated at an elegant writing table. The room was full of ormolu clocks and vases, Gobelin tapestries, several gold and silver tea services, a brass statue of the Virgin Mary and three immense candle snuffers. Deputy Barère waited until the door had closed before offering me a seat. 'I have put myself in jeopardy meeting you.'

I was feeling short of breath. I heard a cheer outside. 'Long live the Republic!' Crowds at the scaffold. I rushed into my speech: 'I am seeking release of my sister-in-law, Citoyenne Marie-Françoise Beauharnais, an ardent Republican. She has been imprisoned in Sainte-Pélagie, due to her ex-husband's defection. Yet she divorced him long ago and is not of his party in any way—'

'Citoyenne Beauharnais!' Deputy Barère silenced me with a wave of his hand. 'I cannot help your sister-in-law. I have family of my own in prison – I cannot help them! I have consented to meet you only out of a past regard for your husband. You must warn him – he is in danger of arrest.' This last he whispered. 'And as for you and your children . . .'

The *children – grand Dieu!*

'Please understand that you must be *exceedingly* cautious. I can't emphasize this enough—'

'But Citoyen Beauharnais is in Blois,' I stuttered. 'I can't even write to him to warn him. I have reason to believe that letters are intercepted and read.'

'Quite likely.' Deputy Barère stood, sighed. 'These are . . . *difficult* times. I can say no more.' And he was gone.

Lannoy was alarmed by my condition. She brought me a claret. She admonished me to rest, but I insisted on rising. I knew what I had to do. I had to appeal once more to Deputy Vadier, write a letter, for Alexandre's sake, as well as for Marie's. I had to rise and write this letter upon which so much depended, and I had to do so quickly before courage gave way, before fear took possession of me.

It took one hour to compose the draft. Lannoy brought me cup after cup of broth for strength. In spite of the flaws and imperfections, I copied out the final version. As I sprinkled it with sand I silently recited a chant Mimi had once taught me so many

many years ago, a prayer to the mystères. I sealed the envelope and sent Lannoy to deliver it. If I waited for a courier, I knew I would tear it to shreds.

4 MARCH 1794 – CROISSY

A long walk today, along the river. As I turned back to the château I saw Eugène running towards me, his long legs pumping up and down, up and down.

What had happened?

He was crying when he reached me.

Alexandre has been arrested.

In which I go to the aid of my husband

6 MARCH 1794 – PARIS

I approached the Luxembourg Palace – a prison now – with trepidation, but was soon reassured. Inside, men and women in aristocratic dress mingled freely. Everywhere there were tête-à-têtes, gatherings, the sound of laughter and games. Some of the rooms were elaborately furnished. I saw a woman in a striped polonaise attended by a valet in livery.

I was told to wait in an elegant antechamber. I was offered tea – *real* tea, so rare now. Shortly, Alexandre arrived. I was moved to see him. He was bronzed from country life, his fair hair blonder than usual.

We embraced and exchanged news much as if we were sitting at home in the parlour, not in a prison. He confessed that he was suffering from indigestion, but not from the food, which he said was excellent. He'd met an old friend, an officer with the Esterhazy Hussars, and they'd stayed up most of the night drinking wine and playing billiards.

'All the best people of Paris are here,' Alexandre said, as if proud to be included. He gave me a list of books he would like and requested money – a considerable sum, for the privilege of being so comfortably detained cost dear. 'I will be out soon, no doubt, but until that happy day, I intend to put this time to good use.'

'I wish I had your faith,' I said.

After a midday meal, which I ate half-heartedly, I decided to call on Princess Amalia and Frédéric. I was in need of the princess's sweet temper, Frédéric's droll wit.

Approaching Hôtel de Salm, I was puzzled by the National Guard standing at their gate. I was allowed to enter the courtyard, only to be turned away at the door by a footman. Princess Amalia was indisposed, he said.

'And Prince Frédéric?'

The valet looked confused. He told me to wait in the anteroom and disappeared into one of the palatial rooms. He returned shortly after. 'The princess will receive you,' he said.

He led me to a bedchamber on the second floor where I found Princess Amalia, her eyes red, her wig on the carpet: Frédéric has been arrested, she herself was under house arrest. Hence the guard at her gate.

We collapsed onto the sofa together. I felt numb. All my fears had come to pass. Were it not for me, Frédéric and Princess Amalia would be in England, safe from harm. 'Where are they holding him?' I asked.

'I don't even know!' she wept.

9 MARCH

The children and Lannoy will arrive by coach at three. I gathered up my meat ration cards to enable Agathe to purchase a hare. We'll have a meal and then walk over to the Luxembourg to visit their father – a prisoner.

14 MARCH

Alexandre has been transferred to the convent of the Carmelites. My heart sank when I heard. Slovenly, haunted – the Carmes was said to be one of the worst prisons in Paris. I thought of the massacres that had happened there, the stories Abbé Maynaud had told me.

So it was with trepidation that I went today. The gate creaked as the guard opened it. Even from the courtyard, I could smell the stench. I followed the guard through an archway and up some stone steps to a small room. There I was told to wait. Along one wall were dark stains – bloodstains, I realized, where the murderers had leaned their sabres.

Alexandre was ushered in. He looked shaken, uneasy. He wasn't wearing a cravat. I told him I'd still not succeeded in finding out the reason for his arrest. For the first time, he showed impatience. 'But there must be a reason! They can't just hold me!'

I left even more determined to find answers.

SATURDAY, 15 MARCH

Deputy Tallien is back in Paris, thank God. I sent him a message: it was urgent that I see him. He returned a note within an hour. I was to come to his office – in disguise. I was to give my name as a Citoyenne Gossec, a perfumer, witness to a shipment of grain that had been destroyed outside the city walls.

The need for disguise puzzled me. I borrowed a dress from Lannoy. By putting a small pillow into a corset I was able to give the appearance of a woman with child. That together with a veiled hat made me sufficiently mysterious.

I arrived at Tallien's office at precisely two. I was let into the anteroom. When Deputy Tallien came to the door, he looked at me without recognition. I smiled and then he realized who I was.

Once within the privacy of his office – which had been elaborately refurnished since I had last been there – we were able to embrace.

'No, I am *not* with child,' I smiled, in answer to his questioning look. 'Why the necessity for disguise?' I asked, accepting my friend's offer of a glass of Clos-Vougeot.

'I am watched.'

'*You?*' He did not look well. 'You've returned to Paris unexpectedly.'

'Been *recalled* is more accurate.'

'Was there a problem?' I thought of the things I'd heard, of the terrible things my friend was rumoured to have been responsible for: a *massacre* in Bordeaux, hundreds of aristocrats executed. Was it possible? I could not believe it.

'You should know that your wish has been granted.' He placed his hand over his heart.

'*My* wish?'

'I now know what it is to love.'

I could not but smile at such a solemn confession. 'That grieves you?' I asked. His expression was one of profound misery.

'The possessor of my affection has an untamed heart – for which I love her all the more, I confess. But I will die as a result, if not of a broken heart then by the loss of my head on the scaffold.' He sat solemnly with his hands before him, his long fingers clasped.

'Pray do not keep me in suspense, my friend.'

'The captor of my heart wrote a letter to Citoyen Jullien, Robespierre's nancy boy sent to spy on me in Bordeaux. In it she gave *him* her undying love, and complained of me, "the tyrant"! She even tried to persuade him to escape to America with her!'

'She sent this letter to Jullien? How did you come to know of it?'

'The saga, my friend, gets worse.' He downed his wine and poured himself another glass. 'Jullien forwarded this missive to the Committee of Public Safety. Now it is a public scandal and I'm cast in the role of a fool.' He looked forlorn.

'Perhaps it is a plot by Jullien and Robespierre to discredit you. Have you considered that possibility?'

Deputy Tallien shook his head. 'I examined the letter. It is in her hand. There can be no mistake. She, the angel who has claimed my heart, she alone is the author of my defeat. Jullien has accused me before the members of the Committee of being her bondservant; I cannot deny it!'

'Where is she now? This angel of yours . . .'

'I've just learned that she is back in Paris. I cannot tell you how it torments me to know that she is near.' He stood and began pacing, waving his glass of wine around wildly. 'You know her, no doubt. Her name is Thérèse . . . Thérèse Cabarrus.'

I was stunned. Thérèse Cabarrus? I had met her at a salon years ago. Even as a girl she had been known for her extraordinary beauty – and her height: 'Amazon' she'd been called. She was the daughter of the Treasurer to the King of Spain. Her family was both powerful and wealthy. Thérèse had been one of the few women admitted to Club 89, an exclusive group whose members included Mirabeau, Lafayette, Sieyès, Condorcet . . . Of course the gossips contended that her contribution was not *philosophical* in nature and had even published a pamphlet to that effect.

Suddenly I understood my friend's lament. Young Deputy Tallien, the humble son of a lowly valet, had given his heart to the wealthiest, most beautiful, most *spirited* woman in all of Europe.

'What a terrible affliction you have wished upon your friend!' he cried. 'It is not the guillotine I fear, but the loss of her love!'

I sighed. There was little likelihood that my friend could be attentive to any of *my* requests for help — not in his agitated condition. 'Perhaps I can be of assistance,' I offered.

And *then* I would see about Alexandre, Frédéric, Marie . . .

16 MARCH

Thérèse Cabarrus was at her toilette when I entered. It was nine in the morning. She was drinking champagne before an open window that looked out on the Seine. A young woman (I would guess her age at twenty), and strikingly tall, she was wearing a revealing dressing gown with no attempt at modesty. 'May I help you?' she asked, turning to greet me. She spoke with a slight Spanish accent. Her voice was deep, soothing, without the ostentation so common to her rank.

I glanced around her bedchamber — everywhere, in and among numerous flowering plants, there were paintings, sculptures, works of art. In the corner was a harpsichord. By the window an unfinished painting on an easel. The abundant trimmings were elegant, yet the effect of the arrangement was unique, bizarre, stimulating to the imagination.

'I am here on behalf of a mutual acquaintance,' I began, accepting the offer of a chair.

The chambermaid slipped the dressing gown from Thérèse's shoulders and began massaging her neck. 'And who might that be?' Thérèse asked. Her eyes were huge, black — not without wisdom.

'A man who loves you very much.'

Thérèse looked at me with a playful expression. 'Ah, but there are so many.'

I smiled. I believed her. I believed it entirely possible for all the men of Paris to lust after such a creature.

'You find me vain?'

'I find you disarmingly honest,' I said.

'Does this disturb you?'

'I appreciate honesty.'

She looked at me for a long moment. 'We shall be friends,' she said.

We finished the bottle of champagne. I informed her that Deputy Jullien had forwarded her letter on to the Committee of Public Safety.

'*Grand Dieu!*' She put her hands to her heart. 'My intention was to discredit Deputy Jullien, for I had discovered that he was spying on Tallien and reporting back to Robespierre. I had intended to tempt him into foolishness.'

'You are aware of the danger this puts Deputy Tallien in?'

'Will he ever forgive me?'

'He will forgive you *anything*.'

20 MARCH

Deputy Tallien leaps about. He cannot believe his good fortune, cannot believe that a woman as rich and as beautiful and as aristocratic as Thérèse could love *him*. He is beside himself with fretfulness, overcome with sentiments of tenderness, writing sonnets and sighing all day long. It is difficult to keep him focused on my petitions, but I persist. Daily I visit Alexandre. Daily I visit Frédéric, Marie. The situation worsens.

3 APRIL

I've become ill. Every day brings news of arrests, deaths. I've exhausted myself begging audiences, writing appeals. Deputy Tallien warns me to be more circumspect in my endeavours. 'You will be arrested if you persist,' he cautioned. 'You'd best think of yourself. Your children need a mother.'

'My children need a father,' I said, fighting back tears.

19 APRIL

Tonight, at dusk, three men came to the door. Fortuné growled. I recognized one of the men from the section office. The other two were unknown to me. I was alarmed lest they enter and find evidence of the Easter drawings I had made the children.

They handed me a paper. 'What does this mean?' I asked. It was a search warrant.

Uninvited, the men proceeded into the front parlour.

'The drawings are in the fire,' Lannoy whispered.

The men were not gentle with our possessions. They began in the basement and worked up to the attic, where they were excited to discover a locked desk, which they forced open. It was with disappointment that they discovered only patriotic letters from Alexandre (which I had intentionally placed there). They left dejected, having found nothing incriminating.

It is dark now. The flame from the candle sputters. I cannot sleep. I know they will return – for *me*.

LATER

It was four in the morning when the banging on the door began. This time they had a warrant for my arrest.

'And for what reason?' Lannoy protested.

'They need no reason,' I whispered. To resist would only make it more difficult. I asked Agathe to gather together a few things.

I went to the children's room. I intended to wake them, bid farewell. I thought of their tears. I could not disturb them, sleeping so. I kissed them each, pulled their bedclothes over them, silently said a prayer.

Agathe and Lannoy both began to weep. 'Take care of them,' I said, as the men led me out of the door.

In which my husband and I are reconciled

I was thankful it was night. I would not have wanted witnesses.

My captors were ordinary men, doing a job. One, Citoyen Delmer, the more outspoken of the three, had a sick wife, and was anxious to get home. I was the last call and he was glad it was done. He didn't like taking mothers from their children. 'It's good you didn't wake them. It's better that way.'

They took me to the convent of the English Ursulines. The turnkey, who smelled of liquor, said there wasn't a chair to sit on, much less a bed.

'Where are we to take her?' Citoyen Delmer saw more work ahead.

The turnkey scowled. Delmer suggested the truckle bed in the guardroom.

'That's *my* bed,' the turnkey said, but he agreed finally.

The next day I asked to be transferred to the Carmes.

'You *want* to go to the Carmes?' The gaoler was a small man with pockmarks on his face.

'My husband is there.'

'It's crowded and none too pleasant.'

Nonetheless, he complied. At noon, after ham, eggs and dirty water, which made me nauseous, I was loaded into a covered cart along with three others. One was a boy of about fifteen. The other two, a man and wife, were puppeteers, arrested for making a puppet of Charlotte Corday.*

There was straw in the cart, some of it soiled. The cart had been used to bring in prisoners from Versailles the night before, our guard explained. As we made our way through the streets, people looked

* The young woman who murdered Deputy Marat.

in at us and cursed. A boy threw a rotten egg. I turned my head in shame.

At the Carmes we were required to wait as the turnkey, a heavy man named Roblâtre, grumbled over the documents. 'Every day they change how it goes,' he cursed. 'And if I don't get it right . . . !' He rolled his eyes. It was evident from his flushed visage that he was overly fond of the juice of the grape.

We were led down a narrow stone corridor. The smell from the open latrines made me choke. Roblâtre opened a door to a narrow room. The floor was lined with straw pallets, all in a row. Clothing was hung everywhere. The smell of mould was strong.

I was assigned a pallet facing one of the barred windows. To one side a young woman reclined, her golden hair fanned out over her pillow like a halo. 'Citoyenne Madame Custine,' she introduced herself. 'You may call me Delphine.'

'Custine? The General—'

'The great General Custine was my husband's father.' She had a high, musical voice and spoke in a studied manner, like an actress, with exaggerated feminine flourishes.

'My husband served under General Custine. Alexandre Beauharnais. He is here.'

'Oh – Citoyen General Beauharnais! You are his *wife?*'

'You know him?'

'He is my husband's bosom friend.' She lay back down on the bed and sighed, her hand over her heart. 'General Beauharnais has been drawing my portrait.'

A bell was rung in the corridor. I followed Delphine and the others down a labyrinth of stairs into the rectory. There, under the vaulted ceilings, under the scratched-out images of Christ and the Virgin, crude plank tables had been set.

I sought a place on a bench. Bent cutlery was stacked in piles. I sat down facing a stained-glass window. To my left were the wooden steps to the altar.

'That's where they read out the names every night,' a woman behind me said. The voice sounded like that of Aimée.

I turned. It *was* Aimée. I burst into tears. She squeezed in beside me. She handed me a teacup. 'Here, drink this,' she hissed. It was whisky. 'I bribed the turnkey.' Her cheeks were flushed. I suspected she'd had a bit.

A scrawny woman with dirty fingernails handed me a metal plate of boiled haricots and sardines.

'Ugh, this again.' Aimée made a face at the food. 'One meal a day and it's garbage.'

'What names?' I asked.

'Of the condemned – who goes, who stays, who lives, who dies. It's the nightly entertainment – quite dramatic, I must say.'

The lard on the beans was rancid. I put down my fork. The woman threw a basket of coarse black bread on to the table. Aimée tore off an end and tucked it down her bodice.

I felt dazed. 'When did *you* . . . ?'

'Yesterday morning – but already it seems like a year. They took us all. Jean-Henri – he's over in the men's quarters. Even Lucie, poor child. She's asleep right now, upstairs.'

Lucie? After losing her first, the girl had quickly become pregnant again – by her husband this time, fortunately.

'She's sick, too ill to eat – if you call this *eating*. I think it was the eggs we ate yesterday – laid under the Ancien Régime.'

'We were all arrested at the same time. Curious.'

'Do you know why?' she asked.

I shook my head. 'Have you seen Alexandre?' Before Aimée could answer, the woman was taking our plates, and our tables and chairs were being moved. The sound in the chapel was deafening. The big double doors opened and a group of men entered. They were unshaven, in dirty shirts and breeches. One wore a kerchief round his head.

'And now the excitement begins,' Aimée sighed with mock reverence. 'Alexandre is probably outside. I beat him in a fencing match last night.'

'*You* beat Alexandre?' I followed her through a wide corridor that opened on to a walled garden. It was a hot, humid night. The smell of mint was strong. Next to an oak tree I saw Alexandre standing with another man. He looked up as we approached.

'And so it is that fate unites us.' Alexandre kissed my hand. 'I was told you were here. I can't say that I'm *happy* to see you.'

I was introduced to Boyce Custine, a young man with glowing pink cheeks and an eager look. 'Welcome,' he said, bowing gallantly, 'to what we bucks and bloods once termed a frolic. *C'est bizarre, cela.*'

'I met your wife,' I told him. 'We share sleeping quarters.'

'Perhaps we could trade places,' he said mournfully.

'He's an eager lad, but his wife is reluctant,' Alexandre explained. 'I've been trying to persuade her to rendezvous with her beloved in the Lovers' Suite.'

'The *Lovers'* Suite?'

'A private chamber reserved for married couples,' Aimée said, 'the rights to which are much coveted, as you can imagine.' She had stripped a lilac branch of its leaves and was using it as a makeshift sabre.

'*Except* by the beautiful Delphine,' Alexandre said.

'Alas!' Boyce Custine exclaimed theatrically, and we laughed.

We were allowed to mingle in the garden until ten. It seemed strange considering the setting. I was introduced to a variety of people of different political persuasions, from the aristocratic Duchesse Jeanne-Victoire d'Aiguillon to the radical Jacobin, General Santerre.

'*The* General Santerre?' I whispered to Aimée. The tavernkeeper who had proposed killing all the dogs and cats of Paris? The monster who had led the invasion on the Tuileries, who had silenced the King on the scaffold, ordered the drums to roll when the King began to speak?

'All the ladies call him Consoler,' Aimée said. She put her arm through his. Apparently the burly tavernkeeper had become the favourite.

'General Santerre,' I said, 'I am surprised, I confess, to see a man of your political persuasion *here*.'

The Consoler grinned sheepishly, adjusting his red cap. 'As I see it, this way, when they really need me, they'll know *exactly* where to find me.'

'Frankly, if you're *not* in here, you're suspect,' Alexandre said.

23 APRIL

For two mornings now, Lannoy has brought the children and Alexandre and I have been permitted a short visit. But this morning, Roblâtre would not permit us to see them.

'Tomorrow?' I asked.

Roblâtre shook his head. 'There's a new rule.' It was morning, yet already he was drunk.

'You mean we may not see them at *all*?' Alexandre demanded.

Roblâtre shrugged. 'No longer.'

Alexandre struck the chair, sending it flying.

[UNDATED]

I've become ill. Everyone has. We think it was the soup and bouilli last night. Duchesse Jeanne-Victoire d'Aiguillon said it was made from diseased horses' flesh and would not eat it. Others say worse.*

LATER

I am weak, confined to my pallet. This afternoon Alexandre brought me the parcel of clean linen Lannoy had delivered. In a petticoat I discovered my fortune-telling cards and a letter written by Eugène. Overcome with joy, I began to weep. Alexandre held me to his heart.

25 APRIL

Now the children are not able to *write* even — our parcels are searched.

'How are we to know how they are, Alexandre?' I wept. There are rumours that the children of prisoners will be taken by the state, placed in the care of 'good' Republicans. 'They might be ill, they might be dying! We wouldn't even *know*!'

26 APRIL

This morning, as is our custom, Alexandre and I went to the office to collect our parcel of clean linen. The turnkey checked off the items against a list of the contents. He was about to throw the list into the fire when Alexandre asked to see it. The turnkey looked at him suspiciously, but handed it to him nevertheless. Immediately I perceived it was in Eugène's hand.

* Some prisoners believed they were fed human flesh.

'Thank you, Citoyen.' Alexandre handed the list back to the turnkey, his hand trembling only slightly.

27 APRIL

Every morning now there is a list with our parcel of linen. On one day it is in Eugène's hand, on another in Hortense's. I can sleep now.

28 APRIL

This morning, as I returned from breakfast (pickled herrings — again*), I heard yelping. Suddenly, at my feet, there was a runt of a dog.

Fortuné!

I picked him up. He must have slipped past the guards.

'What is it? Is it a dog?' my companion asked uneasily.

Fortuné had a big black ribbon round his neck; it had become entangled in his collar. With some difficulty I got him to hold still so that I could straighten it. Then I felt something. There, concealed under his collar, was a folded piece of paper.

Quickly, I slipped the paper out, hid it in my skirt. 'What an ugly dog. It looks like a rat – don't you think?' I put Fortuné down, pushed him towards the gate, my heart pounding. 'Go! Go home!'

It wasn't until Alexandre and I met in the private room that I had the courage to read it. It was a letter from Eugène. They are well – they send their love. I collapsed in tears.

[UNDATED]

Alexandre and I are reconciled.

* Pickled herrings were given to the prisoners in great quantities, provided to the French government by the Dutch in lieu of payment on a debt.

In which my worst fear is realized

30 APRIL 1794
Citoyen Boyce Custine's name has been called. Delphine fainted when she heard, falling on to the stone floor. We carried her to her pallet. There I cooled her brow. Then she opened her eyes and started screaming. The others became angry. A show of grief upsets everyone, and is considered selfish.

I went to the rectory in search of Alexandre. 'Delphine is beside herself,' I told him. 'She is upsetting the others. I thought I might take her into the private room.'

When I got back, Aimée had her arms round Delphine, restraining her. 'She was pounding on the wall,' Aimée said.

'Come.' Together Aimée and I were able to control her. Once in the private room Delphine began to calm. I rocked her like a baby. All the while my tears flowed.

3 MAY
Today, at last, Delphine ate some 'bread' – a barley concoction that makes our throats ache. She accepted it without complaint. It has been three days.

4 MAY
Delphine sat up this morning. 'I will require black,' she said. She composed a note to her woman-in-waiting. By afternoon she had a new wardrobe, striking black robes, quite becoming against her fine blonde hair and light blue eyes.

'You look like a princess,' I told her.

'I prefer goddess.' She rolled her hair in the reflection of the water bucket.

I take it her time of grief is over.

9 MAY

Delphine has been composing verses which she reads to me each night. 'But will *Alexandre* like it?' she asks anxiously when I assure her of its worth.

LATER

This afternoon, as I entered the garden, Delphine and Alexandre quickly moved. It was the briefest of movements, no more than a rustle, but Delphine's ready smile told me there was more, told me everything.

[UNDATED]

Delphine cannot suppress her joy. She glows. She sighs. In the night she moans, moves with desire. I know of whom she dreams.

11 MAY, A HOT AFTERNOON

Alexandre's eyes follow Delphine's every move, and I, the aged, lonely wife, must sit idly by and watch this passion unfold, this grand love.

Jealousy possesses me. Jealousy, anger and loneliness — a lethal mix.

12 MAY

It is unbearably hot. We lounge about the corridors in the most shocking state of undress. The men rarely shave, for water is dear. The women let their hair down, forget modesty. In every dark corner there is a couple seeking the last consolation.

I sit by the slits of windows, taking in air. From a shadow, under a stained bedcover, I see movement. I hear a woman moan, hear a man whisper endearments.

I lean my head against the damp stone wall. *Besoin d'être aimé*.
I shall die unloved. I shall die alone.

13 MAY

Today, two newcomers: Madame Elliott, an English gentlewoman
(the Duc d'Orléans's mistress and a spy for the English, Aimée
insists), and General Lazare Hoche — the hero of the Revolution.
I could understand why Madame Elliott had been arrested, but
General *Hoche* . . . ? A former stable boy, he had demonstrated
brilliance on the battlefield. All the Jacobins sang his praise.

'But if you don't *win* the battles . . .' General Hoche made the
gesture we have come to know too well: the quick movement of
the fingers across the throat.

He is an exceedingly comely young man — thin, tall and with thick
black hair and well-defined features; all the women are in a faint over
him. It doesn't help that to get to his quarters he must pass through
our dormitory. Tonight, as I was reading a journal out loud to the
others, Aimée made a swooning gesture as he went by. I cautioned
her, glanced up. General Hoche was standing on the stone landing,
looking down at me. The sabre scar between his eyes gave him a
quizzical look.

14 MAY

This evening, coming through our sleeping quarters, Lazare Hoche
glanced towards me. He made a small movement with his head.

I looked over at Madame Elliott. 'Going calling?' she asked, in
English. She smiled and demurely looked away.

I summoned the courage to stand. My cheeks were burning.
Quickly I slipped up the stone stairs.

At the top there was a narrow passageway leading to another
door, heavily bolted. Lazare Hoche pushed it open.

His chamber was small and very deep. At the top of a great wall
there was a small window. 'My dungeon,' he said, lighting a candle.
He pulled a dustsheet over the straw pallet. On a board was a bottle
of whisky.

'You have a private room,' I said.

'Generals are allowed certain privileges — even in prison.'

'Even in death?' Why had I said that?

He took a battered metal camp cup out of a wooden crate and filled it from the bottle. He offered me the cup. 'May I call you Rose?' he asked.

I took a sip and coughed. The liquor burned my throat. 'I am older than you.' It was a stupid thing to say. But suddenly I felt so unsure. How old *was* he? Twenty-four, twenty-five? For all he had seen of the world, he seemed but a boy. And I? I felt as old as the earth.

He finished the cup and set it down on the board. 'I would like you to stay.'

I did not answer. He approached me as one approaches a horse that might shy – firmly, but calmly, with confidence. His skin was rough; his touch gentle.

[UNDATED]

Every night some of our number are called. We fall into each other's arms, embraces given, taken, as if they were the last. They are the last.

I play out the cards. They say: this is Heaven, this is Hell. It is as one.

16 MAY

I've become a night animal. I sleep through the days. Not eating, my body bone, I cleave to my lover, disappear into the stars I see fleetingly through the narrow metal grate.

Lazare. *Hold me!*

For I am dying.

17 MAY

This night I went to his room. The door was open, the bedclothes in a bundle on the floor.

Citoyen Virolle came to the door. 'You could come to *me*.'

'Where is Lazare?'

'Among the chosen,' Citoyen Virolle said, slurring. He was drunk.

'*Lazare's* name was called?' I retched on to the stones.

19 MAY

Delphine has complained to the turnkey. My weeping keeps her awake. Duchesse Jeanne-Victoire d'Aiguillon has suggested I move into her cell. There is a vacancy now that her cellmate has been called, a hammock of leather webbing.

'A hammock?'

'So the rats won't get you,' Jeanne-Victoire said.

23 JUNE

I am thirty-one today. I put on my best gown, in spite of my resolve to save it.* In the garden Alexandre presented me with a drawing he had made of the children, an excellent likeness.

He told me to meet him in the private chamber. 'It is not what you think,' he added.

'The children – are they . . . ?' Alarmed.

'I dare not speak.'

We stood in the private chamber facing one another, our backs against the stone walls. 'There is a spy among us,' he said. 'I have reason to believe I will be called.' He told me he would be sacrificed for his country, that he had come to accept his fate. He said he was prepared to die. He asked me to dedicate my life to clearing his name. He had only one wish, and that was to see the children one last time. 'Delphine can arrange it.'

'Oh?' I have become weary of Delphine.

'One of the rooms upstairs overlooks the garden next door. There's a little house there – a gardener's house. Were the children to be taken there, and were we to stand in the window . . .'

'But what if they were discovered? What if we were seen? It's too dangerous, Alexandre! Surely—'

'It has already been arranged.'

I fell silent. It was hot in the little room.

'I thought you'd be pleased.' He was irritated.

'Do I have a choice?'

'Tomorrow, at two in the afternoon.'

---

* It was common for the women in the prisons to put aside their most elegant ensemble to wear on the day of their execution.

24 June

Alexandre and I waited by the window looking out on the garden. After a short time, we noticed movement on the second floor of the little house. Hortense and Eugène stepped into view.

We stared at one another without moving: parent to child, child to parent.

They looked so *very* beautiful.

Hortense cried out, held out her arms. I heard a guard shout, 'Who goes there!' The children were pulled back into the shadows.

It was over as quickly as that.

9 July

Tonight eighteen names were called. So many! We are as sleepwalkers, numb. In the garden, Alexandre accused Citoyen Virolle of being an informer. The little man did not say a word. An hour later his body was found in the rectory. He had been strangled.

17 July

Tonight it was announced: fifty names will be called.

Fifty!

Is it possible? Fifty of our number — *to die?*

We begin to comprehend.

We will *all* of us die.

18 July

Two young men, brothers from Normandie, were the first names called. Hands joined, they leapt down the stone stairwell to their death.

Two more names were added to the list.

21 July

Names:

Maurice Gigost

Louise Dusault

Armand-Thomas Paré
Alexandre Beauharnais

The sky darkens and the heavens break open with a violent crack.
A stray cat trembles, seeks protection under a bench.

A feeling of dreaminess has come over me. I lie in my hammock,
swinging, humming a song from my youth. I can smell the sea.

23 JULY
Alexandre has been taken to the Conciergerie to stand trial. On
Delphine's finger, his talisman – the stone I had given him. This
does not matter.

24 JULY
I have fallen ill. After supper, Jeanne-Victoire came with food, a
little wine. There was no news, she said.

'But there must be,' I insisted. 'What happened at Alexandre's
trial? What happened at the Conciergerie?'

'His trial has been postponed.' She turned to the window.

[UNDATED]
The ace of spades. Death. I slip it under my pillow.

Turn and turn again, the flower turns to blood. Lovers touch and
there is life. A name is called and there is death.

They say I cry. They say I weep.

There is no escape.

[UNDATED]
I rise from my hammock, trembling with fever heat. I go to the
window, lean on the grate, press the cold metal bars to my forehead.
I search the streets for a sign. '*Someone* knows,' I whisper.

I wander into the halls. 'Tell me.'

Aimée turns her eyes away. 'Sleep,' she says, guiding me back to
my hammock. She spoons bitter wine between my lips, smooths my
forehead with a damp grey rag. I hear coughing, voices, far away:
'She is resting, now,' Jeanne-Victoire says.

Resting, now.

THE MANY LIVES & SECRET SORROWS OF JOSEPHINE B.

In the dark I rise. Fever gives me the vision of a cat. I float through empty halls on cat's paws, feel the damp cold of the stones, the air on my skin. All around me spirits hover, caressing.

'I have to know,' I say. 'Tell me.'

They guide me to a paper hidden under a stone. They give me the strength to see. It is there, on the list of the dead, his name: *Alexandre*.

In which Death calls, and I listen

[UNDATED]
Aimée slips a pair of rusty scissors into my hand. The metal is hot, hot.

I know what has to be done. I set to work, hacking at my hair, clearing a path for the knife. Clean, clean, I sing, watching the pile grow.

[UNDATED]
Aimée comes to me. 'Are you dead too?' I ask.

'You are ill,' she says. 'You have a fever, fever thoughts.'

'I hear angels singing.'

She puts her head on my bosom.

'Your tears, my friend, anoint me,' I say.

'Rose, your name was called,' she whispers. 'The doctor told them you are too weak to go.'

'Did he tell them I was dead?'

She nods, coughs. 'He told them soon.'

'It's better this way.' Better than the mob.

'The angels sing one way or another.'

I reach under my pillow, push the wad of hair into her hand.

'For the children?'

I nod. I dare not speak their names. Not with Death so close. Not with Death listening.

'The card too?'

The ace of spades. 'No!' I grab it back.

Her hand is cold on my arm. 'Rose, don't listen to the angels . . .'

I feel the air turn, the walls begin to crumble. A witch is at my side, her long fingers grasp my wrist. I cry out, pull away. It is the soothsayer, her old black face, her old white hair. I know her, know her . . .

Remember what I said! she says.

[UNDATED]
The angels do not sing. The earth pulls me, the stench of the chamber pots, rotting food. I float in, out. Voices come, voices go. Hot hands, cold hands. Cold hands. Cold hands.

Remember what I said! she says.

26 JULY (I BELIEVE)
I sat up this morning. Jeanne-Victoire gave me her day's wine. My lips are blistered, my face a mask. 'Is it the pox?' I asked, feeling my cheeks. Even so, fear was not with me.

'No, an ague,' she said. 'We thought you would die.'

'I did. Several times.'

'Your name was called.'

'Aimée told me.'

I told you! the soothsayer hisses.

I bat my hands about my ears. *Go away! Go away, old woman!*

27 JULY
I am better today. 'Don't get up,' Aimée warns, 'or they will call your name.'

The prison seems almost empty, so many have been called. Even our turnkey has gone to the scaffold, Aimée says. He was too kind to us. Poor drunk Roblâtre.

Now we have Aubert, a Septembrist. He strangles stray kittens with his bare hands, for sport. Each night after supper, he locks us in. No matter.

Outside, I hear drums, great cannonading, hurried footsteps on the cobblestones.

'Something is happening,' Jeanne-Victoire says.

Something is happening, the soothsayer whispers in my ear.

28 JULY

At sunrise the turnkey came for my hammock. I stood by the window and watched him take it down.

'But what will Citoyenne Beauharnais sleep on?' Jeanne-Victoire demanded.

'I guess she'll not be needing it any more.' He laughed.

Jeanne-Victoire turned pale. As soon as he left she burst into tears.

'Do not cry,' I told her.

But she only wept harder. 'Forgive me. I am so weak,' she said. *Remember what I said!*

I remembered: I would be unhappily married. I would be widowed.

There is more!

'Look, you do not even tremble.' Jeanne-Victoire took my hand.

Say it!

I took a breath. 'I will not die.'

Jeanne-Victoire put her arm about my shoulders to comfort me. *Say it — all of it!*

'I will be Queen,' I said. The words came from some other place in me.

'Hush, Rose, there is no queen now,' Jeanne-Victoire said sweetly, as if to a child. But the look on her face was uneasy. She thought me mad.

'And you will be my lady-in-waiting,' I said.

'You are in a fever still.' She pulled me to the window for air. Weakly, I leaned against the bars. I heard musket shot, cantering horses. In the street a woman was jumping up and down. She picked up her skirt and then a stone, her skirt and then the stone.

'She is trying to tell us something,' Jeanne-Victoire said.

The sky was red. Already the heat shimmered over the stones. The woman picked up her skirt, pointed to it.

'*Robe.*'

'*Pierre,*' Jeanne-Victoire said, for the stone. 'Robespierre. She's saying "Robespierre".'

THE MANY LIVES & SECRET SORROWS OF JOSEPHINE B.

The woman drew her hand across her throat and began to dance wildly.

Jeanne-Victoire turned to me. 'Robespierre is dead.' She looked uneasy – frightened. 'You are saved!'

Remember what I said! the old woman said.

V

La Merveilleuse

In which I walk among the living & the dead

28 JULY 1794, EVENING
Mirth without bounds. It bubbles forth from the cracks in the stones.
With a crackle and a boom, our cell lights up like the day – more
firecrackers follow, one upon the other.

The light from my candle throws shadows against the walls.
The spirits of this place, this time, are freed. They dance in the
shimmering heat. I tie my bundle of cut hair into a knot and toss
it between my hands. So close it came. My head.

Grief speaks the refrain. For those who missed the lucky stroke
by one single passing of the sun and moon. Grief . . . for Lazare,
the old puppeteers, the others, too numerous to list. Grief . . . for
Alexandre.

And fear, too, for the bars still close behind us, the guillotine
still stands.

WEDNESDAY, 6 AUGUST
Today two men came through the gates. Deputies. We, the faint,
the tattered, gathered like cattle, watching silently. Outside, on the
cobblestones, the mob – drunken, gay, dressed in musty ball gowns,
tattered silks splattered with mud.

We were herded into the chapel. One of the deputies mounted
the pulpit, a sheet of paper in his hand.

Aimée put her arm round me. 'Are you all right?'

I laughed; others turned to stare. I laughed without cause. I was
one of *those*.

The deputy cleared his throat. 'We have come in the name
of liberty.'

A man cried out. Has not all that has passed and is passing

still been done in the name of liberty? We knew liberty – liberty meant *death*.

The deputy continued. 'What I have here is a list—'

We trembled. We knew lists. The movements of this ritual were well known to us.

'—a preliminary account, we must assure you, of those whom the new members of the Committee of Public Safety deem innocently accused. The following citizens are free to leave . . .'

'Do you understand?' Aimée whispered.

'I am not a child,' I told her. They thought me mad.

'Citoyenne Rose Beauharnais.'

I looked around, frightened. My name had been called.

Aimée clasped my hands. I looked into her weeping eyes. Faces turned to me, friends encircled me. My knees gave way.

I woke on top of a plank table. Someone was stroking my forehead with a damp cloth. I heard a cough, then the words, 'She can hear me.'

I opened my eyes.

Aimée's eyes reassured me. I looked around at the others.

'Don't you understand, Rose?' Aimée said. 'You may go home. You are *free*.'

I listened to her words with fear in my heart. *Free?* What did that mean? 'Will you come with me?' I asked.

'Soon,' she assured me, smoothing rouge over my cheeks. She handed me a basket – my linen, my comb, a handkerchief enclosing my bundle of hair, my tattered cards. 'Quick, before they have a change of heart,' she hissed.

'I can't leave you here.'

'Don't cry! Your children need you.'

My children.

My friends all crowded around me, helping me to the gate. The mob out on the street was cheering. Four men in the uniform of the National Guard were trying to hold them back. Would they set upon me, tear me limb from limb?

Trembling, clasping my basket, I was pushed out on to the street. The big metal gate closed shut behind me. I looked back. The faces of my friends were wet with tears.

'Where would you be going, citoyenne?' a woman called out from behind me. Her breath smelled of liquor. She was wearing a court hat, a purple creation covered over with dirty silk flowers and tattered ribbons.

'To the river?' I could not recall.

Rue Saint-Dominique was wider than I remembered, an empty thoroughfare. On the big wooden doors a paper had been posted. Sealed, by order of the law; enter on penalty of death. *Death*. I turned away, panic filling me. Where were my children? Where were Hortense and Eugène?

I stumbled down Rue du Belle Chasse. The dogs in the lumberyard growled at me. At Port-de-la-Grenoüillere, I held my hand to my eyes. Light glittered off the river. Across, on the other side, a crowd was gathering in Place de la Révolution, around the guillotine. Still?

I turned towards Princess Amalia's, towards the Hôtel de Salm. Daily the children had gone there to visit, I knew.

The gates to the courtyard were bolted. I shook the bell rope. The chambermaid came running. She peered through the metal bars.

'Citoyenne Beauharnais,' I said. I did not say: the *widow* Beauharnais.

A short man appeared between the portico columns. His yellow satin waistcoat glittered with gems. 'What is it?' A peasant, by his accent. He was holding a thick horse whip.

'I wish to speak to Citoyenne Amalia Hohenzollern.' A feeling of weakness came over me. I grasped the metal bars for support.

'The princess? She and her kind have run across the Rhine, along with all the other vermin.'

Princess Amalia . . . in *Germany*? 'Her brother, Citoyen Frédéric, is he—'

The maid made a quick motion of one finger across her throat.

Frédéric – *guillotined*? Mon Dieu.

The man commanded the woman to get back to her chores. I grabbed her sleeve through the bars. 'Where are my children!' I demanded. 'Where are Hortense and Eugène?'

'Their great-aunt came—'

The man cracked his whip.

'Citoyenne Renaudin?'

'No – the short one,' she hissed, running.

Fanny? Was it possible?

*   *   *

THE MANY LIVES & SECRET SORROWS OF JOSEPHINE B.

293

It was Jacques, Fanny's man-of-all-work, who opened the big wooden doors to the courtyard. He suffered a moment of confusion before he realized who I was. I took his leathery hands in mine. My heart was beating wildly. 'My children – are they here?'

I followed him into the house. Fortuné came scurrying into the hall. I scooped him up in my arms; he was a mass of wriggling, his little tongue licking my cheek.

Lannoy appeared at the upstairs landing, Agathe not far behind. 'Who is it, Jacques?' Lannoy asked. She regarded me with haughty disapproval.

'Citoyenne Rose!'

'Madame?' Lannoy looked down at me with an expression of disbelief.

I heard a familiar voice behind me. I turned. It was an old woman, her face heavily made-up.

Fanny. I put one arm round her shoulders, touched her cheek with my lips, her dry, papery skin. 'Thank God you survived,' I said, fighting back tears. How long had it been, the nightmare we had endured? Was it possible it was over?

'Mon Dieu, child, you're so thin.' She stood back to look at me.

'I've been ill. The children—'

'They're here.' Fanny put her fingers round my wrist. 'There's hardly anything to you. And your hair . . . !' She smiled, in spite of herself.

'Aunt Désirée? The Marquis? Are they . . . ?' *Let them be alive,* I prayed.

Then: *Be merciful, let them pass. Please do not ask them to endure the pain of Alexandre's death . . .*

'They are back in their house now – in Fontainebleau. Before they were in hiding. Charlotte put them up in her basement.'

'The cook?' I tried to imagine Aunt Désirée and the Marquis in Charlotte's brusque care. 'Do they . . . have they been told?' I held on to the banister to steady myself. Did *Fanny* even know?

'About Alexandre?' Fanny whispered.

I nodded. Yes.

I heard a girl singing, the sound of a harpsichord. 'Hortense?' I went to the door of the music room. Hortense was sitting at the instrument, her back to me. Eugène and Émilie were seated close by. Eugène turned to look at me. His expression said, 'Who is this woman?'

Hortense stopped playing. She turned and stared.

I stopped, confused. 'Do you not know me?' I let Fortuné down. He stayed by my feet, whimpering to be taken up again. 'Fortuné knows who I am.'

'Maman?' Eugène's voice cracked.

'It is not,' Hortense said.

'They do not believe it is me,' I told Fanny. I managed a smile.

'Mon Dieu, it's no wonder – you look like a stray cat!' She ordered the children to approach.

Eugène came up to me bravely, permitting an embrace, followed by Émilie, who burst into tears. Hortense refused, standing behind Eugène. She watched me, her big blue eyes not revealing any emotion. Her father's eyes.

Fanny chided her goddaughter. 'Your prayers have been answered and look how you behave.'

'I understand,' I said. 'I'm—'

A sick feeling swept through me, violently this time. I doubled over. Fanny called out to Jacques, who helped me to a bench. 'Would you take a dish of broth?' Fanny asked.

I shook my head. I felt too ill. 'I need to wash,' I said. I took a breath, sat up. The pain had passed. The children – alarmed, no doubt – were standing in a silent clump by the harpsichord, watching. 'I'm all right,' I told them.

'Fill the copper tub,' Fanny told Jacques. 'Make it hot.'

'There is little wood,' he protested.

'Do what you can.'

Lannoy helped me up to Fanny's bedchamber. Then she helped me undress, making little clucking noises of dismay. Tears filled her eyes.

'I couldn't wash,' I told her, embarrassed by my filth, my bones. 'There was no water.'

She helped me into the big laundry tub, which Fanny had made fragrant and healing with herbs. Afterwards, Fanny brought me a shift, pretty with lace.

I protested. 'I am infested.'

Fanny shrugged. 'So are we all.' She led me to a stool.

Slowly, she combed the nits out of my hair, talking – of hiding in an attic in Valenciennes, of returning to Paris to try to get her daughter Marie out of prison (without success), of her own imprisonment in Port-Royal, of Michel de Cubières's heroic rescue.

I listened without hearing. In front of me was a looking glass, framed in ormolu. The woman I saw was a stranger to me. Her gaunt face was lined, aged, without colour. Her teeth were black, her eyes sunken — furtive, fearful eyes.

It was no wonder the children did not know me. This woman was not their mother.

Who, then, was she?

I did not want to know.

As I write this, now, it is almost five in the afternoon. I'm sitting at the writing desk in Fanny's guest room. I've slept, performed a modest toilette, put on one of Fanny's gowns — it hangs loosely from my shoulders.

Outside, on the Rue de Tournon, I hear a bell — a rag-picker's wagon. The sound brings back memories, memories which seem more real to me than this room I inhabit, memories of the Carmes, of the prisoners — my dearest friends — who at this very moment are lying on their straw pallets listening for the sound of the guard's footsteps, listening for the peal of his bell announcing supper.

Strangely, I long to be with them. Here, outside the prison walls, I do not know my place. I am of this world, but not of this world. I am like a zombie, risen from the dead.

LATER THAT DAY

I rise, dress, eat — go through the simple routines of my day. It is not real; I am performing a part in a play. Yet it is through these simple acts — tying a sash, fastening a button, reading out a sentence in a reader — that Hortense and Eugène begin to know me again. How I long to take them in my arms, *touch* them, but even now I must refrain. I must not alarm them.

8 AUGUST

I am stronger today, ready for realities. 'Tell me,' I told Fanny.

'It is too soon,' she said.

'Nothing can wound me.' Indeed, I feel I am already dead. I do not tell her this.

She went to her desk and pulled out a blue silk kerchief, folded. There was something inside.

I opened it – hair, long and wavy, chestnut in colour.

'Alexandre's,' she said.

I looked up at her.

'I asked the gaoler for it.'

'You . . . you were *there*?' I felt a prickly feeling in my hands. 'You *saw*?' Did I want to ask? Did I want to know?

'I did not think Alexandre should die alone.'

I pressed my face to my knees, fighting back tears. How I revered this woman, her feisty, quirky, stubborn strength.

'Rose! Are you ill?'

I sat up, took a breath. 'Forgive me, I was overcome.'

'You would have done the same,' she said.

Was it true? 'He knew you were there, I am sure.'

'There's more.' Fanny handed me a pamphlet.

I turned it over in my hands. Alexandre's name was on it. 'What is it?' I asked. 'Alexandre wrote this?' I noticed my name. 'It's written to *me*?' I scanned the text:

I am the victim . . .

The brotherly fondness I have for you . . .

Cherish my memory . . .

The words shifted and moved before my eyes. 'Where did you get this?' I turned the printed sheet over in my hand. One sou, it said, in the lower right-hand corner. 'Did you *pay* for it?'

'I got it by the Luxembourg gates. A young man in a toga was selling them. He had a basketful.' She paused. 'Apparently it's Alexandre's last statement – to you.'

Goodbye, dear friend . . .

Console yourself for the sake of our children . . .

I was having difficulty breathing. I stood and went to the window. How like Alexandre to arrange to have his last words *published*, I thought.

'Rose, he was thinking of the family honour, of the children.'

'I understand,' I said. Two women were helping a drunken man walk down the street. 'He'd fallen in love with Madame Custine – General Custine's daughter-in-law.'

'Delphine Custine? That silly blonde thing?' Fanny scoffed. 'That couldn't have been pleasant for you.'

I lowered myself on to the little upholstered stool in front of the fireplace. 'I can't recall,' I said.

6.00 P.M.

Eugène was withdrawn this afternoon – he remained silent throughout supper. 'It's nothing!' he insisted.

I followed him to his room. 'Something is weighing on you.' I sat down next to his table of military figurines.

He shrugged, repositioning four cannon, kneeling to assess the angles.

'Eugène, please, talk to me. It's something to do with your father, isn't it?' No response. 'Did anything happen at the workshop this morning? Did Citoyen Quinette say something?' Citoyen Quinette is an excellent cabinetmaker, but known for his temper.

Eugène shook his head.

'Who then? The other lads who work there?'

He would not look at me.

'Did they say something to you?'

I reached to touch his shoulder. Abruptly, he twisted away. 'They call me the son of a traitor!' He hid his face in his hands.

'Do you believe them, Eugène?'

'He lost Mainz! He never attacked – instead, he ran!'

'Is that what they say?'

He nodded, tears bursting from him. He wiped them away, embarrassed by his weakness.

'And what do you tell *them*?'

'What *can* I say!'

I studied my son's face. His father – a man he revered, a man who had stood for all that was noble and good – had been put in prison, tried, found guilty, condemned to death. 'I will tell you, then,' I said, taking a breath. 'In war, as in love, it is always complex. You are old enough to begin to understand.' I told him of the condition of his father's troops – farm boys without training, without food. I told him of the enemy – professionals outnumbering his father's troops ten to one. I told him of Alexandre's reluctance to lead his men to slaughter.

'To many, to be a hero one must bask in the blood of others. To many, your father should have led his men to death, risked their lives for the sake of glory. But to me, it proved your father's courage – his courage to risk condemnation, arrest, death even, in order to stand by what he knew to be right. Is *this* not heroic?'

Eugène looked at me with a steady expression.

'You are the son of a good man, Eugène, a man who loved you very much, a man who loved his *country*. A man who lived – and died – for what he believed in. A *hero*. You must never forget that. Your father's memory will be cleared – I promised him that – but it must begin in *your* own heart.'

And in my own.

9 AUGUST

I don the clothes of the widow Beauharnais. The dull black suits my soul, reflects the death I feel within. Even my children cannot wake me from this slumber. Stiff white gauze tickles my throat. A veil of taffeta covers my boyish curls. I am a ghost. I am a survivor.

I set out for the Faubourg Saint-Antoine. 'Place du Trône *renversé*,' I tell the driver.

He puts me down at a corner. I instruct him to wait. I walk the edges. This is where my husband died.

It is a cloudy, hot day. Everywhere children are playing. Did they skip around the guillotine? Did they sing?

I dodge horses, carriages – make my way to the centre. There, despite the curses of the carters, the threat of their whips, I stand. Is *this* the spot? I am only a moment, waiting. Only a moment, long enough to know that he is not there.

I return to the carriage, instruct my driver once again. This time we head out to the country, outside the city walls. I have been told the way; in any case, my driver seems to know.

He regards my dark robes, my short-cropped hair. 'I go often, myself,' he tells me. He is wearing a tall hat with yellow tassels. 'My son is there. My wife went once, but no more.' He needs to talk.

At last, we stop. It is only a farmer's field. It has been dug, mounded, turned. But for that, one would not guess its use.

'The King and Queen are here,' the driver tells me. He is proud of this. 'It is said they share a pit with Robespierre.' He takes down the step. I accept the offer of his rough hand. He wants to be helpful. He has been too much alone in this place.

There are others in the field, four diggers, a pile of lime, a cart nearby. Bodies. Heads.

'Still?' Still more to bury?

'The mountain meets the earth.' The driver laughs at his joke. He nods towards an old woman in a spotted muslin dress, sitting on the ground. 'She's always here,' he says. He twirls a finger at his temple, meaning: crazy.

Unlike the rest of us, I think with irony.

I scan the broken earth, the weeds. So this is where Alexandre lies. And the others – Lazare? Frédéric? The dear old puppeteers? It comforts me to think of them all together.

I head out across the field. I do not have a plan. At the centre I pick up three stones. One for Hortense, one for Eugène, one for myself. I feel the smooth surfaces. Tokens.

Is that all there is? Is it true, what the Jacobins say – that death is eternal sleep, no more, no less?

The soothsayer said: *you will be unhappily married. You will be widowed.*

I watch as two birds fly through the air – a pair. I wait for some sense of meaning. But there are no answers, only this . . . this awful emptiness.

In which ghosts come to life

10 AUGUST 1794

The dawn was breaking when I set out, accompanied by Jacques. The beggars on the Rue de Vaugirard were still asleep. In front of the Luxembourg a grocer was whipping a donkey in an effort to make the old creature move. We made our way round the quarrelsome pair.

It was a short walk to the Carmes, I knew, but one which bridged two worlds. There are degrees of courage, and I was unsure if I had the will to enter those prison gates again. I was thankful Jacques was with me.

A guard I didn't recognize opened the gate. Jacques knocked on the heavy plank door to the turnkey's office. I heard someone coughing inside. Within, by the light of one tallow candle, the turnkey was hunched over a journal, scowling. A very pregnant Lucie was slumped sleepily on a chair, bursting her seams. Aimée was sitting in the far corner. I was struck by the animal look in her eyes.

She burst into a crazy laugh, which in turn gave way to a rattling cough that stole her very breath. 'Am I so very frightful?' she gasped, when she could breathe again.

Jacques took her basket, her meagre possessions. 'Ready?'

'What about Jean-Henri?' I asked.

'Croisoeuil?' The turnkey leafed through his papers. 'No.' Lucie shrugged.

Out on the street an old man came up to us. 'Welcome.' He handed Lucie a flower.

'How does he know?' She watched the man hobble away.

I took Aimée's hand. I could feel the bones. 'We are staying at my Aunt Fanny's on Rue de Tournon,' I told her. 'It's a short walk from here. Are you strong enough?'

'We're not going to Rue Saint-Dominique?'

'It's been sealed.'

'I can't go home?' I saw something crumble within her.

'Come,' I said.

EVENING

'Are you sure you're all right?' I asked Aimée as I helped her to bed. She seemed strange to me yet.

'I pretend,' she said.

I sat down on the bed beside her. It seemed a curious thing to say.

'You're pretending, too. Only you've convinced yourself,' she said.

Tears came to my eyes. She was right. I did pretend. I did not speak of the horror I have known. 'It's different out here, Aimée. *We're* different.'

'The craziness, you mean.'

'More than that.' I pulled the sheet over her, kissed her forehead. 'Sleep.' I closed the curtains, blew out the candle on the mantel.

'You didn't say what it was, Rose,' she said, in the dark.

I stood for a moment. What *was* it? 'Shame,' I said. In the dark, one word. Shame that we broke down, grovelled, *begged*. Shame for crying out, weeping, beating our heads against the stones. Shame for losing hope, faith, for being willing to forsake everything, *anything*, in barter for life. Shame for knowing fear, its sickening grip.

The shame of the survivor.

'Yes,' Aimée whispered. 'That too.'

11 AUGUST

This morning I met Citoyen Dunnkirk, my banker, to attempt to put my finances in order. The news is not good. Martinico has threatened to go over to the British rather than submit to the revolutionary government in France. Citoyen Dunnkirk has reason to believe that Mother has opened her home to the British forces, offered support to the enemy.

'To the *British*?' I thought of Father, of a life spent in battle against '*les Goddams*'. Had Mother offered British officers my father's bed? I was thankful he was dead.

'I assure you that this information will be held in strict confidence. I am aware of the dishonour this could cause you, the suspicion—'

'She is well?' I interrupted. 'The plantation, is it . . . ?'

'I don't know if you are aware that your father left a substantial debt – one hundred thousand livres.' Citoyen Dunnkirk sneezed into an ugly green kerchief.

'Why was I not—'

'We just found out ourselves. Your mother – a resourceful woman, by all accounts – made an arrangement with her creditors whereby the debt would be paid off over a period of time. Fortunately, the crop was good this year, in spite of the civic turmoil. So good, in fact, she was able to pay off the debt and is reported to have hosted a celebration party for everyone in the village.'

'*Mother?*' Surely he was talking about another woman. 'Are you sure?'

'Quite sure, citoyenne. In fact, we are given to believe that your mother is comfortable, perhaps even well-off. She should have no difficulty providing you with the interest on your holdings – if she can get it to you, that is. Due to the war, *any* correspondence will prove difficult, of course.'

'I can't write to her?'

'You could *try*,' he shrugged. 'Is she aware of your . . . situation?'

'She knows nothing.' Nothing of prison, nothing of Alexandre's death.

We reviewed my accounts. I have a sizeable (and growing) debt to Citoyen Dunnkirk, who so kindly advanced funds for the care of the children while Alexandre and I were in prison. 'I will repay you,' I assured him – but *how*? 'I have gems hidden in my rooms on Rue Saint-Dominique. I can sell them, when . . .'

When . . . When the seals were removed. When would *that* be?

'It will take time,' Citoyen Dunnkirk warned, sneezing again. 'The wheels of bureaucracy have always moved slowly, and now . . .' He threw up his hands.

'What about La Ferté?' I asked. Alexandre had invested all of his inheritance in his country estate.

'Your husband's properties have been sequestered. Items of any value have been sold by the government at auction.'

'Sold?' There was a painting of Alexandre as a child – I had wanted it for Hortense and Eugène. 'And when might *that* sequestration be lifted?'

Citoyen Dunnkirk looked at me uncomfortably. 'I hate to be the one to tell you this, citoyenne, but the law gives the government full possession of the property of the condemned. Even if the sequestration were to be lifted today, the estate would not accrue to you *or* your children.'

Slowly I grasped the situation. According to law, Alexandre died a criminal. The children have been robbed of their inheritance. They face their future with nothing but the clothes on their backs and a blackened name.

I returned to Rue de Tournon shortly before noon. There were a number of people gathered on the street. A woman with a hurdy-gurdy was standing in front of the door to Fanny's hôtel.

'Something is happening,' I told Fanny, putting my basket down in the hall. Crowds frightened me.

'They're releasing prisoners at the Luxembourg today.' Fanny was holding a stack of books in one arm. 'And making a spectacle of it – speeches, a parade apparently.'

'Where are the children?' I asked.

'Up at the corner.'

I sighed. Watching prisoners being released had become a form of entertainment. 'Lucie as well?'

'She consented to go, in spite of the fact that the dress I provided was not judged suitably flattering.'

'Neither prison nor pregnancy have dampened that child's vanity,' I said. 'And Aimée?'

Fanny nodded towards the double doors leading out on to the balcony. 'She only just got up. Were you able to get coach tickets to Fontainebleau?'

'I'll try again in the morning.' Two times already I'd tried to get a pass.

I stepped outside on to the balcony. Aimée was leaning out over the edge, her hair hanging down loose and long. I thought to say something to her, to caution her against immodesty, but held my tongue. What did it matter, any more?

I put my arm round her shoulders, kissed her forehead. She'd slept for over twenty hours, the sleep of the dead, but even so, she looked exhausted.

'Good,' she said, answering a question I had not voiced. She put her hand to her mouth to still a cough.

I looked out over the throng. A woman with a child at her breast was wearing a dress made from a flag. Four young men dressed in togas were making their way slowly down the street carrying a banner proclaiming '*la nation*'. Everyone cheered as they passed.

'This seems like a dream to me,' I said. Now and again a wind carried a faint scent of honeysuckle.

Aimée laughed. That awful prison laugh, Fanny called it.

A carriage pulled by a team of old bays turned on to Rue de Tournon. Two open carriages followed. A tall, young man bedecked with red, white and blue ribbons was standing in the last one. The woman in the flag dress began yelling joyously, holding up her baby as if for a blessing.

'Isn't that Tallien?' I asked. Tallien's signature had been on my release form. A stunning young woman sat beside him, scantily dressed in a white toga, a sash with the words '*la liberté*' draped across one shoulder. Her curly black hair was cut short, like a boy's. 'And Thérèse Cabarrus!'

For days the children had been telling me the story: how a beautiful young woman had sent Deputy Tallien a note from prison, hidden along with a dagger in a cabbage, how for love of *her* he had brandished her little dagger in the Assembly, challenged the tyrant Robespierre, ended the Terror.

'Your friends – the new King and Queen,' Fanny said, joining us. 'That could be useful.'

I picked a blossom from a potted rosebush and attempted to toss it into the carriage. I missed and tried again, calling out this time. Thérèse glanced up. She tried to say something to Tallien, but it was too noisy on the street, the crowd too demanding.

Shortly after there was a pounding at the gate. Jacques returned with a message. 'A boy,' he said. 'He said to tell you that the lady with Deputy Tallien invites you to see her.'

'Thérèse? Did he give an address?'

'Nine Rue Georges, Chaussée d'Antin. Tomorrow afternoon at three.'

'You will see about Marie?' Fanny demanded, grasping my arm.

12 AUGUST

A thin boy, only a little older than Eugène, answered the door.* I followed him into a room full of potted flowering bushes. 'She will be with you,' the boy stuttered, and disappeared.

I heard a woman singing – her voice was lyrical, slightly melancholy; it had a haunting quality. Thérèse Cabarrus stepped into the room. She was dressed in a loose white tunic drapped in the Roman style. Her short, jet-black curls framed her face, her tresses shorn, short and boyish, like my own . . . but for the same reason? I wondered. It did not seem possible. The grey pallor that marked the victims of the Terror, the shadow that enveloped our souls seemed not to have touched her. Was it possible she had even been in prison?

'You do not bear scars,' I said, after exchanging civilités. It was bad form to refer to the horrors of the past, but I felt somehow compelled.

She slipped a foot out of a white silk slipper. 'See these?' She touched three spots on her toes. 'From *rats*.'

I put my hand to my throat. I had seen what rats could do.

'May I confide in you?' Her touch on my hand was light, caressing. 'When I was taken to La Petite-Force, I was held in a room by eight guards. I was told to remove my clothes.' She recounted her tale without emotion. 'I knew the danger I was in. The turnkey, a little man with a repulsive face, claimed authority. He ordered the men away. But then he demanded his due.'

I looked at her – her clear white skin, her young flushed cheeks. She looked a child, an infinitely vulnerable but voluptuous urchin.

'I used to believe in love,' she went on, 'but no longer. Perhaps *that* is my scar.' She examined my eyes with surprise. 'You weep? For *me*?'

---

* This is Guéry, the fourteen-year-old son of one of Thérèse's business acquaintances, released the day before from the Luxembourg prison.

'Yet love makes great deeds possible,' I said. 'I am told you refused on threat of death to sign a statement that would have compromised Deputy Tallien.'

'I am cast in the role of a heroine. I enjoy the part, I confess. The lines, the costume, the applause have a certain charm − don't you think?' She smiled, fanning herself. 'Forgive me for indulging in theatrics. It is a weakness of mine. But I promise I will always be honest with you. It was not love that inspired my loyalty. It was simply that death ceased to frighten.' She closed her fan with a snap. 'And *that*, my friend, is *true* freedom.'

I heard the sound of a man's voice in the entryway, footsteps. Tallien entered. Close behind him was Deputy Barras, his long sword trailing.

'Rose!' Tallien exclaimed with a boyish grin. He embraced me.

'How good to see you,' I said, unexpectedly moved.

'You recall Deputy Barras?' Tallien asked.

'Of course,' I said. 'The two of you came to my salon on Rue Saint-Dominique, several years ago.'

'Citoyenne Beauharnais, what a *pleasure*,' Deputy Barras said, taking my hand and kissing it tenderly, in the old style. He smelled of spirit of ambergris. 'Has it really been so very long?' he asked, his eyes mournful and tender. He'd gained weight since last I saw him − his leather hunting breeches were tight on him. Even so, he defined elegance.

'Young Guéry showed you in?' Thérèse asked.

Deputy Barras embraced her fondly. 'He looks too thin,' he told her. 'Send him over to my place; I'll fatten him up.'

'I'm not letting him anywhere near *you*.'

'Unfair!' Deputy Barras lowered himself into a plush pink arm-chair.

Tallien stood in front of the fireplace. 'My condolences, Rose. I was grieved to learn about your husband . . .'

I nodded.

'How unfortunate. Only a few more days and . . . If only . . .'
If only . . .

'We are all of us in mourning,' I said. All of us in shock. 'Everyone lost someone dear.' I accepted the glass of cherry brandy the maid offered. I raised my glass to propose a toast. 'I would like to express my gratitude. First, to you, Tallien, my dear friend. It was *your* name on my release form.'

'I'm sorry I couldn't get you out sooner,' he said.

'And, second, to the three of you. I am under the impression that together you saved us from Robespierre, *le tyran*.'

'We "blood-drinkers" — as he was so fond of calling us — finally got a bit of his.' Deputy Barras downed his glass of brandy.

'Tallien and Barras deserve the credit,' Thérèse said.

'Didn't you send Tallien a note and a dagger hidden inside a cabbage?' I smiled. 'That's what my children tell me.'

'I love that story,' Thérèse said.

'In truth, we'd been plotting for some time,' Tallien said.

'The tip-off was when Robespierre began taking riding lessons,' Deputy Barras said, tapping tobacco into his pipe. 'When a *politician* begins to ride, prepare for battle — an elementary lesson taught to all students at any military college.'

'So Thérèse didn't send a note to Tallien?' I asked.

'You mean the one that refers to our friend's "notorious coward-ice"?' Deputy Barras laughed. Tallien gave him a menacing look.

'I did send a note,' Thérèse said. 'The gaoler's wife smuggled it out for me. I fabricated the story of the cabbage in order to protect her. It makes a good fable, don't you think?'

'I especially like the part about the little dagger,' Deputy Barras said, his big, sorrowful eyes droll.

'I'm amazed people believe it,' Tallien said. 'How could one possibly keep a dagger in prison?'

'Ah, but the French love a good story,' Deputy Barras said.

'Not that there aren't good stories to be told,' Thérèse said.

I put my hands to my ears: I'm listening!

Then the stories began: how they had plotted; how Tallien had brandished a dagger (his own) in the Assembly, confronted Robespierre ('I still can't believe you did that,' I told him. 'I can't believe it either,' he said); how Deputy Barras had boldly taken charge of the military, been the one to arrest Robespierre; how in the middle of the night Deputy Barras had stormed the Temple, seen the Boy — the King's son — alone in his cell.

'You *saw* him?' I asked, interrupting.

The *Boy*. I almost said *King*. 'How old is he now? Ten?' He was only a little younger than Hortense, I recalled, who was eleven now.

I remembered seeing him at the theatre, sitting on his mother's lap. I remembered his sweet distress over his mother's tears. How horrible it must be for him, so small a child, an orphan now, alone in a prison cell.

'The Little Capet is small,' Deputy Barras said, 'too small to be King. *Fortunately*. But ill. He'd been badly tended.'

Thérèse tapped my hand with her fan. 'I should caution you, Rose. Every time the subject of the Boy comes up Deputy Barras begins to weep.'

Deputy Barras laughed. 'It's so unbearably sad! When I saw him he was dressed in grey rags, lying in this tiny cradle – he refused to sleep in his own big bed for some reason. His face was all puffed up, his hands swollen. Frankly, I've been terrified he might die, so I've ordered him examined, put under care. No sign of rickets, the doctor assures me.' He shrugged. 'But I'm not sure how old he is, frankly. As for Madame Royale, his sister, she's,' he cupped his hands, indicating breasts, 'healthier, although not in the head. She has difficulty speaking. I've been told our dear departed Robespierre paid her a visit. No doubt she owes her life to his . . . *interest*, you might say. If we're not careful, we'll be having a litter of would-be kings and queens to worry about. Can you imagine a Capet-Robespierre combination? *Terrifying*. But the boy . . . ? Yes, well, nine, eight perhaps? A sweet child. I wish . . .' He sighed.

'Poor Paul,' Tallien said, handing him a handkerchief. 'Who would have thought that becoming a public parent of the state meant becoming a *parent*.'

Deputy Barras wiped his eyes, sighed wryly. 'It's a job. The crown jewels, the crown prince and princess,' he rolled his eyes, 'the *crown*.'

'Don't say that!' Thérèse said.

A footman came to the door with a note on a silver tray.

'Speaking of jobs,' Deputy Barras shoved in his lorgnon and squinted at the note, holding it at arm's length. He handed it to Tallien. 'You read it,' he said. 'You have young eyes.'

'They've changed the meeting to this afternoon,' Tallien said. 'At four.'

'The Committee?'

Tallien nodded.

Deputy Barras groaned, pulled out his timepiece. 'We'd better get over there.' He stood, stretched, his hand on the small of his back. 'I'm getting too old for this.' He put on his velvet toque hat, adjusting the tricolour plume. 'If we leave that group alone for even a minute, there will be another takeover — only our heads will be the ones to roll this time.'

'Hold on a moment.' Thérèse was rummaging through stacks of loose papers on a writing desk.

'I'll get the horses ready,' Deputy Barras said. 'Au revoir, citoyenne.' He bowed and kissed my hand.

'My pleasure,' I said.

'Here it is.' Thérèse handed Tallien a scrap of paper.

'*Another* list?' He groaned.

'The ones with the stars are the most urgent.'

He slipped the note into the pocket of his striped redingote. 'I'll see.'

I stood, withdrawing a list of my own from my velvet bag. Tallien smiled ruefully when he saw it. 'I'm surrounded by angels of mercy.'

'It's about my cousin,' I said. I pointed out Marie's name. 'Citoyenne Marie Beauharnais — remember? We'd been working to get her out before I was imprisoned. But she's still—'

Tallien put up his hands: stop!

'And Jean-Henri Croisoeuil, my friend Aimée's son-in-law,' I went on, regardless. 'He's in the Carmes, and—'

'I will do what I can,' he said, taking my list. 'I *promise*. But it's difficult. Robespierre may be dead, but his followers live. They're a tenacious lot.'

'If anyone can do it, *you* can,' Thérèse said.

Tallien put his hands to his chest, mocking the pose of a hero.

'You jest,' I said, 'but were it not for your courageous act, we would not be alive today.' Tallien smiled uneasily. He was more comfortable in the role of a rogue. 'I owe you my life,' I said, kissing his cheek. 'I will *never* forget it.'

7.00 P.M.
Thanks to Tallien I was finally able to obtain seats on a post coach to Fontainebleau. We leave in the morning.

THURSDAY, 14 AUGUST

The children and I have been to Fontainebleau and back. I'm exhausted.

It was unsettling to see Aunt Désirée and the Marquis. Aunt Désirée is over fifty now, true, but she looks even older. And the Marquis, at eighty, is an invalid. His mind has begun to wander, his memory weak. Mercifully. Several times he called Eugène by Alexandre's name.

They are back in their own house now. The place had been ransacked, their belongings ruined – but this is trivial in Aunt Désirée's eyes. Her grief for Alexandre is without bounds. I fear for the effect the violence of her feelings will have on her heart. The loss of all of their worldly goods would be enough in itself, but none of it means anything to her. Her one consuming grief, and it is incessant, is the fact of Alexandre's death.

Aunt Désirée was not Alexandre's mother, but she loved him far more than his own mother did, more than I ever did. It is for her I weep.

THAT EVENING

So many are being released, one would think the prisons were empty now. Yet even so, Marie remains. 'You must be patient,' Tallien told me.

'Patient!' Fanny cried out when I told her.

I understood. I was in prison for four months and it very nearly killed me. Marie has been in for over nine months. How much longer can she hold on?

FRIDAY, 15 AUGUST

Lucie's husband Jean-Henri has finally been released. He, Aimée and Lucie will be returning to Croissy in a few days. I'm hosting a small gathering on their behalf – a reunion of sorts, in spite of Aimée's ill health. General Santerre and my former cellmate Jeanne-Victoire d'Aiguillon will be coming, as well as a number of others recently released from the Carmes.

Lannoy has threatened to quit if 'that beast Santerre' sets foot in her house. I reminded her, gently, that this is not her house, that we are guests of my aunt.

Fanny has been trying to console me about my hair. 'You look like a Greek shepherd. Even your Creole accent is fashionable now.'

I nodded, not hearing, examining myself in the looking glass, my cropped hair: '*coiffure à la victime*' it is called.

'Short curls suit you,' Fanny went on. 'They make you look young.'

Young?

Never. Never again.

EVENING

The gathering began with discomfort. We were strangers to one another, ill at ease in this world. But with time (and wine) we discovered we could be ourselves again, speaking a language few others could understand, the language of prisoners.

Towards midnight General Santerre introduced a bawdy game of charades that had us howling with laughter. We fell upon one another weeping. It was at this moment that Jacques entered. He whispered something in Fanny's ear.

Fanny glanced at me, made a gesture I did not understand. I cocked my head to one side: pardon?

Everyone in the room grew still. 'Mon Dieu,' Aimée whispered, looking towards the door. I saw the colour drain from her face.

'Rose?'

It was a man's voice – a familiar voice. My heart jumped. I turned. Lazare Hoche stood before us.

In which I must bid farewell to those I love

Lazare smiled. 'I am *not* a ghost,' he said. 'I wish everyone would stop treating me like one.'

I stood, approached. In a moment I would faint, I knew.

'Don't, Rose.' His voice had that tenderness – that same tenderness I remembered.

'Lazarro?' Speaking helped. I put my hands to my face. 'It's just . . . we . . . I thought . . .' Tears flooded my eyes.

He leaned his sword against the wall, took off his hat. 'Are you not going to embrace me?' Teasing.

I pressed my cheek against the scratchy wool of his jacket.

Aimée and the others crowded around us. Lazare bowed, a mock gallant. 'You ask, is he dead? Alive?' He laughed.

He was as handsome, as vital as I remembered him. I leaned against the wall. A feeling of light-headedness had come over me.

'I take it this is the *famous* General Hoche.' Fanny gave him a beguiling look, a look she reserved for handsome young men, and slipped one arm through his. We followed their slow progression into the salon. 'You were said to be dead, General. No doubt you have a story to tell. Perhaps you could entertain us with an account of your resurrection. We have come to love miracles.'

Lazare helped Fanny to the sofa by the fireplace, then lowered himself on to a leather armchair close by. I sat with Lucie and Aimée on the sofa opposite. A whirlwind of emotions filled me. I held myself in check, fearful lest my strong feelings became too evident. Lazare. *Alive.*

He seemed a crude man in Fanny's elegant salon, his humble origins evident. And young. Younger than I remembered. A tall man, thin. That had not changed. But pale, I thought. What had happened to him?

General Santerre stood in front of the fireplace, his hands clasped in front of him, a bemused expression on his face.

'You knew about this?' Aimée asked.

General Santerre and Lazare exchanged looks. Lazare accepted a glass of port from Jacques. Then he related his story. He had been kept in a dungeon so deep he'd been forgotten. On the fourth day of August the bars to his cell had been opened. He thought his time had come. He emerged into the light, surprised that there were no guards, no guns, no tumbrils waiting. 'The turnkey had his feet on a table. He was singing a rude camp song. I thought of escape, but before I could make a move he gestured: out! As if shushing a stray cat away. Then yesterday, midday, I ran into our friend, General Santerre, in a cabaret in Les Halles. He told me of this gathering and we devised this little surprise.' Lazare caught my eye and dared to wink.

I looked away, my heart beating foolishly. We had been lovers, true — but in that other world, that world of shadow and desperate need. Out here, the rules were different; everything was changed. Out here, Lazare was a former stable groom; I a former vicomtesse. Out here, Lazare was a handsome young man, married, a general with a brilliant future . . . and I? Who was I but an impoverished widow, a mother of two, no longer young, no longer pretty.

As the guests departed, I stood back, unsure what to say. Fanny had long since retired, and Aimée, no fool, disappeared without a word, leaving Lazare and me alone together.

He leaned against the door, looking at me, saying nothing.

'You must not stare so,' I said.

'I was grieved to learn of your husband's death.'

'He was one of the unlucky ones.'

'He was a good man, a good general.'

'Did you really think so?'

'You do not know that?'

'A wife sees her husband in a different way.'

'And how do you see me?'

'You are as forthright as ever.' I smiled.

He put on his hat, took his sword. 'If I were to call . . . ?'

I looked towards the stairs. 'My children, it is still very . . . I don't know.'

'Could we meet? At the Café Lutte in the Palais-Égalité, perhaps?'

'Palais-Royal, you mean?'

He nodded, slipping on his cape. 'If you wish to see me, I will be there tomorrow, at one.'

SATURDAY, 16 AUGUST

Fanny warned me that the Palais-Royal had changed but even so I was unprepared for what I saw. Booths and tables were set up in the courtyard, selling everything that could be imagined: confiscated church relics, silver tea services, candlesticks, snuffers, used clothing of every description, much of it clearly from the closets of aristocrats now dead, banished or merely impoverished.

And the noise! It was early in the afternoon, but even so, the dance halls and gambling rooms were packed. Young women in transparent gauze gowns hung about the fountains, posing to attract the attention of the young men, themselves dressed outrageously in tight silk.

It was with some relief that I slipped into the quiet of the Café Lutte. A violinist played in one corner. A waiter moved silently over the thick carpets. Even the most scarred among us looked fresh in the soft candlelight.

Lazare stood as I was shown to his table. 'You came,' he said. It was with some pleasure, I confess, that I noted relief in his voice.

'You thought I might not?' I asked, allowing him to slip my cape from my shoulders.

He kissed the back of my neck.

I turned to face him. I had prepared a number of things to say: that I was only recently a widow; that it was too soon, my children required all my attention; that it was too complex, not right; that I was ill still, not yet strong; that he was himself married; that what had begun in a prison, under the threat of death, might not be the same now, here, in this other world . . .

Yet words escaped me. I lost all will. I found myself accepting his attentions with gratitude. We spent a very short time together in the café. Then I went with him to his rooms.

17 AUGUST

I've never known a man like him. Honest, open, boisterous . . . He does not disguise the fact that he was raised in a stable. No, he is proud of it! Crude, bold, gentle – he takes life by storm.

THE MANY LIVES & SECRET SORROWS OF JOSEPHINE B.

He is a big man: big in heart, big in body, big in soul. He has the power to chase the shadows away, banish ghosts.

He has no patience for etiquette, intellectual games, social protocol. 'I am a Republican!' he says proudly. He is a believer, in spite of all he's suffered.

His heart knows no limit. Nor his courage. He is said to be a genius. Young. Fearless. Bright.

'You *know* General Hoche?' Eugène asked, incredulous.

'He is a friend,' I told him. Proudly.

19 AUGUST

'It's tomorrow you leave, is it not?' I asked Lazare, trying not to show my disquiet. I had known for some time that he would be going to Thionville, to see his young wife. I also knew that he loved her . . . knew the first time he told me of her, knew by the way he spoke her name – *Adélaïde* – that I had no business in his life. Yet I could not turn him away; my need was too great. 'When? In the morning?'

We were in his bed, the bedclothes crumpled, sweaty. I stretched out over the pillows, a film of sweat cooling against the oppressive summer heat, the pungent sweet smell of love heavy in the air.

'I wrote to her this morning.' He stroked my arm, my neck, touched my damp hair. 'I told her I wouldn't be coming – that I've been delayed.'

'Why?' I dared to ask.

A hint of a smile played around his lips. 'You want to know?'

I nodded. I needed to know.

'You want me to answer truthfully?'

'We have agreed to be truthful with one another.'

'The truth is I couldn't bear the thought of leaving you.'

I buried my face in the pillows, hiding my tears.

He began to make love to me again, but I stilled him. There were things I wanted to tell him, things I could not say. How I woke every night, drenched in sweat, gripped by fear; how at times a faint feeling came over me, a feeling of sickening helplessness; how at dusk I sometimes saw the faces of the dead, pressing at a window; how I felt a lingering shame, still, as if somehow I had deserved to be imprisoned; as if, somehow, it had been *my* failing, *my* weakness, *my* fault. But the worst, the most haunting pain, was the cold that had entered my heart. I feared I could no longer love. Not even *him*.

But how could I tell him such things? 'Does your wife love you?' I asked instead.

'Is that what you were thinking – of Adélaïde?'

Adélaïde. A hard name to speak without tenderness.

'No,' I said. 'But I hope she does love you, for if she doesn't . . .'

If . . . if . . .

'She loves me.' Lazare turned on to his back. He rubbed his chin with his hand. He turned towards me. 'I don't come to you lightly, Rose. I come because . . . What we've seen, felt, been through – it has scarred us, somehow, set us apart. I—' He stopped. He could not find the words.

'You don't have to explain,' I said. 'I understand.' I pressed my face to his chest. Yes. The shame of the survivor.

THURSDAY, 21 AUGUST

Lazare has been reinstated as Chief of the Army at Cherbourg. He leaves in two weeks.

Two weeks . . .

23 AUGUST

Eugène will be thirteen soon – he is coming of age so quickly.

'He should start his military training,' Lazare said.

'He should be at *school*.' Even I was appalled by his spelling. Yet it was all I could do to pay for his boots.

'I could take him.'

Lazare's words registered slowly. '*Take* him?' I asked.

'He could work on my staff – as an apprentice.'

'He'd be working, for *you*?' I began to understand. 'You'd look after him, keep an eye on him?'

'I like your son, Rose. He's an honest boy, forthright. I wouldn't suggest it if I didn't think he'd do a good job.'

'Very well,' I said, fighting back tears.

THE MANY LIVES & SECRET SORROWS OF JOSEPHINE B.

Saturday, 30 August, 3.30 p.m.

The days go by too quickly. Already, Lazare is preparing to leave.
And now Eugène, too, is packing.

31 August

This afternoon, I said to Lazare, 'I will see you tomorrow?' There
were only a few more days.

He cleared his throat. 'Adélaïde is coming. She's bringing my
horse. My sword and pistols. I will be needing them.'

Suddenly I felt frail. *Tomorrow?*

He reached to take me in his arms.

1 September

Eugène will be leaving in the morning – the day before his
birthday.

Hortense and I made a birthday cake for him. Without any eggs
and very little sugar it was a miracle we could even eat it. We
surrounded it with flowers from the garden. 'At least these are
free,' I said.

He has polished his boots three times. My son, thirteen –
a soldier.

Later

No word from Lazare. I sent him a note: 'Am I not to see you
before you leave?'

He arrived two hours later.

'You love her,' I said.

He took my hand. His eyes spoke of profound confusion.

Tuesday, 2 September

They are gone, Eugène, Lazare.

Eugène did not look back.

How could I say: *take care.*

How could I say: *protect my heart.*

In which friends comfort & distress me

SATURDAY, 6 SEPTEMBER 1794

Thérèse and Tallien persuaded me to go out last night, to a concert at the Feydeau. 'A cure for melancholy,' Thérèse said.

The *Feydeau* — it was easy to be persuaded. Most people had to wait in line three days to get tickets.

Thérèse lent me a hat with long silver plumes, a matching silver wig and a necklace shaped like a snake.

'Are you going to go out looking like *that*?' Lannoy demanded when she saw me preparing to leave.

'You should see what Thérèse is wearing,' I said, amused by her disapproving look.

'It's what Madame Cabarrus *doesn't* wear that attracts notice.'

At the theatre there was a terrible crush. The Feydeau is known for its excellent orchestra and the best soloists in Paris, but that isn't the main attraction. 'It's the audience,' Thérèse said — and she was right. All the fine ladies of Paris arrive as if on to a stage, looking rather like courtesans. No corsets at the Feydeau!

I felt like a star, the crowd lined up three deep to watch the parade, with applause for the most dramatic, the most outrageous. Thérèse, who would look spectacular in a nun's habit, was the obvious favourite.

'You should have been an actress,' I told her. The press of the crowd frightened me.

'I *am* an actress,' she said.

Inside, it was like a private reception, everyone going from loge to loge, so unlike former times when it was considered improper for a woman even to move from her chair. Fortunée Hamelin was there, an ugly seventeen-year-old Creole well known for her ribald wit — 'and a body that makes men weep,' Tallien moaned. And sweet-faced Madame de Châteaurenaud ('Minerva'), looking like a cream puff in white gauze. And even sweet little Madame de Crény was there, wearing an amusing headpiece with a giant feather sticking straight up. I last saw her when we were both living at the abbey de Penthémont – a saltpetre factory now.

It was an amazing scene – all the aging aristocrats, the former elegant men and women of taste, together with their now grown children who, having come of age in the Terror, have cast aside all restraint and dress outrageously. 'It reminds me of Carnival in Martinico.' I looked out over the audience. We were sitting in Thérèse's luxurious loge, sipping excellent champagne.

'Isn't that Citoyen Loménie's son?' she asked, indicating a youth in a checked coat and an enormous green cravat. 'Is that a blond wig he's wearing?' The 'Gilded Youths', they were called, our outrageously dressed young men.

'It's the half of thirty-four crowd gone to seed,' someone said.

Thérèse turned, spilling her champagne. 'Citoyen Fouché! You are for ever creeping up behind me.'

I attempted to disguise my surprise. Fouché, 'the mass murderer of Lyons', the deputy who had signed the most death warrants. Yet the man who stood before me was a slight, ill-kempt, and pockmarked human being with gaps between his teeth and unruly red hair. I'd been told he went mad with grief when his daughter died. How could such a man be a monster?

'Half of thirty-four?' I asked. 'I've heard that expression before. What does it signify?'

Thérèse explained: 'Half of thirty-four is seventeen. The Boy in the Temple is Louis XVI's heir, seventeenth in line . . .'

'Seventeenth in line for the throne.' *The Boy*. Le Petit Roi. 'The Little Fellow' was what Hortense called him – an orphan of ten sleeping alone in the Temple prison with rats. And now, according to some, *King*.

Thérèse filled our glasses. 'Are not the words "*Révolution Française*" an anagram for "*La France veut son Roi*"?'*

I looked at her. For a brief, treacherous moment I doubted my friend's Republican conviction.

'Royalists!' Citoyen Fouché cursed. He took a box of snuff out

* France wants her King.

from his waistcoat pocket. 'They are stupid, greedy, entirely without morals – and *all* here tonight.' With his eyes half closed, he inhaled the fine powder.

'You jest,' I said.

Citoyen Fouché brushed the snuff off his waistcoat, smiling slowly. The smile of a man who did not jest.

'Citoyen Fouché knows *everything*,' Thérèse said. 'He makes himself useful in this way.' She leaned towards him, her low décolletage revealing. 'It is rumoured you have eyes and ears in every salon, citoyen.'

Citoyen Fouché snapped shut his snuffbox lid, making a sound not unlike a pistol being cocked. 'Is there something you wish to tell me, Our Good Lady of Liberty?'

Thérèse tapped Citoyen Fouché's hand with her fan. 'You could profit at the gaming tables, you dissemble so well.'

The musicians began to warm their instruments. A group of people in the lower levels clapped, then laughed.

Citoyen Fouché turned to go. 'Good evening, citoyennes. I see the concert is about to begin.'

'A curious man,' I said, after he left.

Thérèse fanned herself languidly. 'Did you notice that Iva Théot is here tonight?'

Iva Théot is an older woman, a former duchesse, prominent in society. 'Is that significant?' I asked.

'Iva Théot reports to Citoyen Fouché.' Thérèse finished off her glass.

'Iva?' Bumbling, matronly Iva Théot – a *spy* for Fouché?

Thérèse laughed. 'Rose, you are so easy to shock.'

'Conspiring, ladies?' It was Deputy Barras, arm in arm with Tallien.

'Oh, it's the mischief-makers.' Thérèse made a face behind her fan. 'You both look . . . *bright*, shall I say? Deputy Barras, have you been leading my darling astray?'

'Just a little contraband coffee, my dear – six cups.'

'Coffee!' Thérèse groaned. 'And you didn't bring me any.'

Deputy Barras greeted me gallantly, then stooped to kiss Thérèse's hand. 'You look exquisite tonight, Thérèse, my child. Good enough to eat. Caution lest you excite an old man's interest.'

'Doesn't she?' Tallien put his long fingers round Thérèse's neck.

'What's that unpleasant odour?' Deputy Barras sniffed the air.

'Citoyen Fouché was just here,' Thérèse said, and they laughed.

'Have you ever met his wife?' Tallien asked. 'The ugliest, the most stupid woman . . .'

'Yet he's devoted to her,' Thérèse said. 'I find it touching.'

'Citoyenne Beauharnais, you *elegant* creature,' Deputy Barras said, filling my glass with champagne, 'what do we hear from our beautiful man in Cherbourg?'

'General Lazare Hoche is already spoken for, Paul,' Thérèse said.

'Alas.' Deputy Barras lowered himself gracefully into the chair next to mine. He turned to me with a plaintive expression. 'Such is the thanks one gets for saving the man's life.'

'*You* saved General Hoche's life?' I was confused. 'I thought it was Deputy Carnot who arranged for his release.'

Deputy Barras made a theatrical groan. 'Carnot! When General Hoche was in the dungeon I was approached by the executioner with a list of the condemned. *I* was the one who scratched out our dear Lazare's name – but you need not tell *him* that. One wouldn't want him to feel beholden to me, *would we?*'

'Hush,' Thérèse whispered as the soloist began.

After the concert we went to Garchy's on Rue Richelieu (I had an apricot ice with almond biscuits – *delicious*) where the gaiety continued into the small hours. Deputy Barras entertained us with stories that had us aching with laughter. In company he is the spark that makes a gathering memorable, the master of comedy, of wit. It is hard to believe the rumours one hears. 'A man who knows how to play his cards,' Thérèse told me in the powder room, referring not to the sport of the gaming tables – a passion both Deputies Barras and Tallien share – but to his unerring instinct for strengthening his political hand.

From Garchy's the men persuaded us to go to a gaming house in the Palais Égalité (I won two livres – in coin – playing faro), and from there, after Tallien lost more than was wise, to the Café Covazza, and *then* to Madame de Châteaurenaud's (*Minerva*'s, that is), where we played 'magnetism' games, debated reform and gossiped about love.

At dawn we all headed over to a little café on Rue Saint-Honoré where we encountered a number of people who had been at the theatre: wild Fortunée Hamelin and two of her party (*not* her disapproving husband, I noted), tiny Madame de Crény with a tall man named Denon, as well as Citoyen Fouché, oddly enough, sitting alone at a table at the back, an untouched bowl of broth in front of him.

'Do you not enjoy your broth warm, citoyen?' I asked, stopping to exchange pleasantries.

He shrugged. 'Have a seat, Citoyenne Beauharnais?' In spite of the hour, he was sober. Unlike myself.

I took the chair he offered. He asked the waiter to bring a glass, which he filled from the bottle of lemon water on the table. 'Have you been working, perhaps?' I asked. 'You do not have the air of a carefree man.'

'Yes, I believe I have been working.'

'You are not sure?'

'The line between work and play is never entirely clear.'

'It is the nature of your work that is not clear.'

He looked at me with a steady expression. 'You are a woman who appears to speak truthfully, yet in this instance I feel I can be confident that you are fully informed as to the nature of my work. I can only conclude that you are one of those women who gives the impression of candour, all the while concealing your hand.'

I cocked my head to one side. 'I generally win at the gaming tables, too.' I smiled.

'Not many regard an ability to dissemble an attribute. Yet it is one of the truly indispensable talents.'

'I did not know you were a philosopher.'

'There are many things you do not know about me.'

'There are things I know that would surprise you.'

'Such as?'

'Oh, that you feign not to care, yet your heart is tender,' I ventured, 'and that this distresses you.' I observed his look. He appeared amused rather than upset. Perhaps foolishly, I went on. 'That you put on an undisturbed air, yet your imagination is easily heated, so you guard against it.'

He sat back in his chair and looked at me. 'I understand you are in need of money.'

I felt heat in my cheeks.

'Forgive me, I have offended you,' he said. 'You must understand that such matters do not mean anything to me. You are a woman without the protection of a husband – this is not a *fault*, although some would have it so. Your family is distant and in all likelihood impoverished. You have two children to provide for. Furthermore, you play in the company of the rich and reckless. This costs – of course – a great deal, but it also pays, does it not? Contacts, properly cultivated, are an invaluable asset. No doubt the balance is to the good. Over *time*, of course.'

I glanced towards the table at the front. Deputy Barras was observing us.

'Furthermore,' Citoyen Fouché went on, 'I am aware of the contributions you give to your relatives, as well as to a number of friends. Not to mention neighbours, street beggars, common ruffians. Indeed, your hand is too frequently open. I would advise you to be more cautious.'

'You do know everything.' I was embarrassed. Was nothing private?

He did not smile. 'I will take that as a compliment – but alas, much eludes me. I am in need of assistance in this respect. If you are ever in need, do come to me. I would be most grateful for the services you could provide, services that would be of benefit to the Republic, I should add. I know you to be a sincere patriot.' He glanced towards my table, where Tallien was speechifying rather loudly now, Thérèse laughing. 'Unlike *some*.'

I rose to go, uneasy. 'We are all of us patriots, Citoyen Fouché.'

'You are leaving me.' He refilled his glass with water. 'I confess my imagination *has* been heated. You seem to understand a great deal.'

'My friends claim I am naive.'

'They are mistaken. You see through the masquerade to the true spirit of a man. I have been disarmed. Like a gallant knight in days of old, I am for ever at your service.'

I smiled. 'I believe you mean it.' I gave him a kiss on the cheek and returned to my friends, who teased me at length about my new conquest. I endured, enjoying their good humour – yet I confess that this one brief interchange has disturbed my repose. Citoyen Fouché's words linger still.

Last night, just after midnight on Rue des Quatre Fils, Tallien was attacked by a ruffian with a pistol. He fell, wounded. When the assassin hit him on the chest with the butt of his pistol, Tallien let out a cry that woke the neighbours. He was taken to his mother's home, close by.

When I saw him in his mother's humble apartment, I was shaken. He was resting on a bed in the tiny salon, behind a canopy of patched curtains. A bullet had gone through his left shoulder. He'd been bled, but even so, he continued to suffer pain.

'Remember when I said that in a revolution men must not look behind them?' he asked. 'I was wrong.'

'It was a Jacobin who tried to kill him,' Thérèse told me as we helped Tallien's mother clear the teacups. Six days earlier Tallien had been expelled from the Jacobin Club for being too liberal in his views.

'You don't think Carrier had anything to do with it, do you?' I asked. Deputy Carrier was President of the Jacobin Club. He was the one who had had Tallien expelled.

'Carrier wouldn't do his own dirty work.' Thérèse put a soup bowl down on the wooden table. 'He would hire some thug to do it for him.'

Dirty work. It was rumoured that during the Terror, Carrier had ordered over ten thousand executed in Nantes – drowned in the Loire River. *Ten thousand.*

I heard voices.

'It's the National Guard!' Tallien's mother cried out, hastily drying her hands on her stained muslin apron. 'There's a crowd out on the street!' Her cheeks were pink.

'I'll talk to them,' Thérèse said.

There were a number of visitors throughout the morning. The police came twice. Several journalists begged entrance, which Tallien refused, making an exception for a friend who writes for the *Moniteur*. At the end of the day Deputy Barras arrived, laden with spirits and a port pudding he insisted he'd made himself. His eyes filled with tears when he saw his friend's injury. He was accompanied by two fashionably unkempt Gilded Youths, not too much older than Eugène, I thought.

'Bonjour, Monsieur,' one of the young men greeted Tallien. He lisped as he talked, as was the fashion, so that it sounded: *Bonzou, monsez.* His breeches were stretched and thin ribbons fell in long curls from the knees.

'We'll kill the assassin for you,' the other said. His coat-tails were ragged and the pockets of his waistcoat had been stuffed to make him look deformed. 'Just tell us who.'

I was chilled by his words. I knew him to be the son of the Duc d'Annonay. He must have been twelve or so when his father was murdered, hacked to death in front of the family home. How could such a thing not scar a child?

'Baptized in blood,' Thérèse whispered, after they had left. We were in the kitchen, helping Tallien's mother prepare a tincture for wounds.

'It makes me sad,' I said. An entire generation, orphaned by the Revolution, hardened by violence, schooled on the streets. What was to become of them now?

'Did you notice how they talk? Barras says they babble nonsense rhymes while beating Jacobins to death. It's a bit strange, don't you think?'

Revenge. Would the violence never stop? 'If only there were a way of putting the past behind us,' I said.

'Try telling that to Tallien,' she said.

By evening Tallien was feeling well enough to begin formulating a plan of attack against the Jacobin Club — against Carrier. 'I'm going to demand that hearings be conducted into the atrocities at Nantes,' he said, 'hearings into Carrier's crimes there. *Thousands* murdered in cold blood. It shouldn't take much to convict him, put him away.' This idea gave him strength.

Thérèse and I exchanged looks. 'Is this wise?' she asked.

'Shouldn't our goal be to unite all parties?' I suggested, gently, I hoped. 'Factions have been our ruin.'

'Justice must be done,' Tallien said.

'But what if the Assembly becomes enthusiastic about this notion of hearings?' Thérèse asked. 'If they decide to look into what happened at Lyons, it will be Citoyen Fouché they put on the stand. If they look into Marseille, it will be our friend Barras.'

And if they look into Bordeaux, it will be Tallien himself, I thought. Thérèse didn't say that.

'Who among us is innocent?' she went on.

SANDRA GULLAND

'You.' Tallien slid his hand up under her petticoats.

'Innocent!' She laughed.

Quietly, I left, without bidding adieu.

9 September 1794 – Cherbourg

Dear Rose,

Forgive my messy scrawl. I did not have a writing master when I was young. The grooms at the stable were my masters and I wouldn't want to tell you what they taught me.

Your son is a fine lad – he will make a good soldier.

I know I did not handle things very well when I left. Can you forgive me? I do love you.

Your soldier, Lazare

SATURDAY, 12 SEPTEMBER

Tallien has recovered – enough to make an appearance at the Odéon Théâtre. 'My public demands it!' he said, adjusting his sling of red silk.

'*Our* public.' Thérèse was dressed in a simple white shift, quite revealing. A string of diamonds threw flecks of dancing light over her breasts.

'*Your* public.' Tallien regarded her with devotion.

The theatre was packed, the applause deafening as Thérèse and Tallien entered. People got up on their chairs to see them, cheering and screaming. I felt awed, proud – and frightened.

In which I am witness to a wedding

22 SEPTEMBER 1794

Day One, Year Three of the Republic. I am writing this on a writing desk in a small but elegant suite of rooms on Rue de l'Université. I'm leasing them at a reasonable rate from Madame de Crény ('The Little Woman' Hortense calls her). Hortense and I moved in this morning. It didn't take long – we have so little.

Lannoy has agreed to stay with me in spite of the fact that I am unable to pay her. Agathe will work for board, as will an old man I hired today, Citoyen Gontier, who insists he is strong enough to carry water buckets. So we're settled . . . for the *moment*, in any case. Dear little Madame de Crény is willing to wait three months for the rent. If only, by some miracle, I could get through to Mother . . .

27 SEPTEMBER

Lannoy's brother-in-law has made a fortune buying estates for very little and then selling them at an inflated value. On Lannoy's suggestion, I've appealed to him for a loan – for fifteen *thousand* livres. It seems like a great deal, but how long will it last? I remember when that much money would have kept an aristocrat in pheasant and champagne for three years. Today it won't keep us in fowl and bitter wine for three months.

SATURDAY, 4 OCTOBER, EVENING

At Fanny's this evening. She's ill, having succumbed to the vapours brought on by her grief over Marie, I believe – so little success has she had in her constant efforts to get her daughter out of prison. 'Can't you do *something*?' she pleaded, breaking down.

What more *can* I do? I've already made several attempts to help Marie, all without success.

'What about that criminal friend of yours?' Fanny persisted. 'I bet he could do something.'

'Criminal friend?' I grinned. '*Which* one?'

6 OCTOBER

Deputy Barras pared his fingernails with a penknife as he listened to my appeal. Tall, baby-faced Citoyen Botot, now his secretary, sat by the window taking notes.

After I finished reading my petition, Deputy Barras looked up at me and said, 'You sang beautifully at Madame Tallien's last night. You have an unusual voice. Innocent, yet suggestive.' He was wearing a double-breasted coat of striped pink silk. His hair was powdered and gathered at the back into a black bag.

'You flatter me . . .' I felt ill at ease. I had conversed with Deputy Barras on a number of occasions – at the theatre, salons, in my own home – but always in the company of friends. He coquetted with me (as is his way with women), yet even so, I feared I was making an imposition asking a favour. I was relieved he'd so warmly agreed to hear my appeal.

'And you are surprisingly accomplished at billiards,' he said. 'You won three games against Tallien, I noticed.'

'Our friend Tallien excels at many things,' I said, 'but billiards is not one of them. I do not believe it just to surmise that I have any ability at the game.'

'Yet you won against Citoyen Rosin as well. You know him, I gather?'

I nodded. I'd met Citoyen Rosin some time ago, at a Freemason meeting. A Creole banker of extraordinary means, he'd managed to get his wealth out of Saint-Domingue before it collapsed.

'And his Swiss banker friend Perré, the man with the burn on his face?'

I nodded. Although disfigured, Perré was particularly charming, I found.

Deputy Barras adjusted his gold-rimmed lorgnon, examined the document before him. 'With respect to your cousin, Françoise-Marie, Citoyenne Beauharnais . . .' He shrugged.

'Can nothing be done?'

He made an exasperated gesture. 'You must understand, governments come and governments go, but the bureaucracy stays the same. No matter who is in charge, there are papers, review boards, committees, procedures. It's an obsession in this country.' He cleared his throat, squinted at the paper again. 'I see here that her husband, François Beauharnais, *Marquis*, is an émigré, an officer in the Prince of Condé's army. Wounded in the Vendée,' he added absently, reading.

François *wounded*? In the Vendée? I longed for details, but I dared not ask, dared not reveal my concern. 'Perhaps you recall meeting her,' I said, 'at my salon on Rue Saint-Dominique.'

Deputy Barras put his fingers to his chin, a posture that displayed to advantage the fine point lace of his shirtsleeve ruffle. 'But as the wife of an émigré, and one who has taken up arms against us—'

'Marie divorced her husband some time ago,' I protested. I glanced over at Citoyen Botot, intent on his notes.

'Many aristocratic wives divorce their émigré husbands in order to save their fortunes,' Deputy Barras said, '*and* their empty heads. It means little, I'm afraid.'

'My cousin is a Republican, she belonged to a number of the revolutionary clubs. She and her husband separated for this reason,' I persisted.

Deputy Barras sighed. 'I will do what I can,' he said. He nodded to Botot, who rose and left the room.

'How can I thank you?' I asked. I clutched my silk bag. I had come prepared to pay, but I could not offer much.

'As a matter of fact, there is something you *could* do for me,' Deputy Barras said, removing his lorgnon. 'I'm involved in a number of fairly large . . . undertakings, I suppose you'd call them. I have need of bankers with a flair for *risk*, shall I say? Citoyens Rosin and Perré have been recommended, but of course without an introduction, a recommendation . . .'

'I'd be delighted to arrange something,' I said, rising. 'An evening at my home?'

He took my hand with exaggerated delicacy. 'Will I have the pleasure of your company at my salon tonight?' he asked.

I answered him with a bow, honoured.

'On condition you join me in a game of billiards,' he said.

'Perhaps we should place a wager on it,' I said.

'I take it you intend to win.'

'Always.'

'You wicked lady.'

'Quite,' I said, smiling.

As I left I paused to have a word with Citoyen Botot. 'Is there any hope?' I whispered.

Startled, Citoyen Botot looked up from the piles of papers covering his desk. 'Citoyenne Marie Beauharnais will be released tomorrow – at eleven in the morning,' he said, lisping only slightly.

29 OCTOBER

I encountered Citoyen Fouché at Deputy Barras's salon. 'What brings you into these circles?' I asked. He was wearing a mismatched, stained, and ill-fitting ensemble, in spite of the elegance of the gathering. The ribbons on his knee breeches had come untied.

'I could ask the same of you, Citoyenne Beauharnais,' he said. 'Although a woman who so willingly listens is always welcome among men of power.'

'You are droll citoyen. You evade my question.'

'Are you trustworthy?'

'You who know everything about me ask if I am trustworthy?'

'Last night two deputies were roused from their beds to go to the Temple. Perhaps you know this already.'

I shook my head. '*Why?*' The Temple was the prison in which the King's orphan children were being held – Madame Royale and the Boy were there.

Citoyen Fouché looked over his shoulder. 'There is a rumour that the Boy – "King" according to the treacherous among us – is no longer there.'

'*Was* he there?'

'There was, indeed, a boy there. But was he the King's son? *That* is not certain.'

'But if the Boy is not in the Temple, where is he?' A child, the trump card of nations. So much depending on so small a head.

Citoyen Fouché shrugged. 'You tell me. The Royalists want him alive. The Jacobins want him dead. And whoever holds the Boy, holds power over them both.'

I saw Deputy Barras coming towards us. I motioned to Citoyen Fouché to be silent.

'So I ask myself,' Citoyen Fouché went on, ignoring my caution, 'who might want that much power? Who might that be?'

TUESDAY, 11 NOVEMBER
Mobs in the streets. Deputy Carrier, President of the Jacobin Club, the executioner of thousands, has been arrested for 'excessiveness' in the line of duty. The Gilded Youths are howling for his head. Restrained from tearing him limb from limb, they set upon the Jacobin Club.

Then Thérèse arrived to close it down.

Thérèse. She took the key to the club herself, fearless of the brawling men, of the violence in their hearts. Thérèse, slipping the key to the Jacobin Club into her bodice, closed the door on history.

'Were you not frightened?' I asked her, astonished. I was reading aloud a report in a news-sheet: 'Such a woman as that would be capable of shutting the gates of Hell,' a journalist had written.

'I will tell you my secret, Rose.' She put her hands to her belly. 'God walks with me. I am with child.' She burst into tears.

14 NOVEMBER, LATE AFTERNOON
Thérèse and I stood at the fortune-teller's door for a time, yelling through the delivery slot. There was a chill wind.

'I do not tell fortunes any more!' Citoyenne Lenormand insisted. She refused to open the door. During the Terror she'd been imprisoned for foretelling the death of Robespierre. Ever since she's been reclusive. She would not allow us in.

'But it's me, Thérèse Cabarrus de Fontenoy – I am the one who got you released!' Thérèse cried out.

Finally, the doors opened. Citoyenne Lenormand was a small woman, younger than I imagined, with small dark eyes, quite deep-sunk, under a dirty lace cap.

'I have seen you before,' she said to Thérèse. She paused. 'Dressed as Liberty . . . when the Luxembourg prisoners were set free.'

'You have a good memory.' Thérèse untangled her hat strings.

'You have an unforgettable face,' the soothsayer said. After civilités, Lenormand instructed Thérèse to sprinkle water over a looking glass placed on a table laid with three cloths. 'You are about to make an important decision,' she said, examining the glass. 'It is destined that the union be made. You know of whom I speak?'

Thérèse nodded. her look was resigned.

'Your path is not an easy one. To your credit, much good will come of this alliance – but you will be the one to pay the price.'

Thérèse made a face. 'I know.'

'You are gifted with vision.'

'Cursed.'

'Yes,' Citoyenne Lenormand said. 'It *is* a curse.' She turned to me. 'I believe I have foretold for you before.'

'When I was in the Carmes, a few of us contrived to send you information, from which you deduced our futures.'

'Yes. And you *are* a widow now.'

I nodded.

'I also predicted that you would remarry, I recall, and that your second husband would be an extraordinary man, known throughout the world.'

'That part hasn't come true.' I smiled.

'You make light, yet your heart is heavy. Ask me what you wish to know.'

'Tell her more about this extraordinary man,' Thérèse suggested, grinning at me mischievously.

Citoyenne Lenormand laid out some cards. After a long silence she said, 'He will be younger than you. Brilliant, yes. A military man – a general, likely.'

Thérèse winked. 'I wonder who *that* might be?'

On the way back to Rue de l'Université, Thérèse lectured me. 'General Hoche is a rising star, he will do great things.' We were in her new red carriage. A gang of children, street urchins, were chasing after us.

'It is true,' I said. A miracle worker, people were saying; a genius of war, a genius of peace.

'What I am saying is that he is your rising star – your *extraordinary man*.'

I groaned.

'Give me your hand, Rose,' she demanded.

'Tallita, you are a Gypsy,' I complained. 'Confess. A Gypsy queen.'

Thérèse smiled, then grew serious. She traced the lines in my palm. 'Citoyenne Lenormand is right. You *will* marry a general.'

'General Hoche is already married.' I pulled my hand away.

'Soldiers get married and divorce once a year, to suit their newest fancy.'

'It is not as simple as that. Lazare cares for his wife – I believe he loves her.'

'You would be more beneficial to him. You could help him advance in his career.'

'Lazare doesn't need my help.'

Thérèse made a noise in her throat – an expression of impatience. 'May I be frank with you, Rose?'

'Are you ever *not* frank with me?' I smiled.

'You are not getting younger. Your children are charming, true, a credit to you in every way, but in need of an education. Sooner than you think, your daughter will be in need of a dowry, your son a position. This will cost, cost a great deal. It is *them* you must think of.'

'You talk as if there were good prospects everywhere.'

'What of Marquis de Caulaincourt? At the Thélusson Ball I saw him following you everywhere, drooling on your shoulder.'

'He's been married for two decades, he has eight children, he's almost sixty—'

'He's rich and he dotes on you.' Thérèse pulled the fur blanket over her knees.

'Yes, Maman,' I said. Thérèse made a playful face. 'But what about you?' I asked, changing the subject. 'Did you find out what you wanted?'

Thérèse sighed. 'I have known since the moment I met Tallien that I was destined to marry him, destined to help others through him.' She paused, looked out of the window. We were coming to the river. The spires of Notre-Dame – the 'Temple of Reason' now – stood bold and beautiful against the sky. 'Destined to soften the rule of his fist,' she said softly.

'Tallita!' I was shocked by her words.

'Forgive me. I know you care for him.'

'And you *don't*?' Did she not call Tallien her 'Lion Amoureux'?

'There are things about him I find distasteful.'

I smiled. 'You were raised to be a princess,' I said. And, certainly, Tallien was no prince.

'I was raised to be a courtesan, but we need not get into that. No, I must confess that I entertain the affections of our friend for a number of reasons, but love is not one of them. Not even passion, which is often mistaken for love. Rather, I feel a bond of obligation towards him. He saved my life and the lives of many of my family and friends. And he has suffered as a result.' She paused. 'I shouldn't be telling you these things.' She let down the glass, in spite of the cold, put it back up again.

'You'll not marry him then?'

Thérèse sat back, her eyes brimming with tears. 'No,' she said. 'I will marry him.'

'I don't—'

'Have you ever had the feeling you were part of a larger plan?' she asked, interrupting.

I wondered about that. The fact that I was a widow now, that this had been foretold – did that mean that my marriage to Alexandre had been part of a larger plan? Was Alexandre's untimely death *meant* to be?

The coach pulled into the courtyard of my hôtel on Rue de l'Université. 'Do you believe this to be so with Tallien?' I asked. I found the idea of destiny both comforting and terrifying.

'When Tallien and I were together in Bordeaux, each night, as I went to bed with him, I liked to think of the lives I had persuaded him to spare that day. In this way I discovered the purpose of my existence.'

I did not know what to say. Thérèse was so young, such a carefree soul – and yet there was this, always *this*, this terrible responsibility she had taken on. Not a day went by that she wasn't pleading for a life. It was a commitment we shared – our religion, some said. 'Ladies of mercy,' Tallien called us.

'Thérèse, you are an angel,' I said, taking up my basket.

The footman opened the door, let down the metal step.

Thérèse touched my shoulder. I turned to look at her. 'Will you be godmother?' she asked.

'*Me?*'

She nodded, her cheeks glistening.

'I would be honoured,' I said.

10 November 1794 – Cherbourg
Rose,

   We are in the process of moving to new headquarters in Rennes. I will be coming to Paris to arrange for supplies. The only consolation in this wretched business is that I will once again hold you in my arms.

Your soldier, Lazare

SUNDAY, 16 NOVEMBER
Lazare!

MONDAY
Lazare brings news of Eugène. Carefully I put forward questions. I do not want to nag. 'You're not working him too hard? He's not in any danger? Is he eating? Are you watching over him?' I have been sleepless with concern. Rennes is in the heart of the Vendée region. I'd heard stories of a civil war there – peasants and aristocrats united against the Republicans. I'd been happier when Eugène was in Cherbourg, facing the British. I didn't want him fighting Frenchmen. It wouldn't be right.

   Lazare laughed, lacing up his breeches. 'Of course I'm working him hard. Of course he's in danger. It's the army!'

   'He's only a boy!'

   'Do you not see that *I* feel pride in him? A father's tender care?'

   This silenced me. A *father's* tender care?

   Lazare held out his hands in a gesture of helplessness. 'I have come to love your son, Rose,' he confessed, 'to regard him as my own.'

19 NOVEMBER
Lazare spends his days in meetings with the Committee of Public Safety; nights he spends with me. I take the time I am allowed greedily, my hunger overwhelming.

20 NOVEMBER

Lazare is gone. He was here for only three days — three whirl-wind days of passion and tears. Will I ever grow accustomed to such parting?

19 November 1794 — Rennes
Chère Maman,

We got to Rennes — on foot! My boots are worn through. (I've enclosed a tracing of my foot and the measure of my leg, for a new pair.) Everyone has lice. But at least I haven't got scabies. We put up in the woods. Yesterday the artilleryman was murdered in town. We are regarded as the enemy!

A thousand kisses, your son Eugène

20 NOVEMBER

An associate of Citoyen Dunnkirk is sailing for America. There is hope of getting through to Mother, so I have spent the day writing and rewriting a letter, writing and rewriting what I must tell her, what she must, in any case, know: that I am a widow, that Hortense and Eugène are without a father, that we are all of us without any means of support.

I am so deeply in debt I know not where to turn. What *are* my choices?

28 November 1794 — Rennes
Rose,

My troops are bored — they long for battle. They fail to see glory in an olive branch. Swords are more heroic, I grant you.

The peasants only want to pray to their saints. Should we murder them for this? The politicians in Paris insist they go to a Temple of Reason instead. What can these halfway minds be thinking? Faith cannot be legislated.

As a result, Royalist sentiment here is strong — a shocking number have hopes of seeing the Boy on the throne of France. This thought disgusts me! What have we fought for, suffered for, if not for Liberty? If the Boy is put on the throne, I'll be sent back to work in a stable.

Your soldier, Lazare

I went with Thérèse to see her country house this afternoon — La Chaumière she calls it. It is a long drive, outside the city walls. Nevertheless, she is intent on living there. She loves its humble aspect. 'No one can understand what I see in it.'

It wasn't easy. I was myself surprised. It even has a thatched roof.

'It's bigger than it looks,' she assured me.

'The setting is lovely.' At the far end of Allée des Veuves, not far from the river, set in the midst of forest, fields, it has a wild, free feeling. I closed my eyes, inhaled the fresh, cold air. Yes, I thought — I *could* understand.

'The first time I came here a hen laid an egg on the doorstep. A sign, no doubt . . .'

'But of *what?*' I asked, laughing. For Thérèse sees signs everywhere.

16 December

Three Jacobin leaders were guillotined this morning, their heads displayed above a cheering crowd.

'It's starting again,' Lannoy said, watching out of the window anxiously.

'They say this will put an *end* to it,' I said. I could hear someone playing 'Ça Ira' on a trumpet.

Lannoy threw me a piercing glance. 'Your friends — the "blood-drinkers" — are they so very different?'

Saturday, 20 December

I encountered Citoyen Fouché on Rue Saint-Honoré this afternoon. He asked if I'd heard anything more about the Boy.

'Nothing.' Aside from Hortense's constant chatter.

'No whispers at Barras's?'

I shook my head. 'Why?'

'Yesterday, three deputies examined the child. Deputy Luzerne is convinced that he is a fraud, that the real Boy has been kidnapped . . . perhaps even killed.'

Killed. The Boy — *murdered*? 'Why do you tell me these things?' Tears came to my eyes.

Citoyen Fouché tipped his hat. 'To caution you, citoyenne. Not everything is as it seems.'

26 DECEMBER

Tonight, Thérèse and Tallien were wed. A small gathering of friends.

'To happiness,' I said, embracing Thérèse. At four months, her belly was just beginning to show.

'To Madame Tallien.' Tallien raised his glass in toast. 'To our Lady of Mercy.'

I recalled Thérèse's words: *I am destined to help others through him, destined to soften the rule of his fist.*

The rule of his fist. Was it a bruise her heavy make-up hid?

In which I learn the true value of friendship

FRIDAY, 2 JANUARY 1795

Daily I cross the river to the Assembly, seeking to have the sequestration removed on our belongings, seeking to clear Alexandre's name, seeking restitution, compensation . . . *seeking*.

All along the quay they are there, the thin children, bewildered men, desperate women with babies at their breasts – excrement soiling their clothes, vermin crawling in their hair. I am moved by the defiant look in their eyes. How is it that an entire city can succumb to such misery? How many souls crying out to Heaven, how many prayers? After all that we have suffered, how can we be asked to suffer still? Take my bread, I pray, spare that child. And that. And that. The little hands reaching out, the sunken eyes: this is torture beyond measure.

Defeated, I returned home. Agathe, Lannoy, Gontier were at their work, Hortense at her studies. On the kitchen counter was the one small loaf of bread we were all of us allowed – two ounces per day per person. I slipped it into my basket and returned to the bridge, to the sickly woman with a baby at her breast, four young grabbing at her skirt. I put the loaf in her lap. The children turned to their mother – was it permitted? She tore into the crust like an animal. I averted my eyes.

Later, at home, I heard Agathe cry out: 'The bread! It is gone!' She had waited in line for two hours to get it, endured the cold. The small loaf had been there, earlier, she *knew* that, on that very counter, she insisted. Her voice trembled with emotion.

'It can't have disappeared,' Lannoy said. Perhaps the bread had been eaten; perhaps Agathe herself was the guilty party, she implied.

'I took it,' I told them, stepping into the fray.

Lannoy turned to me with a bewildered expression. 'Madame?'

'I gave it to a woman on the Pont-Royal. She had four children. She needed it more than we do.'

Agathe burst into tears.

THAT EVENING

By day I pick my way through evidence of the most appalling poverty. By night I coquette with the newly rich in exclusive salons. Deputy Dumont, a former fowl fattener, is now fattening himself on confiscated church property. Deputy Nerval, a leather-seller, recently purchased one of the mansions of the Marquise de Neufchâteau – fully furnished, including the horses and carriages – on profits made supplying wormy pork to the army in the east. Who would know people are starving?

6 JANUARY

Lannoy returned from the milliner's with an ashen face. She went directly to her room. 'What happened?' I asked Gontier, who had accompanied her. He goes with her everywhere now, a knife concealed in his coat.

He shuffled his feet and stared at the floor. It required patience to get Gontier to speak. I waited. 'A woman jumped in the river,' he mumbled finally.

'Mademoiselle Lannoy saw this?' Every day people threw themselves into the Seine. Tallien claimed that there were so many now, at Saint-Cloud the job of pulling the bodies out had become overwhelming.

'She had a child strapped to her.' Gontier stopped, shifted his weight from one foot to the other. 'A big girl . . . like ours.'

Like ours. Hortense, he meant. A girl as big as that, fighting for her life.

THURSDAY, 8 JANUARY, 7.00 P.M.

At La Chaumière there is an atmosphere of creative confusion. A work crew toils under Thérèse's direction. She maintains her energy in spite of her pregnancy. She is exacting, she knows what she wants — but invariably it is something unusual. The workmen simply cannot comprehend. Often it takes several attempts before they get it right.

We stay late into the night, going over fabric samples, walking through the rooms. She wishes to create a theatrical, artistic, witty atmosphere: *almost* overdone (this is challenging). It fires my imagination. Now and again we come up with an idea that sets us both dancing.

Later, we stand at the doors to the garden, listening to the wolves howl, the wind whistling through the trees, talking of love and life. Another world, so far from the misery that is Paris now — but for the hungry wolves circling, watching and waiting.

2 January 1795 — Rennes
Chère Maman,

I will be needing a new uniform soon. New gaiters, too; mine have entirely worn at the heel.

Your son, Eugène

8 January 1795 — Rennes
Rose,

Forgive me for not writing more often. I am not a man of letters, as you know. Also, it has been quite the job here; our provisions are terribly inadequate. We do what we can, what we must — and that on very little.

I am pleased with Eugène's progress — he is a fine boy.

Your soldier, Lazare

MONDAY, 12 JANUARY

Under Thérèse's guidance I've realized an excellent profit speculating in saltpetre. Aunt Désirée was horrified. 'It is unbecoming for a woman to involve herself in commerce,' she scolded. *Until* I told her how much profit I had made (five thousand livres!), and then her own interest was sparked. I intend to reinvest the money in a purchase of lace from Britanny, which I can resell in Paris, yielding an additional twenty per cent.

THE MANY LIVES & SECRET SORROWS OF JOSEPHINE B.

Citoyenne Rose Beauharnais – *profiteer*. At least now I can send Eugène money for a new uniform.

15 January 1795 – Hôtel de Caulaincourt, Paris
Dear Madame Beauharnais,

I am writing to inform you that thanks to your recommendation, General Hoche has kindly awarded my eldest son, Armand, a position as lieutenant in the Army of the Coast. Also, thanks to your efforts, my second son, Auguste, is now gainfully employed as a clerk. I am indebted to you.

At your suggestion I have made an appointment to speak to Deputy Coligny about the three years' pay due to me as a retired general. I will keep you informed as to the outcome. Thank you for approaching him on my behalf.

I would say more, but even in amoral times such as ours it is deemed unseemly for a man of my advanced age and marital status to write words of 'appreciation' to a lovely widow. Perhaps I will see you chez Talliens?

I remain, most gratefully and as always,
Your dearest and most foolish friend, Marquis de Caulaincourt
       'a slave to the devil of middle-aged passion'

THURSDAY, 15 JANUARY
Marquis de Caulaincourt has insisted on awarding me ten per cent for my efforts.

'I did it for friendship,' I protested.

'I will pay you in coin,' he said.

Gold. 'If you must.'

16 JANUARY
Tallien has been advising me on how best to draw up a petition requesting that the seals be removed from my belongings on Rue Saint-Dominique. This afternoon I made my presentation to the Committee of Public Safety. Tallien spoke in support. 'Certainly it is certain,' he began, repeating his words, as was his custom, 'my fellow deputies-in-arms are beginning to comprehend that together

we must cleanse the wounds of the past, right the wrongs in order for the Tree of Liberty to have fertile ground in which to root.'

I repressed a disloyal smile. 'Lukewarm water tap' is what my friend has been nicknamed in the Assembly, he does go on so.

WEDNESDAY, 21 JANUARY

Festivities throughout the city, in celebration of the day the King died, two years ago. This in spite of the cold.

I would have stayed in, with Lannoy, who not so secretly mourns the King, but for a ceremony at the Palais-Égalité where Tallien was to be honoured. So I went with Thérèse, who was bundled in an enormous fox cape.

The speeches droned on, followed by singing. The Gilded Youths, resplendent in their crazy finery, dragging heavy clubs, demanded that the band play 'Death to the Jacobins'.

'There may be trouble,' Deputy Barras said.

I suggested we go back to my apartment, which was not far. I was shivering from the cold. Also, I was concerned for Thérèse — at five months she continues to be delicate.

It was cold in my parlour; the fire had died down. We could see our breath. I was about to pull the bell for Gontier to stoke it when Tallien insisted on doing it. 'After all, this used to be my father's job,' he said.

'Well,' Deputy Barras said, lowering himself on to a stool by the fire. He rubbed his hands together. 'Two years ago today.'

Both Deputy Barras and Tallien had voted for the death of the King. I didn't like to think of that.

The fire caught. 'This last year has been infernal.' Tallien glanced in my direction. 'Pardon my language, Citoyenne Beauharnais — I forget you are a lady.' He stood, brushed his hands.

'And what about me?' Thérèse asked, stretching out on my daybed which I had recently moved into the parlour due to the cold.

Tallien leaned over her, whispered something in her ear. She laughed.

'Perhaps we should request a demonstration.' Deputy Barras accepted my offer of a brandy. I filled his glass from a bottle Marquis de Caulaincourt had given me.

'Really, Deputy Barras, you are *so* perverted,' Thérèse said.

'Imagine, and in Thérèse's condition . . .' I feigned shock.

'I'm *trying* to imagine, that's my problem.' Deputy Barras made a funny face.

Smiling, I threw a fur coverlet over Thérèse.

'Our good, innocent Rose,' she said. 'Are we embarrassing you?'

'How innocent can she be, I ask you, with a bed in her parlour?' Deputy Barras asked.

'My mother keeps a bed in her parlour,' Tallien said. 'All the peasants do.'

'And sleep there?' Deputy Barras asked. His green-and-black-striped coat had big square buttons with hunting scenes painted on them.

'No, it's only for love-making,' Tallien said. (In fact, he used a cruder term.) 'When company comes for tea.'

'Citoyenne Beauharnais, if I may be so rude as to inquire, why *is* there a bed in your parlour?' Deputy Barras downed his glass.

'It's the only warm room.' I took a seat by the fire.

'The other rooms are *colder*?'

We all laughed, but in truth I was beginning to regret having invited them. Seen through their eyes, my small, albeit elegant rooms looked quite humble. Rose, *their* Rose – the former vicomtesse who sipped their expensive champagne – this woman was a fraud, was she not?

'Do you not have fuel?' Thérèse asked, fingering a cameo Tallien had recently bought her for 'only' six thousand livres.

'It's difficult to find in quantity now.' I did not add, and frightfully dear.

Tallien groaned. 'Why didn't you ask? There is more than enough. You'd think there was no fuel to be had in all of Paris, the way people talk.'

'Or *bread*,' Deputy Barras added. 'Of which there is little, you have to concede.'

'The people are too damned lazy to work, and then they come to *us* to complain,' Tallien ranted.

I looked from one to the other. How much was in jest? I wasn't sure.

'My friend has become cynical, I'm afraid,' Deputy Barras said, in answer to my questioning look. 'It is one of the dangers of public life. People expect their representatives to be as gods, to make the foul weather go away.'

I sighed, relieved. We were on to safer ground: the weather. I set up a game of faro. We played, laughed, gossiped and gambled (I won seven livres). They left just before midnight, in good spirits.

'We'll be back next Tuesday,' Thérèse announced as they were leaving. 'For your *salon*.'

'I couldn't,' I said, horrified.

'Rose, be realistic. You can't afford *not* to. Imagine, *Chez Rose* — the most enjoyable salon in all of Paris.'

Chez Rose? I smiled. 'It sounds like a brothel.'

'With a bed in the parlour and everything,' Deputy Barras said.

'The better to get the deputies to come,' Thérèse said.

And so it is set. Next Tuesday. Every Tuesday.

23 JANUARY

Oh, it is cold, but we've been warm. Deputy Barras arranged to have a load of wood delivered. There's a huge pile of it outside. Gontier must stand by it to keep the neighbours from stealing it.

I sent Deputy Barras a note: 'How can I thank you?'

He sent a note back: 'Recommend me to banker Citoyen Rougemont.'

31 JANUARY, AFTERNOON

By some miracle, I have succeeded. Like a stage director I have assembled the props, moved furniture, created *ambiance* — that mysterious aura that disguises the stains on the sofa, the hole in the rug, the less than exquisite fixtures.

My costume I created out of an outdated brocade, Lannoy and I cutting and reassembling the panels into an elegant Grecian design. It took some cajoling to entice her to take up her needle and thread, to use her refined artistry for such a 'shameless' dress. Too much arm, too much leg, but worst of all, no corset!

LATER

Chez Rose was a success!

Who came: Tallien and Thérèse, of course. Deputy Barras, in the company of old La Montansier (who lived up to her wild reputation). Tiny Madame de Crény and Denon, her beau. Citoyen Fouché, skulking around. Deputy Fréron, raving and drunk, and in the company of an actress. (It is rumoured they have three children.) Fanny, with *both* her current favourites: Michel de Cubières and Rétif de la Bretonne who got on well with La Montansier – *pas de surprise*. Fortunée Hamelin, half naked as usual, and her grumpy husband, who fancied no one. Marquis de Caulaincourt, who *also* got on well with La Montansier, I noticed. Voluptuous Minerva in gauzy white, with a man she introduced as her *fiancé* (that was a surprise). Two of my 'prison family': the elegant Grace Elliott, for a short time, and Duchesse Jeanne-Victoire d'Aiguillon – in the company of Mesdames de Broglie, Valance and Bizet, who smoked opium in the water closet, Thérèse claims (I don't believe her). And dear sneezing Citoyen Dunnkirk, who came with fellow bankers Citoyens Rougemont, Hottinguer and Perré. (I introduced them all to Deputy Barras.) And last, but certainly not least, my dear Consoler, the wild, radical and wicked General Santerre.

An entertaining, *very* mixed group. 'A miracle, no bloodshed,' Thérèse said.

I would have run short of food had it not been for Caulaincourt who supplied pâté de foie gras from Strasbourg, larded pheasant and an enormous carp stuffed with truffles from Périgord. Not to mention a crate of freshly baked beautiful bread and a basket of fruit (in February!) from Citoyen Dunnkirk. Even Deputy Barras arranged for a half-barrel of excellent red wine to be delivered.

'Celebrating, darling?' Thérèse asked, watching Barras's footman carry in the barrel.

'Celebrating what?' Deputy Barras asked. He looked unusually serious in a Quaker-coloured silk coat and an old-fashioned pig-tail wig.

'Being elected President of the Assembly.'

'Oh, *that*.'

'You've been elected President?' I recalled when Alexandre had been elected President of the Assembly, remembered our excitement, our pride. How young we were then.

Deputy Barras shrugged. 'A nuisance, if you ask me. No, if anything, I'm celebrating the profit I made on the sale of a property two days ago. Five hundred thousand. *Net.*' He grinned, his charming crooked smile.

Five hundred thousand! I could not comprehend such a sum. I practically had to sell my soul to get a loan of a mere five hundred.

'That confiscated church property on Rue Jacques?' Tallien asked, overhearing.

Deputy Barras smiled, crossed himself. 'And the good Lord *was* smiling on me,' he said.

At around midnight Barras's secretary Botot came by, in the company of another man, Citoyen Laurent. Lisping, Botot asked if he could speak to Barras. I urged them to come in, but they were reluctant. I wondered if something was amiss.

Deputy Barras came to the door. He stepped outside to talk to them. When he came back in he looked drawn.

'Has something happened?' I asked.

'Nothing,' he said quickly. Too quickly, I thought.

'Did I not hear Laurent's voice?' Thérèse asked, coming into the hall on Citoyen Fouché's arm.

'He was just here, with Botot. They had a message for Deputy Barras,' I said.

'It's rather late for messages,' Thérèse said.

'Ah, Laurent and Botot,' Citoyen Fouché said, catching my eye. 'The Temple Twosome.'

The Temple? The *Boy* is in the Temple . . .

5 FEBRUARY

At *last*, thanks to Tallien and Deputy Barras, my petition has been approved, the seals removed from my belongings on Rue Saint-Dominique.

I went there this morning – alone. That was how I wished it.

It was strange opening the doors. The rooms were dark, the shutters nailed over the windows. I lit a lantern – and was sickened by what I saw: everything had been pulled to the floor. Vandals.

I walked through the musty rooms, stepping through the litter of my life. My broken and soiled possessions brought forth an abundance of memories. Clothing, scarves, paintings, my guitar – things I had loved. Now ruined.

I gathered my courage and went into the parlour. Gently, I pried away the loose stone in the chimney. I blew into the hole, lest some creatures had taken up residence. Overcoming fear, I put in my hand. Papers. They were still there. Thank God.

Slowly, and with a great sense of relief, I drew out my treasures – my journals, letters, Manette's tapestry, my Bible, a container of earth from Martinico, my childhood rosary, marriage contract, a little cloth bag of gems. And, at the last, Alexandre's will, sealed with wax.

I lowered myself into an armchair. I was enveloped in a cloud of dust. All that remained of my life was in my lap. I sat for a time thus, as still as the mute objects that surrounded me. How little it all meant, in the end.

My eyes fell upon an object in the corner – my needlework frame. The tapestry I had been working on was still in it, a design of roses, half completed. Miraculously, the needle was still in place. I had the most eerie sense of a life abruptly stopped, a curtain drawn in the middle of a play.

The ghosts began to stir. Not even a year had passed since I had been taken in the night, herded on to a wagon and into a cell. Stripped of my dignity, my health, my faith. Stripped of my youth, my life.

6 FEBRUARY

I sat across from Citoyen Dunnkirk, grasping my basket. There was an uneasiness in his expression that cautioned me.

He cleared his throat and sat forward in his worn leather chair. 'I'm afraid that your husband's will is not going to be of much use to you,' he said, sneezing into a linen handkerchief.

'What do you mean?'

'Well . . .' He paused. 'He has not left anything to you.'

I sat for a moment without responding. Surely I had mis-understood.

'And second,' he went on, mistaking my silence for composure, 'do you know of a Mademoiselle Marie-Adélaïde de la Ferté?'

'La Ferté is the name of Alexandre's country estate.' But Citoyen Dunnkirk knew that.

'This is a child, a girl born in June of seventeen eighty-five, near Cherbourg.'

'Perhaps you mean Adélaïde d'Antigny.' Adélaïde d'Antigny was Alexandre's illegitimate daughter, whom Aunt Désirée and I were doing our best to support, in spite of the hardships. Nine years old now, she was a beautiful child, quite bright, with Alexandre's features. 'But Adélaïde d'Antigny was born in seventeen eighty-*four*, in Paris.'

'This is a different girl, born the following year. Your deceased husband has left her an annual pension of six hundred livres.'

Another illegitimate child? *Two* Adélaïdes?

'And six hundred livres a year is to be paid to Movin, your husband's servant, two hundred a year to Richard, the groom, and a one-time payment of an additional two hundred to Sauvage, the second groom—'

'And *nothing* for Hortense or Eugène?' I interrupted. 'No mention of *my* name?'

'No doubt he assumed that they would be well provided for by your Island holdings.'

I felt short of breath.

Citoyen Dunnkirk cleared his throat again and adjusted the lorgnon in his eye. 'You understand, Madame Beauharnais, with respect to Marie-Adélaïde de la Ferté, there may be a way to get round it—'

'Honour it,' I said sharply. I was already contributing to the support of one bastard child. How many were there? I thought wearily.

In which I am warned

10 FEBRUARY 1795

La Chaumière has become *the* place to go. Thérèse has had to hire a
guard to oversee the door; crowds of hopefuls line the courtyard.

At first there were whispered comments on the absurd location,
jokes about the peasant life. But there could be no doubt that
everyone is charmed, for inside this modest château is a gem
of a palace – the door opens on to a theatrical world of marble
columns and Greek statues. The originality of the décor, the
artistry that is evident, not to mention the abundant fare and
inspired entertainment, certainly make an impression.

But at heart, it is Thérèse everyone seeks. We are as moths
to a flame. She embraces us as if it is months since we last met,
not last night or the night before that. She is, always, astonishingly
beautiful, wearing a simple toga or shift that makes no attempt to
hide her growing belly, her swelling breasts. She draws us into
the parlour, whispering, 'Monsieur Monroe is here, the American
Ambassador. And Citoyen Ouvrard, the brilliant financier . . . Let
me introduce you.'

Within, guests whisper, ever watchful for others. Contacts are
made, broken, alliances formed. After the Assembly's night sitting
closes, the deputies arrive in their top hats. The heated debates go
on until dawn. *This* is the government, it is said.

12 FEBRUARY

'Thank God you're here!' Thérèse grabbed my hand this evening
as I came into the hall. 'Deputy Renan drank the water out of
his finger bowl, Citoyen Maurois blew his nose on the tablecloth.
Already there have been two fist fights—'

'In the Middle Ages, it fell to the Romans to reform the barbarians,' Deputy Barras said. He looked particularly elegant in an embroidered blue satin waistcoat. 'Today it falls to Thérèse to demonstrate to the new ruling class *proper* etiquette.'

Angry voices burst forth from the parlour. Thérèse raised her eyebrows in exasperation. 'But I need help taming this mob!'

And so, my role has been defined: peacemaker. It's a job I apparently do well. I select the most heated guest, engage him in quiet conversation, lure him away – to a walk in the garden, perhaps, if the weather is fine, or through the premises to view the art. Soon my 'victim' is calm, his desire to commit murder only moments before forgotten.

Around four in the morning the last guest finally left. Thérèse and I collapsed on the sofa, laughing to tears over these ardent revolutionaries, trying so hard to be rich.

13 FEBRUARY
Thérèse and Tallien persuaded me to go with them to the 'Bal des Victimes' at Hôtel Thélusson. I went to Thérèse's early to prepare.

'Your hair is already perfect,' she said, fastening a red ribbon round my neck, symbolizing the path for the knife.

'This is bizarre,' I said. She was wearing flesh-coloured tights under a revealing gauze gown. As tall as she is, and with her huge belly and breasts, she looked spectacular.

'This is the dance.' Thérèse began doing a strange wiggling movement, her head shaking back and forth as if it might come loose.

The streets in front of Hôtel Thélusson were jammed with carriages. Beggars crowded around the entry, vying for attention.

'Doesn't it remind you of the days of the Ancien Régime?' Thérèse whispered. 'Of the opera balls?'

A street urchin grabbed the hem of my skirt. Tallien threatened him with his fist. The boy fell back against the dirt. I stopped to make sure he was not hurt, gave him a coin.

'Are executioners allowed in?' someone yelled as Tallien entered.

'It is as *liberator* I am greeted now,' Tallien said, attempting a jest.

15 FEBRUARY
I fear Thérèse and Tallien are not getting along.

'Is something wrong?' I asked. Her left cheek was heavily made up.
There were the beginnings of tears in her eyes. 'I don't understand.
He loves you so much.'

'His love is killing me!' she cried.

15 February 1795 — Rennes
Rose,
    My efforts to negotiate peace may meet with success. Pray
for me — soon it may be even legal to do so. I long for you.
                                              Your soldier, Lazare

18 FEBRUARY, 11.00 A.M.
Lazare has succeeded in negotiating peace with the Vendée rebels,
succeeded where so many before him have failed. In exchange for
freedom of worship, they will lay down their arms.

'But what about the rest of us?' Lannoy grumbled. 'Don't we get
freedom too?'

21 FEBRUARY
There is great excitement in the streets. Freedom of worship has
been granted — to all of France.

'You can put out your little Madonna now,' I told Hortense.
'Are you sure?' She is a fearful child.
'The time of hiding is over.' Thanks to Lazare.

TUESDAY, 24 FEBRUARY
Thérèse has not been well; her pregnancy is slowing her down. As
a result, she has asked my help in organizing a reception in honour
of the Turkish Ambassador. It's to be held next week at Barras's
château in Chaillot. Thérèse and I have been going out there every
afternoon.

    Everything about Deputy Barras is old money: the hounds, the
horses, the snifters of fine cognac . . . the degenerate morals.

(Marquis de Sade is his *cousin*, he claims: '*mon cher cousin*'.) He even suffers now and then from a mysteriously aristocratic nervous condition that requires hot baths. ('The French pox,* do you think?' Thérèse whispered.) Yet he is not without conscience. He seems to take pride in identifying the coming young men. At first I suspected a prurient interest, but I have found it to be otherwise. In the same way he chooses the winning horse at the races, he enjoys predicting who will hold the political trump card in the years to come. This is not without self-interest – nothing Deputy Barras does is without self-interest – for in this way he assures himself support. He is a master of survival.

Yes, an amusing man, mannered, witty, generous – but with a side to him that is so truly shocking. A libertine, he provides Thérèse and me with daily accounts of his conquests. Were it not for his wit, his stories would surely strike one as sordid, but Thérèse and I end up laughing gustily at his portrayals of coy seduction between grown men. Really, it is all *so* bizarre.

SATURDAY

What a night! The partridge arrived foul, the fruit did not arrive at all, the violinist arrived drunk and the Turkish Ambassador sent word that he would not be able to attend. Perhaps that was a blessing . . .

TUESDAY, 3 MARCH, LATE EVENING

Thérèse, preparing for confinement, has been urging me to become more involved in Barras's affairs. 'You are exactly the type of woman he needs – aristocratic, elegant, with impeccable taste and social skills. Your contacts could prove useful to him. There is *no one* better than you. I told him so myself.'

'You told him that?'

'He rewards a woman well, Rose, of *that* I can assure you. And the only thing you have to do is listen to his stories of amorous adventure.'

I smiled.

* Syphilis or gonorrhoea (thought at the time to be the same disease).

'And keep your son away from him, I should add.'
I stopped smiling.

FRIDAY, 13 MARCH

I'm exhausted, but pleased. The reception at Barras's went well. Most of the evening was spent around the game tables with a separate area set up for conversation and canapés. At midnight I had a meal served, prepared from Barras's estates: rabbit from his hutches, vegetables from his gardens, wine from his vineyards in Provence. After, I persuaded everyone to play l'hombre. 'A child's game!' the guests (including bankers Rosin and Perré) complained before reluctantly consenting – then becoming boisterous participants.

Overall, a success. Deputy Barras seemed pleased. 'We will leave pretension to the nouveau riche.'

It is late now, time to sleep. Ideas swirl – I am filled with fantasies of theatricals, concerts, balls, of elegant meals until dawn. Entertaining on an unlimited budget – *this* is a task I enjoy.

SATURDAY, 28 MARCH, 3.00 A.M.

It's late. I'm still at Barras's in Chaillot. The roads are too muddy to risk the return into Paris. Deputy Barras just came in to say goodnight. He was wearing the high-crowned beaver felt hat he reserves for serious gambling. Tonight he'd adorned it with pink and lavender ribbons.

'Your confessions?' he asked, noting my journal. 'Put in something scandalous about me. For posterity.'

'I've put in what an angel of virtue you are.' He smelled of spirit of ambergris, a scent he favours.

'Ah, that *v* word,' he groaned, sinking into one of the plush velvet chairs and tossing his hat on to the floor. 'Let's not be on about *virtue* again. We had quite enough of that from our dear Robespierre, don't you think?' He took a long sip of whatever it was in the glass in his hand. Spirits probably.

'What did you make of Deputy Valen's comment tonight?' I asked.

'About the Boy?' He bent down to pet Toto, his miniature greyhound.

I nodded. At supper, an elegant affair for twelve, Deputy Valen had expressed the view that it would not take much to install the Boy as King on the throne of France – a shocking statement, under the circumstances.

Deputy Barras dangled the silk tassel of his robe in front of Toto's nose, to tease him. 'I think we've had quite enough of kings,' he said, smiling at Toto's antics.

'It is rumoured you favour a return of the monarchy,' I persisted, my heart pounding.

'Only a fool would admit it.' He looked over at me. 'Even to a friend.' His big eyes were impossible to interpret. 'In any case,' he yawned, 'I prefer to talk of men, not kings.' Toto jumped up on his lap.

'Did Citoyen Lumière not stay?'

Deputy Barras sighed, scratching Toto behind the ears. 'Alas, no. His wife was expecting him. His *wife*!'

'And now you only have me.'

'And lectures on virtue . . .' He made a comical face.

'How tiresome,' I laughed.

1 APRIL

Agathe returned from the market in tears. Riots in the marketplace – she'd seen a child trampled. Then, as I was preparing to leave to go out to La Chaumière, I thought I heard musket shots. Nevertheless, I sent Gontier for a hackney coach. The driver, dressed in mismatched livery, insisted on a fee three times the normal rate, and that in coin.

'Only fools are out tonight,' he said when I objected to the fare.

'What has happened?'

'The Assembly has been attacked.' He was a young man, but with no teeth.

The Assembly!

At the end of Pont-Royal there were a number of National Guardsmen on horseback. The coachman cracked his whip; our horses galloped down the quay.

At La Chaumière, coaches and horses filled the courtyard. I saw Tallien, still in his deputy robes. 'You're safe!' I embraced him.

He told me what had happened: a mob had invaded the Assembly, demanding food. The Gilded Youths were summoned, who proved cowardly (for all their talk). Then the National Guard had been mobilized. Finally, the instigators had been arrested and peace restored.

'Who was behind it?' I asked.

'Four men.' Tallien puffed on his pipe. '"The Four" they are called now – the alumni of the Terror.' He recited the names: Billaud-Varenne, Collot d'Herbois, Barère, Vadier.

'Deputy Barère? Your old *friend*?' Barere and Tallien used to come to our gatherings on Rue Saint-Dominique. I remembered Deputy Barère's support of Alexandre in the Assembly, his fear of helping me when Marie had been arrested. And Vadier, certainly . . . Deputy Vadier had signed my arrest warrant. And yet, years back, they'd all been colleagues of Alexandre's, idealists working together for a better world. Now Alexandre was dead and they were on their way to prison – or worse, Guiana.

'Yes,' Tallien said with a satisfied air. 'Strange, is it not, how history turns?'

2 APRIL

This morning Agathe came to me in an agitated state. 'There's a curious man at the door. He insists on speaking to you.'

'Curious in what way?' I asked. There had been sounds of violence, shots fired. I felt uneasy. Today was the day The Four were to be deported to Guiana, expelled from the city on carts. Half of Paris wanted them guillotined, the other half wanted them set free.

'He smells, and he seems nervous,' Agathe said.

I went to the door. I could hardly see the man's eyes for the scarves he had wrapped about his face.

'Citoyenne Beauharnais, it's me.' He put down his fur muff and unwound one of the scarves.

'Citoyen Fouché?'

Agathe hovered nearby. 'You may go,' I told her.

'I have come to bid farewell,' he hissed, after Agathe had withdrawn.

'I don't understand.' I took his arm, urged him in.

'The Four have been arrested, deported. As you know. What

you might not know is that were it not for Deputy Barras, it would have been "The Five". I've been spared, but on a condition. I'm to disappear, as it were.'

'Disappear? *You*?' I invited him to take a seat beside me on a little bench by the door. 'But why?'

'Too much snooping around, I suppose.' He shrugged. 'I'm going to be a pig farmer now.'

I smiled. It was difficult to imagine him thus. 'I like pigs,' I said.

'I forget that you're a farm girl.'

'But where will you be? You and your pigs.'

'Not far.' He handed me a piece of paper. An address was written on it, in a neat hand. He stood to go. 'You are aware, no doubt, of the incident at the hospital, at the Hôtel Dieu?'

'The miracle, you mean?' A dying child had been cured overnight. Hortense had been telling me all about it.

'There are no miracles any more, citoyenne. You know that.'

'You sound sad.'

'It's a hoax, with children for pawns! The sick child was moved from the hospital to the Temple, to *pose* as the Boy.'

'But where *is* the Boy?' King . . .

'That's what I want to know. Your friend, Lazare—'

'General Hoche?'

'General Hoche stands to be hurt by this. The peace treaty he negotiated with the rebels – I understand that part of the agreement was that the Boy would be restored to the throne.'

'General Lazare Hoche would *never* agree to such a thing!'

Citoyen Fouché nodded. 'But Director *Barras* might,' he said. 'Promise, and then not deliver.'

I felt a strange tingling feeling coming over me. I could close my eyes to any number of things, but could I close my eyes to this? I only wanted peace.

'How convenient,' Citoyen Fouché went on, 'if the Boy – or rather, the child everyone *thinks* is the Boy – how very convenient if he were to *die* . . .' Citoyen Fouché bowed and left, wrapping his face in his scarves.

In which a child is born & a child dies

17 MAY 1795
I was awoken this morning by Fortuné growling.

'Citoyenne Tallien's footman is at the door,' Agathe informed me.

'Thérèse! Is it—' I stumbled into my clothes, threw on a wig, a cloak.

The horses were snorting and pawing at the stones. Thérèse's footman helped me into the new barouche. Immediately the horses pulled forward. They were a fast team. I closed my eyes and held on.

When we arrived at La Chaumière the *accoucheuse* was already there. I went to Thérèse's bedside, touched her hand. Thérèse squeezed it hard. Already her nightclothes were soaked.

'Where's Tallien?' I asked.

'He went out last night. With Barras.'

I did not ask the obvious. Deputies Tallien and Barras shared a weakness for 'the gaming tables of liberty', as they put it. 'Well, you'll have a nice surprise for him when he returns,' I said.

I fetched cloths and a bowl of water. For hours I stroked her brow, caressed her, spoke words of calm. Shortly before noon the baby came. 'I saw her in a dream,' she said. There were tears in her eyes. 'Rouge me?' she asked.

'You look beautiful as you are.' I coloured her cheeks as she requested.

She fell into an exhausted sleep. I took the baby — Thermidor-Rose she has been named — and held her in my arms. My goddaughter. She cried for only a moment, a little animal squawk, and then quietened. My breasts responded with a familiar tingling sensation. I sat thus in the rocking chair by the window for some time, looking into the face of this precious little soul, so pure and so new.

If I ever remarry, would I have another? *Could* I?

3 JUNE
Dr Desault, doctor to the Boy, died suddenly three days ago, of brain fever – or so it was reported. The streets have been buzzing with rumours. For once Agathe and Lannoy agree: the doctor was poisoned.

I tell them such stories are entirely without grounds, but now the doctor's nephew has spoken, claiming that his uncle the doctor *was* poisoned, and all because he'd discovered that this child was a fraud, not the Dauphin at all.

'There, you see!' Lannoy and Agathe said in unison.

8 JUNE
At La Chaumière I was met by Tallien. He pulled me into the study. 'The Committee of General Security has gone to an emergency meeting. The Dauphin died,' he whispered.

'The *Boy*?' I sat down. It was only a week ago that the Boy's doctor had died . . . and now the Boy himself? He was only ten years old.

I recalled Citoyen Fouché's words: *how convenient if the Boy were to die.* I felt a sickening sense of helplessness. 'When?' I asked.

'At three this afternoon.' It was six now. 'You're not to tell *anyone.*' He looked around uneasily. '*Especially* Tallita.'

9 JUNE
This afternoon there was an enormous reception planned: an orchestra, a seven-course meal for three hundred (every dignitary in Paris invited), a ball later, all to celebrate the passage of a law allowing restitution to victims of the Terror. It was a significant achievement, deserving of festivity. The new law would begin to heal the wounds of the past. Now Alexandre might be declared unjustly accused, unjustly condemned, his possessions and property returned to his family.

But even so I did not want to go; I could not shake the gloom I felt. However, I had promised; so at midday I set out.

I was greeted by Minerva, her cream-puff cheeks pink with excitement. 'Isn't it wonderful!' Her gauzy skirt billowed up around her. 'We'll be wealthy again.'

She was stopped by the lack of gaiety in my expression. 'What's the matter, Rose? After all the work you and Thérèse did to get this law passed, I should think you would be happier than anyone.'

It was true. Thérèse and I had worked hard. 'There has been a disturbing development,' I told her. News of the Boy's death was to be announced in the Assembly that morning, I knew. Soon everyone would know. 'The Boy died yesterday.'

'You mean the King's *son*?' Minerva sat down on one of the lawn chairs, fanning herself furiously. 'Oh, dear.'

I saw Thérèse approaching, Tallien holding her arm. They were followed by a swarm of men and women, like courtiers to a king and queen. Thérèse was weak still, moving very slowly.

'You should be in childbed.' Minerva took her other arm.

'I refuse.' Thérèse smiled weakly.

A gentleman rushed to get her a chair. Another held a pastel blue sun umbrella over her.

I glanced at Tallien. 'How did they take the news?' I asked.

'The deputies? They were quiet.' Tallien looked out over the festive grounds. The manicured gardens opened on to a small lake, where colourful boats floated lazily. A string orchestra was being set up on a floating platform.

'It's the shock of it,' I said.

'I'm not sure.' He brushed a mosquito off his cheek.

'What else could it be?'

'Suspicion.'

I I JUNE

Late at night, last night, a child was buried – quietly, *quickly*.

'What do you think it means?' Thérèse demanded, her baby in her arms. We were walking in her garden. The flowers were blooming, it was a glorious afternoon. 'Now everyone's saying that the child that died wasn't really the Boy. Yet it would have been so easy to prove. Why didn't they ask Madame Royale? If anyone would be able to give a positive identification of the Boy's body, one would think it would be his sister.'

'Perhaps they didn't want to upset her.' I never told Thérèse about my conversations with Citoyen Fouché, my growing uneasiness . . . my suspicions.

'Because they're so tender-hearted? Because they *care* so much about the royal family?' Thérèse gave me a scornful look. 'Rose, that makes no sense. Even Barras is being evasive. Why do they have to be so secretive? I don't like it.'

I put my arm round her. 'Tallita, you shouldn't be thinking such distressing thoughts. You should be resting.' I led her back towards the house.

13 JUNE

I've been at Deputy Barras's all afternoon, preparing another reception. 'Are you evading me?' he asked, finally. I was in the study writing out the invitations.

I put down the quill. How could I respond? It was true, I *had* been evading him. Ever since the death of the Boy I have had a feeling of disquiet.

Deputy Barras put his hand to his forehead in a theatrical pose. 'And even to this, this little query, she remains silent. One hates to contemplate the magnitude of her despair.'

'This is not a matter for comedy,' I said.

He placed a chair beside me and sat down. 'Tragedy?'

'I can't talk about it.'

'It's all these nasty rumours. Isn't it?'

'There are always nasty rumours.'

'But these you believe?'

I looked away. I would have given anything not to be in this position, talking to Deputy Barras now, but I had begun and there was nothing to do but continue. 'It is said you have consorted with the enemy – with the British.'

Deputy Barras looked at me with an amused expression. '*Les Goddams?*'

'Is it *true*?'

He smirked. 'I dare say the espionage force of an entire nation couldn't have gleaned as much.'

'How can you joke?' I cautioned myself to be calm. 'Do you think this is a game?'

'This *is* a game, Rose, a complex game. Do not presume to understand.' He was angry now.

'You admit it?' I sat back, suddenly short of breath.

'The facts are correct, but the intention mistaken. How better to know the enemy than to be in their league? Or, at the least, to have them *think* you are in their league. A dangerous pastime, true, for one risks condemnation from all sides, but risk has long been my friend, and what risk is too great for the good of the Republic?'

'*Did* you murder the Boy? Did you poison the King's son?'

Deputy Barras made a sigh. 'There are things you would prefer not to know,' he said.

I felt short of breath. 'You—'

He put up his hand. 'It's not what you think.'

'Then?' My mouth was dry.

'The unpleasant truth is that that child's dear uncle, the Comte d'Artois, paid a considerable sum to see that this was done. He rather fancied the throne for himself, should the opportunity present itself.'

I was silent a moment. 'The Comte d'Artois?'

Deputy Barras nodded.

'Offered to *pay*?' For his own nephew's *death* . . .

'Paid.'

'Paid *you*?'

Deputy Barras nodded again, slowly.

'You did then,' I said coldly, starting to rise. 'You—'

'Stay,' he said, putting his hand on my arm. 'I did *not*. The child – a good lad, you might like to know, a boy I came to be fond of, in my fashion – died naturally of a fever some time ago. On that count I am innocent.'

'Why not make it known? Why all this secrecy?'

'Spain would never have signed!' He threw up his hands.

'The peace treaty, you mean.'

He nodded wearily.

'So the child who just died was *not* the Boy?'

'*That* child was sickly, deaf and dumb, the son of a nail-maker – a decoy, you might say, kept alive for the purpose of forging a peace with Spain. He was destined to die in any case. Nature did our work.'

There was a moment of silence. Still, I would not look at him.

'Rose, look at me,' he said.

I turned to face him. He did not look like a devil. He looked like an aging, ordinary man.

'You don't believe me,' he said, his eyes sorrowful.

'I do believe you,' I said. But there was reserve in my heart.

'The question is not *did* I do it.' He stood abruptly, walked to the window. 'The question is—' He pulled the curtains shut. 'The question is *would* I have done it.' He stood for a long moment, his back turned to me. 'And the truth is . . . *yes*,' I heard him say.

I waited for him to move, say something. 'Paul?'

He turned to me, his eyes brimming with tears.

'I don't believe you,' I said.

16 June

This morning Barras came to call. It was early; I had a scarf wrapped round my head, Creole style. He invited me outside. 'I have something to show you.' In the courtyard were two handsome black horses harnessed to a gleaming dark green carriage.

'What do you think?' He slapped one of the horses on the flank. 'Fine specimens. Hungarian.' He opened the door to the carriage. The upholstery was a lush red, the colour of royalty.

'Velvet?' Such luxury is rare now. But then, Deputy Barras never had anything but the best. 'It's beautiful. When did you get it?' I asked.

'It's yours.'

'Mine?'

'In compensation for the carriage and horses your husband left behind in Strasbourg.'

He noted my shocked expression with satisfaction. 'There's a cow as well – a milk cow. I didn't bring her along. Too slow, you know.'

'A *cow?*'

Barras leaned back against the carriage, taking care not to soil his coat on the wheels. 'I got them to throw her in.'

I began to laugh. A *cow* – we could have butter, milk, cheese.

We could have too much, more than we needed. We could have excess – to sell or trade. 'But where would I keep her?'

'Must you be so practical?'

'I'm serious.' A carriage, two horses, a cow . . . I had no groom, no driver, no hay, much less a barn.

'You can stable the horses down the road. And the cow can go to Croissy.'

'Croissy? But I'm not renewing the lease.'

He looked confused. 'Why not?'

I rubbed my thumb and index finger together, meaning *money*. Barras had his estates, his wolfhounds, his English thoroughbreds. It was hard for him to comprehend.

'Why didn't you tell me? I've made a small fortune as a result of the meeting you arranged with your friends Rosin and Perré.'

And so it is agreed. Barras will take over the Croissy lease.

In which intrigue is the rule of the day

20 JUNE 1795
A note on my door: 'The émigré fleet has left the coast of England,
headed for France. They are planning to attack at Quiberon Bay.'
Unsigned.
I looked through my writing desk. Finally I found it, the scrap of
paper, the one Citoyen Fouché had given me with his address on it.
The handwriting was the same.
War. The émigrés are on their way.
I sent a mounted courier to Rennes with a message for Lazare. At
the end I hastily penned the words: 'Send Eugène home. Quickly.'
Quickly.

WEDNESDAY, 1 JULY
The émigré forces have attacked. Tallien left for Quiberon Bay in
the middle of the night.
Where *is* Eugène?

THURSDAY, 16 JULY — FONTAINEBLEAU
I have come to Fontainebleau to escape the tension in Paris, the fear
in my heart, my thoughts of Lazare . . . my worry about *Eugène*.
Only to be assaulted by my aunt.
'Soon it will have been one year,' she said.
One year. I knew what she was going to say. One year since
Alexandre died.
'It is time to think of remarrying, Rose.'
'I am too old to marry,' I said.
She smiled uneasily. There is truth in my jest.

As I climbed the stairs to my suite of rooms, Agathe came running to greet me. 'What is it?' I asked.

'Nothing, Madame,' she said, falling in behind.

She never called me 'Madame', so I was suspicious. I entered the parlour. There, sitting on the sofa, was Eugène, dressed smartly in a dark blue uniform with silver and red trim. Tears came to my eyes. He looked so like my father.

I embraced him, trying not to cry. He had grown since I last saw him over ten months ago, tall for a fourteen-year-old. 'When did you get here?' I asked, sitting down beside him on the sofa.

'Two hours ago.' His voice has not yet deepened.

I took his hand. He pulled away. 'Is something the matter?' I asked.

'Why did you make me come back! Just when things were starting to happen!'

It was hot in the room. I stood and went to the window, opened it wider. The air outside was heavy too; it made little difference.

How was I going to answer? Tell him he was too young to kill, too young to die? That I would not allow him to take up arms against French *émigrés*? That I could not bear the risk of losing him?

'I need you here,' I said.

'You have your men friends to help you!' Abruptly he stood and stomped out. I heard the front door slam shut behind him.

20 JULY

Eugène mopes about the apartment, resentful that I have 'caged' him, kept him from the excitement of army life, the glory of war. He takes to the streets where he spars with a rough-looking group.

What am I going to do with him?

THURSDAY, 23 JULY

It was early, not yet nine when I summoned Eugène. 'Do you know the significance of this day?'

He shrugged.

'One year ago your father died.' This startled him. 'I have

something for you.' I got down Alexandre's sword from on top of the cupboard, put it on the table in the dining parlour. 'This was your father's sword. He would have wanted you to have it.'

Eugène touched it, picked it up, withdrew it from its sheath. On the handle was engraved the Beauharnais family motto, Serve No Further, and under that, a heart. The family crest had been scratched over with the words '*la nation*'.

'It pleases you?' I asked.

A blush of emotion had spread across his cheeks.

I put my hand on his arm. 'Wear it with honour, Eugène.' Quickly, I left. I did not want him to see my tears.

23 July 1795 – Quiberon

Rose,

Victory! I carry your ribbon close to my heart.

Your soldier, Lazare

Note – Tell Eugène that Sébastien Antier was killed in battle. Eugène and Sébastien were close. Tell him Sébastien died honourably.

27 JULY

Victory at Quiberon Bay! Immediately I set out for La Chaumière. It was ten in the morning, early, but already the courtyard was jammed with carriages.

'You've heard?' I exclaimed the moment I saw Thérèse. Through the open door I thought I saw Tallien's bristly head. 'Tallien is *back*?'

'He arrived late last night.'

'For the banquet tonight?' It was the first-year anniversary of the overthrow of Robespierre.

Thérèse nodded. She looked grave.

'Something is wrong?' I asked. 'Is it Lazare—'

'No.'

'What is it?' I felt a panic rising within me.

'Over seven hundred prisoners were taken,' she whispered.

I did not understand. 'Is that not good news?'

'There is talk of execution.'

'Of the *prisoners*?'

Thérèse nodded.

'They were taken in battle?' I asked.

'They surrendered, they put down their arms.'

'Then by law they cannot be executed.'

Thérèse snorted. 'There is fear in the air! They will be slaughtered!'

'You are thinking of the past.' I put my arms round her. She'd risen from childbed too soon.

'We are the past,' she said.

28 JULY

I was awoken in the middle of the night. It was Thérèse, in distress. She'd had an argument with Tallien, been forced to flee. Indeed, there was evidence she'd not escaped soon enough, for her lip was swollen and her cheek bruised.

'I don't understand.' I pressed a cold compress to her face. 'I know how much he loves you.'

She looked as if she would begin to weep again. 'It's my fault. I thought I could reform him. I allowed myself the sin of pride.'

'Tallita, please! Don't speak in mysteries.' I poured us each a large glass of claret. 'What started it? What was the fight about?'

'Have you not heard? About *Sieyès*?' She looked at me incredulously.

I shook my head. Deputy Sieyès was in Holland, I thought.

'He claims he's discovered documents that prove that Tallien is in league with Royalists, with the leaders of the émigré fleet that attacked at Quiberon Bay.'

Tallien? 'But that's not possible, Thérèse.' That would mean that Tallien was on the side of the enemy – the very men Lazare fought against in battle.

'It's true, Rose. I knew by the look on his face when I confronted him, but the worst of it is . . . the *worst* of it is his fear of being found out. Now he will go to *any* length to prove himself an anti-Royalist, to prove to the Assembly that he is against the émigrés, even if it means *massacring* the prisoners he vowed to save!' She broke into sobs. I held her in my arms. The sun was rising when she finally fell asleep.

* * *

SANDRA GULLAND

372

It was almost midday when we awoke. Thérèse hurriedly began her toilette, covering the bruise on her cheek with rouge.

'Where are you going?' I did not trust her mood.

'To the Assembly,' she said, tying her hat strings.

The doorbell rang.

'It's Deputy Tallien,' Agathe informed me.

'You stay here,' I told Thérèse.

I went to the front door. Tallien blocked the sun. It was hard to see his face against the bright light. 'I have come for Thérèse,' he said.

'I don't think it wise for you to see her now,' I said. He smelled of liquor.

Suddenly Thérèse appeared behind me. She attempted to push her way past, out of the door. 'Where are you going?' Tallien grabbed her arm.

'To the Assembly.' Thérèse shook herself free. She cursed him in the Spanish tongue.

'It's no use!' he cried.

'What do you mean?' She stared at him, her breathing heavy.

'It's over!' A motion had been passed that morning: the prisoners would be executed.

'Who made the motion?' Thérèse demanded.

Tallien did not deny it. 'You don't understand!'

'*You* don't understand. Over seven hundred lives have been sacrificed to save *one* – yours. How can you live with that!'

'You would have *me* sacrificed?'

'Yes!' And louder: '*Yes!*' She ran back to my bedchamber.

'Surely something can be done?' I asked, shaken.

Tallien shook his head. He turned his back, hat in hand, a ruined man.

31 July 1795 – Rennes
Rose,

You can imagine my disgrace. I *promised* these men life – now all are to perish! Yet they *surrendered*, they put down their arms! Tallien knows this well – at my request, Sombreuil put his sabre in Tallien's hands! My men saw it! We gave Sombreuil our *word* that his men would be treated as prisoners of war.

When Tallien left for Paris, he was determined to secure their safety. Now I am told it was Tallien who made the motion in the Assembly to have them executed, that it was Tallien who waved a dagger through the air, calling for their blood! I cannot comprehend!

I am too angry to write words of love. Be cautious . . .

Your soldier, Lazare

2 AUGUST

I called on Tallien. I had heard rumours – that he had lost over ten thousand livres in a single game of faro, that he was drinking heavily. In spite of all that had happened, I felt an obligation towards him. He had been a friend to me when I needed a friend most. He had saved my life. Now it was my turn.

'Get out!' he yelled when he saw me. I backed away, sickened. Empty wine bottles littered the bare wooden floor.

'I come as a friend!'

He threw a glass against the wall. 'I do not need you!'

Quickly I left.

3 AUGUST

I summoned the courage to call on Tallien again. I found him ill. He was sober, however – we talked for some time. 'I know my demons,' he confessed.

'Yet you do not know your strengths.'

'I am a coward. I do not deserve to be alive.'

'Was it a coward who confronted Robespierre?'

'I was in fear of my life!'

'And Thérèse's?'

He put his hands to his face and wept. 'And now I've lost her!'

'*This* is your demon,' I told him, holding up an empty wine bottle.

I gave him news of his baby daughter, for whom he displays a sincere devotion. We parted with a tender show of feeling.

EVENING

A victory reception at Barras's, thirty-seven guests, many bottles of champagne consumed.

'Army champagne,' Barras said, doing the honours.

'The army is supplied with champagne?' I asked. Even water was dear.

'Only *victorious* armies, which of course ours are.'

Shortly after nine I was astonished to see Thérèse. She was dressed in a *very* revealing gown, her enormous milk-filled breasts exposed. It was a hot, sultry summer evening and looking at her raised the temperature even higher. Every man in the room regarded her with an expression of both disapproval and lust.

'Should you be here?' I whispered. She smelled of tobacco.

I looked to Barras for help, but found he was filling her glass.

'She should go home, Paul. She may do something she will regret.'

'She is not a child.'

Shortly before midnight I heard Thérèse's musical voice in the game room: 'My entire ensemble weighs no more than two six-livre pieces.'

I went to the door. The men had gathered around her. Three women were watching from chairs by the fireplace.

'Including the jewels?' Deputy Nabonide asked.

'Yes.' Thérèse's face was flushed, her eyes glazed. '*Everything*.'

'I'd bet a louis on that.' Deputy Verneuil threw the coin on to a table.

'Any others?' Thérèse posed seductively. There was silence but for the sound of coins hitting coins.

Barras, grinning, ordered a servant to bring a scale.

Thérèse took off her earrings, her rings, handed them to Barras. Then she slipped a sleeve over one shoulder.

I left the room. Soon I heard a cheer, heard Thérèse's cry – of victory I presumed . . . or was it defeat?

Shortly after, Barras, a young man and Thérèse left together.

My heart sank. I do not have the heart for this life.

4 AUGUST

This morning I set out for La Chaumière. I intended to arrive early so that I could talk to Thérèse.

I found her in her boudoir, splashing cologne on to her silk sheath, to make the thin fabric cling to her naked breasts.

'You come with disapproval in your eyes, my friend.' Her own eyes were glazed. Laudanum, I thought.

'I come out of concern, for you.' I could hear the baby crying in the other room. 'I think you should be cautious. Grief is chasing you. Let it catch you. It will hurt less, in the end.'

'You envy my hot blood. I recommend a diet of truffles and celery soup for you, to heat you up.' She laughed, a laugh without joy.

'Tallita, I love you, but I can't talk to you when you're like this.'

Tears came to her eyes. 'See what you've done!' She threw herself down on to her bed.

'Why do you weep?' I sat down beside her, took her hand. It was soft, without any sense of bone.

'Will you forgive me – for Barras?' she asked.

'Do you care for him?'

'He's an odd duck, but he amuses me.'

'In all the world, Tallita, you are probably the only woman who *could* seduce our friend.'

'One has to be imaginative,' she said wearily.

I smiled. 'Rest.' I kissed her forehead.

'A pox on these men,' she said, closing her eyes.

In which I am introduced to a strange little man

6 AUGUST 1795

Everywhere there is talk of divining, cartomancers, fortune-tellers, soothsayers . . . that mystical realm so much the passion now.

'Rose is always told she will be Queen of France,' Thérèse announced at Minerva's this afternoon. She was stretched out on the chaise longue wearing an ivory silk robe and a green wig – the effect was bizarre, startling. (*'Les merveilleuses,'* they call us, the amazing ones.)

'Why, that's horrible,' Minerva said, adjusting her white gauze petticoats.

'Only once,' I protested, 'as a girl in Martinico. The other time, in the Carmes, I was simply told that I would marry a man who would astonish the world.' I shrugged. 'But what does it mean? My fortunes are extraordinary, yet my life is mundane.'

At that moment Barras was introduced. With him was a curious-looking man with short legs and a big head. Minerva stood to greet them.

'Who is that man with Deputy Barras?' Fortunée Hamelin asked, watching the two approach. 'Another protégé?' She made a face.

'I may have seen him at the Feydeau,' tiny Madame de Crény said.

'If you had, you would *surely* remember,' Thérèse said.

The man was remarkable, it was true, but for all the wrong reasons. His long, limp hair hung down around his ears in a sorry attempt at fashion. His skin was sallow and his figure so thin his threadbare breeches seemed to hang.

'Whatever can Barras have in mind?' Thérèse whispered.

We were silent for the introductions. 'Citoyen Buonaparte, la veuve Beauharnais . . .'

'You are a widow,' the stranger said. His accent was rough – unpleasant. Italian? I could not be sure.

'The Republican general, Vicomte Alexandre de Beauharnais, was this lady's husband,' Barras said.

Citoyen Buonaparte clasped my hand. His eyes were large, grey in colour, striking. His teeth were good. But there was an intensity in his expression that forbade levity. I was relieved when he was introduced to the others in our group, who seemed to respond to him as silently as I. He took a seat and said no more.

'Well!' Minerva exclaimed. 'Perhaps we should play charades?'

It seemed that nothing would leaven the mood. The presence of the man in the corner had a sobering effect on us all.

'That Barras!' Thérèse exclaimed in the privacy of Minerva's boudoir. 'He takes his projects too far.'

'Deputy Barras pressed me to introduce Citoyen Buonaparte into our circle,' Minerva told us. 'He is new to Paris and in need of social contacts—'

'He is in need of social *manners*,' Thérèse said. 'What is he – Corsican or something?'

'Napoleone Buonaparte . . . Why is the name familiar?' I asked.

'He was the general who saved Toulon,' Minerva said. 'Remember?'

Toulon?

'Two years ago, when the British invaded.'

I remembered. The festivities, the dancing, the toasts throughout the night. 'So *that's* how Barras knows him,' I said. 'Wasn't Barras in charge at Toulon?'

'It is impossible for me to believe that that man could be a general, much less a hero,' Thérèse said, dusting her face with rice powder.

'My dear citoyennes, is it possible you are blinded by this man's poverty, his lack of breeding?' Minerva asked. 'Stand as my witnesses: I predict he will have a great future. I see it in the shape of his chin.'

Future or not, Thérèse and I did not stay long – we left on the excuse that her baby was ill.

'What a miserable evening,' Thérèse groaned, settling into her carriage. 'I hope Barras knows better than to drag that Corsican with him everywhere. Next thing you know, he'll be insisting I introduce him at La Chaumière.'

7 August

It is just as Thérèse feared – Barras is intent on making a project of the Corsican. He and the strange little man showed up at La Chaumière and now Citoyen Buonaparte comes on his own. Thérèse, ever the soft heart, has offered to help him obtain fabric for a new uniform. 'If he's going to be coming here, he should at least have proper clothes,' she told me.

'Take care, Tallita, I think he is in love with you,' I whispered to her.

'It would seem that Citoyen Buonaparte falls in love easily,' she said, rolling her eyes. 'He's engaged to marry a girl in Marseille, he talks endlessly about a girl in Châtillon, and now Barras informs me he intends to propose to La Montansier.'

'The lady Barras rents his town house from?'

'*Lady?* Rose, you are too kind.'

La Montansier was proud of the fact that she had started her career as a prostitute. The loges in the theatres she manages are furnished with extra-wide divans. 'But she's over sixty,' I protested.

'And with three million livres hidden under her well-used mattress.' Thérèse raised her eyebrows. 'In Corsica, apparently, they make no pretense of such matters.'

Tuesday, 9 August

Last night, close to midnight at La Chaumière, Thérèse came to my side. 'Meet me in my boudoir,' she whispered.

I extracted myself from my group. When we got to the privacy of her room, she fell on to her bed clutching her sides. 'Buonaparte . . . !' She burst into laughter again.

'The Corsican?'

'He's made a proposal of marriage!'

'To *you?*' I stared at her. I smiled imagining it. Thérèse was so much taller than the Corsican. 'Just now? In the parlour?'

Thérèse nodded, making a great effort to control herself. 'I was with Fortunée, Madame de Crény and Minerva. He came up to us and said, "Citoyenne Tallien, may I speak to you . . . in private?" So I retired with him to the entryway. And it was there he said, "Now that you are free, I would like you to consider me." At first I did not understand. He became a bit impatient. "I am making you an offer of marriage," he finally burst out. Then he said, "Together we could have a great future, for Fortune smiles on me."'

'He said *that*? That Fortune smiles on him? What a curious thing to say.'

'Especially for a man who is in such dire need. If Fortune smiles on him, she should start paying attention.'

'What did you tell him?'

'I told him he should consider *you* instead,' Thérèse said, adjusting the pearl ornaments in her hair in the looking glass.

'No!' She was teasing – surely. 'Tallita?'

She never did say. But now the Corsican watches *me*.

10 August

It has been hectic at Barras's. He complains he has no time for the gaming tables, the hunt. 'Democracy!' he cursed. 'It's so time-consuming! All these tedious meetings.'

I pushed a guest list towards him. For two days, I had been trying to get his approval.

'Citoyen Buonaparte? Is he not included?' he asked, looking it over. 'The ladies have wearied of my Corsican protégé? You do not perceive his brilliance for his long and, I admit, distasteful hair, his smelly boots. I assure you, he is an ambitious man – he will go far.'

'I perceive his ambition,' I said, 'his ambition to woo every woman of standing in Paris. He shows no moderation in his passion – for women of wealth, that is.'

'Moderation be damned. Moderation belongs to the past. Napoleone is in need of a wife. Perhaps *you* should oblige him.'

With that he was gone. I sighed and added the Corsican's name to the list. I will hear more on this matter, I fear.

12 August

Barras came to my salon last night in the company of the Corsican.

'Do Corsicans never laugh?' Thérèse complained. 'He is *so* serious.'

Towards the end of the evening I found myself sitting beside

Citoyen Napoleone (an *impossible* name to pronounce). In an attempt to make conversation, I complimented him on his valour at Toulon. 'It is said you are a genius,' I told him.

'Yes,' he said.

'You have a large family in Marseille? I am told one of your sisters is particularly charming.'

'Who told you that?'

'Deputy Fréron,' I said.*

Then abruptly he stood and left the room!

'Is he angry?' I asked Barras. Had I said something to offend him?

'He's a little strange sometimes.' Barras took my arm, drew me into the entryway. 'I'd like you to befriend him. Get to know him,' he whispered.

'He is not an easy man to talk to,' I protested. 'I don't know if I—'

'If anyone can, Rose, you can,' Barras said. He took several coins out of his pocket, slipped them into my hand.

'What's this for?' The three gold louis were worth over seventy livres.

'I can count on you?' he asked.

15 AUGUST
'Napoleone has become a member of your salon, I see.'

Barras and I were enjoying a private lunch in his garden.

'I am getting to know him,' I said. 'A little.' Napoleone Buonaparte was a complex person; one moment, he talked openly, and the next, he did not say a word. 'It is difficult to know where one stands with him.'

'And how would one *like* to stand?'

'Why do you ask?'

Barras ordered his butler to bring the dessert. 'Did you discuss politics with him?'

* Louis-Marie-Stanislas Fréron had met Buonaparte's thirteen-year-old sister Maria-Paola in Marseille two years before. They wanted to marry, but met resistance from Madame Buonaparte. An educated aristocrat turned violent revolutionary, Fréron was over thirty, inclined to drink and had had three children by an actress.

'He supports the Republic,' I said, 'if that's what you want to know.'

'But with *who* running it?'

'I believe him to be more of a leader than a follower — at least in his own mind.'

Barras laughed as he filled my glass. 'And *that's* why we must keep our eye on him, my dear.'

In which I find a home

16 AUGUST 1795
I have fallen in love . . . with a *house*.

Julie Carreau's, to be precise, on the slopes of Mont-Martre. One approaches it by a long walled-in drive opening on to a most charming setting: a small hôtel, a carriage house, a stable with a garden behind. A tiny, perfect world.

It was a hot day, but cool there, the breeze coming up the mountain from the city. 'This is like a country home,' I told Julie, 'yet close to the heart of the city.' I was enchanted.

'I will miss it,' she said.

'You are moving?'

'It's small. I can't keep enough staff here. And there's only room for one carriage.'

I walked down the garden path. There were rosebushes on both sides. 'Are you selling it?'

'Leasing.'

'I'll take it.' I did not ask the price.

17 AUGUST
I signed the lease. Ten thousand livres a year — almost half my allowance from Mother, if it ever comes through. I move in five weeks, on the Republican New Year. I've made arrangements to have my cow brought from Croissy. A house, horses, a cow, garden, staff. A modest establishment, yet even so, so much to attend to — so much to *pay* for.

WEDNESDAY, 19 AUGUST
Thanks to Tallien my appeal for compensation on Alexandre's La

Ferté property has been granted. We are to get back the books in his library (an extensive collection), the silver that was confiscated, as well as an advance of ten thousand livres (only!) against the value of the property, which the government sold.

'It will take time for the paperwork to go through,' Tallien warned. 'It's unlikely that you will see anything until spring.'

'How can I thank you?'

'You have done enough already, Rose.'

I looked at him with a question in my eyes.

'You are perhaps the only person who overlooks my more visible weaknesses in favour of my more hidden strengths. That is thanks enough.'

17 August 1795– Rennes
Dear Rose,

The post is being watched. Give letters and parcels addressed to me to Deputy Barras. The government couriers are secure.

I love you.

Your soldier, Lazare

27 AUGUST

In the post this afternoon I received a hand-lettered bulletin regarding a school for girls in Saint-Germain-en-Laye, next to Collège Irlandais, a school for boys.

I showed the bulletin to Lannoy. 'Madame Campan is running it,' I said. I had known Madame Campan's brother and his wife in Croissy – the Augiés. Hortense often played with Adèle, their daughter.

'Ah, Madame Campan!' Lannoy whispered reverently. As former lady-in-waiting to our poor departed Queen, Madame Campan was close to being royal herself, in Lannoy's eyes. 'That would be the perfect school for Hortense,' she said.

And the Collège Irlandais next door for Eugène.

But for the cost . . .

SUNDAY, 30 AUGUST

Today the children and I visited the two schools in Saint-Germain-en-Laye. Eugène succumbed with resignation. His is a Spartan institution, as one expects in a school for boys. He liked the playing fields.

Madame Campan's school is situated in the adjoining Hôtel de Rohan, a beautiful if run-down estate on a rambling country property. Hortense and her friend Adèle Augié ran about in a fever of excitement. I rejoiced seeing them together again; one would never know, hearing them laugh, that Hortense had not so long ago lost her father, Adèle her mother to the violence of the Terror.

Madame Campan greeted me with elegant simplicity in the foyer. 'Please, call me Henriette.' She is a plain woman with heavy features. She was wearing a simple black dress, severely cut. Mourning? I wondered. For her sister, the Queen, the Boy? I had heard stories of what she'd been through, her own narrow escapes from death.

She invited me into her office. I was surprised to see a framed copy of the Rights of Man on the wall above her desk. Noting my expression, she slyly turned it over to reveal a portrait of the Queen.

'Comtesse de Montmorin has told me of the heroic efforts you made to save her husband,' Madame Campan said, taking a seat beside me.

'Would that I could have saved him from death.' And others. 'I was grieved to learn of your sister-in-law.' I remembered Madame Augié as a sweet-tempered, somewhat distracted woman, always trying to keep track of her three active young daughters.

Madame Campan offered me a cup of weak tea in fine china, slightly cracked. 'I tell the girls their mother died in her sleep.' Her cup began to rattle in its saucer. Quickly she put it down. 'I am mother to them all now. An invalid husband, a son, three nieces to look after as well as a school for one hundred girls.' She picked up her cup again, took a sip. 'I don't have time to mourn.'

She outlined the school's programme: the girls would be given a classical education with special attention to art (Jean-Baptiste Isabey, a portrait painter I admire, will be teaching there) and history. She glanced at the Queen's portrait. Although hers was a well-to-do establishment, she assured me the girls would not be indulged — they would be taught to cook and to clean up after themselves. 'And, as well, in spite of the fashion now, *my* girls will be taught good manners and the art of conversation.'

I heard a child shriek. I looked out of the window to see Hortense wildly chasing both Eugène and Adèle across the lawn. Manners? *Bonne chance*, I thought, smiling. 'Hortense has a cousin, Émilie, the daughter of an émigré,' I said. 'Her family is ruined, now, of course. She's in need of education; I'd like to provide for her, but—'

Madame Campan agreed to take both Hortense and Émilie, charging only for Hortense. She also offered the use of second-hand uniforms. 'Adèle speaks so often of your daughter, I regard her as one of the family. I must beg your forgiveness for charging at all.'

6 SEPTEMBER

I had a meeting scheduled with Barras at his house in Chaillot but the afternoon proved to be too hectic. He'd just come in from a hunt and his excited spaniels were running up and down the rooms barking at Toto, the miniature greyhound. There were two men waiting in the hall and a courier with an urgent message to respond to. 'Come back at six,' he suggested. 'It will be quieter.' I gave him a letter to forward to Lazare (none for me again, alas) and left.

In the evening, however, it was not much different: messengers, men waiting. Barras told them all to go away. 'If it isn't the Jacobins, it's the Royalists,' he cursed. 'We put down one, only to be attacked by the other.'

'You're anticipating violence?' I'd noticed an increase in the number of National Guardsmen posted near the Assembly. Now, too, one had to apply for a special pass even to go into that neighbourhood.

'I dare say the worst is yet to come.'

'Who is behind it?'

'Sometimes I think it's Royalists disguised as Jacobins. At other times, Jacobins disguised as Royalists. It's the damnedest thing.'

'Why do you smile?'

'The fact is, who cares? The people are exhausted. How many turned out for this last election? One in thirty? But announce the results, and the rocks come flying.'

After supper he got around to the subject of Buonaparte.

'I haven't seen him lately,' I said. 'Not at any of the salons, not even at the theatre.'

'I dare say he's been busy. I got him a job in the topographic department, making maps. Strategic stuff – his passion. A curious enthusiasm.'

'Yet you respect him.'

'I just wish I could trust him. He's impoverished, with a huge family to support. One wonders what he might do for money. And certainly the Royalists have plenty to throw around. If Buonaparte went over to them . . .'

'It's hard to imagine. If anything, he is a bit of a Jacobin.'

'Yes, he's got the rhetoric.'

'You doubt his sincerity?'

Barras shrugged. 'There is nothing more dangerous – or perhaps the word unpredictable is more accurate – than a revolutionary in want of a fortune.'

12 SEPTEMBER – FONTAINEBLEAU

I've been two days in Fontainebleau, without the children – already Eugène and Hortense are involved in school activities – yet I spent the entire time talking about them. Aunt Désirée and the Marquis were charmed by my reports of what Hortense's teachers were saying, how she is doted on by Madame Campan ('La Petite Bonne,' she has been named). 'She loves school,' I told them. 'I don't think I'll ever get her to leave.' I've become a little jealous, I confess; Hortense speaks reverently of Madame Campan.

We had a good visit, without Aunt Désirée's customary lectures on the sins of idleness, revels and reading romances. But as I was preparing to leave, she came to my door. I knew by her manner that there was something she wanted to say. Finally, with some hesitation, she confessed she was concerned about rumours she'd heard about Madame Tallien. I assured her Thérèse was an angel, a friend in every way.

'And you're not having anything to do with these criminals who are running the government now, I hope.'

'Criminals?'

'Deputy Barra . . . Bassar . . . You know who I mean.'

Barras, she meant. I kept quiet. I did not have the heart to tell her that it was 'this criminal' who was paying for Hortense and Eugène's education.

15 September 1795 – Hôtel de Croisoeuil, Croissy
Dear Citoyenne Madame Beauharnais,

My mother has asked me to respond to your letter, as she is not well. She regrets that she will not be able to come to see you. She asked me to congratulate you on acquiring the Talma residence, but also to express her sorrow that you will be giving up the château at Croissy. Do you plan to move your cow? We hope to be seeing you soon. Mother is in need of diversion.

Citoyenne Madame Lucie Hosten de Croisoeuil
Note – Maman asked me to tell you that she recommends Citoyen Callyot, an excellent cook who can make Creole dishes. (I recommend him too!)

18 September – Croissy

A rainy, melancholy weekend at Croissy, sorting and packing. And going twice daily to visit Aimée.

She is much weakened. It is distressing to see her confined to bed, a situation she does not take to happily. 'If I want so much as a dish of tea, I have to ask my daughter for it,' she complained. 'Fortunately Lucie is still under the impression that I have some authority over her, but soon, no doubt . . .'

'I'd like to meet the person who can succeed in dominating you, Aimée.'

She cursed lustily. There is life in her yet.

23 September

The New Year, the new constitution proclaimed. Fireworks late into the night. Thérèse and I watched the display from my garden – my garden! I am exhausted from the move, but happy. I love my new home. I call it Chantereine.

25 September

I worked all day in the garden. Fortuné sniffed every mound of earth, barked at every bug. Lannoy has begun making curtains for the bedroom (blue nankeen with red and yellow crests). The drawing room looks like a seamstress's studio, the floor covered with scraps.

I am having six wooden chairs and a small couch upholstered. I purchased a Renaud harp (only three strings missing) and a marble bust of Socrates at a second-hand shop. Little by little, my home begins to come together. The effect will be simple, but elegant (I hope).

I've hired Callyot, the cook Aimée recommended. He is a Negro from Sainte-Lucie.

Agathe ran off with a fowler from the Midi but quickly saw the error of her ways (he stank of chicken) and returned, not with child, we hope.

Gontier is staying on, dear old soul. Fortunately, for he's the only one who can coax milk from Cleopatra, my cow.

Now all I need is a coachman and a gardener. I am hoping we can manage on that — for a time. Funds are tight, even with Barras's generous contributions.

26 SEPTEMBER
A hot day, but a breeze was cooling. I worked in my garden again. Mosquitoes hovered, dragonflies circled. Now and again I heard popping noises and a faint ringing sound — a tocsin, perhaps? The ferment of Paris seems so very far away . . .

In which we are at war again

MONDAY, 28 SEPTEMBER 1795
It is so peaceful at Chantereine I was shocked to learn that there
had been a riot at the Assembly yesterday. Several hundred people
were killed.

'Several *hundred?*'

'Even the Jacobins are beginning to think that only a monarchy
can save us.' Barras's sword clanked against the fireplace. He had just
come from the Military School where he'd been training a group of
men — 'My private fighting force, my "Sacred Battalion".'

'Not the National Guard?'

'Too civilized,' he said. 'Upstanding citizens, men of property.
How many have ever killed a man? In a conflict, how many will
bolt? Half, I predict. They're good for a parade, but not much
else. No, I need seasoned killers, men with the smell of blood on
their hands.'

'And where does one find "seasoned" killers?'

'In the prisons, of course — thugs, murderers, the occasional
terrorist.' He accepted my offer of another brandy. 'I've got fifteen
hundred of them already. I've virtually emptied the prisons.'

'No—'

'*My* men,' he grinned.

I remembered something Thérèse had once said: *Barras prefers his
men coarse, his ladies refined.*

'And the more the merrier, thank you,' Barras said, as if reading
my thoughts. He pulled out his timepiece. He had to go. But
first there was something he wanted to ask: would I seek out
Citoyen Buonaparte? 'There's a rumour he's been in contact with
the Royalists. Whose side is he on? I must know. Things are
heating up—'

'But he's busy, you said — with this business of maps.'

'You women have your ways. Invite him to your home. Surely this is not a mystery to you.'

The project struck me as distasteful.

'Consider the fate of the Republic,' Barras insisted, 'your *children's* future.'

4 OCTOBER

Citoyen Buonaparte was better clothed than I was accustomed to seeing him, dressed in a new blue uniform. Even so, he looked sickly, his skin sallow, his boots huge on his spindly legs.

I invited him into the garden. I asked Agathe to bring us café au lait. 'Made with coffee beans from Martinico,' I told him, 'and milk from my cow.'

He accepted, although he was in a hurry, he said. He could not stay for crêpes. He has been toiling day and night — on a plan to liberate Italy from the Austrians, he said.

I smiled. 'You say this in all seriousness.'

'One need only believe.'

'Is it that simple?' He did not answer. He was absorbed in an examination of the sundial. 'You do not credit destiny?' I prompted him.

He turned to me abruptly. 'One can become accustomed to appeasing destiny rather than controlling it.' He had a strange way of putting things, rather in the manner of proverbs.

'I believe I am of the first party, Citoyen Buonaparte.' Although I wasn't sure what he meant.

'*Brigadier-General* Buonaparte,' he corrected me.

'Forgive me, I thought—'

'Actually . . .' He smiled. He is almost charming when he smiles. 'You may call me Emperor.'

'Emperor Buonaparte?' I bowed my head, amused.

He stared at me, his eyes grey, cold but inflamed, unsettling. 'I mystify you,' he said. 'That is understandable. But what I don't understand is why you induced me to call. I confess I have developed something of an attachment for you. Nevertheless, I am under the impression that this feeling is not, at this time, reciprocated.'

I stooped to pick a rose. A thorn pricked my finger. Tears came to my eyes, an embarrassing weakness.

'Barras has something to do with this,' he persisted.

I turned to him, angry for being so bluntly challenged. 'It is clear you favour directness, General Buonaparte. Very well then, yes, it was Deputy Barras.'

'And how much did he pay you?' He put on his hat.

'Don't go—'

'I do have pride, citoyenne.' And was gone.

I set out for Barras's in a nervous condition. I was expected – to review social plans, financial arrangements . . . I had an agenda of my own, however. I wasn't going to do his bidding any longer.

Barras burst into laughter when I told him about my exchange with General Buonaparte.

'I regret I do not see the humour,' I said.

'Rose, you are so charming in this mood.'

I stood up. 'You are not taking my position seriously.'

He put his hand on my arm. 'Sit, relax. You can't leave now. I asked the cook to make meringues.'

'I do not care for dessert.' I sat nonetheless.

'Very well, I will eat your share. Your disposition is sweet enough. I, no doubt, could use a little *douceur*. Ah, there, you see? I knew I could coax a smile. But please, my friend, accept my apologies. I have caused you distress. I regret to tell you that there have been no letters for you from Lazare. Soldiers are so cruel. But tell me about your children. Do they like their schools? By the way, that Creole banker you introduced me to has proved to be a *most* profitable contact, did I tell you?'

In short, Barras made himself entirely agreeable. I softened and we talked: of his most recent romantic conquest, the tragedy by Corneille opening at the Comédie-Française in two days, his rabbits.

It was as I was finishing my second meringue that a messenger came.

'Do you recall where the convent of Filles de Saint-Thomas is?' Barras asked, squinting to make out the writing.

'Rue Vivienne, I believe. Why?'

'Apparently it's full of armed men.' Barras cursed. 'Royalists.' He looked at his timepiece, sighed. 'And I'd hoped to get some sleep tonight.'

I left as he was strapping on his sword, ordering a horse saddled, 'getting into war gear', as he put it. I gave him a good-luck kiss. 'Take care,' I said.

He stopped for a moment. Then he smiled, that crooked smile that makes him so endearing. 'So tell me, Rose. *Can* Buonaparte be trusted?'

5 OCTOBER, MIDNIGHT

I'm at Thérèse's. I didn't think she should be alone tonight.

Lieutenant Floraux was just here, cantering dramatically into the courtyard, his horse lathered with sweat. 'The National Guard has rebelled!' he cried out, still breathless. He took off his helmet. His hair was short, as is the fashion with the young now, in what is called a Brutus crop. 'They've turned on the Assembly, on the deputies, joined the Royalists!'

'The National Guard?' I asked, incredulous. 'Joined the *Royalists*? Are you sure?' I urged him to sit down.

'Not all of them.' He gulped down the glass of port I offered him. 'Three out of four.'

How could a defence be mounted without men? 'How many Royalists are there?' I wondered if Jeanne-Victorie d'Aiguillon's nephew was among them. Or Régis de Saale, the Marquis de Caulaincourt's friend. Or Madame Campan's young cousin, only seventeen.

'It is thought they are forty thousand strong.'

'*Forty* thousand — mon Dieu!'

'Forty thousand what?' Thérèse asked, coming into the room. She'd been helping the nanny put the baby to bed.

'Royalists,' I said weakly, taking a chair.

6 OCTOBER, DAWN

We were awakened by the sound of pounding on the gate. Thérèse's footman ran to answer it, yelling for the intruder to be silent. This set a horse whinnying.

It was Lieutenant Floraux again. The government had rallied, he told us. He helped himself to a glass of port. 'They've named Deputy Barras General.'

'But without the National Guard, who does he command?' I asked.

'He's got some men, a tough-looking group, the Sacred Battalion he calls them. "Battalion of the Terrorists" others would have it.'

A battalion of murderers let loose on the streets of Paris. I was thankful the children were in Saint-Germain-en-Laye. 'And General Buonaparte? Is . . . is he involved?' I asked.

'The little Corsican? He's second-in-command apparently.'

'*Second*-in-command?' Thérèse groaned.

'He may surprise you,' I said. *One need only believe.*

'We could use a surprise.' Lieutenant Floraux downed his glass.

10.00 P.M.

At supper, we thought we heard gunfire . . .

'Can that be *cannon*?' Thérèse asked, walking the baby back and forth across the room.

We heard a second blast, and another.

Thérèse pressed the infant's head to her heart. 'Surely not.'

'They wouldn't use *cannon*,' I said. 'Muskets, but not cannon. Not on citizens.' My words were silenced by a volley of ominous booms.

In which my heart is broken

Blood on the cobblestones. In front of a church, a market woman wailing, 'The butchers! The butchers!'

It is as we feared – a slaughter.

'On *citizens*!' Lannoy ranted angrily. 'Your friends, your *virtuous* Republicans, fired *cannon* on citizens!'

What had happened? I set out for Minerva's.

'Have you talked to Barras?' she demanded. 'What's going on?'

I shook my head. 'Anyone we know hurt?' *Killed*, I meant to ask, was afraid to ask.

'Only rumours. Everyone's upset.' We joined a group by the doors to the garden.

'It was the Corsican who gave the command to fire the cannon,' Deputy Renouvier was saying.

'That's not what I've been told,' a man standing next to him said.

'Corsicans are ruthless,' Madame de Méchain argued. 'Entirely without morals. Everyone knows that.'

'And now, have you heard? He has set up strict supervision of all the theatres and cafés – even the meeting places around fountains are under surveillance. The fountains!'

'I was at the theatre,' a sweet-faced young man said, his voice high and tremulous. 'There were sentries at the doors of all the boxes. If anyone *dared* voice a request for any but the most *correct* Republican tune, there were over a hundred grenadiers there ready to pounce!'

'Is it not critical that the government gain control?' Deputy Renouvier asked.

'Did we not have enough of control under Robespierre?' the

sweet-faced young man argued. 'The Corsican is a Jacobin I am told.'

'A close friend of Robespierre, I heard,' Madame de Méchain said.

'Not exactly.' Minerva looked to me for support. 'He was a friend of Robespierre's brother.'

'Ah, *Bonbon's* friend!' the sweet-faced young man said, and everyone laughed.

The group fell silent. I looked towards the door. It was General Buonaparte, looking over the room with a haughty expression. He took off his hat. The tricolour plume fell off. He stooped to retrieve it, his sword knocking against the door.

As he stood, he spotted me.

'Citoyenne Madame Beauharnais,' he said, coming directly to my side, 'I—'

'Would you care to walk in the garden, General?' I interrupted him. 'I feel the need for air.'

Outside, I fanned myself, feeling somewhat faint. 'I am fine.' I sat down on a stone bench. 'Thank you.' A man and woman passed. The woman, recognizing General Buonaparte, turned her head in disdain.

Buonaparte broke a branch off a bush, began tearing off the leaves. 'The French have a strange way of treating their heroes.'

'You feel your actions are beyond reproach, General?'

'I am a military man, not a politician. I do what I am told.'

'But perhaps too well, and too quickly.'

'The Royalists needed a lesson.'

I stood, my cheeks burning. 'I do not know the customs in Corsica, General, but the French, as a rule, do not fire cannon on their citizens.'

I returned to the parlour, trembling.

I was in the game room with Minerva when Barras arrived. 'Congratulations on your victory,' Minerva told him, putting down her cards.

He was flushed. He threw himself on to the sofa. 'As we soldiers say, when the wine is opened, it must be drunk. To *their* butts,' he said, raising his glass. 'For once.' He laughed and took a long drink.

I looked away.

'Damn your tears!' He threw his glass into the fire. It made a sharp, musical sound.

12 OCTOBER

It was not yet noon when a member of the National Guard came to my door. All arms were to be turned over to the military authority of Paris. Upon penalty of death.

Eugène, home from school for two days, clasped his father's sword.

'You must do as you are told,' I told him. I could see defiance in his eyes.

I asked the guard to excuse us. We went into the parlour. Eugène would not relent. I returned to the guard. 'How might one obtain an exemption?' I asked. 'This sword means a great deal to my son. It belonged to his father, a Republican general who died little over a year ago.'

'Only General Buonaparte can grant an exemption.'

Every day it seemed, Buonaparte was promoted. Now he was Military Governor of Paris, and controlled everything.

'You will come with me?' Eugène asked.

'Better to go without me,' I said, recalling my last angry words to the General.

13 OCTOBER

At noon I was surprised by a caller. 'General Bona-something,' Agathe said.

'General Buonaparte?'

She nodded.

I stood abruptly. What would I say? Our last meeting had not been gentle.

But I had no time to prepare. He was already standing in the door. 'Post this at your gate.' He thrust a piece of paper into my hand.

It was a notice of exemption. 'Does this mean my son may keep his father's sword?'

General Buonaparte nodded. He paused. 'On the twelfth day of Vendémiaire,* most of the guns were loaded with blanks. I took

---

* A reference to the Republican calendar.

care that the citizens had areas available to them that afforded the greatest protection.'

His declaration was followed by an awkward silence.

'Surely my opinion cannot matter to you, General,' I said.

'You are correct. It does not. Nevertheless, I wish you to understand that I am not entirely without conscience.'

'Thank you, General.' But already, he had departed.

26 OCTOBER

The election results have been announced. Under the new constitution, five 'Directors' will rule. Barras is one.

'They behead the King, put five in his place,' Lannoy grumbled. 'And your friend Barras the worst of the lot.'

'Hush, Lannoy!'

TUESDAY, 3 NOVEMBER

The five Directors had a meeting in the Luxembourg Palace this morning. In the afternoon 'Director' Barras gave Thérèse and me a tour.

The palace is in frightful repair, its recent use as a prison all too evident. I recalled my visits to Alexandre there. How different my purpose now. There was no furniture, only a few kitchen chairs and one rickety table. And cold, too – Barras sent a footman out for wood.

The five Directors will move in next week, each into his own suite. Already Barras has a work crew covering his walls with silk. His rabbit hutches have been set up in the gardens, his English thoroughbreds are already in the stable.

'What good a king without a palace?' he asked, surveying his shabby domain.

'What good a palace without ladies of the court?' Thérèse echoed, taking my arm and his.

4 December 1795 – Fontainebleau

Dear Rose,

Thank you for your letter. How wonderful that the children are doing so well in school. I miss seeing Hortense at the weekends, although I must admit that a Sunday confirmation class with Madame Campan is possibly the only excuse I would have happily accepted.

Your new home sounds delightful — small but charming. I am impressed that already you have had vegetables from your garden. Your mother would be proud. I read your account of getting your cow freshened to the Marquis. We both had a laugh over it. If it weren't for the sad state of my own health and having to tend to the Marquis so religiously, I would accept your invitations to come for a visit.

No doubt you have heard about Fanny being sued by some woman claiming to be her daughter — what a scandal! I don't know how Fanny manages to be so cheerful, especially now with Marie *marrying* a mulatto. I don't dare tell the Marquis — the news would kill him.

I know how busy you are, dear, but even so, we long to see you. Do remember what I said about keeping good company.

Your loving Aunt Désirée

WEDNESDAY, 9 DECEMBER

I've been going to the Luxembourg every day, presenting petitions on behalf of friends, and friends of friends — émigrés, for the most part, wishing to return to France.

'You spend too much time on the welfare of others, Rose,' Director Barras said to me this morning. 'It is time you considered your own wellbeing.'

'Meaning?'

'Meaning you should be thinking of marriage.'

'You have someone in mind, *Père* Barras?'

'Buonaparte.'

'I am not wealthy enough for him, I'm afraid.' Rumour had it General Buonaparte had just proposed to the recently widowed Madame Permon, a woman old enough to be his mother — but quite well off.

'I've assured him he would be well rewarded.'

I looked to the window, took a breath. Perhaps I had not heard correctly.

'I see you are alarmed.' Barras leaned back in his red velvet chair

– his 'throne' he called it. 'Very well, I will explain. Buonaparte has requested command of the Army of Italy. He wishes to pursue a plan to push the Austrians out of Italy.' Barras made a gesture meaning: insane! 'Of course my fellow Directors do not trust him. They find him abrupt, abrasive . . . overly ambitious. They suspect in him a desire to rule, so they are naturally reluctant to grant him an army, even as pathetic an army as that of the Army of Italy. But they are fools, I say. Buonaparte *will* try to take over, it is in his nature – unless, of course, he is kept busy. Unless, of course, he is *controlled*—'

'Unless, of course, he is married to a very good friend of yours,' I said.

Barras smiled slowly. 'I might not have put it *exactly* that way, my dear.'

'How exactly *did* you put it?' I felt an alarming emotion rising within me.

'I explained to Buonaparte that the French Republic was reluctant to promote foreigners to positions of power. I suggested that if he were to marry a Frenchwoman – a certain French widow, for example – perhaps then the Directors would trust him more, and – who was to say? – perhaps *then* the Army of Italy might very well be his.'

'You told him that!'

'Think about it, Rose. Buonaparte may be a Corsican, and impoverished, I grant you, but he is a man with a future. I am in a position to guarantee it.'

I stood to leave. I was offended by his meddling.

'Rose, must you always be so emotional! You know it is time you married. It's not easy at your age.'

I headed for the door.

'I offered him an army!' he yelled after me. 'I'm *giving* you a dowry, for God's sake!'

10 DECEMBER

I have been hours at my toilette. Tiny wrinkles have begun to line my face. My teeth, never well-formed, are turning black. I have lost two in the last year. I smile, and it's a fishwife's grin I see.

I threw my brushes down in despair. The herbal remedies have not succeeded in restoring any regularity to the flowers. Now and again, too, I am weakened (and embarrassed) by frightful flooding.

I am aging.

Marry, my friends say. Soon.

Friday, 11 December

At Minerva's last night, General Buonaparte declared his feelings for me. This rather publicly, in the midst of a game of fox and goose. I tossed it off as a jest, but left soon after.

Tuesday, 22 December

Minerva came to call. After a glass of wine, news (Madame Royale, the King's unfortunate daughter, has been released from the Temple and sent to Vienne) and idle gossip (Citoyen Léon is taking a mercury treatment*), she asked why I had not been to her salon recently. I confessed my discomfort with the attentions of General Buonaparte. I was reluctant to go to her home lest I discover him there.

'Do you not consider General Buonaparte an acceptable suitor?'

'My heart is taken,' I said.

'General Hoche, you mean.'

I nodded. My feelings for Lazare were no secret.

'Rose, if I may be so bold, there is something I must tell you. It is your *lover* who is taken.'

I put down my glass.

'When the émigrés landed in Quiberon Bay, General Hoche saved the life of a Monsieur de Pout-Bellan. I have it on good authority that he has fallen in love with this man's wife.'

I stood, went to the window recess. Lazare, in *love* with another woman?

Minerva came up behind me, put her hand on my shoulder. 'Surely you knew that Lazare would never marry you, especially not now, not with his wife expecting a child.'

A *baby*?

'Due soon, I believe,' she said.

I bit my lip, fought back tears. Why hadn't he written?

* Venereal disease was treated with mercury.

THE MANY LIVES & SECRET SORROWS OF JOSEPHINE B.

'You will come to my salon, Rose?' Minerva asked. 'Tonight?'

THAT EVENING
I've just returned from Minerva's. General Buonaparte requested the honour of my company at the opera tomorrow evening. I gave him my consent.

In which I am courted

General Buonaparte called for me at nine. He was nearly an hour late, and a bit dishevelled, his sash ill-fitting. 'I was in a meeting.' He did not apologize. He stood in the parlour before the fire cracking his knuckles. He took out his timepiece. 'The curtain rises in a few minutes.' He leapt for the door. I followed after, bewildered and somewhat offended.

His coach is new, a garish yellow with gold trim, very showy, in bad taste. Inside was no different – the seats were covered in gold brocade, the shades tasselled with pink silk.

We took off at a terrific pace, the coach careening over the bumps and round the corners at a frightful speed. I was momentarily overcome by paralysis. Terror had rendered me speechless. I gripped the sides to steady myself. Finally I summoned the strength to cry out, 'Stop!'

General Buonaparte signalled his driver and the coach came to a sudden halt. I fell forward on to the facing seat. I began to laugh.

'We are late.' He pulled out his timepiece again. 'What is it you want?'

I could not speak for the laughter that had gripped me. Tears ran down my cheeks. Buonaparte regarded me with a puzzled expression. 'Too fast?'

I burst into laughter again, nodded through my tears.

Hesitantly, he smiled, a bit unsure. He signalled the driver to go forward again, this time at a more civilized pace. By degrees my laughter came under control. I took several deep breaths. An evening with General Buonaparte – it was not as I had imagined.

It was an enjoyable performance, I thought, yet on the way home

General Buonaparte expressed discontent. 'The French can't sing, their music has no melody. It grates on the ear. *You* sing for me.'

'Here?' We were at the intersection of Rue de Richelieu and Rue Neuve des Petits Champs.

'This is the trouble with the French. They think they cannot sing anywhere, at any time.' He launched into an aria I was unfamiliar with. A chimney sweep turned to stare. 'Now you,' he commanded.

'I am not a singer.'

'Yet you have a lovely speaking voice.'

He would not be refused. Quietly, I sang a short refrain from Mozart.

He regarded me seriously. 'Not bad. What's your name?'

'You know my name.'

'Your full name.'

'Marie-Josèphe-Rose.'

'Joseph is your father's name?'

'Was.'

'Was he a good man?'

I smiled. Hardly. 'A very good man.'

'Very well, I shall call you Joséphine, after the heroine in *Le Sourd*. Have you seen it?'

'My name is Rose.'

'You are mistaken.'

26 DECEMBER

'Why do you insist on calling me Joséphine?' Buonaparte and I had just come from Barras's salon and were on our way to the theatre, to a performance of a work by Molière.

'Do you not find it an attractive name?'

'I am told this is your way with a woman. First you ask her to sing, then you give her a new name.'

'You have been talking to your friend Thérèse,' he said, disgruntled.

'You can keep no secrets from me, Buonaparte.'

29 DECEMBER

'What is it you *do* all the time?' Thérèse demanded. 'You were almost an hour yesterday in the garden.'

'We just talk.' It was true – driving in the Bois de Boulogne, walking along the quay, sitting in my garden, or in his.

'*Just* talk? Whatever about?'

Music, science, religion . . . there was little that did not interest him, little that escaped his notice.

'You know what people are saying, that he is mad for you.'

'We are friends.'

'No doubt,' Thérèse said, smiling capriciously.

30 DECEMBER

It was approaching noon when Thérèse's red coach pulled into my courtyard. 'Maybe you shouldn't come to La Chaumière tonight,' she said, letting down the glass.

'But I must, it's arranged. Buonaparte is coming for me at nine.'

'Lazare is back. He will be there tonight.'

Lazare?

'I thought you should be warned.'

Buonaparte and I arrived at La Chaumière shortly before ten. I was relieved that Lazare was not yet there. Even so, I could not be at my ease.

It wasn't until midnight that Lazare arrived, in uniform, in the company of several aides. He saw me and turned away. I took Buonaparte's arm and asked if we might go into the garden for a moment.

'But it's freezing.'

'Only for a little air.'

After a few moments I was able to compose myself. I had to address Lazare, I knew, had to find the courage to address him. Upon returning to the drawing room, Buonaparte was accosted by Madame de Crény and Fortunée Hamelin, demanding that he read their palms, a magical art for which he claimed to have some talent.

Lazare was standing nearby in front of the fire, watching. 'How good to see you in Paris,' I said, congratulating him on his recent promotion. He regarded me with cold dignity – an expression so chilling I was relieved when Buonaparte joined us.

'And you, General Hoche?' Buonaparte demanded. Lazare put

forth his hand. Buonaparte examined it and grinned. 'General, you will die young – and in your bed,' he said.*

'Alexandre the Great died in his bed, did he not?' I took Buonaparte's arm. 'I believe Thérèse wants us in the game room,' I said, pulling him away. 'That was unnecessary,' I hissed.

Buonaparte looked at me. 'Do you think me blind?'

I pulled my shawl round my shoulders. 'Take me home, Buonaparte,' I told him. 'I feel quite ill.'

It seemed a very long ride back to Chantereine. Buonaparte and I sat silently. 'How are you feeling?' he asked as we turned on to Rue Mont-Martre.

'I lied about being unwell,' I said.

'I was curious to see how far you would take the charade.'

'That's not kind.'

'I never said I was a kind man.' He paused. 'You have an attachment for General Hoche.'

I arranged the fur coverlet about my knees. I was thankful for the dark. 'I knew him in prison.'

'And now?'

'And now General Hoche has a family of his own. Would you care to come in?' I asked as we pulled into my courtyard.

'Would you care to have me?'

I thought for a moment. 'Yes,' I said. I did not speak untruly. I felt overwhelmed by a feeling of sadness, a feeling that I was too much alone in this life. The cold look in Lazare's eyes had disturbed me in a way no words ever could.

Buonaparte stayed for over an hour. I drank several glasses of Chambertin. Before he left he said, 'I would like permission to kiss you.' It seemed a harmless request.

His touch was tentative, unsure, and then urgent. I pulled away. He walked around the room at a vigorous pace.

'Buonaparte?' His manner alarmed me.

Apparently he did not hear, for he did not answer. Then he smiled, a curious smile, I thought, as if he held a great secret. He kissed my hand and was gone.

* Lazare Hoche would die in his bed on 17 September 1797, at the age of twenty-nine.

'Are you lovers?' Thérèse demanded, pulling a robe on over her head. She was trying on a variety of ensembles. In two weeks there is going to be a feast at the Luxembourg Palace in honour of the third anniversary of the death of the King and Thérèse was planning her toilette. Robes, petticoats and shawls were strewn all about the room.

'Not in the sense you mean.' I held up a shawl for her to consider, a luxurious white lace Barras had given her.

'What other sense is there?' She laughed.

'He intrigues me.' General Napoleone Buonaparte was like a tropical day, at one moment exuberant, at the next quiet and moody. He did not inspire respect; rather, he commanded it. I never knew what to expect of him.

'Barras is intent on you marrying him,' Thérèse said.

'I don't belong to Barras.'

'We all belong to *Director* Barras, my dear.' She fastened the pearl buttons on her sleeve. 'So what would you answer if Buonaparte proposed?'

I sighed, sat down. '*Marry* Buonaparte?'

'I think our friend the Director is right. I think you should consider. How old is Buonaparte — twenty-six? Remember what Lenormand predicted, that you would marry a brilliant military man, someone younger than you?'

'Hortense weeps at the thought of me getting married again,' I said.

'Has she even met Buonaparte? Why not bring her to the fête at the Palace? She is almost thirteen, it's time she started coming out into society.'

SATURDAY, 9 JANUARY

At first Hortense was thrilled at the news that we were going to a formal dinner, especially when I showed her the dress Lannoy was making for her.

'It's at the Palace,' I said, thinking she would be impressed.

'The Luxembourg?'

I nodded. 'Director Barras is hosting it.'

'We're going to a reception given by Director *Barras*?' She had a scornful expression on her face. 'But, Maman, it was men like him who *murdered* father!'

'Where did you hear such a thing!' Ever since Hortense had started school, she'd begun to have 'notions'. I'd intended to talk to Madame Campan about it, but withheld, sensing that it was possibly Madame Campan who was the cause. 'Were it not for the help of Director Barras, we would never have succeeded in getting back your father's properties,' I lectured her. 'You owe it to be kind to a man who has done so much to help us.'

Finally, she relented; she would go. 'But I refuse to speak to criminals and rogues. After all, I'm a Royalist.'

I slapped her. We both burst into tears.

21 JANUARY, MIDNIGHT

I'm exhausted. The gala dinner celebration at the Luxembourg Palace was a tremendous success, but it was hardly enjoyable for me. Buonaparte was particularly intense, following my every move. He ate quickly, often with his hands. Hortense sat between us, sullenly refusing to speak.

All the way home Hortense was silent. At last, in her night clothes, she cried out, sobbing, 'If you marry that horrid little man, I will never speak to you again!'

I took her in my arms. 'I won't,' I told her. 'I promise.'

I promise.

In which I must decide

FRIDAY, 22 JANUARY 1796

Buonaparte has made a proposal of marriage. I told him I would consider.

'For how long?' He began pacing the room.

'I will give you an answer in two weeks.'

'One week.'

'Then the answer will be no.'

He smiled. 'You are stronger than you look, Joséphine. I like that in a woman.'

'My name is Rose.'

SATURDAY, 23 JANUARY

Eugène stood at attention when General Buonaparte came to call. As for Hortense, she turned a cold shoulder. Buonaparte tried his best to charm her, but with little success. For most of the evening Hortense stayed in her room, refusing to come down.

'Try not to be hurtful,' I suggested to him.

'I was only teasing.' He had accused Hortense of being a bigot because she was preparing to be confirmed.

'She's not a child one can tease. She takes everything seriously.'

'Then we *shall* get along.'

29 JANUARY, 6.00 P.M.

'But Thérèse, I am not enamoured.' Thérèse and I were walking along the quay. It was cold but invigorating, the water grey.

'You care for him as a friend,' she said. 'He cares for you. Is that not more important?'

'You do not credit love?'

Thérèse scoffed. 'Tallien loved me and all I got were bruises.'

'He knows he wronged you.' I had been waiting for an opportunity to talk to her about Tallien.

'You've seen him?'

I nodded. 'He has changed.'

She said nothing.

'He worships you, Thérèse,' I persisted. 'And he is such a loving father.'

She turned on me. 'Don't you know how it pains me?' she cried, her eyes full of emotion. 'A marriage can survive without passion, Rose, but not without respect. Tell him I'm sorry, but I can't – I just *can't*.'

30 JANUARY

'She expresses regret.' I tried to soften the news. Tallien had looked so hopeful when I arrived. 'She cares for you.' This was true.

'But?'

I shook my head.

I stayed for a time. We played piquet, like in the days of our youth, days before the Terror, days that seem so far away. I talked to him of General Buonaparte, of my doubts and confusion.

'He's an ambitious man,' Tallien said. 'He will rise. Of that there can be no doubt.'

'So Barras says.'

'He cares for you? And the children?'

'Yes.' Indeed, he seemed to like Hortense and Eugène. 'I believe he would be a good father to them.'

'And, as a general, a help to your son's military career, no doubt.'

'True.' That was an important factor.

'Yet you are unsure?'

'We are not lovers.'

'That's not difficult to resolve.'

'It is not always easy for a woman.'

'Is fidelity an issue? Perhaps . . .'

I shrugged. It was customary for married men and women to take lovers – but did I want to live like that?

'I advise you to accept,' Tallien said. 'It is a gamble, but then . . .' He groaned as I displayed my cards. 'But then you have always had a talent for winning games of chance.'

31 January 1796 – Hôtel de Croisoeuil, Croissy
Dear Citoyenne Madame Beauharnais,
    Come quickly – Mother is not well.
                Citoyenne Madame Lucie Hosten de Croisoeuil

1 February 1796 – Hôtel de Croisoeuil, Croissy
Dear Citoyenne Madame Beauharnais,
    Forgive me for alarming you. Mother is stronger today.
                Citoyenne Madame Lucie Hosten de Croisoeuil

TUESDAY, 2 FEBRUARY – CROISSY
It was just past noon when my coachman put me down in front of Hôtel de Croisoeuil. Lucie came to the hall with an infant in her arms. 'Madame Beauharnais!' She greeted me most sincerely. 'Did you get my second note?' she asked. From somewhere I heard a child laugh.

'How is your mother?' I asked after complimenting her on the birth of her second child – another boy. 'What does the doctor say?'

We were interrupted by a scream – a child's. Lucie looked up the stairs. 'Quiet!' she yelled. She turned back to me with an angelic expression. 'We've moved her downstairs,' she said, distracted by the now howling infant in her arms.

It was dark in the music room; the curtains were drawn, the windows closed. The smell was more touch than sense, a thickening of the air. Gently, I pulled the bedcurtains back. Aimée's eyes were open.

'Aimée.' I took her hand, sat by her side. I stroked her damp forehead, studied her face. I did not like what I saw.

'You came.' Her voice was husky, hoarse.

'Lucie wrote to me.'

'She didn't need to.'

'Does talking hurt?'

'I'm so tired.'

'I'll rub your feet. Would you like that?'

She nodded. 'Tell me news. How is everyone?'

'I am considering an offer of marriage.'

'Lazare?'

I shook my head. 'General Buonaparte.'

'The man in the journals?'

I nodded.

'Isn't he Italian, Rose? Italians are so unclean.'

'He's Corsican.'

'That's even worse.'

'I wish you could meet him.' I longed to tell her of the confusion in my heart, but already she was becoming drowsy, her eyelids fluttering, closing. I sat back down beside her, took her hand. You can't leave me like this, Aimée, I thought. I need you.

Lucie came into the room, a chamber pot in her hand. I stood up. 'She sleeps more and more,' Lucie said.

'It will heal her.'

'Yes.' But neither of us believed this to be so. I took up my basket, my hat. At the door, I turned, looked back. Lucie – so young, so fresh – was standing at the foot of her mother's bed with a resigned look on her face.

'Give her my love,' I said. Pray for her soul.

3 FEBRUARY

'I've had a proposal of marriage,' I told Fanny. I was at her hôtel on Rue de Tournon, arranging for a delivery of wood.

'You would throw away your liberty?' She looked shocked.

'Liberty to do without.' Liberty to sleep alone. 'Eugène and Hortense need a father.'

'Is it that Corsican I met at your salon?'

'You disapprove?'

'He tells a good ghost story. I rather liked him.'

'Most people don't.'

'Let them hang. I know the aristocratic matrons of Saint-Germain will stick their noses up over a man with a name they can't pronounce, but who cares about *them* any more?'

'What will Aunt Désirée think?'

'You haven't told her?'

'I haven't the courage.'

'She wants you to marry.'

'But a Corsican?'

Fanny laughed. 'She'd get used to it. Compared to Marie marrying a mulatto, it might even look good. Do you love him?'

'No.'

'That's a relief.'

4 FEBRUARY

General Schérer, Commander of the Army of Italy, has resigned.

'Why?' I asked, alarmed. Any mention of the Army of Italy brought on an attack of nerves in me.

Buonaparte and I were in his horrible coach, in the Bois de Boulogne. I had persuaded him that in order for me to enjoy the ride, it must be taken at less than full speed, and somewhat reluctantly he had ordered his driver to lay off the whip.

'Director Carnot sent him my plans for the campaign in Italy,' Buonaparte said. 'It would appear that General Schérer didn't care for them. He said only the idiot who thought them up would be able to make it work.'

'So he resigned? Just like that?'

'Moved over, let's say.'

'For you?'

'We shall see . . .'

'What do you mean?'

'I must have an answer. *Soon*.'

6 FEBRUARY

I felt restless this morning. I decided to go for a drive. On an impulse I asked my driver to take me out to the field where Alexandre was buried.

It looked different from before. Here and there, in patches, grass had grown, now brown from the frost. The wind blew over the hard lumps of earth. The crazy woman was there, again, in spite of the cold.

I headed out into the field, out to the oak tree in the middle. I leaned my head against the gnarled trunk. How old was this tree? I wondered.

I thought of my life, of the decisions before me. I thought of Hortense, of Eugène. I would turn thirty-three this summer. How many offers of marriage would there be?

'The children must have a father,' I said out loud. Could Alexandre hear me? 'I cannot manage on my own!'

The crazy woman turned her head towards me, grinned.

I went to her. She was crouched in the dirt. I stooped down beside her. I was surprised to see how young she was, younger than myself. Her clothes were in rags, filthy with excrement. She was shivering.

'You will catch your death out here. Do you have a home?' I asked. 'Somewhere you can go?'

'Caesar is coming,' she said.

'The Roman?'

'He said he would meet me here.'

'You should be inside.' Her skin was grey from the cold.

'I am waiting.'

I slipped my cloak over her shoulders. 'He told me you were to go home,' I lied.

'*He* told you that?'

I hesitated. 'He told me to give you this.' I slipped my little bag of coins into her hand.

She fingered the bag. She looked up at me. Her eyes were deep-set, a dark blue – Alexandre's eyes. Shaken, I turned away.

SUNDAY, 7 FEBRUARY

Another sleepless night. The wind blows against the shutters. I have come to my writing desk by the fire, pulling a patchwork counterpane around my knees. Tomorrow I'm to give Buonaparte my answer. I don't know what it will be.

I get out my cards, hidden away since the Carmes. I feel their worn surfaces, feel the sadness in them still. With fear, I lay them out. At the centre, Conflict. To the future, Union. And the controlling card: Fate.

8 FEBRUARY

I have given Buonaparte my answer.

SANDRA GULLAND

In which I have cause to regret

9 FEBRUARY 1796
Eugène took the news philosophically. In fact, I think he was pleased.
Hortense, however, was inconsolable. I have betrayed her, she said.
She stayed in her room, refusing to eat.

18 FEBRUARY
The banns will be published tomorrow morning. 'Have you told
anyone?' I asked Buonaparte. 'Have you told your family?'

Buonaparte's enormous family: his widowed mother Madame
Letizia (whom he worships), his elder brother Giuseppe (whom
he loves), Lucciano (who shows such promise), Luigi (whom he
regards as his son), his sisters ('the three Marias') Maria-Anna,
Maria-Paola and Maria-Anunziata, the 'baby' Girolamo — twelve
now. All of them in Buonaparte's care, all of them needy.

'I've only informed Giuseppe,' he said. We were sitting by the
fire eating preserved cherries in thick fresh cream. 'I wrote to him
two weeks ago.'

Two weeks ago? I hadn't given Buonaparte my answer two weeks
ago. 'And what was his reponse?' I asked.

'He's furious. He said he should have been consulted, since
he's the eldest. He insists I honour my commitment to marry his
wife's sister.'

'The girl you were engaged to last summer?'

'And now Giuseppe has written Mother.'

'And?'

'And now *she* demands I break it off.'

'Is this not going to be a problem, Buonaparte? Perhaps we
should—'

'No!' he said angrily. 'I am my own master.'

19 FEBRUARY

Buonaparte has been talking to Barras, Barras has been talking to Thérèse, Thérèse has been talking to me. In this way I have learned that Buonaparte's brother Giuseppe has threatened Buonaparte with a lawsuit for not marrying his sister-in-law!*

'Corsicans spend half their life in court,' Thérèse said when I told her. 'It's their favourite sport. Ever heard of a vendetta?'

'What am I getting into?'

'Don't worry, Rose. You could charm a snake.'

'But Corsican in-laws?'

Thérèse made a doubtful face. 'Maybe not.'

20 FEBRUARY

I've been to see Citoyen Calmelet, my family adviser, regarding my baptism certificate, which is required for the marriage licence. 'I think you are doing the right thing,' he told me.

'Not many say so.' General Aubert-Dubayet, the Minister of War, had had the audacity to tell me I'd be making a fool of myself if I married Buonaparte. Even Grace Elliott had asked how I could consider marrying a man with such a terrible name.

Citoyen Calmelet nodded. 'General Buonaparte is not one to stand on ceremony. This offends some people. But he shows promise and he seems to care for you sincerely. One can see it in his eyes.'

'Will you come to the ceremony, be one of my witnesses?'

'I'd be honoured. When is it?'

Seventeen days.

MONDAY, 22 FEBRUARY

It was almost noon when I heard the sound of a horse trotting up

* Bernadine Eugénie Désirée Clary would later marry Bernadotte, who became Crown Prince of Sweden, making Désirée Crown Princess. Ironically, their son, Oscar I of Sweden, would marry one of Rose's granddaughters.

the drive. I looked out to see Lazare dismounting from a splendid grey. He handed the reins and his riding crop to my coachman.

Quickly I went to my mirror, rubbed some colour into my cheeks.

Agathe came into my wardrobe. 'General Hoche is here to see you.'

'Yes, I saw him.' I removed my apron. I had intended to work in the garden and the simple muslin gown I was wearing was not flattering.

'Shall I tell him that you will receive him?'

I thought for a moment. Should I? No. 'Tell him I am indisposed.'

A few moments later I heard a commotion in the hall. I looked up. Lazare was standing in the door. 'I want my letters back,' he said.

I scoffed. 'What letters! I've not had a single letter from you since *August*.' I pulled my shawl round my shoulders. 'Since you *rescued* Madame de Pout-Bellan's husband.'

'Monsieur de Pout-Bellan? What does he have to do with this?'

'It is said that you fell in love with his wife.'

Lazare waved his hand in a gesture of impatience. 'Madame de Pout-Bellan? There is nothing! Nothing, at least, to compare with the way you and Vanakre—'

'Vanakre? Your *footman*?'

'You need not take that aristocratic tone. Vanakre is my aide-de-camp now.'

'That's not the point. You thought I'd had an amourette with *Vanakre*?'

'I have *proof*!'

'It would amuse me to see such proof, General Hoche.'

Lazare began to pace. 'And now you with this,' he cursed, banged his fist on the side table, 'this little *police* general! How could you!'

'Do not speak of General Buonaparte in that way.'

'Did you know that only last year he was transferred to an infantry brigade under *my* orders, but he refused, *pretending* to be sick. Did you know the Committee had him demoted for insubordination? And that he offered his services to the Turks! He's an opportunist! He can't be trusted. He only wants the promotion Barras has offered him.'

'It has nothing to do with Barras!' I put my hands to my ears.

Lazare grabbed my hands, pulled them away. 'Buonaparte's reward for marrying you is the Army of Italy. It is *that* he wants — not *you*.'

'Whosoever is appointed to command the Army of Italy will be appointed on the basis of merit.' I was trembling. '*All* the Directors must approve it, as you well know. In point of fact, it would appear to be Director Carnot who is promoting General Buonaparte.'

'Tell me you love him,' Lazare demanded.

'I have given him my word.'

He stared at me for a long moment. 'That's it?'

I turned to the window, took a breath. 'I understand congratulations are in order. You are a father, I am told.'

'I am. A girl.' There was pride in his voice.

I turned to him. 'I was never unfaithful to you,' I said.

He took my hand. 'You're trembling. Do I frighten you?'

'Don't make me cry, Lazare.' I pulled my hand away. His touch was gentle. He had always been so very gentle. 'Please go.'

At the door he turned. 'It is true that I have fallen in love with another woman,' he said. 'My wife.'

'You always did love her.'

He bowed and was gone. Shortly after I heard the sound of his horse's hooves cantering up the drive.

I sat for a time by the window, looking out at the grey winter day. Agathe asked if there was anything I wanted.

'Nothing,' I said.

LATER

I was digging in the garden when a message was delivered. It was a note from Citoyen Dunnkirk: 'Come and see me.'

Was it Mother? Immediately I called for my coach, arriving at Emmery's office shortly before five.

'I am glad you could come so promptly. There is something I think you should know. Your fiancé has been to see me.' It was cold. He was sniffling, as usual.

'General Buonaparte?'

'Yes. This morning.'

'But *why*?'

'He was inquiring into your financial affairs.'

'I have no secrets! He didn't need to ask you.'

Citoyen Dunnkirk shrugged.

'What did you tell him?'

'The truth.' He blew his nose on a dirty blue handkerchief.

'And?' I didn't know who I was angrier with, Buonaparte or Citoyen Dunnkirk.

'He thought you were wealthier than you are.'

I sat for a moment in silence.

'I know it is not my place, citoyenne, but . . . are you sure this is the man you should marry?'

'I must go.' I stood, in fear of my emotions.

THAT EVENING

'It's off!' I yelled the moment Buonaparte entered. I had not intended to explode in this way, but the words escaped before I could control myself.

Buonaparte looked behind him. Was I addressing someone other than himself? 'Joséphine?'

'And I will *not* be Joséphine! I am *Rose*.' I paced the room.

Buonaparte threw his hat on to a chair. 'Perhaps you could tell me what this is all about,' he said, '*Joséphine*.'

I struck out at him. He caught my wrist, hard. 'I warn you never to strike me,' he said.

Lannoy came running to the door. Gontier was behind her. 'Madame?'

'Leave us alone,' Buonaparte commanded. He was not as calm as he pretended.

I nodded to them both. 'It's all right.'

After they left there was a moment of silence. Outside, a horse whinnied.

'Now, if you would be so kind as to explain?' Buonaparte jabbed at the embers with an iron.

I sat down, clasped my hands in my lap. 'I have decided to call off our engagement.'

'That much I have gathered. Would it inconvenience you to provide a reason?'

'You have been to see my banker.'

'I have.'

'You could have come to *me*.'

He did not respond.

'You have no affection for me, Buonaparte. In marrying me, you seek only promotion.' I would not look at him. 'Nothing you can say can persuade me otherwise. Do not try to defend yourself.'

'And *you* – are you so . . . ?' He stood. 'So free of self-interest? Can you claim that it is only out of *affection* for me that you have consented to marry?'

'So much the more reason to abandon this ill-fated union.'

He left abruptly. There were tears in his eyes. I do not feel relief.

In which we begin again, & yet again

I was still in bed when Agathe informed me that General Buonaparte
had arrived.

'I heard the horse,' I said. Agathe brought me my white muslin gown. I tied a red scarf about my head and put rouge on
my cheeks.

I wasn't looking forward to this meeting. 'Stay near,' I told
Agathe, slipping a shawl round my shoulders, 'in case I need you.'
I shivered from the cold.

Buonaparte was waiting in the drawing room. He was standing by
the window examining the bust of Voltaire. He turned to face me
when I entered. I could see from his eyes that he had not slept.

'Good afternoon,' I said.

'Is it?' He was wearing a dark embroidered coat with a high
stand-up collar.

I took a seat to the left of the fire, gesturing for him to take the
seat to the right. His boots, which he is in the habit of polishing
with some obnoxious substance, threw off a strong odour. I asked
Agathe to bring us coffee and toast. 'And rum.'

Buonaparte and I sat in uncomfortable silence until Agathe
returned. She placed the urn and goblets on a serving table and
left. 'Coffee?' I asked. He refused. I poured myself coffee from the
urn, added rum, cream, two heaped spoonfuls of sugar. My spoon
made a scraping noise on the bottom of my cup.

'The time has come for truth,' he said. He stood. I braced
myself for recriminations, justifications. 'You have accused me
of self-interest in proposing marriage to you. I will answer your
charges.' He clasped his hands behind his back and then across his
chest, and then back behind his back again. 'In the beginning, yes, I

was attracted by the advantages marriage to you would offer. I saw that you were a woman of influence, a woman who was at ease with men of power and wealth, a woman who bridged both the old world and the new. These qualities would be an asset to me, I knew. And of course there was the plum of the Army of Italy. The Army of Italy! I would have married the most lowly of the market prostitutes to gain command of the Army of Italy.'

'You need not insult me, Buonaparte.'

'*Insult* you!' He fell to his knees before me. 'I intend to honour you as no other woman has been honoured!'

'Rise!' I said, alarmed and embarrassed.

'You *must* hear me!' He took the seat beside mine, grabbed my hand. 'Don't you see? I have fallen in *love* with you!'

'Yet you went to see my banker!'

'I will not deny it. It was the act of a coward.' He stood back up again. 'I was seeking reasons, cause and effect, premise and proof. I was seeking escape.'

'From *what*?'

'You. From the emotion that has engulfed me.'

I sat back in exasperation. 'I dislike riddles,' I said.

'You don't understand! When I am with you, it is as if a curtain has been opened, and all that has gone before has been merely an overture. Is this not frightening? I have held a dead man in my arms. I have walked to the mouth of a cannon set to fire. I have faced my mother's fury. Yet *nothing* is as frightening to me as the tenderness that comes over me when I look into your eyes.'

Abruptly I stood, went to the window. Fortuné was by the garden wall, by the rosebushes there, digging at something.

'Will you not marry me?' There was desperation in his voice.

I came back to my seat by the fire. 'You know I do not love you,' I said.

'Yes. I know that.'

'You know I am . . . older than you, that I have loved another.' Love another still. I did not say that.

'I do.'

'Yet even so, you wish to marry me?'

'I wish to worship you.'

'Must you be so droll, Buonaparte?'

'You think I jest.'

'Surely, you must.' I smiled.

'Forgive me?'

I took his hand. I had never noticed how fine his fingers were, how smooth his skin.

'Join me for a promenade?' he asked.

I stood. We were almost the same height. I felt he was a brother, a companion — 'my spirit friend', Mimi would have said. 'I will not give up Chantereine,' I said, opening the doors to the garden.

'My hôtel on Rue des Capucines is more prestigious,' he said.

'This is my first real home. It is everything to me.'

He looked about. 'After I liberate Italy, I will require a larger establishment.'

'And when might that be, General Buonaparte?' Teasing.

He looked at me with an amused expression. 'Shortly after we are married, Joséphine.'

WEDNESDAY, 24 FEBRUARY

'I announced our betrothal to the Directors,' Buonaparte told me this evening.

'And what was the response?'

'Positive.' He seemed pleased, strutting around. '*Very* positive.' He slapped his hands together.

2 MARCH

Buonaparte's footman unloaded a crate of papers into my hall, Buonaparte coming in after him. 'Behold,' he said with a dramatic flourish. 'The Commander of the Army of Italy.'

'It's official now? Were you not expecting it?'

'One can never be entirely sure of such things.' He rummaged through the crate of papers.

'And now?'

Buonaparte flipped through the pages of a report.

'And now?' I touched his arm.

He looked at me with a distracted expression.

'And now?'

'And *now* the work begins.'

8 March

Buonaparte called for me at noon. I was ready. Together we went to my lawyer's office on the Rue Saint-Honoré. Buonaparte waited in the entryway while my lawyer went over the marriage contract.

'Are you familiar with this contract?' Raguideau asked when I sat down. His dusty office was cluttered with papers and legal forms. The windows looking out on to the Rue Saint-Honoré were covered with grime.

'I am.'

'Nevertheless, I am required by law to go over it with you.' He is a small man, yet he has an exceptionally deep voice. 'Your finances will be kept separate. You will each contribute equally to the costs of maintaining a household. Even the cost of getting married will be shared between you.' He spelled out the terms: 'Your husband assumes no responsibility for your debts. Other than paying you a nominal sum of fifteen hundred livres a year, you will receive nothing from this union.'

He put the papers down on the desk, took off his thick spectacles. 'Citoyenne Beauharnais, I must be frank. This man brings you nothing but a cloak and sword. I'm afraid I cannot, in good conscience, advise you to sign this contract.'

I felt heat in my cheeks, in spite of the chill. 'I have come to sign this contract, Citoyen Raguideau, not to question it.'

'Please understand, it would be a *disaster* for you to marry this man.'

'So be it.' I took up the quill.

Buonaparte was waiting outside. He seemed amused. 'Only a cloak and sword?'

'You overheard? Are you not offended?' I was angry. Was nothing predictable with him?

'We shall see what a cloak and sword can do!'

Later

The parish bells had just struck four. I was standing by the window, looking out at the garden, when I was startled by a noise. Behind me was Lannoy with a worn leather valise in one hand.

'Are you going somewhere, Lannoy?' I asked. I did not recall that leave had been arranged.

A vigorous tip of her head almost dislodged her hat, a modest straw creation overpowered by a white-and-blue-striped bow. 'I cannot serve that Jacobin!'

'You are leaving me? *Now?*'

'Farewell!' she wailed, throwing herself into my arms.

9 MARCH

Barras and Tallien arrived shortly after seven. Tallien had on his black coat and top hat. He was carrying an umbrella instead of a sword. 'His funeral ensemble,' Barras said, who was dressed more traditionally in velvet and lace.

I smiled uneasily.

The three of us headed off in Barras's coach. Agathe and Gontier had attached little bouquets of flowers tied with white ribbons to the horses' bridles.

It was exactly eight when we entered the township office, a once elegant white and gold drawing room decorated with frolicking cupids, now headquarters of the second arrondissement and covered with dust. A fire was dying in the marble fireplace. It was dark: a single candle flickered in a bronze sconce. The large gilt mirrors reflected 'only shadows.

My adviser Jérôme Calmelet was already there, seated in one of the hard leather chairs. The registrar, Citoyen Leclerq, was going through papers at the desk. A thin lad with a wooden leg sat slumped beside him.

But no sign of Buonaparte. 'No doubt he's been held up,' Barras said, removing his cape.

We waited. After almost an hour, the registrar stood, yawned, put on his cloak. 'I leave you in charge, Antoine,' he told the young lad. Citoyen Antoine manoeuvred his wooden leg under the big desk and regarded us with an attempt at authority.

'No doubt he thought he was to be here at nine.' Tallien shifted in the uncomfortable chair.

'It is past nine now.' My little bouquet of flowers had begun to wilt. 'I insist that we leave.' I stood. I was angry. I was more than angry; I was humiliated.

'Wait,' Barras commanded.

It was past ten when we heard footsteps on the stairs. 'He's here,' Barras said.

Buonaparte burst into the room followed by a youth in uniform. He went directly up to young Antoine and shook him. 'Wake up!'

The lad sat up, blinked.

Buonaparte grabbed my hand, pulled me to my feet. 'Marry us,' he commanded the lad, pushing a gold band on to my ring finger.

It was over in a few minutes.

We rode back to Chantereine in silence, Buonaparte and I.

'I have decided to change my name. Bonaparte. Napoleon Bonaparte. It's more French. Do you like it?'

I said nothing.

'Is something wrong?'

'If Barras hadn't insisted, I would have left. I don't know why I stayed!'

'So, divorce me in the morning.'

'Perhaps I will!'

We didn't exchange another word all the way to Chantereine. I headed immediately up the stairs. I threw the flowers off my bed, embarrassed by the fuss Agathe and Gontier had made. Fortuné growled when Buonaparte entered the room.

'Your footman put your bags in there this afternoon.' I nodded towards the wardrobe.

'What about the dog?' Buonaparte asked, returning in his night clothes. He was wearing a cotton nightcap with a silly-looking tassel on it.

'The dog stays.' Fortuné was in his usual place at the foot of the bed.

'I will not sleep with a *dog.*'

'Very well, then, you will sleep on the settee.' I blew out the lantern.

Buonaparte stumbled towards the bed in the dark. I heard Fortuné growl. Then I heard Buonaparte curse loudly in the Italian tongue.

I sat up, my heart pounding. Fortuné was snarling. 'What happened!'

'That dog should be shot!' Buonaparte held up his hand. In the moonlight I could see something dark on it.

SANDRA GULLAND

'*Mon Dieu!* Is that blood? Did he bite your hand?'

'My leg.'

Agathe came running into the room, holding a lantern. Buonaparte's leg was covered with blood. Buonaparte pressed a bedsheet to it to stop the bleeding.

Fortuné was cowering under a chair, baring his fangs.

'A basin of hot water and some bandages,' I told Agathe, grabbing Fortuné by the scruff of the neck and shutting the snarling little thing in the wardrobe.

Gontier came to the door, his ruffled nightcap falling into his eyes. 'Go for a surgeon,' I told him.

'No surgeon will be necessary,' Buonaparte said.

'Don't attempt to be a hero over this, Buonaparte,' I said. 'There is nothing to be gained by it.'

'Do you think heroism is something that can be put on, like a cloak?' He turned to Gontier. 'I am master of this house now, and I am telling you, do *not* go for the surgeon. I've spent too much time on the battlefield attending to my own wounds to be coddled like a tailor by some ignorant youth.' He took one of the bandages Agathe had brought and dipped it into the steaming water. 'If your girl could bring some salt?'

'Her name is Agathe. Ask her yourself.'

Buonaparte glared at me. 'Are we to spend the rest of our lives quarrelling?'

'I believe so.' I nodded to Agathe. 'If you could fetch the salt? And the cognac,' I added.

Buonaparte cleaned and dressed his wound, securing it with two stitches of strong silk which he put in himself, gritting his teeth against the pain. I persuaded him to lie with his leg propped up on a pillow.

'You may go now,' I told Agathe and Gontier, who were standing at the foot of the bed, trampling the flowers. 'Take Fortuné with you.'

'I'm to be woken at six,' Buonaparte instructed Agathe.

'That's only a few hours from now,' I said.

'I have taken too much time already.'

Agathe and Gontier withdrew, taking away the lanterns and a still-snarling Fortuné.

By the light of a single candle I poured two snifters of cognac. I handed one to Buonaparte. He put his hand up in refusal. 'I must keep my wits about me,' he said.

I sat down on the bed, took a sip of the cognac, sighed. I had wanted a father for my children, security; now it seemed so much more complex.

'You doubt the wisdom of what you've done,' he said.

What I've done. Yes. 'Must you for ever be telling me my thoughts?' I was being churlish, I knew. 'I'm sorry,' I said. 'It has not been a romantic evening.' Suddenly I felt tears pressing. Is one allowed to go back, begin again? Can mistakes be undone?

Buonaparte pulled at a pillow.

'Allow me,' I said. I put down my glass and adjusted the pillow behind him. He put his hand on my wrist. 'There is something I haven't told you.'

'Please, no.' It was too late for confessions. I pulled my hand away.

'A fortune-teller told me that a widow would be my angel, my lucky star.'

I thought of the fortune I'd been foretold. *You will be Queen.*

'You scoff,' he said.

'I'm no angel,' I said. I lay down beside him.

'You think the woman I love does not exist. You don't believe in Joséphine.'

His grey eyes were so intense. I looked away.

'Do you believe in *me*?' he asked.

I regarded his profile by the light of the candle. He had a haunted look. What was it that fired him, drove him? It would never give him peace, I knew.

'Are you cold?' He pulled the sheet over me.

'Yes,' I said. I stilled his hand against my breast.

He seemed unsure what he should do. I felt unsure myself. Should I blow out the candle? Take off my gown? I felt my age, his youth.

'I have read that if the tip of a woman's breast is touched in a certain way, she will go mad with pleasure,' he said. He sounded like a schoolboy, reciting a lesson. 'I amuse you?' he asked, observing my smile.

'You have a scientific mind,' I said.

He cupped my breast in his hand, examined it. 'Your breast is a perfect example of its kind – round, firm.'

'Buonaparte!' A warmth had come into my heart.

I leaned over him. His breath on my face was sweet.

'Truly, you—' He stopped, unable to speak.

I touched a tear that was running down his cheek. It tasted of the sea. 'Yes,' I said. 'I do believe in you.'

DAWN

The sun has tinted the sky the most delicate shade of pink. It reminds me of the mornings of my youth. I listen for the animals stirring, the cock, the cow.

Buonaparte, his leg wrapped in a bandage, is asleep. I listen to the sound of his breathing.

I am married. Again.

My husband is not the man I dreamt of as a girl, not my *grand amour*, and certainly not the king the fortune-teller had foretold. Only Buonaparte, strange little Napoleone. Now Napoléon.

And I? Who am *I*?

He calls me Joséphine. He says I'm an angel, a saint, his good-luck star. I know I'm no angel, but in truth I have begun to like this Joséphine he sees. She is intelligent; she amuses; she is pleasing. She is grace and charm and heart. Unlike Rose: scared, haunted and needy. Unlike Rose with her sad life.

I slip off my wedding ring, a simple gold band. Inside, I see an inscription. I hold it to the light: To Destiny.

Chronology

YEAR	DATE	
1760	28 May	Alexandre is born in Fort-Royal, Martinique.
1763	23 June	Rose in born in Trois-Ilets, Martinique.
1764	11 December	Rose's sister Catherine is born.
1766	13–14 August	A hurricane destroys Rose's home.
	early September	Rose's second sister Manette is born.
1769	15 August	Napoleone Buonaparte is born in Ajaccio, Corsica.
1777	16 October	Rose's sister Catherine dies.
1779	11 April	The marriage banns are published in Martinique.
	12 October	Rose arrives in France.
	13 December	Rose and Alexandre are married.
1781	3 September	Eugène is born.
1782	6 September	Alexandre leaves for Brest (en route to Martinique).
	30 November	Alexandre sails for Martinique. Laure Longpré is on board.
1783	10 April	Hortense is born.
	27 November	Rose moves into the convent of Penthémont.
	8 December	Rose begins legal proceedings against Alexandre.

1785	5 March	Court decision in Rose's favour.
	July	Rose and the children move to Fontainebleau.
1786	3 September	Eugène, five, is now in his father's custody.
1788	2 July	Rose sails for Martinique.
	11 August	Rose arrives in Martinique.
1790	6 September	Rose sets sail for France under cannon fire.
	29 October	Rose lands at Toulon.
	7 November	Rose's father dies.
1791	20 June	King and family flee Paris.
	21 June	Alexandre President of Assembly.
	25 June	King and Queen are returned to Paris.
	31 July	Alexandre President of Assembly for a second term.
	14 September	King pledges oath of allegiance to the new constitution.
	4 November	Rose's sister Manette dies.
1792	20 April	France declares war on Austria. Alexandre joins army.
	25 April	First use of the guillotine.
	August	Alexandre appointed Chief-of-Staff of the Army of the Rhine.
	10–13 August	Insurrection. King and Queen are put in prison.
	28–30 August	Night house searches begin – thousands are arrested.
	2 September	French troops at Verdun fall to the enemy. Panic in Paris.
	2–6 September	September massacres. Over 1,000 in the prisons murdered. Rose sends children away with Frédéric and Amalia. Alexandre commands children return to Paris.
	20 September	Divorce is made legally possible.
	22 September	The Republic is proclaimed.
	26 December	Trial of the King begins.

1793	15 January	King declared guilty.
	21 January	King beheaded.
	29 May	Alexandre made Commander-in-Chief of Army of the Rhine.
	21 August	Alexandre's resignation is accepted.
	17 September	Law of Suspects passed.
	26 September	Rose moves to Croissy.
	16 October	The Queen is beheaded.
	29 October	Fanny's daughter Marie is arrested.
1794	2 March	Alexandre arrested in Blois.
	20 April	Rose is arrested in Paris.
	23 July	Alexandre is beheaded.
	28 July	Robespierre is beheaded.
	6 August	Rose is released from prison.
	2 September	Hoche leaves Paris for new command. Takes Eugène.
	9 September	Attempted assassination of Tallien.
	7 October	Marie is released from prison.
	26 December	Thérèse (21), pregnant, and Tallien (27) are married.
1795	21 February	Religious worship allowed in private dwellings.
	17 May	Thérèse gives birth to Thermidor-Rose.
	8 June	The Dauphin (10) dies in prison.
	23–27 June	Émigré forces land at Quiberon Bay.
	16–21 July	Battle of Quiberon Bay. Hoche leads French troops to victory.
	17 August	Rose signs lease on house on Rue Chantereine.
	28 September	Rose invites Buonaparte to call on her.
	4–6 October	Right-wing insurrection defeated by troops under Barras and Buonaparte.
	26 October	Barras and four others elected Directors of France. Buonaparte takes over Barras's position of General-in-Chief of Army of the Interior.
1796	21 January	Gala dinner at Luxembourg Palace.
	19 February	Banns for Rose and Buonaparte's wedding issued.

2 March	Buonaparte is made Commander-in-Chief of Army of Italy.
8 March	Marriage contract signed.
9 March	Rose (32) and Napoléon (26) are married in a civil ceremony.

Select Bibliography

Castelot, André. *Josephine, A Biography*. Trans. New York: Harper and Row, 1967.

Catinat, Docteur Maurice. 'Une lettre inédite de la future impératrice Joséphine.' *Bulletin, 1991*. Rueil-Malmaison: Société des Amis de Malmaison, 1991.

Chevallier, Bernard, and Christophe Pincemaille. *L'impératrice Joséphine*. Paris: Presses de la Renaissance, 1988.

Cole, Hubert. *Joséphine*. London: Heinemann, 1962.

Cronin, Vincent. *Napoleon*. London: Collins, 1971.

Dictionnaire de biographie française. Sous la direction de M. Prevost et Roman d'Amat. Librairie Letouzey et Ané, 1954.

Dictionnaire Napoléon. Sous la direction de Jean Tulard. Fayard, 1987.

Epton, Nina C. *Josephine: The Empress and Her Children*. London: Weidenfeld and Nicolson, 1975.

Jones, Colin. *The Longman Companion to the French Revolution*. London and New York: Longman, 1988.

Knapton, Ernest John. *Empress Josephine*. Cambridge: Harvard University Press, 1963.

Le Normand, Mlle. M. A. *The Historical and Secret Memoirs of the Empress Josephine*. Vol. I and II. Trans. London: H. S. Nichols, 1895.

Minnigerode, Meade. *The Magnificent Comedy; Some aspects of public and private life in Paris, from the fall of Robespierre to the coming of Bonaparte July, 1794 – November, 1799*. Murray Hill, New York: Farrar and Rinehart, 1931.

Rose-Rosette, Robert. *Les jeunes années de l'impératrice Joséphine*. Martinique: Publié avec le concours de la Fondation Napoléon, 1992.

Turgeon, F. K. 'Fanny de Beauharnais. Biographical Notes and a Bibliography.' *Modern Philology*, Aug. 1932.

Wagener, Françoise. *La reine Hortense (1783–1837)*. Éditions Jean-Claude Lattès, 1992.

Whitham, J. Mills. *Men and Women of the French Revolution*. New York: The Viking Press, 1933.

Acknowledgements

For help both general and specific: Eleanor Alwyn, Nathalie Bedard, Gale Bildfell, Elena Diana (Amaritha), Dr John Goodman, Paul Kropp, Jackie Levitin, Corine Paul, Charis Wahl, John Williamson, and the Golden Girls Plus Bob, especially Robert Zentner. For editorial suggestions, my main readers: Peggy Bridgland, Judy Holland, Marnie MacKay (ever-patient librarian), Fran Murphy, and especially Sharon Zentner. For nourishment and wisdom: Janet Calcaterra, Thea Caplan, Pat Jeffries, Kathlyn Lampi, Jenifer McVaugh, Joanne Zomers. For significant teachings at important crossroads: Margaret Atwood, Matt Cohen, Janette Turner Hospital, and especially Jane Urquhart. For help in the historical labyrinth: William R. Beall, Bernard Chevallier, Dr Robert Rose-Rosette, and especially Dr Maurice Catinat and Dr Margaret Chrisawn. For fuelling the passion: fellow Napoleonic enthusiasts Tony Kenny, Dr John McErlean, Derwin Mak, Helen Smith and Robert Snibbe of the Napoleonic Society of America, and especially deceased Society member David Goudy. For being there from the beginning, Jan Whitford. For being such great editors, great publishers: Iris Tupholme, Maya Mavjee and the rest of the gang at HarperCollins. For being even more pernickety than I am, Bernice Eisenstein. For enthusiasm and understanding: Carrie and Chet Gulland, and especially Richard Gulland – without whose unquestioning and steadfast support this book never could have been written.

Now you can buy any of these other
Review titles from your bookshop or
direct from the publisher.

FREE P&P AND UK DELIVERY
(Overseas and Ireland £3.50 per book)

Hens Dancing	Raffaella Barker	£6.99
The Catastrophist	Ronan Bennett	£6.99
Horseman, Pass By	David Crackanthorpe	£6.99
Two Kinds of Wonderful	Isla Dewar	£6.99
Earth and Heaven	Sue Gee	£6.99
Sitting Among the Eskimos	Maggie Graham	£6.99
Tales of Passion, Tales of Woe	Sandra Gulland	£6.99
The Dancers Dancing	Éilís Ní Dhuibhne	£6.99
After You'd Gone	Maggie O'Farrell	£6.99
The Silver River	Ben Richards	£6.99
A History of Insects	Yvonne Roberts	£6.99
Girl in Hyacinth Blue	Susan Vreeland	£6.99
The Long Afternoon	Giles Waterfield	£6.99

TO ORDER SIMPLY CALL THIS NUMBER

01235 400 414

or e-mail <u>orders@bookpoint.co.uk</u>

Prices and availability subject to change without notice.